THE BLUE BELL VILLA

I0668760

HSD

Become Shakespeare .com

First published in 2017 by

Becomeshakespeare.com
Wordit Content Design & Editing Services Pvt Ltd
Unit - 26, Building A-1, Nr Wadala RTO, Wadala (East),
Mumbai 400037, India
T:+91 8080226699

WORDIT ART FUND

This book has been funded by the Wordit Art Fund. Wordit Art Fund helps deserving authors publish their work by providing monetary support. To apply for funding, please visit us at www.BecomeShakespeare.com

ISBN: 978-93-86487-54-4

DISCLAIMER

This is a work of fiction. Names, characters, businesses, places, events and incidents are either the products of the author's imagination or used in a fictitious manner. Any resemblance to actual persons, living or dead, or actual events is purely coincidental.

DEDICATION

To the narrator

ACKNOWLEDGMENTS

(Readers may find this section too long)
My family: Your constant support in every walk of life has made the work a reality. I hope I will make you proud one day.
Rajeshwar Rangaswamy: The first person to read through the manuscript.
Lavanya Rajamani: For reading the content with a critical eye.
Vijay Basavaraju: For being the devil's advocate.
M. Bhimsen (VP, Silverpeak Global Pvt Ltd): For the constant encouragement and support in editing the work.
Neha Gore: For considering the request for proof-reading and helping me immensely in correcting the errors and improving the quality of work.
Kalpesh Khairnar: For the feedback and inspiring words.
Maria Alex: For not committing and yet upholding the commitment.
Ganesh Bapat: For taking some time to read despite his Ph. D studies.
Tiju Thomas: For considering a random request and the prompt feedback.
Srikanth (Chiku): For being the most supportive in my venture.
Pragya Hari: For the refining the content to a great extent.
Aman Jhawar: For the support in other aspects.
Rishi Amit, Astha & Mukesh: For replacing Qutub Minar in my memory when I think about New Delhi.
Krishna Kashyap and Krishna Simha: For being great friends despite not being great readers.
Vikas Chandra, Apurva Singh and Ankit Tripathi: For the indirect support
Harish Munidev: For continuous backing throughout the work
Amol Kulkarni: For not starting to read until published.
Ravi and Priya: For designing the cover exactly the way I wanted. More importantly, for the patience.
Appachu Chottangada, Harshita: So lucky to have Kodava friends!
Hanoch Mario Tauro: For everything.
Malini Nair, Likhita Puthran and team: For publishing the work!

I also express my gratitude to the unknown hands that have worked hard to bring the book to the readers.
Lastly, and more importantly, thank you reader!

CONTENTS

1 A BRIEF HISTORY OF MINE

Hi there, dear reader!

You may not know me but I know you well. I am with you even as you open the very first page and begin to read. I know you inside out. I know the moments you felt happy and sad. I know the mamories that make you nostalgic. I even know those occasions that make you feel embarrassed, that make you hope those moments be forgotten. I know your family, friends, foes and of course, your crush.

I know what you like, what you hate and what you're confused about! To me you are not a drop in an ocean, you are an entire ocean. There are only two entities that are omniscient, omnipresent and omnipotent. One is God if you believe in God; the other is me, whether you believe me or not. I'm beyond your belief; beyond your imagination. I'm formless, lifeless and priceless. I'm TIME!

That is the name given to me by your race-The Human Race. You have interfered into almost every entity you have found on your planet, including me. You tried to define me, travel through me and more importantly, race with me. You failed and failed and failed until you accepted me. You tried to win me but pity you still don't realize that you can win me only when you stop fighting me!

You don't agree? Well, I don't care! Don't think that I'm criticizing you too much. I am only a slave... Of my slaves!

I'm sounding harsh because I usually don't get a chance to educate you on utilizing me for your own good.

Anyway, let's keep all this aside. Let me take you through a story. A story so memorable, it might be too long in my standards to overshadow it. I want you to give me freedom to toggle between periods while narrating the story because I can simplify it only to an extent of making it uncomplicated. Nothing more than that...

So let me begin...

2 THE BOYS PLAYED WELL

"Hold him... Tight..."- a thug frisks the pockets of an unknown gentleman in the foggy night on a dark, isolated street. Three of his friends have arrested the movements of that person. The man's briefcase is lying open on the road. There are drops of blood all around. His nose is bleeding. His eyes are swollen. The thug has snatched the wallet, the watch and a dazzling gold ring. The gentleman is in pain.
"Drag him here..."-frustrated, he orders his friends to bring the man to a car parked nearby. He is being mercilessly dragged to the car. The man lifts his feet to exert his weight on those dragging him. It is hardly of any use. They are strong although he is quite well-built too. He is lifted and brought in front of the car. The thug stands arrogantly in front of the gentleman. After a brief lull, he holds the neck of the gentleman and pushes backwards against the bonnet. The rest of the gang now holds the man's arms tightly. He is crucified with bare hands. The thug stands on the bumper of the car with his legs spread apart. He holds the forehead of the person with his left hand and brings down his right hand heavily on his jaw!

"Thuddd!"-the noise is pretty loud. The car has started to sound the alarm. The man groans. The thug is not done yet. He takes out a screw driver and a hammer from the briefcase. He inserts the driver between the man's lips, holds it in an oblique manner and knocks the man's tooth out with the hammer!!

The man screams with his throat beating against his neck. The men holding him are terrified, thrilled and puzzled. They loosen the grip. The man falls on the road and starts wailing. The thug tries to recover the man's tooth by shoving his fingers in his mouth. He is unable to find it there. He turns the man around and punches on his neck hoping to bring out the tooth, he thinks, is stuck in the man's throat. The tooth is not found there.

"Search!!"-the thug shouts at his comrades.

They frantically get down to the task. The man rolls across into the darkness of the street. One of the gangsters takes out his cell phone and flashes the torch on. They speed up the search.

"Here..."-he hands over the tooth to the leader. The thug takes it from him hastily, examines it and pockets it with an evil smile. They are looking around. The gentleman is not to be seen. They walk briskly and vanish in the fog.

The gentleman remains flat on his back in a gutter, with a handkerchief stuffed in his mouth to prevent yelling and attracting attention.

The night is quiet again, the sky is deep blue and the moon is crescent with a faint silver lining around it. But the tooth was of gold!

Days roll by. It is dawn and cool. The sky is slowly turning crimson. Birds have just begun their day. But they are not the ones to wake up first every morning. A handful of people do get up very early in this ironically sleepy second-tier Indian city flanked by mountains.

If you see the distant view of this quaint place from amidst the swarm of flying birds and drifting mist, you will see a temple at the top of the mountain that oversees the city. It is the first structure that catches your eye. There is a lake to its left, at the foothills. It is huge, deep and calm. It feeds water to all the life forms there. The grateful residents have aptly named their city 'Sarovar Nagar'- The lake city.

There are paddy and sugarcane fields necklacing the city, strung by canals originating from the lake. A lone boat stands still in the middle of the lake.

Up close in the heart of the city, there are small to medium-sized buildings scattered everywhere, magnanimously paving way for some roads. The Double Road is one of the very few ones that run along the length of the city. It serves as the main artery. At the south end of the Double Road, there is a small patch of land thronged by dense trees on all sides. It is the city playground.

A dark band can be seen moving about in the playground. When you go closer you find that it is a group of men. They are in their twenties and thirties, and have assembled there for an early morning cricket match. Unemployment has driven them to the playgrounds. It is a major source of income for them to play what they fondly call- THE BET MATCH. Every match played there is for money. Every penny earned there is for the next match!

The money is managed by mugging... an act of looting vulnerable passersby... The matches happen every day. Rainy mornings or sunny afternoons, hunger is to be pacified. Money is to be earned. There are also big-budget matches between the two notorious teams-the Killer XI and the Hunter XI. There are other teams too but with lower budgets.

For the Hunters and the Killers, the matches have moved from being bread earning avenues to being a matter of pride, prestige and legacy. Many of the regular players have become rich enough to own cars without loans. Older players have become organizers who remain neutral during the course of a match and also do umpiring. Some still stick to their teams as mentors, coaches and strategists. Their attitude, yet, remains belligerent and money craving.

These days, there are tickets being issued for the general public to view them. The public, after plunging into the whirlpool of IPL, crave for more entertainment off the season. They do not mind local matches. Money flows into the teams. But habits remain. Mugging still takes place off the Double Road when darkness sets in.

The local MLA, who, for five years in his youth, was a pathetic batsman, inaugurates the tournament every time. Both the Hunters and the Killers now own offices in the busy 'Charlie bazaar'. But the other thriving teams still play for livelihood.

These days, the parents of young boys understand that their kids are on their path to transition into adulthood when they see them throw away marbles and pick up the cricketing talents observing the grownups. Every shot is improvised; every delivery is made more lethal. Except the Hunters and the Killers, the other teams do not have proper protective gear. For example, there are no batting pads. Just a couple of thick rags tied on one leg. But there are some costly bats and good balls- investments for a rich harvest of quick bucks. Ironically the abdomen guards, although cheaper than the bats that cost thousands, are shared. Each player brings his own polythene 'cover' in which the guard is put before it is worn!

The betting phenomenon has attracted young adolescents away from schools. The police have been mum on the matter. Most of the policemen were once a part of the one team or the other in their teenage. But they were able to move to bigger cities for education and competitive exams coaching. They do not take much action. They know the players are not as fortunate as they once were. And above everything else, there's the MLA!

A rectangular pillar-stone is being rolled in the middle of the ground by a couple of men. It is going to stand as the batting stumps. It was to serve as a support for fencing in a nearby field. A third guy stands with his right heel touching the now standing stone and starts walking as straight as possible with equally spaced short steps to mark the bowling stumps. He counts 22 yards whispering softly. He leaps long after the 22nd yard.

"Babloo... Here..."-he directs another guy to keep the small piece of brick as the bowling stumps. The brick is a mere half. I don't know why the batting stumps have to be as big as the real ones while the bowling ones are to be one half of a common brick! They, though, have decided logically. There can be no compromise with the batting stumps. But a brick can be a life-saver during run out chances for both teams.

A bat is brought to measure the distance from the stumps to the crease. Babloo sits down, keeps the bat flat on the ground with the bottom touching the middle stump and handle facing the opposite side. He marks a line with his forefinger just touching the handle's free end and pulls the bat to the line marked, with the root of the handle overlapping on the line. He makes another small line just touching the tip of the handle. He gets up, extends the line horizontally to mark the crease! It is called 'one-and-a-half' bat. Strange that a handle is considered half the bat!!

Today is a big match between the Hunters and the Killers. The bet amount has broken all past records. Today it is 6,00,000 rupees per team for a win. It is going to be played in the noon.

For now, the match is between two smaller teams. For breakfast... Bet size-500 rupees... Per team... The third umpire is a cellphone hanging from the main umpire's neck. There is a cell phone on the leg umpire's neck too. Video-recording will be on as soon as the first ball is bowled. These are costly phones with high-end multimedia. Every team that plays there has invested money to buy these. They sign on a register and take these phones for matches if ever they need them. There is a shed at a corner in the ground where all storage is done.

Both teams are now in the middle of the pitch. The main players are finalizing the rules before the start of the battle. Even that is being video-recorded. Boundaries are being fixed. Free hit is being discussed...

"No tree catch..."-Kumar, the captain of one of the teams, is against the catch taken by a fielder at the boundary when the ball falls through the trees.

“Ok...”-Chandu, the opposite team’s captain has no problems with that. “20 over match...”-Chandu is confident of finishing the match before breakfast by picking up all the wickets. Kumar’s is a new and inexperienced side and Chandu is well aware of it.

The coin is tossed. “Tails...”-calls Chandu. Kumar waits anxiously as the coin dances after the impact with the ground.

It is heads!

“We bowl first...”-Kumar has his decision ready.

The openers are out in the middle. The match begins. Runs come as the batsmen regularly scamper about every now and then. Then the boundaries begin at the cost of a few wickets. Kumar is now afraid of losing the bet. He is in a fix whether to check the flow of runs or pick wickets. He decides to try and get those wickets. The fielders close in. The wicket keeper stands right behind the stumps. But disaster strikes. The keeper is injured. He drops out. There is no good player to keep wickets and the byes are proving costly. Kumar walks to Chandu and asks for a spare fielder. Chandu looks around to pick the worst fielder in his side. His teammates look back angrily.

Chandu’s eyes fall on a person sitting at a distance on his age-old black Yezdi motorcycle. The person has been watching the game right from the start. He is about the same age as theirs but looks a lot younger because of his slim appearance. He is tall, has a broad forehead with a scar in the middle and big, dark eyes. He sits on his bike, sweaty, unaware of the goings on, waiting for the innings to restart. There is a big drop of sweat on his nose that is turning into a flow, connecting with other drops. He looks worried. He doesn’t know, worry kills a person quicker than the things people worry about do.

Chandu displays brilliant diplomacy. “How about him?”-he points to the man on the bike. Kumar has no other option.

"Hey... Wfff..."-Chandu whistles for Kumar.

The man turns. Kumar waves his hand. The man gets down and walks to them.

"Can you field for us? Just a few overs left. We'll also let you bat... as the last batsman."-Kumar brings out the best of his courtesy.

The man nods. He is at the square leg, next to the umpire. The match is restarted. The man gets a chance to field the ball after a few deliveries. A batsman flicks to the leg side and runs for a single. The man at square leg is fast. He picks the ball with one hand and aims at the bowler end. The brick half is halved again!

They thought a brick could lower the chances of a run out but it seems that this man could hit even a coin! The batsman is out. Kumar and his team are euphoric!

They celebrate the dismissal and pat the new man.

"Can you keep wickets?"-Kumar offers a promotion.

The man nods again. He is now behind the stumps.

The next batsman tries a paddle sweep to send the ball behind the stumps. The keeper is quick. He stops the ball. The batsman, unaware, steps out of the crease for a run without looking at the non-striker who is showing a 'No'. The keeper flings the ball at the stone immediately. The ball rebounds after hitting the stone and rolls far, far away.

The batsman has to leave. Kumar exults. The team celebrates. After a few more overs, the innings comes to an end.

The target set for Kumar's side is 110 in 20 overs. There is still no smile on the new man's face. Chandu's team is now in the middle, formed into a group connected by arms. Chandu instills some wisdom and polishes their main strategy-a strategy almost all teams follow, thanks to the example set by the Hunters and Killers. "If you can't get a batsman out, get him retired hurt!!"-a pat lands on the back of the main bowler.

The main bowler is a tall and fiery man who looks more like an executioner. He nods. They disperse after loud hysteric shouts and applause.

Kumar's batsmen walk to the wicket, confidently.

"Strike or non-strike?"-asks one of them.

The other batsman looks at the main bowler.

"Non-strike."

All set. The umpires for both the innings were decided to be the players of the batting side whose order of batting was low down. The new man is asked to be the umpire. He does not refuse but does not heed to either. He slowly walks to his Yezdi and lies down on it. Kumar is unable to understand. But the new man has earned his respect. Two other players have been sent.

The 2nd innings begin. The new man is not perturbed by the progress. He is experiencing a calm morning with eyes closed but strangely, something is bothering him. There is occasional applause, whistling and yelling. A few squirrels are squeaking and sparrows are chirping. Their advice, however, is not being considered by Kumar's team as the wickets have started to tumble. Soon, it is the new man's turn. He's the last batsman. Kumar is at the other end.

"Try pushing for singles."-he advises when the required run rate is 18 per over. The new man starts whacking. Every ball bowled is ruthlessly being dispatched. Chandu is anxious to take the last wicket. The main bowler- the executioner, charges ahead like a knight does for his king. He is flogged. Each of his delivery is being toyed away. Deadly yorkers, slow bouncers... Nothing is being spared. Kumar is struck with awe. Chandu is clueless.

The match is tied. One run is all Kumar & Co need to win. The new man launches a rocket! The ball is lost forever! And so is the main bowler's reputation.

"Nothing went my way..."-Chandu is dejected. Well, cheer up dude... At least you finished the match before breakfast!

The new man is fervently patted and hugged but he is emotionless. Chandu's team is still in traumatic disbelief. The noise has now reduced for the most important part. The bet is being settled between Kumar and Chandu. Chandu's disappointment has transformed to boiling anger. He spares a look at the new man. Human nature it is- to vent out disappointment on the very people who are considered favorable and recommended, if they turn out to be otherwise.

Kumar smiles but wisely keeps away from striking at Chandu's ego. He walks away with his players to the farthest side of the ground. He has to distribute cash to them. The players flock around him like famished cubs of a mother hyena. They form a group that spreads around uniformly.

Each one now has money and smile. They all can have breakfast today. How about tomorrow? "There is still plenty of time left."

What a joke! Only I know how plenty is 24 hours.

The new man starts his bike and rides towards the exit of the playground.

"Hey, you... Hey!"-Kumar yells out loud.

The man stops his bike.

"Here..."-Kumar offers him money.

The man shuns, waving his hand. He starts his bike again.

"What's your name?"

There is silence. A silence that, for me, is a prelude... Prelude to a storm that is going to create history... Prelude to a battle that is going to seal fates... Prelude to a ray of hope that is going to stare back into the eyes of the fireball of crime...

"Ayodhya..."

3 WHAT GOES AROUND...

Ayodhya's Yezdi has come to a halt at an old, dilapidated two-storey building. Since a decade, the only painting on the building has been done by patches of green algae.

He scampers along the slippery stairs, three steps at once and unlocks the door. The scene inside is not great.

There is an old, really old, huge brownish transistor on a steel table. Cobwebs galore... There is a TV kept on a stool near the entrance to the kitchen. There is a showcase near it containing some not-so-worthy pieces of broken toys and papers. There is a photo kept in the center, framed and cleaned. The floor was polished ages ago with red which has now turned brown. The lighting is a typical 1960 style with thick wires running all around the ceiling like snakes. There is a huge fan hanging in the middle of it. The walls are chipping out. A dirty curtain separates the bedroom from the drawing room.

"Grandpa..."-Ayodhya unlaces his shoes, sitting on an old, sturdy and long netted chair. There is no reply.

"Grandpa..."

"Appu, you're back?"-his grandpa emerges from the bedroom. He is tall, just like Ayodhya. There are wrinkles on his face that look like solidified ripples on water. He is bald, spectacled and feeble. His eyebrows cover the eyes, and moustache, his lips. He is wearing a Kurta-Pyjama, typical of aged middle-class citizens of Sarovar Nagar.

"Yeah... Played a match today..."

"Bet?"

"Yeah... But between others..."-Ayodhya walks to the bathroom to take a bath.

His grandpa starts doing the dishes. There is no sound other than the sound of of utensils in the kitchen and that of splashing of water in the bathroom.

Clicck...

The bathroom door is opened. The door is broken. It is merely meant to indicate that the bathroom is engaged. Ayodhya proceeds to chop vegetables.

"Do you know the difference between routine and habit?"-his grandpa tosses the cleaned vegetables towards Ayodhya.

Ayodhya pauses the chopping to think over. "Routine is externally compelled and habit is internal."

"One more thing..."-his grandpa adds as he walks out. "... Each one can give rise to the other..."

"What will you have today, Appu?"

"Upma..."

His grandpa has kept the utensil on the gas stove and is now looking for the match box.

"Here... We keep it on the shelf every time. You know that well..."

"Yeah, I know it is routine. But I still search out of habit."

"I'll prepare, grandpa... You go watch TV."

The grandpa walks slowly- "Time is the greatest enemy of mankind, Appu. Because so far, man has been losing... So far... And you know, time conditions you to routine, softens your senses, turns you in to a robot that cannot bear a deviation from routine, a robot that desperately fears those deviations..."

"And then, once you are ready to be devoured, time strikes..."- his grandpa settles slowly on the chair as the clock strikes. "Very violently!"

Ayodhya doesn't know to cook anything other than Upma. It has been about twenty minutes. He comes out with two platefuls of the dish. His grandpa is engrossed in newspaper.

"Here..."

"I talked about routine and habit to make you realize that playing cricket should not become a routine for you. You're a grownup now. You should not end up being one of those men who play for money. You know you're different. We have a name in the city..."

Ayodhya nods. He cleans the photo frame with a cloth. It is his habit- to clean it before breakfast; the only thing that is cleaned every day in the whole house. It is of his parents. He thinks about what he could have done had he been as old as he is now, on that fateful day...

Let me take you through that incident. It's the late 80s...

The heir for 30 acres of land, three farm houses and the Blue Bell Villa is expected to be born any time in the month.

"What shall we name him?"-his father has called up from the office. They have been told by the doctor that it is going to be a boy.

"Ayodhya..."-his mother answers feeling the little pranks going on in her womb.

"Why? It is a place. Not a person."

"It is a habit..."

"... to be unconquerable..."

His grandpa comes out of his room. His siesta is over.

"What name did you say, my child?"-he asks affectionately.

"Oh, you woke up father?"-she turns.

"Ask him too..."-the voice from the office requests.

"Ayodhya... How does it sound?"

"Great..."

"He likes it..."-she answers back.

"Ok... I'm leaving office now, will be home in some time... What would you want me to bring for snacks?"

"Upma..."

"Upma? For snacks?"

"I feel like tasting upma..."

"Ok. I'm on my way..."-the call is cut.

Knock! Knock!!

Someone is at the door. His mother gets up slowly with her hands supporting her waist.

"I'll open the door..."-his grandpa insists.

"No, I'll see."-she walks to the door.

It is her sister-in-law, the grandpa's eldest daughter.

"How is our hero doing?"-she feels the womb of Ayodhya's mother. She has not brought anything for her brother's family.

"He is fine."

"I was just passing by and thought of dropping in to check out our hero."-her vacuous talk begins.

"That is ok. Good to know that you came. What would you like to have?"-asks Ayodhya's mother.

Ayodhya's grandpa looks at her admiringly.

"Just some Besan Laddoos if possible. I'm not insisting..."-the grandpa's daughter smiles broadly.

Ayodhya's mother can't believe it. She blinks for a second. "Besan laddoos?"

"Well it is just that Soman is returning for a holiday from US next week. He loves those laddoos. He told me over phone that he wanted to eat some... That too made by you and only you."

"Are you out of your mind? Can't you see she's pregnant? What kind of a doctor are you?"-the old man loses his cool.

"Why you are so upset, father... It is ok. I told her I'm not insisting. It is only for the poor kid."

"Kid? My foot!! Soman is a spoilt drunkard. Ask him about studies and he'll frown. But he will give you all the details about foreign liquor even without asking. Since when has the mongrel become a poor kid longing for besan laddoos?"

“Father, it is ok...”-Ayodhya’s mother tries to intervene.

“Ok... I’m leaving. How unfortunate I was born as a daughter to a stone-hearted man!!”

She leaves. Everything is calm. The evening is hot, the ceiling fan makes a mild sound and there are some crows cawing out of thirst.

Ayodhya’s mother walks down the stairs of the house to the garden. She carries a small cauldron in her hand.

“Where are you going?”-Ayodhya’s father has just arrived at the gate.

“I just want to fill this thing up with water and keep here in the garden... The birds are very thirsty.”

Ayodhya’s father parks his Yezdi near the well and walks towards her.

“Leave it... I’ll fill it. Don’t strain yourself unnecessarily...”

She walks back into the house.

“Let us not talk about his sister. He is tired...”-she suggests to Ayodhya’s grandpa. Her deep, dark eyes have made the suggestion gentler.

“The whole lineage of mine has been doing some noble deed from centuries that she is my daughter-in-law!”-he thinks.

Three days roll by. It is twilight.

Ayodhya’s grandpa has gone for an evening walk. Only his mother is at home.

Knock... Knock...

She walks slowly to open the door. The grandpa’s second daughter and the second son have arrived with the first one.

“Oh, so nice to see you...”-she welcomes them in.

“So? What do you keep doing all the day?”-the grandpa’s second daughter wants to know.

“Nothing much... I’ll prepare breakfast in the morning and...”

“It is not about daily chores... What do you do at other times?”-the grandpa’s second son interrupts.

She is unable to gauge what is going on.

“I... I... um...”

“Can’t you go for work? Will you remain a burden all your life on my brother?”-the first daughter opens up a topic.

“Look, you have to listen to us... We both are doctors.”-the second daughter boasts. “Does that make you immortals?”-I would’ve asked if I were in the place of Ayodhya’s mother.

Ayodhya’s mother stands shocked. She thought that they had changed for good.

“You didn’t bring anything during or after marriage. We showed some leniency. But don’t take anything for granted. We will extract everything you were supposed to do. Don’t act too innocent.”

“See, I can’t understand why you are so upset with me. I couldn’t bring much gold or cash with me. But I have always remained dutiful and looked after everyone.”

“You acted cheap and ignited the anger of that old man just because I asked you some laddoos...”

“I didn’t act... I was a bit surprised...”

“Oh, have you become so influential that you get surprised if we request something?”-grandpa’s second daughter looks at Ayodhya’s mother and the others, surprised.

Ayodhya's mother feels tired. She sits on the chair, unable to answer. Her heart has become heavier than her womb.

When logic and reasoning fail to convince, you must understand that there is a motive.

"You have the audacity to sit when we are standing?"-the old man's second son shouts out aloud and kicks her hard on her stomach.

She screams but her voice is suppressed by the other two.

She feels extreme pain in her womb.

"Leave her. Job done!"-the first daughter hurries away.

"Help!!"

The doors of the house and humanity are closed on her face. The car speeds away.

"We should have shot her in the head."-the second son is anxious.

"There are always two things in a successful crime. One, accomplish the task, two, escape."-explains one of the sisters.

"Will she survive?"-he asks.

"I felt her womb three days ago. The way you kicked... I don't think she could bear it. The nearest hospital is ours. If, by chance, the oldie returns home in time and she is able to make it, we'll nail her in the hospital."

"How?"

"We are doctors!"

The second son is dropped at the office building where Ayodhya's father works. He is tasked to kill his own brother. A contract killer has been hired two days ago.

Ayodhya's mother is screaming aloud ceaselessly.

The vendor at the roadside stall hears the shouts. He acts quickly.

"Hey Chotu... Leave those tea glasses in the bucket. I'll remove them. Run quickly and call grandpa from the park. Tell him... Aauntie is screaming and bring him here..."

Chotu dashes to the park.

Ayodhya's grandpa returns home in an auto rickshaw. He pays the driver and runs with all his might.

He finds no one at home. A few seconds later the tea vendor returns to Ayodhya's home.

"Sir, I heard madam shout with pain. I immediately called the doctor. She is taking her in the car towards Gandhi hospital."

"Thank you so much..."-the grandpa clutches the tea vendor's hands.

He dials up the office number of Ayodhya's father and informs him of the situation. Ayodhya's father leaves immediately.

"Please take care of the house. I'll return."-the grandpa leaves for Gandhi hospital.

Ayodhya's father pulls out his Yezdi from the parking area. He is about to start.

"Bro..."-the grandpa's second son walks up to him.

Ayodhya's father is surprised. How is it possible that his brother who had broken all bonds ages ago is now walking with a smile towards him?

"You? Here?"-he doesn't stop to talk.

"To see you off!"

A knife quietly slices its way into the stomach of Ayodhya's father!

Ayodhya's father rides to a distance and feels intense pain. He yells and turns towards his brother. He sees his brother approaching to have another go at him. He races through the road.

The contract killer his brother has hired tries to block him with his car. Ayodhya's father takes a sharp turn, bumps out of the divider and rides to the opposite direction.

With meager population in the city, there is no way help could arrive. The roads are empty. The chase is on. Ayodhya's father has held his stomach tightly but the bleeding is unabated.

The killer seems to gain on. Ayodhya's father changes gear. The Yezdi rips through Double Road. The car is not able to keep up the pace.

But he is slowly losing consciousness. After about a couple of kilometers, he sinks on the bike and falls down.

A few seconds later the killer is relieved. He is getting his payment in full!

"Parvati..."-Ayodhya's mother lying on the backseat calls the lady who is driving the car. Parvati is trying to look back at her and simultaneously speed up the car. She is her neighbor. She is a doctor and has been taking care of her.

"At any cost..."-Ayodhya's mother continues amidst pain.

"Ayodhya should survive!"

Her eyes have rolled in. The back seat is full of blood.

Parvati realizes the futility of reaching the hospital. There is an old, broken gate at the side of the road. She takes a violent turn and enters the gate. After a few yards, she stops the car and gets to the backseat with her emergency kit.

She has no other way than to cut open the womb.

She starts weeping mildly as she slowly retrieves the baby. She doesn't want her sobs to disturb her steady hands. Ayodhya's mother is cold... Dr. Parvati finally cries out to relieve her emotions as the baby cries for breath. There would have been eerie silence that late evening if not for the cries...

It is a graveyard!

4 OVERCAST- THE RISE OF GHARIAL

Your world is cyclic... Unpredictably cyclic. Strange, isn't it? Sometimes irony explains better than facts do. You might have memorized poems and found them difficult to remember. I have been seeing the cycle of life since millennia and yet, sometimes, am not capable of predicting the next thing that is going to happen. It becomes even more difficult when it comes to certain people. When the most sinister of entities take up human shape... When evil, in its purest form, dissolves into the unfathomable depths of civilized society... When hell lets itself loose on earth!

While Ayodhya takes another look at his parents' photograph in Sarovar Nagar, the sky is unusually overcast in one of the trendiest cosmopolitans of India. It is three in the noon but looks quite sundown. People, unable to believe their watches and gadgets, confirm the correct time from others-

"Excuse me, Sir... Could you tell me the time please?"

"Three... Difficult to believe right?"

"Yeah, it looks like seven. Is there any eclipse today?"

The real eclipse has begun on humanity... in an old building at the far end of the city... The complex has some retail outlets, some agencies and some apartments. Flat no. 333...

"Your name, Sir?"-the receptionist at the state-of-the-art waiting hall asks politely.

"Gharial!" -a heavy, thunderous voice replies. He is six-two; a long overcoat covers his broad shoulders. A hat refuges his eyes within. His features are difficult to make out.

"Gharial?"-she smiles, amused. The visitor's face seems to be serious.

"Very funny... I mean...Please tell me your real name..."

In a flash, a huge hand lands on her neck and squeezes it relentlessly. Her chair bends backwards. Her head presses against the wall.

Her eyeballs begin to roll inwards. Her hands search for an object around. Nothing seems to come to her help. She succumbs...

He slowly leans forward. His lips are right next to her ear.

"Death!"

He is walking down the aisle followed by two of his comrades.

"Real names don't help... Real faces do."

There is some activity happening around in the small, module-like rooms on the either side of the aisle.

His eyes fall on the girl in one such room wearing a nightgown and holding a cellphone. There is a telephone directory, a few markers, some paper bits lying here and there and a laptop on the floor.

"Am I speaking to Mr. Pavithran Nair?"-her voice is captivating.

"Yes..."

"Hi, I'm Richa Rastogi calling from LIC Corporation of India."

"LIC?"

"That's right... We are pleased to inform you that we are offering personal loans at 2% interest for the customers... You can claim the amount in the name of your son Prinjith Nair. The loan amount is rupees 3.5 lac"

"Really? Hey shut up..."-Mr. Nair silences his noisy son. He wants to know more. A personal loan at this stage is very helpful. More than half of the world drags the body called daily life on the hard floor called loan. The floor bleeds the body but keeps it moving.

"Yes Sir... All you have to do is just submit a cheque of Rupees Fifteen Thousand towards the processing fee in the name of Mr. Lomy Lala. Your name, date of birth..."

"One second... Just hold on... One second... Hey give me the pen..."-he asks his son. His son delays as the pen is not handy.

Mr. Nair slaps him! He slaps the very person in whose name he is going to claim the amount!

'Ms. Rastogi' controls her laugh.

"The second drawer, you brat!!"

"Yes madam... Mr. Lomy Lala, my name, date of birth..."

"Your name, date of birth... Policy number... Right? Credit card details along with the four-digit ATM card pin number and CVV number should be written legibly, in capitals on a separate paper and to be sent along with the cheque within two days to this address... No.333... 4th floor, Marichika Complex... Dweepa"-she gives him the address.

"Once we confirm your credentials, you will receive the amount directly into the bank account."

"Please remember, this facility is only for select elite customers who have been prompt in their premium payments. We request you not to disclose the same to anyone else... Any doubts?"

"No, madam... Ok madam... Thank you... Thank you so much..."-the call is cut.

"I have a doubt madam..."-Gharial comes in.

She is shell-shocked. Her eyes are wide open. Her body has started to tremble with fear. There is a sudden gush of sweat.

He sits down. It looks like a lion sitting in front of a lamb. She slides back on the floor slowly.

"Lomy... Lomy!!"-she tries to raise the alarm. Her voice too is trembling.

"Yeah, one sec..."-Lomy answers from another room.

Gharial gently stuffs a piece of fabric in her mouth. She does not oppose; she can see his eyes from under his hat. Perhaps his eyes are too cold to overcome. He ties a cloth around her mouth.

She is numb with fear. The floor is wet.

He ties her hands to the window grill. One of his comrades spreads a bunch of tissue papers on the floor.

Holding her palm in his, he bites out the flesh from her wrist! Her vein is slit.

She groans but the cloth in her mouth prevents the voice from reaching Lomy's ears.

"Are you insured?"- Gharial wipes his mouth.

He waits for her answer eagerly. Her eyes are red and moist. They are pleading him to release her.

Gharial walks out of the room.

In another room Lomy is busy editing a webpage. His back faces the door. There are some books, an I-Pod, an empty coffee cup and a thing resembling a tennis racquet used to kill mosquitoes.

The webpage reads- 'STATE BANK OF DWEEPA'

It has a 'Home' tab, a 'Login' tab, a 'Contact us' tab. But the link on the address bar is different!!

It does not read the original 'www.onlinesbd.com'

There is something fishy.

Lomy is done with the editing. Now he is busy drafting an email.

It looks official and quite appealing. It is a request mail, the link is mentioned and the recipients are asked to update the KYC or 'Know your customer' information within a stipulated timeframe and failure to do so is supposedly resulting in automatic locking of bank account.

"Know your visitors, Mr. Lala."

Lomy is taken aback. He turns around swiftly.

"Hey... Who... Who are you?"

"Can I hand over the cheque in person, Mr. Lala?"

"Yyyy... Yeah... I mm... mean... Twinkle... Twinkle... Ask... Ask these guys to wait outside."-he tries to appear normal.

"The girl in the other room? She was Twinkle?"-Gharial is feigning a surprise, slowly turning to his comrades.

"Thought she was Ms. Richa Rastogi..."-he looks back at Lomy, slowly.

"Was?"-Lomy is scared.

"Is? Hmmm?"- Gharial turns to his comrade who in turn goes out of sight for a minute and returns.

"Was..."

"WAS!!!"-Gharial confirms to Lomy.

"She is now twinkling in the sky..."

"Please let me go... You... You can take whatever you want. We have lots of money... Take all of it... Here..."-Lomy drags out huge bags loaded with currency notes!

"Oh boy!!"-Gharial exclaims softly digging the money out of the bag with his feet and gently brushing Lomy's hair. Lomy has closed his eyes and his hands are folded. He is sobbing and holding Gharial's knee for mercy.

"You seem to have a good appetite for money..."-he remarks as his comrades zip the cash.

He picks up a pack of thousand rupee notes from one of the bags.

"Bon appetite!!"-he holds a note in front of Lomy's lips. Lomy looks at the note and slowly takes it. Gharial waits... Lomy's eyes squeeze in grief. His sobbing gradually gets louder.

"We are strange people. We don't gobble up what we are hungry for."-Gharial looks around. He spots the tennis racquet. He switches on the power button.

There is current flow through the racquet. He slowly brings it in contact with Lomy's arm.

Lomy screams.

"Eat it!"-Gharial thunders!

Lomy tries his best to chew the note. He spits after a few seconds.

“Please forgive me.”

“Forgiveness always comes with a choice... And ends without a guarantee...”

The racquet touches him again. This time it is longer. He screams out loud. His mouth is wide open. Gharial stuffs the entire pack in his mouth.

“Money can buy you luxury, security, courage, power... Nutritious, isn’t it?”

Lomy wiggles in pain. Gharial now holds the racquet on Lomy’s chest. A few moments later Lomy is motionless...

Gharial and his men exit the apartment.

The overcast has turned into darkness!!

5 THE FRENZIED PURSUIT

"Dude... Look at this..."
"Amazing reflexes... Hey, Akhil... Check this out."
The videos of Ayodhya's batting and wicketkeeping have travelled across Charlie Bazaar like twin lightnings.
"Send me those videos..."
"You are on Shutapp?"
"No, mine is Vada OS..."
"To hell with you..."
A cricket den in Charlie bazaar feels the need for Ayodhya.
"Have the dogs seen these?"-the team manager of Hunter XI asks the captain who has shown the videos. He wants to know whether the Killer XI has seen them.
"I don't think so. The video is of today. Morning match."
"Where does he live?"
"Don't know but Kumar said the guy's name is Ayodhya and he has an old Yezdi. Two days ago I've seen the bike near the 2nd street after Double Road."
"Quick..."
The Hunters XI hunt for Ayodhya. They have clear instructions- to stop all those who ride Yezdi.
"How does Yezdi look?"
"Goggle out..."

Back in the house-
Ayodhya walks down the stairs, towards the well.
"Ayodhya, what are you up to?"
"I'll just fill up this cauldron with water and keep it there... The birds seem to be craving for water"!!
Something tells him to do that. But he is not able to sense it. He can only feel it. And sometimes feelings are stronger than senses.
He returns and closes the door.
His grandpa sits on the netted chair with the newspaper in his hand. It has covered his face from Ayodhya but has not quite covered his mind.
Ayodhya knows that his grandpa is in deep thought and not reading newspaper. It is held upside down.
His grandpa is indeed thinking about the past...
Dr. Parvati has reached the hospital with the baby.
His grandpa has reached there about an hour ago. "What happened? What took you so long?"-he asks her as she walks with the baby.
"Sister, here. I'll come in five minutes."-she gives the baby and goes to the washroom.
As soon as she comes out of the room, she takes the grandpa away to a corner and narrates him everything.
"I'm totally shocked. How could it happen? She was perfectly healthy yesterday."
"My children... I never knew I have raised demons."-he breaks down.
He walks to the nearest seat and sits sobbing, with hands on his forehead.
She perches next to him, gently supporting her temple on his shoulder.
"Shall we go to the police?"
"Doctor..."-a nurse waves her hand.
"Dr. Gopal wants you to meet him."
Dr. Gopal is a leading doctor in Gandhi hospital who conducts autopsy.
"Dr. Parvati, she has not fallen off the stairs. There are no wounds. I can sense that someone has punched or kicked her on her womb really hard."
Dr. Parvati loses a heartbeat!
She leaves to meet the grandpa. "We have to go to the police."
"Can I see Ayodhya?"

Dr. Parvati is surprised that they had named the baby even before he is born. The last words of Ayodhya's mother ring in her mind.
The grandpa's eyes for the first time fall on Ayodhya. He experiences a cold, soothing gush of blood in his trembling heart.
"Where is his father?"-he asks her, holding baby Ayodhya in his arms.
"Did you inform him?"-she questions him back.
"Yeah... He should have come here by now. Can I use the phone?"
He dials the number at his home. There is no response. It has started to rain.
The night ends with minds full of questions.
The grandpa wants to know of his son's whereabouts. Dr. Parvati wants to know how she could protect the baby from the grandpa's children. The grandpa's daughters and the second son want to know what has happened to Ayodhya's mother... and her baby.
The next day the grandpa's daughters enquire in their hospital if any pregnant woman was brought in critical condition. "No."
"Where else could she have gone?"
"Gandhi hospital?"
The tea vendor brings the news of the death of Ayodhya's father. The old man has a bold heart. He listens. He has experienced all the fear, all the sorrow the previous night. The only reason for him to move on is the baby.
People sink into trauma when incidents such as these occur. But there are some who have extreme presence of mind.
"They should not know Ayodhya is alive."-he tells Dr. Parvati. "Yes, even I was thinking about it. We'll never let them know he's born."
The plan is made. Ayodhya will stay in Dr. Parvati's house as her son!
The grandpa deliberately invites his children for the funeral of Ayodhya's parents. He wants them to get convinced that nobody has survived.
Fear of failure makes the celebration of success hysteric. The trio is so happy that they don't make any attempts to dig out information on Ayodhya.
Dr. Parvati and her husband start offering support to grandpa. He stays just a few yards away.

I allow problems in pockets. You need to gather strength, muster courage... And hence my grace is bestowed.
I gave that to Ayodhya's grandpa too.
Three years roll by...
A young Ayodhya has uncanny resemblance to his father. A casual gaze at him can send shock waves across the minds of the grandpa's children who have seen their brother right from childhood. They can barge in anytime. After all, 30 acres of land, three farm houses and the Blue Bell Villa are way too attractive even to a corpse.
Dr. Parvati has conceived. She cannot offer more assistance. She is moving out to another city.
Ayodhya has to attend school. He has started to read some words in his mother tongue and of course, English.
His grandpa sits looking at Ayodhya who is all set for a bicycle race. He waits at the start point along with others. Among the front tires of the bicycles that you see lined up across the street, there is one exception. A bike tire! Of Yezdi! And nothing more!
Other kids have their own bicycles. Ayodhya has a punctured tire from the Yezdi. He is going to run along, rolling the tire while others are going to ride their bicycles. He is barefoot while others are with footwear. He is wearing a woolen coat in the hot sun. The coat is torn where the shirt inside is fine and the shirt is torn where the coat outside is fine.
His grandpa feels the pain. The property is under dispute. His own children have filed a case against him. The revenue from the land is zero. The court expenses are huge. His pension is the sole support.
Ayodhya smiles at his grandpa. He does not know what economic inequality is. He sees only the race. The finish line...
"One..."
Ayodhya crouches. His right hand supports the tire. His eyes are focused on the finish line.
"Two..."
His heel lifts from the ground and the body bends forward.
"Three!!"
He charges ahead. The other kids too, start with all their might.

He hits the tire on its top with such a frequency that his hand appears blurred!
He has beaten two of his contenders. Only one is left. Ayodhya pulls his body to keep in pace with his toes. The race between the two lasts about twenty yards.
The kid with the bicycle finally wins. Ayodhya pants with hands resting on the knees. He turns back to see the other two kids not even trying to reach the line.
"One more!"-he wants to race the fifth time! He wants to race until he wins.
"Ayodhya... Come home..."-Dr. Parvati calls him.
"Ma, just one race. Last one..."
"No... The milk is ready."
He walks back, hitting gently on the tire. It seems he is upset with it- "You could have rolled faster..."
"Grandpa..."-he runs after drinking milk.
"Why don't Rakshit and Suraj ask for another race when they lose?"
His grandpa is amazed by the question.
"Because they are not Ayodhya!"
A few days later the grandpa decides. He will take Ayodhya to a boarding school, a hundred miles away. Ayodhya will study there until my grace prevails.
"Ma, why can't I live here with you and study? Like Rakshit and Suraj... I promise, I'll be good. I won't trouble you. I will help you fetch the groceries. I know how to spend money. Look, one coin of one rupee and another of two rupees make it three rupees and when I give a coin of five rupees, auntie will give me two rupees back with the bunch of coriander leaves."
Dr. Parvati looks at his grandfather and leaves. Her state of mind is better left untold.
Ayodhya is unable to understand.
"Grandpa, I'll press your legs and bring you three glasses of water every day. Can I stay back?"-his eyes are wide with expectations.
His grandpa feels immense pain in the heart. But he is helpless. He can't be emotional. He can't prefer affection to safety.

"Kids are like moist clay. Initially, they take the form we give them and then they get hardened with time."-he really has high regards for me. I am flattered.
"Ayodhya, the school you will be going to is a big one. You will have many friends there. You will even have a bicycle."
"So you want me to go..."-the three-year-old comes straight down to conclusion.
"I'll come there every Saturday."
"It is ok, grandpa. I know you are old. Don't worry too much about me."
His grandpa hugs him tightly.
Ayodhya's schooling begins...
"Disappearance is the first form of security."-the grandpa thinks. It has been five years now. The grace period is over.
Knock! Knock!!
Someone's again at the door.
"You're still alive?"-the eldest daughter asks. The trio is back.
"What do you want?"-the grandpa stands firmly at the door.
"What is stopping you from dividing the property?"-the younger daughter asks, making her way in.
"Soman has finished his schooling. He has to join a college. Management fee is high. Let us sell some property and get him admitted into a good medical college."-the son suggests.
"Why can't we prefer a merit seat?"-the grandpa asks.
"His rank is too low. But you know very well he is lucky enough to have a rich grandpa"-she smiles.
"But do you know there may be poor people unlucky enough to be his patients?"
"I told you the oldie will blabber and drag the matter..."-the second son turns to his sisters in despair. His eyes fall on a toy and a few clothes meant for a kid.
"What are these things doing here?"
The grandpa is caught!
The second son has got a clue that the baby has survived.
"When are you distributing the property?"-the first daughter shouts at

him.
"Very soon."-the son walks out.
The old man is scared.
"Go away. It is my property. I'll give it to whoever I want."
"It is ancestral, damn it. You dare do any such mischief."-the second daughter warns.
"Oh, would you then stab me too?"
There is a sudden lull. The daughters look at each other and walk out. The old man rushes to see what the son is up to.
For his utter shock, he sees the son enquiring about a small kid with the children in the neighborhood. The children seem to be blurting out everything!
The second son turns to his father who still stands at the balcony.
The sisters get in the car. The son slowly follows them and sits in the back seat. The car is still. The old man observes keenly. There seems to be a conversation going on.
Suddenly the car starts. The second daughter drives. The first peeps out of the window and shows her hand indicating a small child. Her next gesture is the reason the old man is worried even today.
She indicates slitting of throat!!
Knock... Knock... Knock
Ayodhya's grandfather is brought down to the present world by someone at the door. Every time there is a knock at the door of their house, there has been an epic turn in their lives. Every person who visits their place seems like the three children of Ayodhya's grandfather or someone sent by them. Ayodhya knows the fear his grandfather experiences.
"I'll see..."-he walks to the door.
There are five members of Hunter XI standing at the door including the team manager.
"He's the one!"
"You're Ayodhya, right?"-the captain asks.
Ayodhya nods.
"We are from Hunter XI. Today there is a match between us and the Killer XI in some time. We want you to play for us."

"I'm sorry."-Ayodhya replies.

It is quiet for now.

"Look... We are not here to request. It is our order. We rule the city."-a haughty remark comes from the captain.

"And I rule my will."

"He'll play."

Ayodhya looks astonishingly at his grandfather.

"Grandpa?"

"He will play. You may go now." The visitors leave.

"Better uneventful than tragic."-his grandpa walks in.

"What tragedy, grandpa? They are just a bunch of delinquents. Five minutes is all I need to fix them."

"Niche qualities are meant for extraordinary things."-his grandpa returns with a glass of water.

"You'll play and return immediately."

"Once I play for them, they will never let me leave. I'll be sucked in."

"You've already started the process, Appu. You played in the morning."

"The unluckiest thing that could happen to talent, beauty and all the good things is..."

"... falling into wrong eyes!"-his grandpa drops on the chair in despair.

Ayodhya stares at his grandfather. There is an air of disbelief. He feels his grandfather doesn't have faith in him.

But there are deep thoughts going on inside the grandfather's mind.

"You will remain calm throughout the match. They are dangerous people. Let us not muddy ourselves."

The Yezdi roars.

Ayodhya is back in the ground. There is pomp and show all around. Push carts are ruling the traffic. The hawkers are having a good time. The sound system is ready for the commentators. Huge speakers are mounted on wooden structures. The boundary is being marked with chalk powder and wet lime. Separate seating arrangements are made based on the spending abilities of spectators.

The MLA is expected to arrive anytime soon. He will bat the inaugural delivery and kickstart the match. The Hunter XI is warming up. The Killer XI is jogging.

"Wfff..."-the captain of Hunter XI whistles and waves at Ayodhya. Ayodhya walks towards them. The captain gives him a new pair of jerseys. Ayodhya walks to the storage shed and returns after a while. He is in the jerseys.
"Who is he?"-the main batsman of Killer XI asks his team mates, jogging, looking at Ayodhya.
"Never seen him before. Must be an extra player. Replacement for Rahul I guess."
Except the second statement, everything else is correct.
The one who comes late and leaves early is the most important person.
The MLA comes, talks, plays, goes.
The match begins.
Ayodhya is the wicketkeeper.
The first two batsmen play long innings. The ball is sufficiently old now. Ayodhya moves up to the stumps.
The batsman commits a blunder. He misses the ball coming at his legs, loses balance and lifts his back leg for a fraction of a second.
The bails come off!
The Hunters XI have their first prey. The batsman looks grudgingly at the celebrations before leaving.
The next batsman comes to the crease. He marks the middle stump line on the crease, walks away from the pitch, stretches his groin, jumps a couple of times and rolls his arms. He returns to the crease, looks around to record the field placement in his memory.
Wicketkeeper? Huh... He is just there to collect wide deliveries. He doesn't care.
The bowler indeed bowls a wide ball on the leg side. The batsman misses and takes out his back leg completely.
Ayodhya dislodges the bails yet again.
"Be careful! The keeper is ready behind you! Don't lift your back-foot. Fix it in the crease."-the team members of Killer XI warn the new batsman.
Cognizance of the aftermath sometimes hastens it. The next batsman too falls for a stumping after a couple of overs.
"Mistakes can be corrected. Blunders are addictive."-thinks Ayodhya as

he sees that nobody is willing to learn from their predecessors' mistakes. After four stumpings, finally the lower middle order steers the run rate. "I can't do anything if they don't give me a chance. It is all about their confidence."-he stands thinking after a batsman walks out of the crease, down the pitch, and whacks a sixer!

They have set a reasonable target.

The Hunters XI start batting slowly. The required runrate is increasing. The only thing that has remained constant is the rate at which the required runrate is increasing. The pressure is immense. The batsmen come to their senses and try some hard-hitting.

Five wickets fall in a heap. The situation is pathetic. The bet money seems to be slipping out of the manager's hands.

"Ayodhya, go..."-the only sensible thing the manager does that evening is the uttering of the two words.

Ayodhya stands in the middle. He resorts to fireworks. The opponents start getting anxious. Negative thoughts creep up their mind.

They decide to go for the most infamous of strategies.

"Spike him!"-the captain orders his bowler.

The bowler hurls a beamer straight at Ayodhya's head. Ayodhya has been noticing his grandpa experience fear every day. He knows what fear is. He also knows that a beamer isn't fear.

He bends backwards and hooks the ball. The ball flies out of the ground. The bowler gets a warning plus a no-ball. The umpire is an ex-Hunter XI.

"Great shot, man. Whenever I take the main umpire position, you may play freely. I won't declare you out for LBW and keeper-catches."

The leg umpire is a former Killer XI. He talks something to the captain. The captain indicates something to his fielders.

Ayodhya thinks- "This is the difference between a sport and a game."

The match continues. Ayodhya soon realizes that the bowlers are trying to get him injured.

But what he fails to understand is that even fielders are!

Ayodhya defends a delivery. A close in fielder charges at the ball even though no run is being attempted, picks it up and hurls an over-arm throw from just a few feet away at Ayodhya. The ball hits Ayodhya on

the arm!
"Bull's eye!"-the captain hides his smile.
They all know that Ayodhya is hurt but they are unpleasantly surprised. Ayodhya is not showing even a speck of pain on his face.
"It's my game now!"
Ayodhya makes his first move by throwing them into confusion. "Was the hit not that hard?"-the fielder thinks.
The next ball is bowled. Ayodhya steps out to hammer it at the same fielder. It hits him on the knee. The fielder falls on the ground instantly! He refuses to get up. He is finally escorted out. A spare fielder comes in. The match continues. Despite constant exhortation by the captain, no fielder is daring to have a go at Ayodhya.
"In the market of fear I am the only seller!"-Ayodhya feels.
The match is slowly getting into the folds of the Hunter XI.
The captain makes a small shift in the strategy. They are now targeting the other batsman.
Ayodhya is compelled to finish off the match quickly by taking risks. Compulsion is the origin of risk. And risk is a tussle between brain and heart. Brain goes by reason while heart, by itself.
Ayodhya's brain tells him to settle for a single while his heart wants a double to save the poor partner. His brain, nevertheless, agrees with his heart for a reason. The leg umpire is ex-Hunter XI!
Ayodhya takes the risk. He forces his feet to cover those 22 yards once more. The ball seems to be getting the better of him. The keeper's eyes are wide, eager to catch the approaching throw. His hands are slowly forming a cup-shape. Ayodhya resorts to the last option.
He dives to save his wicket. He thinks he has not made it. But the ex-Hunter has no doubts!
Ayodhya succeeds. He plans risky runs every alternate over. The perfect blend of brain and heart is called a calculated risk.
The match ends with Ayodhya sealing a symbolic sixer. The Hunters run in from the stands. The people celebrate. The Killers are looking for reasons to assault Ayodhya. He walks for a handshake. The opponents deny. The members of Hunter XI lift Ayodhya on their shoulders.
The captain of Killer XI makes an angry gesture at Ayodhya and hurls

abuses.
The trophy and the bet money are awarded to Hunter XI. People are looking at Ayodhya, pointing their fingers stealthily at him. They are whispering among themselves.
Ayodhya turns at them. They smile. Ayodhya doesn't reciprocate. He has fallen in the wrong eyes already!
The ground slowly begins to lose the head count. Everyone disperses. Small kids walk with their parents, imitating some shots Ayodhya has played.
The Hunters have assembled at the storage shed.
The captain is giving some congratulatory sermon to his team members. He is praising the contribution of his team mates.
As expected, Ayodhya's name comes up. The players give a loud cheer. But Ayodhya is nowhere there.
The situation at the other side is quite tense. The team manager, the coach and all those who 'care for the legacy' of Killer XI, are not anywhere close to know about the spirit of the game and are shouting at the captain like possessed spirits. He stands, hanging his head in shame.
They disperse in their cars. The captain bangs a chair on the ground!
The team members discuss ways to avenge their defeat. "He was runout. But was not given."-the initiator fulfils his duty.
"We'll not let him go."-the captain declares after much animated arguments.
They wait near his Yezdi while Ayodhya slowly walks to the captain of Hunters XI. He returns the jersey and quietly leaves.
"You guys leave, I'll join you. Ayodhya!"-the captain runs to him.
"I am not playing."
"Why?"
"I'm not interested."
"You're wasting your talent."
"None of your business!"
"You dare play for Killer XI."-the captain finally brings out his paranoia.
"None of your business!"
"Ayodhya... We are dangerous people here. You don't know about us. We won't hesitate to even..."-the captain hesitates.

"First learn to blurt it out!"-Ayodhya thinks and walks slowly at the parking area.

There are four members of Killer XI waiting for him at the parking. They are impatient, hungry and tired. Their eyes fall on his bike. "What is this old bike doing here?"

"It's his!"

"Let the rust bite the dust!"-the captain lifts his bat to smash the headlights. He completes the swing but the bat goes missing half way in the trajectory. He looks at his bare hands in shock.

Behind him, inspecting the bat stands a stranger wearing a cap and a pair of sunglasses. A hankie covers his face!

The number three batsman of Killer XI who has newly learnt some aggressive moves charges at the stranger with a stump.

The stranger swiftly takes a step towards him, slides on the ground by his hip, lifts the player by tummy with his feet and flings him behind. The young gun falls at his captain's feet trembling in pain.

The other two run away.

The captain pushes the Yezdi on its side. The stranger is quick. He hurls a log of wood lying nearby, in its path. It gets stuck between two iron bars. The bike rests on the log.

The captain picks up the stump and hurls at the stranger like a spear. The stranger ducks backwards but the throw is accurate. It chips off a piece of flesh from his left shoulder. Blood springs out instantly.

The stranger presses against the shoulder. He stays calm for a while.

The captain's anger turns into fear. The stranger gets up, walks to the captain and kicks him violently on the shin. The captain screams in pain and falls on the ground. The number three batsman runs away. The captain too hops away quickly.

Knock! Knock!!

Someone's at Ayodhya's door.

His grandfather opens it slowly. There are two policemen with the head coach, chief strategist, assistant strategist, mentor and the captain of Killers XI.

"Where is Ayodhya?"-the police constable interrogates.

"He has gone for the match and not come yet."

"The match is over long ago. He's hiding in the house, we know it. Call him at once or we'll drag him out!"-the captain yells.
"Ask him to come to the station when he's back."- the chief strategist is calm. After all, he's a strategist.
"Sir, his bike is here..."-the captain points at the Yezdi parked in the garden.
"We are confiscating it as of now. It will be returned when he comes to the station."-the policeman signals the constables.
The old man doesn't resist.
The men call a towing vehicle. The bike is cleared in a jiffy.
The old man shuts the door. His breath is warm. He settles down on the netted chair.
"What a life, Ramprakash..."-he thinks to himself. A trailer of the last fifty years of his life passes by in front of his closed eyes. Strange, he sees it.
He sees himself in his twenties. The landlady of his house wants the old cupboard to be discarded. He immediately walks down to the bedroom, lifts the cupboard all by himself and takes it out of the house.
"What do you eat that you have so much energy?"-she asks admiringly.
He sees his thirty-year-old self. There is an old man at the railway station. A few men are harassing him for money. Others are just being onlookers. But he rushes to help. There are five of them but he beats them up black and blue.
The scenes seem unending. He opens his eyes to face the reality. The bike- his son's last sign, has been taken away in front of his eyes and he doesn't have the energy to even resist. He blames me for that. I accept it gracefully.
He breathes heavily to overcome the emotions. He doesn't want to know that he could cry. He has dispatched his grandson away to the place he should be working in. So, where is Ayodhya?
Now, follow my directions to sail a few hundred miles away. Take the Double Road and cross the city limits. Keep moving ahead. You'll hit the highway once you zoom under the flyover. Turn right and follow that huge truck. Oh, it has slowed down. Overtake it anyway. You'll see the toll booth. You need not pay there. You're my guests. Stick to the

highway route. You could see the paddy fields and patches of land showing signs of existence of water until recently. No, it isn't the moon. Sail on... Look to your right. A train is running alongside you. You see that man sitting at the stairs of the coach? He is ticketless. He wants to hop out once the train slows down at the next station. Now you see sugarcane fields on the either sides of the road. You smell a pungent odor? Yes, there is a sugar factory nearby.

Keep cruising. There are small, isolated houses here and there whose walls are painted by some brands for advertising. Corasandal cement- for a scent of sandal in cement! Sodafone- where you go, we don't know. Pairtel- unlimited usage for the lovebirds.

You see the roadblocks? Zoom past them. They are not for you. Dogs are signs of human presence. Pigs are signs of extreme human presence. Yes, they are the first ones to welcome you. Never mind, cross the lanes. There is a China Market selling cheap goods-the source of high levels of waste the city is suffering from. Keep moving and you see the main road after a few meters. Take left, fly above the vehicles standing at the signal and cross the circle diametrically. I know we could have just gone tangentially but I love symmetry. Go past the golf course. Be careful, the nets have holes. The golf balls fly through them. There is a bridge ahead, over the seamlessly flowing river. You see a man standing on the bridge wearing an adventure pack on his right shoulder and looking at the setting sun?

That's Ayodhya!

6 THE SPREE

The elections are over in Dweepa. Posters of various political parties are still competing for space on the walls of buildings and pillars of flyovers. Their flags are still fluttering majestically while the tri-color is waving quietly.

The counting is coming to an end. National Strength Front, NSF as it is known popularly is all set for a thumping victory in the state. News channels are displaying the vote statuses of all candidates. There are children who are watching the goings-on in awe. They only know that there is a change in the government and one of those people who had visited their houses uninvited, is going to win.

Crackers are bursting on the streets. The party workers have brought trucks full of people from a nearby village for dancing and singing. They are paid generously. Tons of sweets are being prepared to distribute among the public. NSF is not thinking twice to spend the money. They have the license to loot for the next five years. It is observing a 'free drink' day all over the state as a mark of apology for including a 'drink-free' city in their election manifesto.

There is a huge bar at the end of the road that leads to the Legislative Assembly of the state.

The waiters are wearing Halloween masks for an unusual celebration.

"Free of cost man... Don't think twice."- a young man pats his friend as the liquor is being served.

"It is poison."-the waiter gives a piece of advice.
The young man looks at him, startled.
"I know it is slow poison. Well, I'm not in a hurry."-he smiles.
The two friends gulp a few shots.... And pass out.
"I am!"-the waiter leaves for the storage area.
A few minutes later the entire bar is full of half-dead people. The waiters remove their masks except the one who has gone towards the storage. He comes back with a hat drawn up to his eyes, wearing his overcoat. His men are busy covering with polythene bags, the faces of the people lying unconscious.
"You know, once I bumped into a biology teacher with a few students..."-he turns to one of his men.
"She asked her students what happened when a polythene bag was tied to the leaves of small herbs. While they said that the plant dies, I interrupted and said- 'it makes a wonderful sight!' You know what she said? That I was fooling around without being asked to."
"I told her that I couldn't understand the feelings of plants and I saw them as just things. She insulted me in front of her students."
"I want to observe today. These guys can speak, can't they?"
"I want the address of the teacher. She is still alive. She can't die without witnessing my completing the assignment."
One of his gang members appears nervous at the heap of dead men. Gharial stares at him for a while. "If you're alone and in trouble, you panic. If you're in a group facing trouble, you don't... even if the collective trouble is much higher... That's why I dealt with them together. We are helping them die fearlessly."
"And I don't mind hurting party animals..."- Gharial takes a sharp look at his man. The man smiles obligingly.
"Coz PETA doesn't care..."- Gharial sits on the lounge.
"Keen observation..."-he smiles at another of his comrades.
"Hey..."
He is trying to poke a person lying on the floor by kicking him gently.
"How do you feel? I need a report."
"He is dead."-one of his men replies.
"Eureka!"

It is midnight.
"Hello..."-an old lady receives the call, half awake.
"Madam, what happens when a plant is covered by polythene?"-a child's voice asks innocently.
She is surprised listening to such a question in the middle of the night. It is not exam time.
"Why don't you observe and tell me tomorrow? Don't study too late in the night. What's your name?"
"Gharial!"-an ominous voice replies.
"What?"
"Turn around please..."
She turns to see the shadow of a gigantic figure standing behind the curtains at the end of the hallway. She is scared to death.
"If only the curtains were walls."-Gharial emerges.
"Who are you? What do you want? Please don't hurt me. Sonu... Sonu..."-she shouts for her son, even though she knows that he is in Sweden since the last two years. When death is near, you humans act foolish.
"Loved ones are those who are to be remembered only when in danger."-Gharial nears her.
"Others told you that the plant dies..."
"Sonuuu!"
"I'll make you feel it..."
"Help! Please!!"
"I will show you what happens after the plant dies!"-he forces polythene over her face and ties it at her neck.
He holds it tight until she gives up struggle.
"And the only thing I can observe for you is a two-minute silence."-he stands still, with eyes closed, in front of the lady for an exact 120 seconds.
Two days pass by.
The atmosphere is tense at NSF party office. The son of the chief ministerial candidate is missing.
There are murmurs in the meeting. "Must have gone abroad for party."
"When did he start working for the party? That *** ****!"
"I meant partying!"

"Let him never come back. This father-son duo is a big thorn in the flesh. They somehow needed this jolt."
"Guess what will happen if his son is dead. The father will die of heart attack and we will have our chance!"
I've seen India in this situation since ages. The chief minister, the elections, their talk... All these are dust as compared to how it was just a few hundred years earlier. And the first fresh case that glares in my eyes when I look back is the historical meeting at the outskirts of Murshidabad.
It is the turning point in the history of India. The British Empire was blessed with a son called Robert Clive. His offers could not be refused; strategies could not be defeated. And far, far away from all these was a young monarch lost in his own world.
It is April 1757.
"But I'm sorry, Sir. I do not understand why you have decided to trust Mir Jaffer. You better trust a wily old vixen."-Clive's deputy expresses his discomfort.
"... Mir Kasim seems to be much faithful... And he is young too."
"Officer, there is a reason. Did you observe them when they greeted us?"
"Yes. I did."
"How did they greet us?"
"They bowed down."
"And what did you observe with Mir Jaffer?"
"I'm afraid, nothing..."-the deputy admits.
"He bent down the most!"
The current conversation continues.
"Sir, please listen to me. If you break this news in the media before the swearing-in ceremony it will be a huge embarrassment for our party. The opposition will pounce. You will not get enough time to consolidate your position."
"But where did that brat go?"
"Sir, he must have gone for a fun trip. And he has done this before too."
The chief is somewhat relieved.
It is the day of his oath-taking.
"Where the hell is he?"-the CM candidate is concerned that his son has

still not returned for the ceremony.
"Sir, his cellphone is switched off. His friend too is out of reach. Must have gone for some outing, Sir."
The would-be-CM is not happy. He tries to divert his mind.
"I don't know how to read this properly."-the CM complains throwing away the copy of the oath he has been given to memorize.
"Nothing to worry, Sir. The governor is literate!"
"Do we really have to take the oath?"-asks he.
"Formality Sir, formality. It is just a start point."- his loyal party worker replies.
"Leave me alone for some time."-he sinks on his seat. Everyone leaves. He thinks about the last forty years of his political career. He does not have even the remotest estimate of how many people he has got murdered. He has even forgotten that once upon a time he himself had killed scores of people.
"Why am I remembering all these things just minutes before the swear-in?"-he had believed he had a practical mind. But he is human too.
"I should do away with the oath ceremony. We should have cake-cutting."-he whispers.
"Your wish is my command, Sir."-a man wearing a safari suit similar to those of the bodyguards stands a few yards away in the hall. A large trolley stands next to him covering something with a white sheet.
"Who are you? Wait outside..."-the would-be CM turns.
He is surprised to see a bodyguard wearing a hat. He can't recognize him.
"Who are you? Why are you wearing a hat?"
'SHASHIDHAR'-the name is flashing on the pocket.
"I'll have you kicked out of the job... Get lost!"
"Hmmm?"-Gharial points towards the name plate on his shirt.
"Hmmm!"-he points to the balcony that is visible from the glass window. A man, half naked, lies in a pool of blood.
"Kicked out of the world!"-Gharial's mouth opens wide displaying the huge gap formed by a missing tooth on the upper right of the jaw.
"What are you? Wh... wh... who are you?"
"Ask him!!"-Gharial opens his arms and points his palms towards the trolley.

The CM slowly walks to the trolley.
"Ram... Ram...!"-he trembles, calling his personal assistant.
He slowly lifts the white sheet.
His blood vessels almost burst after seeing the object underneath. His head reels. He is not able to feel his feet. He tries to move back but falls on the floor.
"Aww... The popular CM is floored!!"
"You know what's wrong with Personal Assistants?"-Gharial sits near him. He is panting for breath.
"Ra... Ra..."-he is still trying to call Ram. But his tongue is twisting uncontrollably like a fish out of water.
"They are obsessed with phone calls."
One of Gharial's men has kept the PA busy with a fake phone call supposedly from the party high command. Gharial had initiated the call imitating the voice of the high command, stating that he would be leaving from New Delhi.
Gharial slowly lifts him and drags him to the trolley. Tears flow inundated from his eyes. His son lies on, quietly, his body pieced together as though someone has perfected the art of solving jigsaw puzzle.
Gharial removes a piece of flesh from the waist part of his son and holds it in front of his mouth.
"Congrats, papa...!"
He tries to slap Gharial!
Gharial leans back and twists his hand violently. He shouts aloud but almost immediately the flesh is shoved in to his mouth.
"And they alleged that I was a cannibal!"-Gharial exclaims in a complaining tone.
People have gathered at the grounds to witness the ceremony despite the hot sun.
Media personnel are trying to cover the best of the views.
The party men are getting impatient. They want him to occupy the dais.
"Sir, the governor has arrived. Sir...?"-someone knocks at the door.
"Do you know a fact?"-Gharial asks the CM candidate who is trying to breathe.

"They say that those who see the face of Gharial, die..."
Gharial slowly uncovers his head from the hat.
The CM candidate lies on the floor.
"No, you don't seem to know it."
"Sir..."-the party men throng the entrance to the hall.
"Sir... Can I come in?"-one of the party loyalists seeks permission.
"There is no time. Move..."-the first person to lose patience barges in. Others follow. They see their leader lying on the floor.
"Sir!"-they rush towards him. There is a minute of shock.
"Call the ambulance. Quick..."
"Yes Sir..."-a man who seems to be a party senior with thick spectacles, wearing a dhoti leaves immediately.
The ambulance is just a few meters away. It starts immediately to the hall entrance.
The CM candidate is placed on a stretcher and taken in to the van.
There are shouts coming out from the hall. They have found the trolley and the half-naked body outside.
"Seal all exit. I repeat..."-the security-in-charge speaks in to the walkie-talkie.
"Let the ambulance pass..."
The media get the scent.
"There is a lot of activity going on here right behind me but the authorities are tight-lipped."
"It seems the future CM is unwell. You could see the ambulance making its way out..."
Traffic on all the roads is halted for the ambulance. There is green signal to it all along the way.
The ambulance crosses the city limits. The highway is empty.
Could you see the driver's window?
A dhoti is tossed out!

7 LIFE WITH A DIFFERENCE

It makes a wonderful silhouette- Ayodhya standing on the bridge under the crimson sky.

He is faintly visible from here. Let's go a bit closer. There... His legs are slightly spread apart. His left thumb is hooked into the corner of his jeans. His long hair is dancing to the tunes of the cool breeze. His eyes are on the horizon where the difference between the river and the sky is murky. It is forcing him to think about his past- the past which was different from those of most others. He had struggled to differentiate good and bad, right and wrong.

I still remember. He is in kindergarten. The newly appointed teacher is not able to control the noisy kids. She gives a helpless gaze across the classroom. Only Ayodhya sits silently looking at her, wanting to learn something. She is surprised. "Come here... What is your name?"

"Ayodhya"

"Where do you come from?"

"Sarovar Nagar..."

"What is your father?"

"Doctor. My mother is a doctor too."

"Why didn't you join a school there?"

Ayodhya is mum for a while. "I don't know. They said I needed to join a big school to have more friends."

She smiles. "How many friends have you made?"

Ayodhya does not know how to answer her. He feels uncomfortable. He looks elsewhere.

"Do you know her?"-she points at one of his classmates busy pulling the hair of her friend.

"No."

"Him?"-she points at a kid in rigorous effort to chew down his neighbor's pencil.

Ayodhya nods in negative.

"What do you do all the time?"

"I read."

"Read what?"

"Books?!"-Ayodhya looks at her as though asking 'what else'.

She opens the rhyme book. "Have you read the third rhyme I taught yesterday... Baa... Baa... Black sheep?"

Ayodhya nods. "I've read the whole book!"

"WHAT!!?"

"I finished reading all the eight rhymes."

It was just the beginning.

Ayodhya had just begun to bond with the best friends anyone can get. Books!!

The scene is different on the other side. Whenever a good seed sprouts in the richness of a child's brain, venomous thoughts too get infused elsewhere in corrupted minds. It is the balance of nature.

The old man's children are restless. They have failed over and over again in locating Ayodhya. They have visited, assaulted and threatened the old man a number of times, trying to force him to reveal it. But the old man is still their father. He has pledged everything for Ayodhya's life. Every time he has fallen on the floor with blood dripping from the nose he has become more resolute. "It is better to be beaten a thousand times than be killed in one blow." He knows that once Ayodhya is finished the children would love to reduce the count of old men on earth by one.

He doesn't want to complain to save the respect his family has gained over generations. And the children do not want to kill him because of a clause in the will that in the event of his death all the property would go to his first son and if he too dies then to his son.

The trio wants all of them to be dead. As simple as that...

"One clue... Just give me one clue."

The three children of Ayodhya's grandfather are brainstorming in a restaurant.

"See, one thing is for sure. Come what may, the old man will not deny his grandson education."

"How could you say that?"-the second daughter asks.

"Because he sent you too to school!!"

The second daughter, surprisingly, laughs.

“So we’ll comb each and every school in town. If need be, we’ll fix a man to follow the oldie. He is sure to meet his grandson sometime... Sooner or later...”

So the plan is finalized. A rag picker is in turn picked by the three for the job. They have stuffed so much cash in his dirty pockets that he has turned into their eyes and ears.

A few years have passed by. The trio still waits.

The three of them meet the rag picker once a month near the municipal waste dumping yard. He has nothing more to give them than the daily routine of the old man which does not include his traveling. The old man has been winning the battle of patience. He believes that his three children are having an eye on him. He has cleverly kept himself away from meeting his grandson for years now. Once in a fortnight, he calls the school office and talks to Ayodhya. He advises his grandson on how to behave, how to dress and more importantly how to be vigilant. His grandson’s sweet voice has been nothing less than elixir for a man who is condemned to die sooner or later. In the past, whenever he had fed his children with sumptuous supper, he had never imagined that the energy would someday turn on to him.

Ayodhya’s birth has been a miracle. He has survived infancy. The old man hopes he would go on to see his youth. He prays for my grace. He wants me to give him some leeway in life span so that he in turn can give it to his grandson.

Ayodhya is in class six. He has many friends, all lined up for him. They know only to give and not expect anything. One friend gives him ideas in science while the other in literature. A few friends are such that they contradict one another. They debate through Ayodhya. They try and refute claims and eventually counter claim. Ayodhya’s mind has become a playfield for them.

The phone at Ayodhya’s house rings.

"Hello..."-his grandpa answers.

"Namaste, I am Ravi Mohan... Am I speaking to Ram Prakash Sir?"

"Oh, Namaste Principal Sir..."

"The result of class six exams is out. Ayodhya has topped the exams fifth time in a row now. We are giving away prizes to all the toppers on 26th of this month. I request you to attend the event at least this year."

"Has he been asking for me?"-there is no feel of happiness in the grandpa's voice. The Principal is surprised as usual.

"Sir please don't mind but may I ask why you keep away from meeting your grandson? He's such a brilliant student."

"Has he been asking for me?"

"No, he doesn't interact much with anyone. I have never heard him say he wanted to see you."

"I'm coming this time!"-Ram Prakash wants to take a chance.

It is the 26th. He walks out of his house and locks the gate. His shadow has company!

A long journey by bus has made the grandfather more anxious, more eager. He walks in hot sun, wiping sweat with his hankie. The road is just a muddy pathway flanked by stones. The wind is hot. It is blowing sand with a unique noise of its own. Hawks are prying over his thoughts with their cries, not allowing him to think properly. Probably they are warning him of the impending threat.

The school is in the middle of a huge plot of open space. A banyan tree is the sole hope outside. He sees a swarm of blue at one wing of the building. The students have come in neat blue uniforms. He walks towards them. There is a very lively atmosphere. They are having fun. It reminds him of his childhood. He used to swim across the river to attend school as he did not have money for the ferry. He always used to win the swimming race with Shankar. Shankar is now resting in peace since twenty years now. As you get older, you will have to see your friends die one by one. And you'll have to bear that.

He blindly follows the crowd and enters the titanic Function Hall. The parents have all assembled and engaged in talk. Here and there a few parents share momentary laugh, jerking their necks towards the ceiling.

His eyes look around for Ayodhya. A small, delicate hand clutches his rough palm gently. He turns.

"How are you, grandpa?"

His tiredness has vanished in a second. Ayodhya stands with eyes brimming with affection. He is wearing the same blue uniform as others but there is still a difference- the glittering, cup-shaped, dark eyes.

"Appu!"-he kneels, brushing the silky hair of his grandson.

He holds his cheeks and kisses his forehead. "You still haven't forgotten this old man's face?"

"Old? A uniform is all you need."-a sweet smile appears on Ayodhya's face.

"Ha... ha... ha..." Ram Prakash hugs him.

"So... Would you introduce me to your friends?"

"Sure... This is Niyaz... My classmate... He plays the piano really well."

"Hi Niyaz, keep it up!"-he pats Niyaz.

"She is Aashrita. She is a classical singer. She is performing the inaugural prayer."

"Oh, how nice... All the best!"

"There are many more. You see there? He's Rajat. Football player. That's Kiran. His handwriting is just like print."

"Oh, great! So, who is your best friend?"

"Come here..."-Ayodhya drags his forehand with all his strength. "Easy, easy... I'm coming!"

They enter a huge library, with numerous books all around.

"Not again, Ayodhya. The library is closed today for the ceremony. I told you yesterday."-the librarian's eyes stare at Ayodhya.

"I know, Sir. I just wanted my grandpa to see the library."

"These are my best friends. I like reading a lot!"-Ayodhya swirls a couple of times, giving way to emotions.

Ram Prakash is awestruck!

"This is like a second home for him. He doesn't leave the place even after working hours. A book worm!!"-the librarian adds.

"And he is Bunny Sir. The kind librarian. He doesn't come to library even after the start of working hours!!"

"Hey, don't say that. What can I do if you come half an hour early?"

The grandfather is happy. "What books do you read, Appu?"

"Anything. I've been reading this wonderful book called- 'The Annals and Antiquities of Rajasthan' by James Tod. It is so gripping."

"What will you do reading this book at this age? Others were studying for the exams and he was here reading this huge one."

"Bunny Sir, I topped!"

The conversation ends there. The librarian gets back to munching peanuts. For Ayodhya the text books are peanuts.

“Appu, you’re on the right path. The habit of reading books is a very rare gift. Never give up on this habit.”

“I’m on the right path? Where to?”-Ayodhya is confused. His huge eyes widen to receive the reply.

“A place only a few make it to.”

“Oh really? Which place is that?”

“You keep up the habit. And you’ll soon realize!”

“How does this path look like? I can’t see it. Am I already walking on it or is it just an illusion?”

“What do you know about illusion?”-he is surprised hearing the word from a young Ayodhya.

“It is something that plays with our senses. Our eyes... It is not what we think it is. If we control our mind we can see through it!”

“Where did you read that?”

“Some book over there. In the philosophy section.”

“You’re such a good boy. Then I guess you should have read about the path...”

“Yeah, but I couldn’t make out much. Anyway I’ll read it the ninth time. Probably it might get clear.”-he pulls his grandpa’s arm and heads back to the hall.

The ceremony is inaugurated and prize distribution begins.

“Moving on to class six. Third rank goes to...”-the class teacher of sixth grade is announcing.

"Appu, your turn is fast approaching."-he feels glad but is not happy with his choice of words.

"Yes, grandpa... I'm ready to take it."

"...Fifth time in a row, Ayodhya!"

He walks towards the dais. This time it is special. His grandpa is there to witness. He turns to see his grandfather and feels overwhelmed to see him applaud with raised hands.

The Principal is giving away the prize. "Has your grandfather arrived?"-asks he without congratulating.

"Yes Sir."

Ayodhya walks back with the prize. "Oh, it is a casserole this time!"

"How could you say that? It is still wrapped."-his grandfather is amused.

"I think they are following a trend. It is cyclic since the last five years. Dictionary, Casserole, Water bottle... Dictionary, Casserole, Water bottle..."

"It could be water bottle then?"

"No, the size, shape and the weight say it all. It is a Casserole."-Ayodhya replies calmly, looking elsewhere.

The grandfather can't believe it! His grandson is deducing what a wrapped box contains, by some logic and observations.

"Let's open it."

"Here..."-Ayodhya offers the box to him.

"You open it. It is your prize!"

"But it's your surprise, grandpa."

Ram Prakash smiles and slowly removes the wrapper. It is indeed a Casserole!! And he is surprised!

"What have others got? For second prize and third? Are they too getting cyclically?"

"Why would I think of that, grandpa?"

Ram Prakash likes his grandson's attitude.

"How are mom and dad? You said they went to America long ago. Do they call up? Can you give them the school number?"-Ayodhya asks for Dr. Parvati and her husband.

Ram Prakash looks at Ayodhya. The calm but curious eyes pierce his heart.

He feels he should reveal everything to Ayodhya-about his parents, Dr. Parvati, the trio.

"I can't hide it any longer. Today he has made out what the box contained. It wouldn't take too long for him to figure out my mind."

"Appu, be courageous, ok? I am going to tell you something."

It has been about twenty minutes. And the entire background has been told to Ayodhya. Ayodhya is looking at his grandfather, his eyes telling that he can't believe it.

"Appu, your aunts will come for you. But you have to be brave. Do you know about presence of mind? It is something that will not let you down in front of your enemies. It makes you think of ways of escape than of the end results. Always, Appu, think of what to do next. I am taking maximum care to shield you. But as I have been always telling you, be vigilant. Don't roam around alone. Your life is a bit different from others."

"Grandpa, the only difference is that I don't have parents. That's some kind of a mathematical difference."-Ayodhya wants to appear unhurt.

"Appu, I'm there for you."-he hugs Ayodhya tightly.

"Yeah, grandpa. Let us think about what to do next!"

"Mr. Ram Prakash..."-the Principal is standing at a distance.

"Sir, nice to meet you."-Ram Prakash gets up. After exchange of formalities, praises and brushing Ayodhya's hair by turns, Ram Prakash finally comes down to the serious matter at hand.

"Sir, there is a threat to Ayodhya's life. Let me explain."

The Principal is shocked. "Ayodhya, please go out and meet your friends."-he sends him away. Ayodhya walks some distance and stands.

Forty minutes go by. The Principal now knows the matter. "I'm boosting security as a general measure. The guards will be given special instructions to shield Ayodhya if he's attacked."

"Thank you so much, Sir. I'll take leave now. Appu..."-Ram Prakash hugs Ayodhya.

"Well, Ayodhya. Your grandpa and I had a friendly chat."-the Principal wants to make Ayodhya feel that nothing serious has been talked about.

"Yeah, Appu. Just told him to buy a better gift next time!" The Principal looks on as Ram Prakash exits.

8 WHIMSICAL

Two kids hop over a compound to enter the neighbor's lawn.

"Where did you hit it?"- asks one, getting down gently.

"I don't know. It was a six, right?"

"Let's first find the ball."-they walk towards the bedroom window crossing a small pool of muddy water in the garden.

The TV's volume is high- "The hospital staff says that all the doctors are ready for emergency services but the ambulance has not yet arrived. What should not have taken more than half an hour with traffic lights turned green, seems to have turned out to be an eternal wait for the state. The special plane is ready at the airport to fly the CM to Singapore for enhanced treatment after basic check-ups in the city hospital. The act seems to be of kidnap. The search operation is on. The authorities are still awaiting the call from the kidnappers for ransom. Here's the latest news update from our correspondent, Yami."

The correspondent waits, looking blank into the camera. She suddenly nods a couple of times and starts off- "Thanks Gautam, as you can see in the background, people are unhappy that they are kept in dark regarding the kidnapping of the CM candidate. They feel left alone by the police for not letting them know about the fresh, ghastly killing of the candidate's son and the bodyguard. Let's hear it from them. Hi, what's your name?"-she holds the mic to the man standing closest.

"I'm So-So-Sonu. From Somnathpur."

"So Sonu, what is your opinion? You have come all the way from the opposite end of the state. How do you feel about the situation?"

Another young man fights for camera space with Sonu. They both want to get as close as possible to the gorgeous correspondent. She hopes the mic were a knife!

"He's Motu...."-Sonu finally gives in. "We... We have come from all the way to see the swear ceremony. There is no swearing and we feel extremely... extremely... disapp..."

"Indignated?"-she suggests.

"Yeah... Indignated with the goings-on."

"They... They should have let us see the body of the son of CM!"-Motu speaks but his voice is faint.

"Come, come again..."-she turns the mic to him. Sonu feels that she's slipping away from him. He starts immediately bending into the mic taking a step towards her- "The media is very kind, very supportive. We came to know that the body has been cut and pieced up together. But the media was not allowed inside. We have come a long way from home. We..."

"We wanted to see the ceremony but they should have at least showed us the body. We want to see something..."

"Errr... Who do you think is responsible for such a lapse in security? What is your opinion about the Police? Don't you think they should not have allowed this?"

"I think the police are sleeping. The officers have to shed their uniforms."

"What do you want to tell the city police on this botched up security apparatus?"
"We want them to be more efficient and improve their system..."-Motu intervenes.

"What is your message for the police through this media?"

"We want them to learn from this incident and..."

"No, I mean through your freedom of speech..."

"The ****** *******."-Motu continues.

"***** ** *******..."-Sonu shows his superiority.

"Here you see that the people are extremely upset with the security establishment. Lots of swear words are being used in the swearing-in ceremony. They want justice and that too as soon as possible. As the old saying goes, Justin delayed is Justin denied."- the reporter realizes her mistake immediately.

"I am sorry, justice delayed is justice denied. With cameraman Justin, I'm Yami, NOT NOW!"-she corrects her statement.

The news reader in the studio takes over- "Rightly so, we'll take a short, little break. Thank you gentlemen for being on the expert panel of our program SECURITY BEEF UP..." The sitting ducks in the video conference come to know that the program is over only when their collar-mic is taken off.

The news reader now turns to the camera- "When we come back, we'll take you through our exclusive program WARDROBE GOOF UP... So don't go elsewhere, stay tuned to NOT NOW!"

The kids could not find the ball. They are returning to hop out of the garden. The second kid wants to walk through the muddy pool of water.

Splash!!

He falls down!

He had accidentally stepped on a round thing immersed in the muddy water. "Hey, it's the ball!"

The police headquarters is buzzing with activities.

"No, no, no... We have to stay low for another two to three weeks. The new ACP has joined the department today. We don't know what kind of a person he is. And moreover, the CM's missing. His son's case is pending. One bodyguard too is murdered. It is quite a complicated situation now. Ask him to keep the money with himself for the time being. Then I'll ask my son to go collect it from his son."-a sub-inspector instructs his head constable.

"Ok Sir... Sir... He's arrived!"-the head constable stands in attention.

The sub-inspector turns around. Both of them salute the new ACP-Assistant Commissioner of Police. The ACP walks wearing neat uniform. It is clean and tidy. The police emblem on his beret gleams on his forehead. He has a clean shaven face with brown, cat-like eyes. But he has a frown on his face. The pressure is high. Everyone wants answers. There are too many to follow up and too few to act. "The Indian Police System is just as it was in the British Raj."-he recalls a part of what he had studied during his IPS preparations. Sometimes he feels his efficiency has become his enemy. He'll be transferred wherever grotesque, intriguing and high profile crimes are committed. But he loves the uniform more than anything else. He has given in to the whims of the department.

He looks straight at the sub-inspector. The look is sharp and judgmental. "I'll have to cancel the deal."-the sub-inspector thinks for himself.

The head constable moves his eye balls across the ACP's name plate. SAGAR- it reads.

"ACP Sagar, we don't have enough time. The public, the media and the NSF are demanding a CBI probe into the matter. It is a question of our competence."-a senior officer explains as he enters the briefing area.

"This file contains all the information we've got. The CCTV footages at the ceremony hall are available too. You're heading the team."

"Sir!"-the ACP salutes.

"We need results, officer. Fast and accurate... We need success and nothing else!"

"Sir!"-he salutes.

"To tell is human!"-he feels although he has pledged to catch the fugitive.

He calls the team to assemble.

Officers line up in the hall. He is lost in thought- "I know I can only try. Even if I try, success is not guaranteed. But if I don't, failure is!"

He looks around, getting up from the seat- "Officers, we don't have much time. But that's exactly why we have been selected by the police department. We know how to act under pressure. This is a case many of us would never get in our entire careers. So let's put the best foot forward and give our 100%"

"Sir, I am Head Constable Jackpot. I was on duty at the main hall that day..."-the head-constable who had saluted him earlier steps forward to give some information.

"What name did you say?"-Sagar wants to know his name again. There has been nobody who has not asked him the second time for his name... Nobody ever... Since his childhood.

"Sir, Head constable Jackpot."

"Really?"

"Yes Sir..."-Jackpot knows that he'll have to tell the background to the ACP just like how he had to tell everyone he had ever met... Since his childhood...

"My parents had ten daughters. I was their last child. They did not have enough money for delivery. Somehow, my father arranged for money and took a chance, hoping for a male child. And I was born. They were overjoyed. They thought I would bring luck to the family and hence they named me Jackpot."-he repeats the cliché. The same old thing he has been telling. Ever since his childhood...

"Interesting. Let's hope you bring some luck to the department as well!"

"Sir, that day I was on duty at the hall..."

"Hold on Jackpot, were you really there?"-he gauges from an over-prompt Jackpot.

"No Sir, I was asked to manage extra vodka and chilled beer for celebrations after the ceremony. There were many police personnel available. One of them might have been stationed there."

Sagar is not able to believe his words. Jackpot is talking as though it is normal. Sagar bends forward- "Who asked you to bring liquor?".

"Sir, I think it was from the CM's office. But the Sub-Inspector told me."

The Sub-inspector agrees but he's upset. "Yes Sir, I had told him to take care of that as I could not go. I was at the screening area."

"Why were you supposed to go?"

"Sir the... The... Inspector..."

“Do I have to ask you too?”-Sagar is fed up.

“Sir?”

“Who told you, damn it!”-Sagar bangs the table in despair.

“Yes Sir, no Sir. I was at the main stage near the dais. I was asked to go but I asked the Sub-inspector instead.”-the circle inspector accepts.

“I... I got a call from my senior!!”

“Where’s he?”

“Sir, he’s gone to the bathroom.”-Jackpot replies. He is in a precarious situation. He tries to balance truth with softness. His moustache is wet with fear. His bald head inside the Police beret has started getting itchy with sweat. It always happens whenever he tries to think hard.

“Sir!”-the senior inspector salutes.

“Who asked you to arrange liquor?”-Sagar wipes his face with his hankie.

“Sir, the PA to CM’s office. He called me over mobile.”

“Show me the call log.”

“Here...”-the officer immediately flashes his phone. Sagar sees it and sighs. “How did you decide that the call was his? You have not even saved the number...”

“Sir I’ve spoken to him a number of times. I’ve been on duty at the CM’s office for the last two years.”

Sagar frowns. “It is because of people like you that I’ve been a roadrunner from one city to another. Transfer after transfer...”

“Don’t you feel the basic need to save the number of CM’s office?”

The officer bows his head. The whole department knows that he had the senior officers' recommendations for promotion up to the current rank. But alas, they all have retired... by my courtesy!

"Have you got True Caller?"

"Who's that, Sir?"

Sagar gulps a glass of water. He's had enough on the first day.

"Check whether the number belongs to the PA."

One of the officers obeys and exits. There is nervous silence in the hall. Everyone has something to say. Everyone wants to be heard. But they have all been under the spell of silence. The huge fans high above in the hall too are running silently, swaying cobwebs in their blades. The entire hall has a different scent, that of dusty windows beyond the reaches of cleaners... The stone floor, somehow, has retained the decade old iconic aroma. Sagar feels he's in his ancestral house. The smell is identical. The tall Ashoka trees within inches from the windows are shielding the hall on the first floor from the wrath of the sun. The crows, though, are creating long, throat ripping noise, unable to get their points across to the police.

"Sir..."-a tech expert barges in, not in sync with the mood in the hall. He submits a bunch of papers.

"The number does not belong to the PA at CM's office. But the officer's official cell phone was under tapping as per the protocol. The voice sample that instructed him to bring beer closely fits in with the PA's voice but there is still mismatch in the amplitude. It is a... Kind of... Touch and go!

"We can't say anything for sure."-the expert's voice diminishes.

"Hmm?"-Sagar wants the expert to repeat his statement although he is immersed in thought. The thought is being fed by the words from the expert.

"Sir, we can't really say whether the voice is of PA or not. Here's the amplitudes juxtaposed. The green one is of the PA. The red one is of the caller."

"What does your intuition say?"-Sagar asks an abstract question. Abstraction is the best tool when every other one is exhausted. It does not need convincing.

"Sir... I think it is someone else! The SIM used by the caller is of a missing person. A lady... We have her details. She is a biology teacher in a nearby school. Missing since the last few days."

"Thank you."-Sagar nods.

"Get me the CCTV footages."

He sinks in his seat with the hands supporting his forehead- "This is like a never ending chain"-he starts thinking.

"The guy is not just intelligent, he's a genius."

"He? What is making me think it is a 'he'? Something's telling me. Wait... Yeah... That's it. A female can't imitate the bold voice of the PA. Only a man can do it. My intuition says it. So it must be true..."

"He knows a few basic things. Who the weakest and the most susceptible member in the department is."

"Hey, Jackpot!"-Sagar comes out of thoughts.

"Sir..."

"What's the background of that officer?"

"Sir... I..."-he hesitates, signaling to Sagar that he could ask the superiors like the circle inspectors.

"I won't ask anyone else. From now on, you're going to work directly with me. The inspectors are transferred from police department!"

"Sir?"-he bends forward.

"I mean they'll only transfer information from me to you. If at all needed."

"Sir, why are you so particular to pick me out? I'm only a constable, Sir..."-he brings all the fingers on his right hand touching one another and moves them from lips up to a foot's distance with his back bent. It is to indicate 'just a' constable.

"Head constable."-Sagar smiles.

"Ok Sir, but still... Why not others?"

"I like your name!"

So far, Jackpot has never felt this sorry for his name!!

But the real reason for Sagar to pull in Jackpot is his spontaneity. Jackpot blurts out immediately, not giving time to manipulate the information... By himself or others... And he has been directly involved in the lapse of security. As the last link...

"Sir, the officer has big connections..."-Jackpot begins in a low tone. He brings out the entire life history of the irresponsible officer. How he failed entrance exams, how the offline exams in those days were easily manipulated, how he had passed the physical fitness tests without moving a muscle and much more.

Sagar again sinks into deep thought- "So this guy knew something about that officer. He has neatly picked him as the scapegoat. Bull's eye!"

"And he is a dangerous imitating artist. More importantly, he knows the mindset of police... How the department works. He knows that the constables are made to do menial work for the MLA's and the ministers. Bring groceries, cook for them, pick up their kids from school and college, wash and press clothes, clean rooms and cars, and arrange for exclusive entertainments... And about how the orders from superiors percolate down to the poor constables. Bravo!"

"He has studied the scenario really well. Is he an insider? No way... What would he get? And why would he kill the son and play Chinese puzzle on his body? Why would he dare kill the bodyguard?"

"Sir, the CCTV footages are ready."- the expert asks him to join at the main controls. Sagar hurries along.

"Shastriji, move..."-the expert takes over. "Sir, this is the time when the ambulance exits out of the gate."

The driver is not visible properly. The ambulance slowly makes its way out.

"Nothing much... The driver surely doesn't belong to the hospital. Where was the actual staff?"

The ambulance crew was dragged to the office on the very day of disappearance and beaten up even before the flurry of questions was fired. They were asked to reveal the identity and location of the culprits. The poor driver could not even speak.

Jackpot feels important-"Sir, they were interrogated. But they are not revealing anything"

"Call the driver."

The driver is dragged to the balcony of the first floor. His left eye is swollen. He has to tilt his face and use only his right eye to see. His jaw has turned bluish green. There is brownish patch under his nose.

"What happened to you?"

"Sir, just some hospitality!"-Jackpot smiles.

"Shut up!! Are we police or savages? Who permitted you to beat him up?"-Sagar shouts aloud. A few crows on the Ashoka trees fly away in fear.

"Sir, he's just a driver!"-Jackpot's eyes shine with a smile on his face, trying to make Sagar understand that he is forgetting something.

"Does that take away his dignity!!!?"-Sagar shouts again. Jackpot's heart shivers. He is able to feel a cold, liquid-like thing running down his gut.

"Sir, the circle inspector and sub-inspector have dealt with him."-Jackpot backs off.

"Take him to the hospital right now!"

Jackpot pulls the driver by his collar. Sagar stares in Jackpot's face. Jackpot releases the collar and leads him away.

It has been four hours now. Sagar is sitting on the table. His right leg is swaying to and fro in the air while the left leg is supporting his body. His shirt is all sweaty.

The phone at his desk rings.

"Hello..."-Sagar answers immediately.

"Sir, Jackpot here. The driver is willing to speak..."

"Namaste Sir, I and my crew including the doctor had got a call on the doctor's phone from the chief medical officer in charge that our duty was cancelled. So we didn't go... We left the ambulance in the hospital."

Jackpot takes over- "Sir, the ambulance is intact in the hospital. The caller's number is not the same as that of the chief medical officer. I've sent you the caller's number through Shutapp. And Sir, one more thing... The chief medical officer is a lady."

"Ok..."-Sagar opens Shuptapp, ponders over the number for a brief moment and kicks the chair in disappointment.

The number seems familiar.

It is the biology teacher's!

He sits quietly. He has never been this confused before in a case. He still believes that the caller is a single person... The same, dangerous imitation artist... And a 'he'. Sagar usually banks upon intuition.

"Sir, chai!"-a constable brings tea in a kettle and a number of paper cups. "Don't bring tea again when you're wearing uniform. If you're so interested, I'll have you suspended."-Sagar accepts the tea calmly. His cat eyes are restless. There is an air of discomfort.

But tea has fans for a reason.

"Yesss!!"-Sagar smiles.

"The CCTVs at traffic signals and cross roads. Get me those footages..."

"Yes Sir..."

An hour later the expert returns- "Sir, we have the recordings at these locations but the persons in the ambulance are not clearly visible. The ambulance number is false. After the road reaches the bypass near national highway, there is no CCTV. It is free from the bridge onwards..."

Sagar is disappointed for a while.

"Show me the ceremony footages again..."-he wants to extract some clue out of it.

"Sir!"-the expert displays them.

"And that's the time Jackpot left from the hall to fetch liquor... He has started the van... He is passing through the gate..."

The footage does not show any unusual activity for a long time.

"Fast forward!"-Sagar is impatient.

The van returns after about an hour.

"Call up Jackpot. I need to talk to him."-Sagar has some questions. After sometime the expert informs- "He's on the way, Sir."

Sagar sits examining the video.

"Sir!"-Jackpot salutes from a distance.

"Where did you go to buy liquor?"

"Sir, Sunset Wines. Actually, they themselves supply with their own vehicles. But on that day it was considered risky. So we used our van."

"How long does it take to bring?"-Sagar asks in an interrogative manner.

"Sir, not more than half an hour. But the tire got punctured on the return path. So we had to get the tire changed."

"Who changed the tire?"-Sagar is not convinced yet.

Jackpot's throat is dry. "Sir, there were some people who offered to help. So we sat down at a restaurant for tea. After they changed it we returned."

"Do you remember the faces of those people?"

"Yes Sir, there were three of them. One among them was tall and strong. He hardly spoke. His face was not clearly visible. He was wearing a woolen cap. The other two were changing the tires while he was just checking the chassis at the bottom for damage."

"Was he like this?"-Sagar plays the video he had paused at.

The van is stopped at the hall. Jackpot gets down and stands casually chatting about something very tasty. Two constables unload the boxes.

"All done?"-Jackpot is seen enquiring. One of them signals a 'done' by showing his palms to Jackpot and moving them horizontally away from each other.

But there is more to the cargo. As Jackpot starts the van and drives away, a huge figure as big as an adult crocodile lies flat on the ground where the van had been stopped!

It pulls the hat closer to its eyes and lies still. Jackpot shivers momentarily, witnessing the video.

Jackpot is then seen parking the van at some distance and walking back to the hall. In the meantime, the body is still flat. Jackpot approaches it from the toe end. The figure allows him close. He almost sees it when he remembers he has to fill water in his bottle. He changes direction. The figure, still as it seems, suddenly sits with only the torso rising from the ground.

It then heads inside the hall. A few men covered with caps drag out a wheeled stretcher from the ambulance. One of them gives an overcoat which it wears passionately. It is Gharial!!

They are now out of the camera as they have entered the hall and there is no CCTV inside. Politicians always face this challenge- privacy or security? And some incredulous ones opt for privacy. Because it secures them in a different way.

Sagar is burning with anger. His cat eyes add to the terror. Jackpot is sweating. He doesn't like the way the expert is looking at him. He feels that the look contains a cruel curiosity.

"Why wasn't this part of the footage inspected before?"-Sagar tries to control himself.

"Sir, nobody took the lead."-the expert replies.

"Why?"

"Sir, who wants to risk comfort?"-Jackpot blurts out what he thinks is true. And what he thinks is true. The governor had ordered a coordinated action. And collective responsibility is nobody's responsibility.

Sagar waits for the footage to show Gharial return.

"The guy is an artist."-Sagar's cat eyes have caught the party senior in white dhoti and thick, dark pair of spectacles, who is approaching the ambulance making way through crowded people.

"There he goes, right under our noses!"-Sagar sees the ambulance make its way out.

The people at the hall are seen screaming in fear and shock. Some of them are running out. They have seen the body on the stretcher.

Nothing much is noteworthy after that. Sagar removes his beret and feels his thick, brownish and supple hair between his fingers. He runs his fingers down his head a couple of times and stays still.

"I need to see the body of the son and the bodyguard."-he finally speaks, sipping the last drops of tea.

"Sure Sir..."-Jackpot tries to be too courteous.

The sun has started to set. The sky has a mix of greenish blue color all around except immediately around the sun which is crimson. The parrots are retreating in a formation, flapping their wings intermittently.

Sagar is still at work. He is walking around the body of the son of the Chief Minister. Jackpot can't stand the sight.

"Sir, can I wait outside?"

"Then you'll have to always remain outside."-Sagar still has his eyes on the body.

He stands near the feet of the corpse, deeply observing the cuts.

Jackpot looks elsewhere.

"Jackpot, have a look. Tell me what you feel..."- Sagar wants to amuse himself a bit. He turns Jackpot towards the corpse, holding his shoulders from behind.

"Sir... Errr... Sir..."-Jackpot timidly ponders over.

"The cuts are artistic."-says he.

Sagar's intuition sends a spark!!

"Yes!!"-he pushes Jackpot back and steps close to the body. He bends over and slowly moves from feet to head.

The cuts are made calligraphically!!!

Sagar reads aloud- 'GHARIAL'

"What?"-Jackpot is amazed.

"You see there? From the feet? The cuts start. That's the 'G'"-he runs his forefinger along a cut.

"And 'h', 'a', 'r'"

"But Sir, where is 'i'?"

"You see the flesh missing out there? Near the waist? That is the space between the stick and the dot in the 'i'!"

"Jackpot, you're such a criminal!!"

"Sir?"-Jackpot believes him.

"Seeing art in a macabre killing... It needs a twisted mind!"-Sagar twists his forefinger near his temple.

Jackpot, for a moment, thinks if he's really so. He looks at Sagar expecting him to change his statement.

"I'm joking..."-Sagar pats him and heads out. The bodyguard's body has a few stabs. "Nothing noteworthy..."-Sagar thinks as he walks. He is a bit surprised that ten years ago he wouldn't have imagined seeing a stabbed body and feeling nothing noteworthy. He holds me responsible for it. And he's right!

Jackpot turns, still looking at him, and follows him with a smile.

"I need a detailed history of this thing called 'Gharial'. What it means, how this man on the CCTV is related to it... You got it?"-he asks the expert.

"Sir!"-the expert obeys.

"What's your name?"-Sagar asks the expert.

"Abhilash Chandran, Sir!"-the expert replies.

"Thank you."-Sagar turns. Jackpot stands right behind him.

"Sir..."-he looks timidly.

"What?"

"Am I really that intelligent?"

"Yes, of course. You're a... head!!"-Sagar sets right the beret on Jackpot's head.

Jackpot is silent. For the first time after so many years someone has called him intelligent. And that someone is an Assistant Commissioner of Police is a bonus. The only one who had credited him with intelligence ever before, was Shyamala. Twenty-seven years ago. Both of them got wedded a year after that. It's been twenty-six years since his marriage and it feels like twenty-six minutes for him. The memory of her long hair, partially blocking his view in the city bus, when he used to follow her everywhere, is still afresh.

"Namaste..."-Jackpot had spoken with pounding heartbeat. She had turned, smiled frugally and turned back.

"It means 'yes'."-he had felt. It had made his day. He had started to stalk her everywhere. Once, in a flow of emotions, he had lost track of where he was heading to as she had entered a ladies' restroom. How he was beaten black and blue by other ladies... He does remember the pain but more importantly he remembers how Shyamala had then nursed his wounds. "Are you still feeling pain?"-she had asked after a few days. "Yeah..."-he had shown it on his face.

"If you feel hurt, I feel hurt too."-she had said softly, which had soothed his groin.

"Will you marry me?"-he had proposed immediately. Oh boy! How she had blushed! Her dense hair had again denied him the privilege of seeing her. She had used her hair so efficiently.

"I... Please talk to my family."-she had scampered away like a young deer.

Her father had rejected him. The reason for his rejection by her parents was, of course, his name. Her father did not wish to give his daughter's hand to a person whose name contained any one of the five sinful habits-Drinking, smoking and GAMBLING. Jackpot had never been even close to all these eliminating criteria, except by a minor thing called NAME.

He had summarily refused to even meet Jackpot. "Look at Purushottam. The finest of gentlemen! Like name, like character."-he had thrown away Jackpot's neatly written bio-data.

Jackpot and Shyamala had, secretly met at the Satyam Cinemas, their usual rendezvous. “How about running away?”-she had proposed as her marriage was almost fixed like that of the heroine in the movie. Jackpot had a different idea like that of the movie’s hero. He wanted to wait for the Police Constable Exam results, impress her father and marry with full honor... Err... marry her with full honor. He wanted to hit a jackpot like his father had done. The results had been declared after about a fortnight and he was selected like the movie’s hero! He was happy. He had asked her to wait for a couple of days and somehow keep giving excuses to her parents to postpone her wedding. He had an emergency posting at his senior officer’s wedding.

He was in the police van on the first day of his duty. It had stopped at the wedding hall. He had stood on duty at the side entrance. The rituals were on; he had had a sumptuous meal in the basement dining hall before returning to the side-gate, managing the crowd.

“After this one, my wedding will take place. I’ll book the same hall and receive guard of honor in front of my honorable in-laws.”-he had even enquired about the rent per day. “‘Shyamala weds Jackpot’. How does it sound?”-he was lost in his dream world as every second ticked in his watch on that sultry afternoon when he had readied himself for the gun salute. “I’ll have gun salute too. Shyamala will be so happy.”-he had known for sure that the day was near. He wanted to meet her father soon after duty.

Now her daughter is his son’s classmate!

And Jackpot has taken every care to keep his son away from her daughter to avoid another heart break. “It is genetic, heritage”-he reasons whenever his son argues about it and his son always corrects him as ‘hereditary’ before continuing with the argument. The jackpot Jackpot had hit was hard. The movie climax had come with an ‘anti’ in his life.

Perhaps on that fateful day, his day was too near to be realized. If he had known that the gun salute he was so valiantly offering was for her wedding, if he had known that the banner 'Shyamala weds Purushottam' that stood at the entrance near the main gate was of his own Shyamala and if he had known that he had wastefully paid the hall authorities to retain 'Shyamala weds ' portion for use in his marriage, he would have probably turned the muzzle of the gun towards his own temple or towards her father or worse, towards Purushottam who later denied him promotions.

The shattered dreams of Shyamala had sent him into shambles for a few months. He too got married the same year.

These days Shyamala's father can't walk. He keeps lying on a stone seat in front of his daughter's house in Police Quarters, trying to apologize to Jackpot telepathically. He curses himself every time his son-in-law comes home drunk and throws cigarette butts at him after losing money in a gamble with his colleagues. "I should have selected Jackpot."-the old man regrets.

"What's in a name? Being the boy next door is all that matters."-he turns in vain to catch a glimpse of Jackpot's window almost every day when Jackpot gets beaten to pulp by Komala, his wife!

Abhilash returns after a while. "Sir... The details..."

"Yes Abhilash..."-Sagar and Jackpot follow Abhilash to the projector hall.

"Shastriji.... Please start the first slide."-Abhilash instructs and starts the briefing- "Sir, firstly, about the name... Gharial is a freshwater crocodile found in India. It is a critically endangered species. It has a long, pointed mouth with a round snout. It primarily preys on fish."

"What is its hunting habit?"-Sagar comes to a very valid point.

"Sir it lies in wait for the prey and suddenly attacks when it is in the vicinity."

"Coming to this person on CCTV, it is difficult to make out given his cap. But yeah, one thing we strongly feel is that he is related to the recent vanishing of people. The cell number of that teacher is probably used by him. And she is missing. Of late there are many such similar cases coming from the city and no other city has seen such exponential increase. The graph shows the comparison year-wise and region-wise."

Sagar stands still. The rigorous activity in his nervous system is not visible to Abhilash and Jackpot.

"You're right, Abhilash. It quite seems so. Any relation between the missing persons? Anything in common? Any trend?"

"No, Sir. The first case reported in recent past is of three persons- Lomy Lala, age 24 and his accomplices, Twinkle, aged 22 and Tina aged 20. These guys were running a phishing agency. They were arrested last year but were set free after some initial investigation. The second case is of the Chief Minister's son and his friends along with the entire crew and staff of Mohini Bar."

"What do you mean by entire staff and crew? All of them?"

"All of them!"-Abhilash is sure. "The complaint was filed by the owner who, fortunately, was not present at the time. The manager, waiters, bar tenders, and all the customers who were present at that time on that day. Shastriji, please display the complaint copy... The son's body has been brought by this Gharial guy to the swear-in ceremony."

"Why does he need them and he has not contacted for ransom. We don't even know whether all of them are dead.... Why is he doing such a thing?"-Sagar is clueless.

"Sir, he appears to be doing it randomly. In one word- whimsical!"

"Sir!"-an officer enters, sweating profusely.

Sagar is anxious. "What happened?"

"There was an object found in a huge puddle of water across the road... near the outer ring road. People inspected the thing. And it... it... turned out to be the head of the CM candidate!"

Sagar misses a heartbeat! Everything is still for a moment.

Some silences make eerie noises that become intolerable.

"I'm on your hunt, Mr.Gharial!"-Sagar thinks to himself. His convictions are strong.

Far away from the headquarters there is a McGoBalds Corner. The lights on the display board are dazzling. The 'I love it all' tagline catches the sight of a pedestrian with a long overcoat.

He speaks softly but in a heavy voice- "Same here!!"

9 LONER

The breeze is cool. It is sprinkling moisture on Ayodhya's weather-beaten face, asking him to come out of the past and face the present. On his way along the bridge, even as he tries to walk briskly, his past catches up with him...

It has barely been a few weeks since the sixth class award ceremony. It is late evening. Ayodhya sits under the banyan tree, recollecting the facts his grandfather had narrated him.

"Never wander away alone, Appu."-he remembers his grandfather's words. But Ayodhya sees no fear in darkness. "If it is darkness for me, it is darkness for them too." He doesn't mind the dark. In fact, he prefers it, for he thinks more of them than he does of himself. "If my being in the dark obstructs them, so be it." His thinking has changed. The outlook of the twelve-year-old Ayodhya has undergone a change that has never since then, allowed him to revert.

He has further distanced himself from people.

"They are normal. They have a normal life. Let them live it. I'll look after mine."-he sits under the cover of darkness. All other kids are back in the hostel, doing what normal life expects of them.

Two shadows loom surreptitiously on the school compound.
"Surjeet!!!! Alert!!"- a security guard yells aloud from the main gate. Ayodhya turns frantically.
A couple of gun shots are heard along with flashes of light. Within the hostel, there is continuous sound of knobs being turned, creaky doors being opened and slammed after fractions of a second. The crows on the trees are awakened from slumber. They are creating a ruckus, unable to find their paths in darkness. The bats at the banyan tree are flying in a pattern that indicates threat.
"Nobody comes out!!"-a guard shouts to the students, revealing his hiding location near the security cabin. The intruders attack him from both sides. He sees them, unable to decide the next move. They make his job easier. They take a careful aim. Flashes of light along with gun shots are again heard.
Another security guard crawls from behind. He reaches sufficiently close, stands up, and with a hysteric cry, fires two rounds into the cabin. One of the intruders is silenced. The other one though, escapes into the darkness. He runs directly to the first floor of the hostel. He wants the advantage of height to spot the guard.
The guard searches for him, ultra-cautiously. The guard's hands are having a nervous grip on the gun. The intruder can't enter any room. They are all locked. He thinks of forcing the door open and snatching one of the kids. But he has neither got enough time nor enough ammunition to sustain deviations in the plan. But he has definitely got a prey.
He runs down fast and drags a kid hiding behind a bush. He pulls the kid up in one hand and tries to take out the pistol at the waist. It is missing. He feels that he might have lost it in action or while scaling the compound. It doesn't bother him. He drops the kid on the ground. The guard, who had set to search him, walks closer. He is anxious. The intruder points his gun at the kid who is kneeling with head down.
"Drop your gun and come in front of me! I'm giving you just ten seconds..."-he shouts.
The guard has no other way. This is my strength. When I am short, even the best of the minds give in.

The guard comes in front of him, still pointing the gun at him. "Drop the gun! If you want to see this kid alive..."-the intruder warns.
"So that I could be a turkey?"-the guard is no fool.
"Call Ayodhya! Where's he? Listen... I don't have anything against you or this kid. I just want Ayodhya, grandson of Ram Prakash."
The guard stands without a word, facing the intruder.
"Do you know Ayodhya?"-the intruder presses his gun against the kid's head.
"Y... Yes... He studies in class six."-the kid gives away the information.
"Which room does he stay in?"
"Seven."-the boy reveals Ayodhya's room number.
The intruder now turns to the guard-"Listen, don't act senseless. We can settle it peacefully. I'll just take Ayodhya with me. Go to room number seven and get him."
"I'm giving you twenty seconds."
The stakes are not just high. They are unknown. The value of lives is to be estimated in twenty seconds and a decision has to be taken as to which one is expendable.
The intruder begins the countdown!
The kid under his gun can see the shadow of the intruder falling diagonally to the left. The intruder's face seems to be covered with a cloth. The poor boy continues to kneel even though his knees are hurting, pressing against the hard floor. His neck too, is aching.
"Five!"
"Four."
"Three."
The guard stands with no change in his position. He is not able to think.
"Two."
"See we can settle this peacefully. I am offering you again! But I am not going back on my words if you fail to heed."
"ONE!!!!"
The bullet is let gone. The head is pierced!
The guard still stands with his forefinger on the trigger unpulled!
He knows his gun has run out of ammo long ago.
He only wanted to delay the death of the kid as much as possible. He had

felt that every minute the kid could be offered to live should be offered. Every single breath it could have breathed should have been breathed before the imminent.
The blood is drawn. It flows through the crevices on the ground and forms a pool at a low lying area. The pool gets bigger and bigger. The redness of the blood is slowly getting muddier. The hands of the intruder lay wide apart, his gun lying next to him, partly on his fingers. His forehead looks like a hot spring, oozing blood.
When the intruder had lifted the kid, his pistol was there at his waist. But when he had brought the kid down to kneel in front of him, it was not!
The kid had felt the touch of pistol at the back of its palm. Before it was pushed down, it had quickly removed the pistol. It was kneeling with the pistol all the time in the partially lit area. When the countdown had begun, the kid had a look at the shadow of the intruder's head, the target, and quickly estimated the target's physical location in the three dimensional space.
As the countdown was about to end, it had slowly turned the pistol in its right hand, to point at the estimated target and pulled the trigger when the intruder had counted one after offering a peace deal.
The chance it had taken had hit the bull's forehead! The intruder had fallen on the ground pivoting about his heels, like the falling of a huge tree axed at the bottom. The deal was sealed. The intruder had to rest in peace!
The guard recovers from the numbness. His legs are trembling, slowly getting the blood supply that was choked due to shock. He dashes to the kid.
"Are you ok, son?"
The kid points its right thumb. The knuckle is broken! The pistol's reaction has dislocated its thumb knuckle.
"The joint is dislocated. But it is fine."-the guard reassures.
"What's your name?"
The kid inspects its knees, wiping them of stone particles.
"Ayodhya!"
The next morning is full of astonishment, shock and a strong sense of fear. The Principal stands frozen in front of the intruder's body. The

cloth on the face has been removed. The mouth is open and so are the eyes. The bullet hole is right in the center of the forehead between the eyes. Flies are buzzing around the face, to doubly ensure that it is a dead body. The crows have all lined up along the electrical transmission wires for an early morning feast.

Ayodhya stands among the students. The students and the teachers are looking at the sky, amazed! Ayodhya turns to his eyes to the sky. Not even an inch of it is blue to be called the 'sky'.

It is swarmed by hawks and vultures hovering menacingly, losing patience with every single passing minute. Ayodhya could see that some of them are extremely close; screaming that they are famished... and perilously irate. He could see their eyes, taking turns, threatening him to go back. He could see the sun's rays making its way momentarily through the golden feathers. The kings of the sky are casting their shadows on the gathering, warningly, trying to indicate their intentions.

"One shot can change the skies."-Ayodhya stands bewildered.

The police party arrives tailed by an ambulance. They request the Principal to disperse the students. He waves his hand. The teachers take the students away. The guard stands with the Principal.

The Principal explains to the police that the intruders had come for kidnapping students for ransom. The Police find it hard to digest. Kidnapping students from a hostel needs planning to a much bigger scale, they feel. The Principal somehow manages to convince them. Nothing is spoken about Ayodhya. The guard is complimented for gunning down the attackers. A special ceremony is planned to honor him. Although he was indecisive against the second intruder he had managed to kill the first. The other guard who sacrificed his life at the entrance too is going to be awarded posthumously.

Ayodhya's thumb is hurting. The history class is going on. The teacher is narrating the Jallianwalla Bagh massacre in quite an animated manner. Ayodhya is not very alert. He's pre-occupied.

"... And the park was full of people. There was only one narrow entrance to it and it was the only exit. They were demonstrating peacefully against the misrule of the government that was seated thousands of nautical miles away. General Dyer arrived on his horse, sitting stiff on the saddle.

He looked around like a beast that had satiated its hunger but was craving for blood... Blood for amusement... Blood to satisfy thirst unquenchable by water... There were the children, the women, and the elderly. He saw them and just saw them. His cruel eyes told everything. There was not a moment that could bring sympathy in his heart. He made no announcements. He gave no warnings. The people remained assembled even after noticing him and his men who stood at the entrance. They had no reason to panic. Their overlords whom they had been serving for centuries had come to check violence, that's what they thought.

How foolish! They thought they were British Indians, trying to become Indians. But the man sent from far across the seas thought that they were locusts trying to become humans!

Dyer's murderous eyes scanned the whole area. Again and again... His head became a cauldron of boiling blood spewing fumes of hate. He turned back and batted his eyes across his shoulder. The party took up the formation. The sound of the horseshoe died down but the tail still moved slowly in the thin air. The soldiers looked viciously astonished at the easy. The demonstrators had a sense of satisfaction that they were a part of a greater good. Unfortunately, they thought that sense was a thing. And more damaging was their feeling that their overlords possessed sense. There was dedication in the minds of the demonstrators while callousness ruled the psyche at the other end.

A moment that was going to be a black spot in our history was about to come. The wind stopped blowing and the leaves ceased fluttering. The clouds halted sailing across the sky, to witness in disbelief, one of the bloodiest massacres of civilians.

General Dyer looked to his left. He could see a young locust with beautiful, bright eyes looking on curiously. It held its mother's hand gently. He saw more locusts turning to him in puzzlement. He became steady and signaled his men. They took aim. Each rifle was pointing straight. There was no need to aim, the soldiers knew.

There was an ominous silence. If the General had tried listening, he could have heard a thousand incessant heartbeats pounding the earth. The silence loomed long enough to overcome his patience.

FIRE!!!"
Ayodhya's memory takes him through the previous night, the intruder counting one and the trigger he pulled to hole the forehead. He shivers for a moment. When he comes down to reality, he finds himself drenched in sweat.
"Principal wants you to meet Ayodhya."-the attender stands at the door.
Ayodhya looks on, with trembling limbs. He breathes deep and moves out of the class slowly.
The man walking aling, is more than just an attender. He is meant for a greater role than what he is officially appointed for. Even the teachers respect him. He prepares the visitors mentally to face the Principal. If he knows the reasons for the summoning, he comes out with it and if he doesn't, he'll give an estimate of the mood inside. He is the most underrated spy in this story!
Ayodhya looks at him as they walk along. He gestures a 'don't know' and nods, dancing his head up and down slowly with a piercing look to indicate 'you are awaited... badly'.
Ayodhya smiles at him. He has moved on from being a normal kid to a man who does not give a damn.
"I have worse people to deal with."-Ayodhya thinks as they approach the cabin.
His indifference confuses the peon. "Are my my gestures becoming ineffective to even a small boy?"
Well, you chose a man, mate. Not a boy...
"Come, come Ayodhya. Come."-the Principal shows him a seat.
The guard, Surjeet, is also sitting across the table. The peon leaves. He is entitled only for the audio session.
"Surjeet has told me everything."-the Principal starts off.
"Everything?"-Ayodhya looks at Surjeet.
"Y.. Yeah until the point... I... I saved you."-Surjeet hesitates for an eye contact with him.
"See, Ayodhya. We have lost one guard. We had almost lost you if not for Surjeet. I know how you feel but we don't have a choice. I've spoken to your grandfather. We want you to discontinue."
Ayodhya, surprisingly, maintains his composure. There is no panic, no

disbelief and definitely no fear on his face.
"But..."-the Principal continues with a smile. "...you will continue. Your grandfather is a genius. He has a wonderful plan. We expel you from school for namesake. We want the students to believe that you're no longer here. You will have to continue studies on your own. I'll be there to help you with it but no other teacher will be available. Your grandfather made it a minimum member plan. You will stay in Surjeet's house and will never come out during the active hours. That is to say that you'll study during nights. Librarian Bala will anyway leave the library keys with Surjeet. You may study there during night. Your grandfather was telling me you're fond of books and like to be in the library."
"He wants to speak to you."-the Principal dials as he speaks. "Surjeet, you may leave now."
Surjeet obeys.
A while later the phone call is answered- "Mr. Ram Prakash? Ayodhya is here. I've explained him everything. Just have a word with him."
"Yes Sir... Please."-Ram Prakash requests. The Principal leaves after gently placing the receiver in Ayodhya's little hands.
"Grandpa..."-he hears Ayodhya's calming words after long, sleepless hours. He wants to talk to Ayodhya warmly, make him feel comfortable and drive out his anxiety. But he decides not to. He wants a different Ayodhya; an Ayodhya who believes he is capable of handling anything that comes his way. He wants Ayodhya to start saying 'come what may' and say it more often.
"Appu..."-Ram Prakash almost sobs. His voice trembles. "How could they even think of killing an angel like him?"-he thinks.
"The guard did not kill that killer."
Ram Prakash is surprised- "What? Appu? That killer isn't dead?"
"He is... But the guard didn't kill him."
"Then?"-Ram Prakash fervently hopes there is no new entrant in the game of death.
"I did!"-Ayodhya's voice has a mark of a battle-hardened warrior.
The entry has happened!!
"Appu?!"-Ram Prakash sits on the chair gently. Ayodhya looks at the

door. Nobody seems to overhear. He narrates the entire incident and also the claim made by Surjeet.
"You talked about some presence of mind. Is this what you meant?"-asks Ayodhya.
Ram Prakash wipes his forehead. He turns his head around. There is an idol of Lord Shiva in the prayer room, behind a dimly lit oil lamp. The pristine radiance emanating from the eyes of the Lord fills him with relief.
He looks on, thanking the Almighty- "You made me beg in front of you and when I did, is this how you rewarded me? I asked for you for someone who can take care of Appu. And you gave me the perfect person!"
"Grandpa? Hello?"
"Appu, let it be so. Let the guard be felicitated. Don't spoil anything. You have to remain low. You heard me?"-Ram Prakash bends over thrusting his voice into the phone.
"Yeah, grandpa. Look after yourself. Don't think too much. I can take care of myself. Give me some time; I'll take care of you too."
"Bye, Appu."-Ram Prakash is unable to believe it.
Ayodhya is back on the seat, awaiting the Principal. It has been a while. He's alone. A friendship is on the cards. There is a faint clue of a new relationship kindling inside him. A bond, an attachment... with loneliness...
It, he has started to believe, would help him stay in the present and survive.
The Principal is back. "So? You spoke to him?"
"Yes Sir."
"Ok, let's go."-he takes Ayodhya out of the cabin, gently holding his shoulder.
"I'll issue a memo and expel you out of school. Let us see how it works out."-he talks calmly. "Ok..."
The peon is confused hearing it.
As they approach the class room, Ayodhya falls on the floor as he has been pushed by the Principal.
"Sorry Sir, I will remain a good student!"-Ayodhya starts weeping.

"Please don't expel me."-he falls to the Principal's feet.
"You are out. That's it."-he pushes Ayodhya hard. Ayodhya is thrown near the table. He kicks Ayodhya on the hip. Ayodhya cries aloud.
"How dare you talk to me like that?"-the Principal holds his collar and slaps him hard. The sound is chilling. The history teacher is shocked at the sheer magnitude of assault. Ayodhya is dragged along as the Principal leaves the class.
"Please don't expel me, Sir."-Ayodhya grips the Principal's leg, begging for mercy.
All along the corridor, the Principal drags his heavy leg while Ayodhya hangs on.
"Leave me."
"Promise me that you won't expel me, Sir."
The whole school stands mute witnessing the brutality. They approach the cabin with Ayodhya imploring for sympathy with tearful eyes. The peon stands with a frightful look.
The classrooms are now out of sight. Ayodhya gets up, setting right his collar, wiping tears. The Principal follows him, pushing the twin windows across the door while Ayodhya just ducks under it and goes into the cabin.
The peon is dumbfounded!
"I hope I didn't hurt you badly."-the Principal is apologetic.
"You shouldn't have kicked me. Pushing and slapping were ok."-Ayodhya gulps water. "Getting kicked is the only thing I hate."
"I was doing this for your own sake."
"That's the only reason I swallowed it!"
The Principal is taken aback.
Ayodhya sits quietly as the Principal starts typing the expulsion order.
"Actually, you too are benefitted by this act of ours."-Ayodhya breaks silence. "How?"-the Principal raises his brows, his fingers still on the computer keyboard.
"The bullies in the school... They are tamed!"
The silence is restored.
It was Ayodhya's idea. As they had walked along the corridor, Ayodhya had come up with a suggestion-

"Sir, you have to beat me up in front of the entire class, saying that I misbehaved and hence you are expelling me. This way we can force others into believing I'm gone for good."

"And I felt his grandfather was the most intelligent."

The show had begun.

It has been almost two decades now. Ayodhya has lived a childhood of anonymity. The students had feared his presence in the library during wee hours of the night, imagining a nerdy ghost. The librarian too had, many a time, resigned for the same reason, seeing differently arranged book shelves. Sadly, his resignation was turned down each time!

Ayodhya had not only learnt his academic subjects but also continued his fond association with other books, any book he got his hands upon in a random section. His exams were conducted in a very fair manner, in which the Principal sat in front of him as he had written answers the very evening his classmates had done.

His tenth and twelfth grade exams however, gave some headache to the Principal as the exam center was located elsewhere. For the first time in his life, the Principal had bribed the inspection squad to allow Ayodhya to appear for the exams in a separate cabin as a viral fever candidate.

Ayodhya had scored very high marks in both the exams, standing first in class but sadly the Principal was not able to publish his photo in the newspaper along with other toppers for obvious reasons.

There was another peculiar fondness that Ayodhya had developed, thanks to his staying with Surjeet.

Guns!

While the normal kids were busy with the push-back cars of China, Ayodhya had experienced the recoils of a Russian handgun!

He had become so fond of guns that despite Surjeet's apprehensions, he had cleaned the handgun, rifle and the machine gun for him every day. He had learnt some shooting skills too. Surjeet was under obligations since Ayodhya was the sole person responsible for the fame and respect he had earned after the shootout. That being on one hand, he was also willing to teach shooting to Ayodhya on the other, since there was a constant threat hovering above Ayodhya's life.

He stayed with Surjeet while Ram Prakash's daughters and son moved abroad as they had earned enough money from the hospital. They were involved in issuing false medical certificates, forcing deaths on financially incapable patients and removing their body parts. Soman, another grandson of Ram Prakash, too completed his studies in Psychiatry and landed up in the same hospital... as a doctor. They had everything. They now no longer needed the old man's property. But they still wanted to kill Ayodhya for the sake of it. Habits die only with the person. Ayodhya was an unfinished chapter in their lives. They had pledged to return for him after some years. And they wanted the Blue Bell Villa at any cost. It was a villa whose location Ram Prakash had hidden from his children. There was a buzz within the greater family of Ayodhya that the villa contained treasures from six generations. Years ago, when Ram Prakash's children first fell apart from him, they had made every attempt to locate it but had failed miserably each time.

These days Soman takes care of the hospital. He was made to stay back in the country. Now he has taken the hospital to its 'zenith', opening branches all across the country.

While these developments took place on one hand, on the other hand, Ayodhya had started preparing for engineering entrance exams. His aim was to crack Combined Entrance Exam, popularly known as CEE across the country. It was the kind of an exam, which, even being a zygote was not too early to start preparing for.

He had cleared it in flying colors to get admission in YIT Dweepa. Dweepa was a place that had caused sensation in the general populace. The world was left dazed by the surfacing of a new island about 187 nautical miles off the coast of Karnataka, in the Arabian Sea. There was a series of earthquakes for eight months leading to the overlapping of the tectonic plates under the sea which had finally given rise to the island. The Government of India had immediately dispatched a team of officers and declared the territory Indian by hoisting the tri-color. It was named 'Dweepa'. There was furor all over the nation. The news channels beamed videos after videos but the nation wanted to know more. The geologists and other scientists were dispatched and tight security was maintained around the island. Unfortunately, there were no deposits of minerals or other natural resources found. It was economically of less importance as the salt content in the soil had made it unsuitable for vegetation but an interesting conclusion was drawn after a few months of further examination with sophisticated minds and equipment. The island was declared to be a permanent landmass!

That meant that there was no chance of it going back down. It was then thought to be used as a military base for maritime security. Things changed in a couple of years. Frequent depressions in the sea brought unprecedented rains, dissolving and eroding the island of most of the salt content and the first signs of green sprouted. It was gifted on a platter by nature for poor and hungry Indians. But poor Indians! They didn't know that there were hungrier Indians.

The serenity was mesmerizing. Flora and fauna flourished, migrating from the nearby Minicoy and enriched the biodiversity. The beaches carved out were better than the best in the world. Over the years, the cost of one square inch on the island shot up. Ravenous politicians, hideously wealthy businessmen, imbecile kids of cine superstars, overpaid sports personalities and the self-styled champions of social justice had all been vying for space on the island. But the outcry of the common man successfully led the sane authorities to declare it for the general public and a world renowned Engineering Institute- YIT Dweepa was established. But India has always been a generous country, a country that has not disappointed even plunderers. The big league still has its eyes on the island.

Ayodhya's studies had continued in that institute. He had opted for mechanical engineering. His days there were not too rosy either.

He didn't know the nuances of the student world. He was a newcomer. Everything looked so new to him.

For years, he had not stepped out of the school premises, fearing not death but deviations in life, a life he thought he controlled. He had only played cricket occasionally with a group far, far away from the school. He had mastered one of the rarest qualities of human being- Patience. A quality that involves a brawl with me...

His dedicated patience has successfully extended my grace period, but at what cost? He has not learnt the worldly aspects of life. He has seen most of the world through books. He's been a third party to the happenings all these years. Just like me... A third party... And that is why, probably, despite being dispassionate, I have a soft corner, a penchant, for him. Ayodhya for me is a chaste soul scathed by a different living.

Now for a peek into his college days-

Ayodhya stands watching the sea gulls fly past him above his ferry. He thinks that a new life has taken wings on a new, unblemished piece of land.

"Hey look at him. Ha, ha, ha..."- a senior student sitting on his motorcycle comments on Ayodhya's clothing. Simplicity leads to mediocrity in a shallow world. Ayodhya has just two pairs of cotton clothes for his use. He has a taste for books. But his horrible dressing sense has made his lean, skinny looks more comical. The same, age old hackneyed act called ragging is going to be the first of the challenges he has to face.

"Hey, you... Come here..."-the seniors call him near the parking. Ayodhya continues his walk towards the college, not heeding to their call. He is burning from within.

"How dare they call me? Who are they after all? Should I really tolerate?"-he thinks. But thankfully he recalls the words his grandfather always quoted- "Anger is like a double-edged sword. Wielding is all that makes the difference."

"Hey, cartoon! Are you deaf?"

"They are not worthy to be even my enemies."-Ayodhya walks away.

"Leave him, anyway. Where would he go?"

"What if he gets blown away by the wind?"-a third one asks.

"You would anyway suck him back. You're so good at it, aren't you? Ha, ha, ha"-a fourth answers. "How do you know that?"-another one laughs.

It has been a couple of days. He has joined the Central Library, a few miles away from the college, as a free member. He has offered to render service to the library, like maintaining records, issuing books but not without an exchange in return- a free stay at the library shed- a dusty place where old, worn out books are disposed away. He wants to start a new life in the dust, like a phoenix. The library officer is happy with the deal. He thinks he has got a free servant. He doesn't know Ayodhya is a slave of books.

Ayodhya has skipped the Fresher's Party on the first two days. The classes have started from the third day.

He enters the class and scans the classroom. It is so spacious. He occupies the seat by the window and looks as far as his eyes can see.

The sea!

It is so serene. The classroom is at a height. The coconut trees have hidden the waves battering the shores. All he can see is the tranquil of the distant sea. You, humans, fall prey for the sight more often than any other life form does. More often than fireflies!

Ayodhya's seniors too, have fallen for it.

The first session has ended. Ayodhya is at a roadside restaurant.

"Hey, here is our Mr. Floyd Mayweather!!"-a couple of seniors who had always ragged in the presence of their batch mates for safety, walk to him fearlessly. A seemingly weak Ayodhya lets them come closer. One of them slaps him! Ayodhya's spectacles fall on the floor. "So you don't listen to us when we call you, do you?"

Ayodhya slowly picks up the spectacles and gulps water.

The other senior takes the jug and pours water on his head.

"Om.... svaahaa... Ha, ha, ha."-he chants a hymn looking at Ayodhya who has worn vermillion on his forehead.

Ayodhya's fury is rising gradually just the way the vermillion on his forehead is getting washed away. The table is wet. The hotel cashier is helpless. He decides to remain mum than see his furniture get smashed to pieces. As the water gets poured, Ayodhya recalls the temper he had to overcome as a child. Ever since he had come to know of the sad truth about his parents from his grandpa, he had been fighting fits of anger. His grandpa somehow had managed to sprinkle some sedative thoughts in his mind from time to time. Ayodhya at last had promised to himself that he'll never allow anger have its way.

The water flows through his shirt. He can feel the chillness of the liquid. But he knows his rage could be more chilling. He turns to the senior, slowly takes the jug and places it back on the table.

"Sir, I am a very weak person as you can see. If you try to harm me, my condition could get worsened and you will be responsible for it."

"Boo... hoo... Mummy..."-one of them tries to cry like a kid, satirically mocking Ayodhya.

"Please leave me."-Ayodhya's voice weakens.

In the meantime, the biggest bully- Pony, spots two of his friends take pleasure in ragging Ayodhya. He has a long ponytail and hence the name. He has an odd obsession with overuse of two phrases- my father's and your mother's...

"So, you guys have finally found Mayweather- the greatest fighter in town?"-he makes a sarcastic comment and starts slapping Ayodhya.

"Sir, please don't harm me."-Ayodhya pleads walking backwards, out of the restaurant.

"Why my son, why?"-he drags Ayodhya near the hostel gate and pushes him on the ground. The other seniors stand in a circle. Pony stands in the middle. "Hey Romy, how does he look when he sleeps? Can you imagine?"

"Like a sleeping skeleton!"-Romy laughs. "Ha, ha, ha..."

"Let us see how a skeleton sleeps! Sleep... Sleep..."-Pony keeps slapping Ayodhya who is lying down on the floor.

Ayodhya does not obey. Pony forces his eyes close by pressing them with his fingers.

"Show how you sleep. Or else his father will put you to sleep."-Romy warns Ayodhya. Ayodhya struggles to remove Pony's hands off his eyes.

"No, no, baby. You heard Romy? Do you know who my father is? Hmmm? Do you know who he is?"

Ayodhya shouts in pain. Pony releases him and kicks his back. "Ha ha ha... He is just like a walking, talking corpse. He he..."-Romy comments as they walk away.

It is eight in the night. Ayodhya closes the library doors. The breeze from the sea tries to assist him close the windows. He walks slowly to his home- the library shed. The shed is quiet. He sits down in a corner with his eyes facing the ceiling. His mind has become a dormant volcano-suppressing hot tides of indignation.

He calls up his grandfather and explains everything including his state of mind. His grandpa has only one advice that he has been giving him all along- to never retaliate.

"No Appu, everything will soon pass. Have patience."

"Sometimes we need to act, grandpa. And when I say act, I don't mean complaining to the grievance cell or the police. Some people are immune to every man-made damn thing."

"Whatever you do, make sure that you are not caught."-Ram Prakash gives up. He thinks it is better to allow Ayodhya make his own decisions. "I've reined him for too long... for a considerable chunk of his life. Let me leave him free now." Ram Prakash is lost in running through the past- something he has been doing for decades. He knows he is in some way responsible for the kind of living inflicted on Ayodhya.

"Bye grandpa..."-Ayodhya leans against the wall. It is eleven in the night. He struggles to stay in the present. "I have to play with the constraints-taking action and avoiding any problems later."

He falls asleep, exhausting his energy trying to think of a solution.

A chain of nightmares has slowly started to unwind- a gang of men are charging at him firing guns. He is trying to scale a mound to cross over to the other end and escape them. Pony is kicking him back down the mound, laughing insanely with wide mouth as he rolls on. A few college seniors have gone hysterically excited at his futile attempt. The hawks are swooping down one after the other to peck the flesh out of him even as he attempts fervently to save his skin. His grandfather has been chained by three shadowy figures and is being thrashed with wet grass-"Where is your grandson?" The sea has gone extremely violent and is rising like a monstrous wall of water, ready to bury him underneath!

Ayodhya shakes his head, trying to come out of the nightmare. It doesn't seem to end- his struggle has become more forceful. You can see it through the darkness of the library shed. It is still not over. He clasps his eyelids and tries to scream but is unable to open his mouth.

Suddenly, an act of providence sets in on him!

Ayodhya now knows, being in his nightmare, that he is experiencing a nightmare and in reality he is lying in the library shed. He, delicately and very skillfully, continues the show!

He gives up the struggle. He stands still in front of those trying to gun him down, in front of Pony and the gang. The bullets pierce through him but he still lives on. He looks straight into the eyes of the hawks that are raining towards him. They pluck his eyeballs away like cherries but he is still able to see. He looks at his grandpa whose bare chest has turned violet with the beatings. His grandpa smiles at him. He stands with his heel locked against a stone, in front of the wall of water. The water gushes at him with infinite force but he is still standing and so is the stone behind his heel!

He proceeds towards the gun party, snatches a machine gun and starts firing at will. The men vanish away one by one. He catches hold of a hawk that has charged at him and squeezes its neck. It screams, flapping its wings in agony. The other hawks fly away. He walks to his grandfather, releases him from the chains and touches his chest. The violet fades away. He turns to the shadows and tries to hold one of them. They slip away. He turns around and there's Pony!

He opens his eyes and comes out of the dream. The night is calm. He gets up slowly and reaches for a jug of water. Gulping some water and wearing his woolen jacket and skull cap, he walks down the pathway. It is a full moon night. Dweepa is well lit with milky light all along. A distant howling of a lone wolf fills the moisture laden air. He sits at the shore on a rock. The tides are unusually high. He stays there for a while. He feels better. He feels the wind that appears like a pair of invisible hands brush his hair and sooth his pain. He sits savoring the unique touch of calmness brought by the glow of the moonlight. After sometime, he slowly gets up and walks along the beach.

He sees fire from a distance.

He walks closer, trying to avail the cover of darkness. The fire gets closer. And so is the noise of drums and guitar. He comes so close that he could not only see the fire but feel it too. He hides behind a tent. There is a group of people dancing around. Young girls and boys are swaying around in the partial darkness. The noise is heavy. There is intermittent clapping, turning and jumping. Ayodhya could still hear a voice. He tries to focus... on that dim voice emerging from the noise like snake slipping on through tall grass. The laughter... The very laughter Ayodhya is desperate to hear again has caught his ears.

He could see a ponytail among the thick and the curly masses of hair. He startles! PONY!!

The beach is a regular haunt for Pony, being the only son of a wealthy businessman. He comes there every weekend, grabbing a bottle of beer in one hand and an objectified life in the other.

Ayodhya could feel creepy movements inside his body. His eyes are lit up. The fingers are clutching the soil tightly. He looks at the fire. He feels like shoving the log of fire into Pony's mouth. An inhumane happiness fills Ayodhya.

He waits and waits and waits until the party mood dies. They drop down, one by one, on the beach, inebriated. To Ayodhya's luck, Pony lies a few yards away from the person nearest to him. Ayodhya scrambles towards him!

He sees a pit dug in the sand. The party group has always been doing that- burying the empty bottles of liquor and other used items in a huge pit in the early mornings to escape the beach patrol authorities.

Ayodhya wastes no time.

"Pony!!"-he snarls into the ears of an intoxicated Pony.

He has become extremely wild. One of those traumatic moments of anger seems to have possessed him yet again, after years.

"Hmmm?"-Pony opens his eyes partially.

"Dude by day, nude by night?"

"Who is it?"

Ayodhya starts dragging Pony to the pit by his feet. Pony's head makes way along the sand.

"Leave me... Do you... know my... Do you know who my fff... father is? He won't spare you..."-Pony tries his best to struggle his way out.

THUDD!!

Ayodhya mercilessly pushes Pony down the pit.

"Mummaa!!"-Pony wails feebly.

Ayodhya makes Pony sit upright and slowly starts filling sand into the pit. Pony sits singing his favorite Portuguese song. Ayodhya cements the sand with his feet all around Pony and leaves only his head over the surface.

He walks back to the tent and brings a knife.

"Let me goooo!"-Pony tries to free himself out of sand.

Ayodhya walks to him.

"Look at me..."-he whispers. Pony is unable to turn his eyes upwards. He swings his head-"Hmmm... Let me go..."

"LOOK AT ME!!!"-Ayodhya roars!

Pony shivers. He slowly tries to look at him. Ayodhya doesn't like the sluggishness. He keeps his left foot on Pony's head and turns it upwards in a jerk.

"Don't hurt Ayodhya ever again!"

"Who are you? Hmmm? Do you know... who... my... father is?"

"That's for your mother to figure out!!"

The next morning Pony is woken out of slumber by some kids standing in a circle around him. They are taking his photographs and laughing. Pony's friends have woken up on the other end of the beach.

Pony is now fully sober. He finds out that he was buried in the sand, neck deep, the previous night by some eerie person. He remembers the conversation slightly. But what he is not able to find out is what is stuck in his mouth.

He wants to speak but something in his mouth prevents it. He is not even able to spit it away. He starts making sounds, pleading the kids to help him. The kids laugh away the request. They are not immature enough to give up on a lifetime opportunity.

After an hour a few elderly fishermen spot him and dig him out.

"Thuuuuu!! Thuuuu!!"-Pony spits out the thing, cleaning his tongue with his hand. It is his ponytail!!

It is late afternoon. The atmosphere in the college is tense. The chief security-in-charge for the institute is a retired police officer- Mohammed Asrar. He arrives with another policeman to meet Pony as per Pony's father's request. Pony is sitting with a bottle of aerated drink in his hand. They are trying to make him remember the assaulter. "Give us some clue. We'll drag the bugger out from wherever he is!"-the policeman assures.

Pony thinks hard. "Sir, I don't remember correctly but he was quite tall and... and..."

Ayodhya too stands in the crowd, listening to the testimony. He is not comfortable with the turn of events. He is feeling guilty for whatever he has done. He had not expected it to be blown out of proportions. Now all he can do is keep mum and let the happenings unfurl. He has a strange feeling of joy too. Never had he felt so blissful before. He feels as though he has been rid of an unseen burden, as though he has been suddenly let free after years of slavery, as though he has woken up on a certain promising morning that has ended all his sufferings. But he still wishes that Pony does not recognize him.

"And... quite... you know... well-built. Like Romy."

A ray of hope shines in Ayodhya's mind. He recalls the woolen jacket he had worn the previous night. It had covered his body perfectly and given an impression that he was well-built. "Now there is no chance I would even be suspected."-Ayodhya leaves. Romy sweats!

Ayodhya is back in the classroom. The lecture is on. But he has been thinking of the previous night's adventure. He is gradually arriving at a solution to all his sufferings. "This is a good beginning. I'll tolerate all the stuff they do to me. Later, I'll hunt them down one by one. I need to be as random as possible. If person A hurts me on one day, I shouldn't take action on him the same day. Rather, I have to record it and wait for an opportune moment. Probably until then person B and C might also have hurt me and A would be least expecting a retaliation. I should not leave a pattern or any clue that leads to me."

He improvises his plan further. "To achieve things that are too personal, I need to be as much a commoner as I can. The only things I have to take care of are my appearance and voice."

"More importantly I should ensure I don't miss anyone. Be it Pony and company or those who are troubling grandpa."

"And hence the solution. Any doubts?"-the Professor asks.

"Not at all. Everything is crystal clear now."-Ayodhya thinks.

It is the restaurant again. Ayodhya sits sipping coffee. Pony arrives with his gang. "How long will it take to grow back your ponytail?"-his friend asks him.

"Shut up!!"-Pony isn't happy. He occupies a seat and scans around. Ayodhya notices that Pony has seen him. Pony recalls that the assaulter had said something about Ayodhya. He slowly walks near Ayodhya and sits in front of him, looking sharply into his eyes. Ayodhya looks back timidly- "Good evening, Sir."

"Where were you last night?"
"In the library. I was preparing for the internals."
"Do you know anyone here? Someone like a relative?"-Pony tries to be calm. "Yeah, I have very caring relatives who are always after me."
"So it was your guy. Right?"-Pony holds Ayodhya's collar and pulls him closer.
"I don't know who you're talking about."-Ayodhya looks frightened.
"Ask your relative to meet me when I'm sober if he has guts. Not when I'm drunk."-he pushes back Ayodhya. Ayodhya slowly gets up. Pony's friends leave. Pony turns to follow them.
"Where do you want him to come?"-Ayodhya asks timidly, correcting the position of the spectacles on his nose.
It is half past twelve in the night. Pony's style quotient has a zero remainder. His ponytail is gone. He has come in rumpled clothes with grumpy looks and walking around in Gaanja Park-a park originally named as 'Mahatma Gandhi Park' that had eventually turned into a Gaanja and Hookah hub. There is a bust of the great leader in the center of the park. These days, people dope literally under his nose.
Ayodhya too has reached the place. He knows Pony has got reinforcements. Pony's friends are waiting in his brand new Audi parked a few yards away next to a compound, just behind a tree. They have stored hockey sticks in the rear of the car. Pony waits. Ayodhya is wearing a leather jacket and a cap. He has borrowed a pair of sunglasses from a member in the library in exchange for an extension of a popular book for a fortnight, counter to the rules. He is wearing a hankie across his face. His identity is fairly sealed from Pony & team. But he is unable to decide on how to stop Pony's friends from interfering on Pony's behalf. The car can reverse or take a right. To its left is the compound and to its front is a tree. There is a motel across the road facing the opposite side. Ayodhya walks to the motel and starts talking casually to the man at valet parking. The man looks at Ayodhya wearing sunglasses in the middle of the night and feels that he is just another parvenu who has fallen short of intelligence with sudden wealth.
"Hi, today is my girlfriend's birthday. I have planned a surprise party here. She would be coming any moment now. My other friends are

coming too. So I would like to take your place for about an hour. It is a part of surprise. So could you go out of sight for an hour?"
The man hesitates. "Just go away for one hour. Go, enjoy the beach. Can't you sacrifice just one hour for your bro?"
The man looks at his hotel. He fears the manager. "Sir, but can you inform the manager once?"
"Look, we have booked the entire party hall for a night. You want to cross check? Come in..."
"Sorry Sir... I'll leave. But how about other guests?"
"Every guest is my guest! Thank you."-Ayodhya holds him by the shoulder and takes him in the direction of the beach.
"No, I mean other customers..."
"Do you know who my father is?"
Ayodhya now stands at the road. A customer stops his SUV and throws the keys at Ayodhya-"I'll be back in an hour."
"Yes Sir."-Ayodhya starts the vehicle and takes it towards Pony's Audi. He parks it directly behind the Audi so that Pony's friends cannot reverse their car.
He returns to the motel. This time a BMW stops at him. "How long will you take, Sir?"
"Will leave tomorrow."
He drives it towards the Audi. By now, Romy has come out of the car and is inspecting the rear. "Who the **** has parked the car so irresponsibly?"-he is walking around the SUV. Ayodhya loses no time. He quickly wraps his face with the hankie, wears the cap and drives on. He parks the BMW right next to the Audi so that Pony's friends are trapped, unable to push the doors open.
"Hey, hey... You... How dare you park it like that?"-Romy kicks the BMW to attract Ayodhya's attention. Ayodhya walks swiftly at him and slaps him hard!
"What did you say?"-he snarls threateningly. Romy falls on the ground. His left ear bleeds.
"Sir, I just meant..."-he crawls backwards. Ayodhya bangs his head against the SUV-"Pardon Sir? I didn't understand."
"No, no... I'm sorry..."

"Make no mistakes."-Ayodhya kicks Romy's face. Romy is grounded.
"Ask no apologies."-Ayodhya presses Romy's head against the ground with his foot. He kicks Romy's back, waist and stomach. He lands his foot on Romy's chest. "Never be a bystander when jobs are left unfinished."
By now the other friends trapped in the car have started calling up Pony's number. Pony, has not been able to receive their call as he has switched off his phone to avoid his girlfriend's midnight chatter- "To hell with you, Anca"-he had cursed her in his mind.
Ayodhya casually walks towards Gaanja Park.
A few moments later Pony spots a guy sitting on a stone bench wearing a leather jacket, a cap, sunglasses and wrapped with a hankie across his face.
"Want some?"-a random man offers the masked Ayodhya a syringe. "No. The drug will go on a high."
The man walks away, baffled.
Pony walks towards the masked man with a lit cigarette and sits on a stool meant for the watchman. There are a few young delinquents, looking on at Pony and the strange man.
"Want a smoke?"-Pony offers his cigarette, hoping to see the strange man unmask.
"I don't take butts in my lips."-the reply is cold. Pony gasps for a moment.
"How are you related to that slimy Ayodhya? Look, you are anyway doomed to death. If you give me all the answers I'll make your death a little less painful. I give you my word."-he displays his pistol.
Ayodhya looks at Pony and bends forward. There is less than an inch's gap between their faces. Ayodhya slowly turns Pony's face to the right by holding his chin, and begins in a thunderous voice-
"Are you still called 'Pony'?"
Pony's anger shoots up.
"Or do they call you a pen-drive now?"
"You're in for a painful death!"- Pony swings his hand to slap Ayodhya. Ayodhya doesn't back off even an inch. He just raises his left foot up, thereby lifting the horizontal bar at the base of the stool. Pony tips

backwards and falls on his head. The hand that he had raised to slap Ayodhya stops just short of Ayodhya and follows the body. Pony holds his head and groans. He has suffered a severe hit by the hard ground. His hands clasp his head tightly.

"More painful than this?"-Ayodhya challenges. Pony crawls back, trembling. The young delinquents pack up all their items and take to their feet. "Asrar Sir...!"-Pony has a trump card unknown to Ayodhya. Ayodhya is shocked but not for too long. The presence of mind he has been practicing brings him back to reality in seconds. Elements of surprise have seldom affected him.

"Things seem unknown because they are often behind us."-he turns back immediately. Asrar and a couple of policemen spring from their hideouts.

"Freeze, you're surrounded."-a policeman shouts with a revolver pointing at him. Ayodhya grabs Pony's pistol from the ground and takes shelter behind Pony himself! The police party is surprised. They had least expected Pony to possessed firearms, let alone carry. The element of surprise turns to them.

Ayodhya points the pistol towards Pony's temple and signals them to drop their guns and back off. The policeman hesitates. Ayodhya fires!!

The revolver in the policeman's hand is severely damaged. And so is his hand. The bullet has passed right into the gun!

They move back step by step, facing Ayodhya. After they reach sufficiently far, he signals them to turn around and sit down. They obey. They could only hear a wailing Pony. A few minutes later Asrar turns around. Pony is still wiggling on the ground. There is no sign of the stranger. They rush towards Pony. There is a board supported on an iron tripod kept on Pony's chest. It has been taken from the flower garden nearby. 'KEEP YOUR SURROUNDINGS CLEAN'.

The next day Asrar summons Pony. "How did you get access to pistol?"

"Sir... I keep it for safety. You know my father is a bigshot. So there is always a risk of kidnap."

"Have you got a license?"

"No Sir. My father has..."

"Why didn't you inform us that you were carrying it?"

"Sir... I..."
Asrar waits.
Pony can't hold on to his frustration- "Sir... Cut this crap ok, you were supposed to catch that criminal and you ran away like a coward. How could you even expect me to trust you? Your... your policemen are a waste. Thank God I carried a pistol."
Asrar gets up in rage. The policemen stop him. "Sir... Sir... Please calm down."
"Do you know your foolishness could have cost all our lives? We would have lost Yogendra. Thankfully he has suffered a minor injury."-Asrar shouts.
"God knows why these spoilt brats are born. We have to not only endure them but also protect them!"
His eyes fall on Romy. Romy has some bluish green color under his ear, spread up to his nose. "What's wrong with him?"-Asrar asks.
"Sir, they had accompanied Pony to Gaanja Park yesterday. The same assaulter has hit him on the face and kicked on his chest."-the policeman answers.
Asrar stares at him. "Sorry Sir... Mahatma Gandhi Park!"
He then narrates the entire Audi-SUV-BMW and the assault incident.
Asrar inspects Romy's face. Romy allows diffidently. "Bring me the clothes you were wearing yesterday. Immediately."
"Sir I've given it to the dhobi for washing."-Romy answers in pain. "I want it now!"
Asrar inspects the shirt. It is muddy. He looks for the most obvious clue. The sole marks! Asrar hands it over to the policeman and leaves. Within an hour he has a lead. The shoe belongs to the Puma brand and the size is nine!
Ayodhya, on the other hand, rests back on his chair to review the incidents. He sees no trouble. He decides to be more careful with the scouting, the next time.
"How did you fix an appointment with the assaulter in one day?"-Asrar is surprised. Pony doesn't like to reveal Ayodhya's link. He has taken it as a matter of self-respect, respect of his father, his family and more importantly the clan he belongs to. He has decided to deal with

Ayodhya's companion all by himself. He has even warned his friends against disclosure.
"Met him by chance... I felt he would be there as Gaanja Park is famous for the infamous."-he keeps it simple. The policeman goes from classroom to classroom to pull up students with Puma shoes of size nine.
"Sir, there is a student. First year Mechanical Engineering. Only his shoes match our requirement."
"What's his name?"
"Ayodhya!"

10 SAY CHEESE

Ayodhya stands trembling in front of Asrar.

Pony isn't happy. He considers himself a lion and doesn't like a pack of hyenas snatch away his prey. "Sir, that boy is a good guy. Very studious and moreover we are quite helpful to him."

"Get the jeep."- Asrar leaves.

"Sir, what about the boy?"-the policeman asks.

"Look at his face. He doesn't seem to have even learnt to wear undies. How could you expect him to fire a pistol?"

"Don't think he escaped me. He can get lucky once, twice, thrice... But not every time."-Pony warns Ayodhya. "Sir, I implore you. Please don't harm him. I've nobody other than him. Please Sir..."-Ayodhya begs with tearful eyes.

"Then get one!"

Three months have passed. Ayodhya is being ragged intensely by Pony and his friends knowing that it is their final year in college and the opportunity will not recur. Ayodhya has been extremely patient. He has not resorted to his alter ego, well aware that exams are round the corner. The exam season ends like thin fog under the sharp rays of the morning sun.

His third semester has started. Pony has arrived to fetch the degree certificate. "Where's he? Did he die listening to my warning? Wherever he is I'm going to find him out and kill him! I swear on my clan!"
Ayodhya starts weeping. "Please Sir..."-he folds his hands. Pony leaves.
"Must have seen an old Indian movie."-Ayodhya feels as he instantly ceases weeping.
It is time for the college festival. There is a huge crowd that has gathered to take part in different events. Ayodhya has just come out of his electrical laboratory session. The electrical Professor is a mad man. He hates the students of Mechanical branch tremendously. And so do many of the other lecturers in that department. The students in Mechanical branch too are wary of him and his gang of lecturers- "Don't know why an electrical subject in 3rd semester!"
Ayodhya has failed to obtain the required output in the 'Semi-conductor diode' experiment. The Professor has made Ayodhya stand outside the lab as punishment. Ayodhya is not bothered. He leaves immediately.
He crosses the various stalls arranged in the path, trying not to look at them. His pockets are empty. The only source of income for him is the meager amount his grandfather sends him every month. The Gol Gappas, Juice machines and Coffee makers have personified and laughing aloud looking at his pennilessness. There is also a rose stall to rub thorns on his wound- any boy who wishes to express his love to a girl can buy roses for her from that stall at cheaper rates- provision for an economical romance.
There is also a stall selling jackets with the college name and the name of the college festival imprinted on them. Students are busy buying the jackets of their sizes. They are all beaming in white. Ayodhya suddenly gets an idea!
"If ever I land up in trouble and have to turn into the other-me again, the jacket one would be a perfect option. The chances of my getting caught would be low. Many students have it!"
"How much?"-Ayodhya asks a student from Electronics and Communications department who is selling the jacket. He is a kind of student who loves co-curricular activities than studies. And he has grasped the art of maintaining the jeans just above the knees in order to

prove how much he spends to buy that branded underwear.
There are many like him and college festival is like a revival of their hidden desires.
“150 only. Superb print, it won’t fade away even after a thousand washes”-he shows his marketing abilities. “Keep one for me. I’ll arrange for the money”-Ayodhya looks around.
He walks towards the open space next to the Girls’ Hostel. A gang of men is playing a cricket match. Ayodhya was always discouraged by his grandfather against playing for money. But Ayodhya can’t help it this time. He has to somehow get that jacket.
“What’s the bet?”-asks he to a lad. The lad is cheering his team mate who has just hit a boundary. “25 per head.”-he replies and proceeds, sensing a chance to argue with the bowler that the hit was actually a sixer and not four. Ayodhya walks to the captain of the batting side. “I want to play the next match.”
“Are you good at cricket?”
“Yeah.”
“Prove it.”-the captain asks mechanically, looking elsewhere, with a twisted smile.
“I am quite an experienced player. Because I have what others don’t... apart from experience.”-Ayodhya shows him the shiny sunglasses.
“It costs 4000. I want 150 for a win”
“150? Are you crazy? The five of us get 25 each for win. If our luck is good, we end up at 100 on a day.”
“Today is your day!”
Ayodhya realizes that he has to play six matches. “We’ll play six matches. Keep one of your boys out of the team.”-he is confident.
“But will the opponents agree to continue the play if they keep losing?”-the captain asks showing immense faith in Ayodhya.
“Once a gambler always a gambler...”
The rules are set. Each team gets six overs to bat for. Each player can bat for a maximum of one over unless the rest of the members get out. The runs are only on the leg side and straight runs are considered only if the ball remains within the leg side to the light pole standing straight ahead. Runs cannot be taken by running between the wickets. All scoring has to

be done by making the ball cross a gutter that stretches along as the boundary. If the ball clears the gutter, it is a six. There is a catch though. The ball cannot enter Girls' Hostel- either directly or after bounces. The batsman would be declared out in such a case. The bowler cannot raise his heels while delivering the ball although there is no restriction on the speed of delivery. All the power is to be generated by arms. Rules are subject to change depending on the prevailing situations, on mutual consent.

"Do you want batting or money?"-Ayodhya asks a straight question to his team mates. It doesn't matter on the island whether a person is a park loafer or an international player. Money is the honey.

Ayodhya faces the first over and displays his batting skills. His team mates, completely charmed by his talent get out deliberately, giving him more deliveries to face. Ayodhya walks in match after match, facing the first over, sparing the next over for others to make way for him and destroying the bowling attack for the rest.

He has stumped three of the five batsmen in the second match. In about an hour, he has 150 rupees in his hands. He doesn't like it but he has no other go. "How could you so confidently say you would win even before the start of the match?"-asks the captain, returning the sunglasses to Ayodhya.

"I do face-reading!"-Ayodhya leaves.

But deep down, Ayodhya knows. He couldn't have afforded to lose the sunglasses that belonged to a member in the library. When you drive yourselves to such an extent against losing something, you naturally start winning; because the feeling becomes a part of you like your limb and head... When you play with that added part, you tend to use it since it is within your control just like your fingers. Ayodhya had played with that extra accessory.

He purchases the jacket and walks down the college pathway for some distance.

His cell phone rings. It is an unknown number. Ayodhya's mind immediately alerts him. He does not maintain any contact with anyone other than his grandfather.

"Could it be the three of them about whom grandpa always warned?

Should I receive it? Is grandpa in trouble?"-he looks around. "Hello?"
"Hi, is this Ayodhya?"-a beautiful female voice asks.
"Yes?"-Ayodhya replies with a tinge of suspicion.
"Hi, I'm Pooja from Electronics department. I just found your ID card near our hostel. Could you come to the hostel and get it?"
Ayodhya checks his pockets. The ID card is missing. He realizes that he might have lost it while playing. "Yes..."-he replies. But he doesn't want to go to a Girls' Hostel. "Why can't she just hand over in the office?"-he thinks. But he is on the other side. He can't demand. He looks around. There's his classmate standing at the Gol Gappa center. He is of the same height and physique as Ayodhya, with dark brown eyes and has long, pointed hair. He looks quite different and hence quite good.
"Hi, I'm Ayodhya."- Ayodhya has, for the first time, started a conversation with a classmate. So far, he had only been attending classes and just attending classes. He had been extremely quiet, not even having a casual chat with anyone. His classmate is surprised that Ayodhya has voluntarily spoken.
"I'm Kunj Bihari Yadav. And the name's going to stay."-says he, tired of the taunting by his friends. Being from Bihar in that college is seen as a reason for trolls based on the stereotype about their accent, English speaking skills, looks and ways. And unfortunately for him, his name blatantly conveys his eligibility.
"Don't worry. In India, stereotyping is more pandemic than swine flu."-Ayodhya consoles him. "Why don't you have some Gol Gappa?"-Kunj offers, quite pleased with his words. Ayodhya hesitates. He doesn't want to spend money his grandpa has been earning with such difficulty. Ayodhya had many a time felt guilty for not having earned any money. He had been playing cricket for bets whenever he had shortage. "If you want more money, ask me Appu. Don't ever play for money."-he recalls his grandpa's words.
"What's wrong, grandpa? It supports us. And I'm not stealing. It's like business."-Ayodhya had asked him when he was in school, addicted to bet matches.
"No, Appu. Business has ethics. Betting is gambling. It is bad. Bad things are easy to learn, good things aren't because bad things come with a price

and good things with a prize."
"When you learn a bad thing, you're letting go of some restraint- social, biological, ethical, moral... some restraint. You're letting go of value, which is easy because of the natural tendency of diffusion. It is like opening the tap of a tank and letting the water go. But when you're learning a good thing, you're adding value to yourself which is not easy. It is against the pull of tendencies. Your will, your grit and your determination alone can help you get there. Value addition is hence a prize. Don't ever play for bets."
"What happened?"-Kunj enquires.
"Hmm? Nothing."
"Here..."-Kunj offers him a Gol Gappa. Ayodhya is surprised. "Thank you..."-Ayodhya struggles to come to the matter at hand.
"Did Scooby Doo punish you too?"-he inquires about the Electrical Science Professor. The Professor has a wobbled up face due to constant 'Eddy currents' getting generated in his throat, shouting at Mechanical students. He has long drooping ears too, giving a feel of Scooby Doo-a popular cartoon character.
"Why do you think so?"
"I saw you standing outside the lab."
"That's because he considers me outstanding!"
Kunj is perplexed.
"I get it. You stand out from the rest of the class and hence stand outside..."-Kunj smiles before looking at Ayodhya's new jacket.
"So, you bought the jacket?"
"Yes..."-Ayodhya is still thinking of ways to begin about the ID card. "Could you help me with my ID card? I've lost it near the Girls' Hostel. We... we... need to search!"
"Ok..."-Kunj doesn't think twice.
They reach the hostel area. Ayodhya slowly proceeds to the open space, ostensibly to search for it but his eyes float towards the hostel. He sees a girl standing at the gate swirling an ID card in her hand. She seems to be expecting someone. "Kunj, that girl there has got my ID card."-Ayodhya finally reveals. "What? How do you know?"-Kunj is astonished. He pauses searching in the gutter. Ayodhya narrates everything. "Could you

please ask her?"
"Why don't you go get it?"
"No, Kunj... Please..."
"Ayodhya, I know you're a bit timid but a time will come when you'll have to be bold. Future has got bigger challenges. When will you buck up?"
"Next time..."
"He he he... Just a minute... I'll be back."
"I'll be in college...."-Ayodhya leaves without even waiting for Kunj's response.
He goes to a place despised even by the ghosts-the library. He settles down with a book on Material Science by William Callister. He finds it so engrossing that he forgets all about the ID card. And he has not even taken Kunj's number. It is five in the evening. The buzz at the festival area is gradually getting noisier. Ayodhya slowly peeps out of the window. There is a swarm of students wearing colorful clothes. They are participating in computer games, games that challenge the fitness levels like rope climbing and some less taxing games like collage etc. Some boys are seen head-hunting with roses in their hands. Some are hunting in packs.
Ayodhya realizes that it is futile to look for Kunj. He walks down the library and proceeds towards the college exit.
He feels a pat on his shoulder.
"Hey... Where were you?"-Kunj stands grinning.
"Library."
"Here is your ID card. Strange isn't it? You lost ID card there and I lost my heart."-Kunj tries to get Ayodhya curious but soon realizes that he is more mysterious than previously thought. Ayodhya shows no interest in knowing more.
"Why are you so worried?"
"I wouldn't have got my bus-pass without it. Thank you."- Ayodhya keeps it back in his bag.
"She is a nice girl. Pooja..."-Kunj begins. Ayodhya looks on. "I went for lunch with her."
"Thank you Kunj."-Ayodhya leaves. Kunj stands puzzled at the odd

nature of Ayodhya. He doesn't seem normal.
"Are you an introvert?"-Kunj catches on. Ayodhya turns back. "No... How about you?"
"I'm extrovert. I don't like being gloomy all the time. I think you're facing some difficulties in life. I won't ask you what they are but I can assure you, they'll end. Did you have lunch?"
"No..."
"Come to the hostel. There will be some food left in the mess. Come quickly, the cook would close the mess after five thirty."
Ayodhya walks with him. "Difficulties were after me even before I was born. They will end only with me."-he thinks. "Actually, I am an extrovert too. I interact a lot. And the only person I do with is me, myself."
After food, Kunj requests Ayodhya to return to see the festival unfurl amidst pomp and show. Ayodhya hesitates but soon realizes that Kunj too is looking for a friend who has not laughed at him for his name, native or accent. He has seen genuine friendship in Ayodhya. But Ayodhya's best friend, loneliness, has besieged him into giving it up. Its possessiveness is tenacious. It is highly intolerant. And poor Ayodhya is under attack.
He follows Kunj to college. "What do you love the most?"-Kunj asks him.
"I don't understand what you mean."
"Everyone loves something or someone. You too might love something... other than silence and solitude!"
"Guns!"-Ayodhya speaks up about something he always wanted to hide.
"WHAT!!?"-Kunj is shaken. "Guns? Why?"
Ayodhya realizes his blunder. "Umm... They protect..."-he tactfully brings out a positive point.
"You are strange... I mean... I'm sorry... But you're a bit different. Anyway, let's..."
Bang! Bang!
They hear mild gunshots!!
"Was it a gun?"
Ayodhya figures out immediately- "Dummies... Used for games..."

He walks robotically towards the direction he heard them from. Kunj too, walks along. The noise is now more frequent. There are many students surrounding the area. Ayodhya and Kunj stand on their toes to get a glimpse. A man stands next to a huge, white board, quickly filling dummy bullets in guns of various sizes. Students try their shooting skills on the balloons tied to the board.

"Pooja, Pooja... Why don't you try?"-a girl asks Pooja. Kunj sees Pooja for the second time in the day. She is tall and extremely gorgeous. She walks with a graceful panache to the shooting area. "All the best, Pooja."-Kunj wishes her. "Hi..."-she whispers as she tries holding the murderous looking gun in her delicate pair of hands. Kunj's heart is beating faster. He is not able to resist staring at her. He somehow wants her to have a second look at him. As she raises the gun to take aim, Kunj could see the Cupid raise his bow and aim at his heart. She places her forefinger on the trigger, not able to locate the hole she should be seeing through with her right eye. But the Cupid has a perfect and clear sight. He pulls the string of the bow back up to his shoulder. The balloons sway in the wind just like the Cupid's flickering target pumping juicy blood ready to burst instantly at the first touch of his arrow. The situation is tense. Kunj's blood pressure is alarmingly high owing to the sudden surge of activities in his blood vessels that have been under-efficient all these years. There is a nervous air of uncertainty. Kunj pleads in his mind- "Either look at me with love or turn the gun at me with one eye closed."

Pooja turns her head with a smile at Kunj. "Swoosh!!"-the Cupid lets go of the arrow and Pooja pulls the trigger!! He has hit the bull's eye. Kunj is feeling numb, isolated from all the happenings around. Pooja's shots, though, have missed the swaying targets. She closes her eyes in disappointment- "Nooo!!"

"Ha ha ha..."-a few boys laugh at her. Kunj is upset with them. All the while, Ayodhya has been staring at the various models of guns lined up on the table. Small pellets are heaped in bowls for use as bullets.

Kunj wants to prove his caliber to Pooja and give the boys a fitting response. Ayodhya is quick to gauge that Kunj is deeply attracted to her. He decides to help poor Kunj.

"Hey, listen."-he calls. Kunj turns hysterically with an angry 'did you see

that?' look.
"Come here..."-he has a plan. Kunj agrees to follow his idea.
"Pooja, Pooja..."-Kunj fights his way to reach Pooja who is now enjoying an ice cream.
"Hi..."-she smiles.
Kunj knows he's going to talk foolish but he is getting carried away by rage. The music too is quite appropriate for such a mood.
"I want to avenge your humiliation!"
"Have an ice cream!"
"No, I want revenge!"
"Wh.. what?"-she giggles looking around to see if any of her friends have heard him. They don't seem to. "Pooja, do you have two rupees? We need change."-they ask.
She nods and starts searching in her purse. "Why revenge? On me?"
"No... For you... I did not like the way they laughed at you."
"Who? Those guys? They're my classmates. Don't worry, it was not serious... Had they done that before I began shooting, I would've shot at them!"-she consoles.
"No, Pooja. You need to come with me."-he pulls her by her arm.
"Ok... Ok... Here, your two rupees."-she gives the coin to her other friends and walks with him.
"Bro, I'll take this gun..."-he pulls out a gun and in the meantime, bumps against the table. Three more guns fall on the ground along with a bowl of 'bullets'. "Careful, careful!"-the vendor shouts. "Kids these days don't have self-control at all."
Ayodhya stands nearby, wearing the college jacket. He helps pick a gun and keep back on the table. The vendor picks one more. "Sorry, sorry..."-Kunj holds the vendor's shoulders, shielding Ayodhya from the view. Ayodhya slips back the third gun in to his jacket! He grabs a handful of 'bullets' and leaves.
"Ok, ok... Start. The record is twelve hits out of twenty. If you break the record you can get anything among these gifts."-the vendor forgives Kunj and explains about the game. Pooja stands at a distance holding an ice cream, implying 'I'm bored. Make it faster'.
Kunj confidently walks some distance. "Why are you going that far? You

will miss the target."-she warns.

"No way. Just watch..."

He takes aim and fires. Although he is zero in shooting skills and has missed the target completely, the balloon has been ruptured with a bang! Standing a few meters behind him under a tree within a curtain of bushes is Ayodhya, aiming a gun!!

Kunj sets right his skull cap. He is wearing a Bluetooth device in his ear. He has kept the phone on call to Ayodhya's. Ayodhya is wearing a pair of ear phones.

"Now raise your gun and take aim at the pink balloon to your left."-Ayodhya instructs Kunj. Kunj obeys.

"Three... two... one... Fire!"-Ayodhya whispers. Kunj and Ayodhya fire simultaneously!

Kunj misses the balloon but Ayodhya doesn't. Pooja is getting excited. The crowd is applauding. Two hits in two attempts for Kunj.

"Good! Now for the yellow one to its bottom right. Three... Two... One... Fire!"

Ayodhya continues to hit every balloon Kunj fires at. Kunj is getting nervous. You can see sweat dropping down from his forehead. He has started to become self-conscious. But Ayodhya is as cool as cucumber, lurking behind the tree.

The crowd has gradually started to get bigger and bigger. They have never witnessed such a good shooting display before. Some have already started video-recording Kunj's feat. A girl now moves a bit and stands directly in Ayodhya's line of fire.

"Kunj, there's a girl in my path. Kunj?"-Ayodhya is helpless. Kunj starts trembling. "Go for it! Last shot!"-Pooja is anxious. Kunj wipes his sweat.

"Move away... Let the air come..."-the vendor disperses the students. The girl moves. Ayodhya is back with the aim.

"Perfect, Kunj. All clear. Aim for the violet one. Three... two... one... Fire..."

The violet balloon bursts!!

"Yeah!!!"-the students cheer Kunj. He takes another aim. "That's it. You won!"-the vendor comes ahead.

"No, stay back there. I'm not finished yet."-Kunj shrugs. The students

standing next to him too ask for some more chance for him.
"He has a point to make. Let him continue!!"
The vendor, Pooja and a few others are left bemused. Ayodhya and Kunj continue their show for some more rounds of shots-"Three... Two... One... Fire!!"
"Pooja... Come here..."-Kunj finally returns the gun and clutches her hand. He slowly walks with her as though he is accompanying a queen. She is left dazed at the sight! The ice cream drops from her hand!
The unburst balloons are in a formation that, when seen from the front, reads-'THIS IS FOR POOJA'
Pooja's eyes fill with tears. She turns to him emotionally, carried away by the joyfulness in the crowd and hugs him tightly!! The crowd continues to applaud and record the video that eventually grabs fifty thousand hits on the internet in a single day.
"Hey, one gun is missing..."-the vendor urges the students to search for it.
"Look under the table."-a voice suggests from the crowd!
Ayodhya slowly walks away as Kunj and Pooja sit with their heads resting against each other, enjoying precious moments of privacy near the stairs to the library. "You've got such a perfect aim."-she whispers into Kunj's ears. "You're right. I aimed at the most beautiful girl and got her."-Kunj thinks.
"Why don't you try Olympics?"
Ayodhya walks in twilight. The central library is closed today as it is a Tuesday. He slowly removes his watch and slips it into his bag. He removes his wallet too. And the cell phone... His spectacles follow the wallet and the phone into the bag. He gently places his bag between two parked cars and slowly enters the graveyard, the shortest route to his home-the library shed. He is being followed!
Someone suddenly grips him by the neck from behind!
Ayodhya in turn elbows the man on the neck! The man loosens the grip to recover from pain. Ayodhya turns back. It is the vendor at the shooting stall!
"I set up the shooting stall for you!"-the vendor walks in a circle around him.

"You should have made a wish at the shooting star!"-Ayodhya too negates the encircling. The vendor charges at him and inflicts quick blows on his stomach. Ayodhya retaliates by kicking his shin brutally. But the vendor has got a firm hold on Ayodhya's neck. Ayodhya struggles to free himself. The vendor slides Ayodhya's legs and pins him on the ground. Ayodhya gets hold of a stone big enough to damage a skull. He tries hitting the vendor on the forehead with it. The vendor ducks and kneels on him. Ayodhya pulls off an insane header on the vendor's nose. The vendor falls away. He removes his nose and throws it aside. He slowly takes off his wig and the moustache. Ayodhya gasps!

It is Asrar!!!

"Sir...?"

"I always knew the shooter would show up at the shooting event."-Asrar helps him up.

"The whole purpose of the stall was to catch that person who could shoot into another gun's mouth with a crazy level of accuracy in the dark of the night. When the Kunj episode got over I allowed him to have a few minutes with his girl and once he took leave of her at the hostel I threatened him to reveal the person who was shooting for him."

"How did you know someone else was at it?"

"Initially I could not. Courtesy- your brilliant planning of pinching the gun... But later I saw that he did not return to me for refilling the pellets at the end of four shots. The gun was a smaller one. It couldn't have lasted that long without refills. Then I spotted you amidst the bushes but could not identify."

Ayodhya walks back to fetch his bag. "How did you find out I was after you?"-Asrar asks in astonishment, having seen Ayodhya prepare for the fight by keeping all his valuables in the bag.

"I knew the vendor would definitely do something. After all, in his enthrallment he had dispersed the crowd to make way for me to aim. When Kunj was right there, what was the need to move that girl away who was much behind him?"

Asrar is dumbstruck! "Who are you?"

"Ayodhya."-he does not mean his name.

"That is true but who has trained you in shooting? How did you learn

about observational deductions and planning?"
"I follow my own syllabus!"-Ayodhya merges in the wraithlike darkness.
Asrar stands still.
"Meet me at the grounds tomorrow at six am- Asrar."-Ayodhya receives a text message in the night.
It is half past five the next morning. He is still in bed. Something is preventing him from sleep. He feels a strange voice within himself- "Go meet him, Ayodhya... Go, meet him..."
The voice is repeating ceaselessly. Ayodhya pulls the pillow over his head. It doesn't seem to show any mercy. "Go meet him, Ayodhya... Go, meet him..."
It is six. The mist is settling down gently on the waving strands of thick hair. The air is brushing by the shirt swiftly, creating a flutter. The dim shadow falls on the grass, denying it of the murky view of the rising sun. It is Ayodhya standing at the edge of the ground. Asrar is running the last lap of his morning jog.
He is glancing at Ayodhya every now and then, admiring the personification of enigma. Ayodhya is staring at the ground, unperturbed. Asrar completes the jog with a sigh, wiping a napkin on his face. He walks to Ayodhya- "So? You finally found someone who made you decide to come, I guess."
"Guess work is for the unprepared..."-Ayodhya replies calmly.
Asrar looks on.
"What made you trust me? What if I land you into trouble? I've sided with Pony once already."-Asrar walks towards the tap.
"There is nobody who can always be trusted. And there is nobody who can never be trusted. I follow my instincts."-Ayodhya stands still, without even looking at Asrar.
Asrar washes his face while Ayodhya savors the panoramic view of the ground.
"Ayodhya..."-Asrar pats Ayodhya and starts towards the exit. Ayodhya walks along. "You see people every day. They are all good at something. There is nobody who is not specialized in anything. So, specialization is such an ordinary quality. But there are also people like me who are good at anything... who can manage many tense situations. People like me

have several skills which need to be carried forward. Having specialization in everything is the only special quality. I want to teach you those so that you could be prepared for some out-of-syllabus questions life poses at you from time to time. Not just that, to earn your livelihood you should be an expert in at least one thing others bad at. There are many such things. I'll teach you them. Also, you must use them for the benefit of the society."

"Why do you want to teach me? Why not others? What if I misuse what you teach?"

"I follow my instincts too..."-Asrar replies, sitting on the stairs at the pavilion.

"I was bad at social science. I don't do social work."

"Look Ayodhya, I am not asking you to do anything. I just want to teach you. And once you learn them, you will compel yourself for the work. I saw your fighting spirit and skills. I witnessed your uniqueness. I won't ask you why you've learnt these but I have chosen only you. Just want to teach you some combat skills, some..."

"You..."-Ayodhya interrupts. "...teach me combat skills? You?"-Ayodhya is amused.

"You heard me right..."

"I don't think you've got enough skills after I fought you yesterday. You couldn't hurt me."

"I am supposed to hurt only those who hurt my country."-Asrar tries to explain. "I was only trying to check how much skills you've got in you!"

Ayodhya gets a feeling that Asrar is not just a retired police officer. There is something more to it. "Who do you work for?"

"I work for the school but serve the country just like any responsible citizen."-Asrar gives a veiled reply. Ayodhya, the kind of person he is, does not press further. Asrar understands that Ayodhya has nothing more to inquire.

"First of all, you need to increase your fitness levels..."

The training goes on every morning. Ayodhya has been extremely devoted. He is practicing everything he is being taught. When you get less opportunity for a task you show more interest. You do it more efficiently. The same has happened with his studies-he gets to study less each day. He is studying more efficiently than he did before. He has been taking Kunj's help to keep himself abreast of the happenings in college whenever he has missed classes for some rigorous training sessions in swimming, rock climbing, diving etc. Asrar is conducting dance, singing and music classes too, for him.

It is exam time. The sessions, though, are going on without a break.

"Now for the combat lessons..."-Asrar stands in the center of the badminton court. "There are certain ways to take down an enemy. You're thin. You are not supposed to face the enemy upfront. You should always use your enemy's body mass against him. Use his inertia. Make him hurt himself. And do you know what the first target for you should be?"

"... His feet!! The only vulnerable part in anyone's body that makes the whole body vulnerable."

"There is a method used to hurt an enemy badly with minimum efforts and time and using whatever is available around. Attack me however you want... Go ahead."

"What is it called?"-Ayodhya tries to hit him with a broken racquet.

Asrar turns, disturbs Ayodhya's body balance with his leg and takes him down using the same racquet.

"Krav Maga!!"

The college days sail with me like the ship you can see to the left of the island on the waves of the calm sea. He is now in the third year. It is summer. He stands sweltering on the shore, witnessing the wild tides. The pressure on him is high. His classmates have sacrificed annual visits to their homes to take up 'mini projects'. It is not a part of the curriculum but an age old practice driven by competition. Someone, lost in the pages of history, had carried out a mini-project in some corner of the country and landed up in a top institute for a degree in Master of Technology. It was because the person had thought out-of-the-box and completed an extra project. Well, right now he is in the box, sealed from the rest of the world.

Names get erased but legacy remains. The last few decades have seen a nauseating number of mini-projects and there is a lot of stress physically and electronically for space to store the outcome of this stress-relieving activity. Ayodhya's scuba-diving sessions are over. Asrar plans to give some breathing space to him.

It is the machine design class. "Anshuman..."

"Present Sir..."

"Babita..."

"Present Sir..."

"Sir..."-Ayodhya stands up.

"Bishnu..."

"Yes Sir..."

"SIR!"-Ayodhya is a little louder now.

"Yeah?"-the Professor looks at the stranger standing like a palm tree in the African savannas.

"Sir... Ayodhya... Present Sir..."

"I've been skipping this name every day from the last semester. Are you Ayodhya?"

"Yes Sir..."

"How did you write the semester exams?"-the professor gets angry knowing that a person who has not satisfied session requirements has appeared for the exam.

"It went very well Sir... I scored 81%."-Ayodhya answers.

"I mean how did you get the hall-ticket? You have not attended a single class of mine!"

"Sir I suffered from typhoid twice in the last semester. I had the video sessions of your class. I have virtually attended all your classes from the hospital bed. Kunj Bihari Yadav had video-graphed for me!"

Kunj shivers. But he has to sustain. The Professor removes his spectacles in astonishment. He is impressed at the friendship.

"I hope to see my sessions on BlueTube soon. You know, when I teach my students I put all my energy into it. I teach by my heart..."-the Professor's face brightens up, looking for approval.

"And your students learn by-heart!"-Ayodhya wants to say.

The class is over. Kunj is upset with Ayodhya but he cannot show his anger after all that Ayodhya has been doing for him.

"What is the matter, Kunj? I am sorry I used your name."-Ayodhya apologizes for namesake. He never feels bad. "It is ok. But how did you

get the hall ticket?"
"I showed the attendance certificate to the office attendant. Bunny Sir had given me an entire booklet of attendance certificates with signatures on every leaf. He had told me that I could use it whenever I wanted to."
"Why did he give you?"
"I was the only one selected for the University Cricket team from our college. He said it reminded him of the past glory of our college when seven of our students had consistently been representing the University."-Ayodhya has surpassed Pillu and company, the top players in the College team and his new antagonists after Pony, to seal a place in the coveted University team. Mr. Bunny's gesture has been too rude for them, now that Ayodhya poses a serious threat to Pillu's captaincy of the college team. Pillu and his gang has been waiting for a chance ever since, to drag Ayodhya down in academics.
"You don't come to college but play for University. It is hard to understand you, Ayodhya."
"Try and understand the subjects instead. You may taste some success."
Kunj and Ayodhya have been following the simple rule of mutual co-existence since two years. Kunj helps Ayodhya with the academic rituals like completing laboratory records and paying the lab attendants on behalf of Ayodhya to reveal the titles of group experiments. He has also been planning and maintaining a 'fortnightly schedule' for Ayodhya, making Ayodhya's academics easier. When the next internal tests would be conducted, when the assignments would get checked and other requirements are considered and the master chart is prepared for Ayodhya. On a few occasions Kunj himself has purchased stationery for Ayodhya so that he could smoothly write his exams. Kunj has even written assignments for him. You may call it the instance of a devoted friend. But alas! I won't. And as you already know, I decide, not you. Kunj has an element of selfishness in him. He considers his contribution to Ayodhya's academics an opportunity to put in some extra effort in his own studies, the compensation for spending time with Pooja-real and imaginary.
On the other hand, Ayodhya too has been helping Kunj.
Didn't get it? Let me take you through this incident... Fourth semester...

College festival- the cauldron of happenings, the consummation of girl-boy interactions, the hub of preening old, monotonous relationships and the blooming of new, promising ones is here again. Pooja is completely impressed with the hip-hop performance by her classmates for the song from the movie- Step Up. She has even forgotten that Kunj is with her and is shouting her throat hoarse in vain, trying to encourage them. The lead dancer jumps across two of his partners and completes the dance with a flying kiss at her. Pooja stands blinking her eyes, not able to decide how to react. She steals a look at Kunj popping a question at him through her eyes- "Oh no, you saw that? I am glad though."

Kunj can't bear it. He walks towards the rest room.

Ayodhya is undergoing one of those rigorous fencing sessions with Asrar. "Look at the tip of the sword, not me. If you focus at the point that matters, half the game is won."

"Mr. Lonely... I'm Mr. Lonely... I have nobody..."-Ayodhya's cell phone rings. Asrar turns away, swinging the sword. Ayodhya spares a look at him and walks to receive the call.

"Sir... A personal commitment. Directly related to academics."-he waits for Asrar's reaction. "Go... But you got to defeat me tomorrow if you have to continue with the training."

"Done, Sir!"-Ayodhya has a conviction now, to win against Asrar, just as how he had during the bet matches with the sunglasses at stake.

"Yeah Kunj..."-Ayodhya is standing at a location he is highly unlikely to be found. The college amphitheater...

"I don't know how you'll manage. But I want to beat them in dance performance."

"Who is the organizer?"-Ayodhya has no demands.

"Mohit from EEE"-Kunj names the person from Electricals and Electronics Engineering.

"Ask him to include one from Mech."

Kunj obeys but the result is negative. Ayodhya has no time. He has to somehow get back to fencing practice. He wants to beat Asrar at any cost tomorrow. "He is refusing."-Kunj complains to Ayodhya, emerging from the back stage. Ayodhya turns him around holding his shoulder and walks at the main stage. Mohit stands admiring the beauty of the girl

who is videographing her boyfriend's dancing. "Mohit... One sec... Mohit."-Kunj calls him downstairs. Mohit refuses a couple of times but Kunj seems to come up on stage.
"Wait, wait..."
"Yeah, what's up?"-he asks with chin pointing at Kunj. A gentle pat prompts him to turn back.
SLAP!! A hard, rough palm sends Mohit rolling on ground. He looks around. Nobody is seen except Kunj. His head reels.
"My performance is a must tonight. Else, you will get slapped by unknown hands all this semester."-Kunj warns. "But the Bullford College students are yet to give it their shot. They are in the competition."-Mohit is scared but determined.
"It is up to you..."-Kunj turns to leave.
"Who is performing?"-Mohit gets up. "I am. Download this song."
"The next performance from Mechanical department- KUNJ BIHARI YADAV!!!"
"Whoo... Ha ha ha"-the students go crazy listening to his name. "Is it a Bhojpuri song?"
"When you wear a lipstick..."-they mock, singing a popular street song.
The show begins- Enrique Iglesias' 'Maria'.
'Kunj' performs in hip hop attire that has been snatched away by beating up the Bullford College students. Ayodhya and Kunj have assaulted them, wearing scarves across their faces and robbed them of their costumes. Bullford has sworn never to return to YIT Dweepa for performance!
Pooja stands stunned, seeing her Kunj perform on stage- "C'mon Kunj... Way to go!!"
The dance is electrifying with gravity defying moves. The crowd is mesmerized. The dancer is wearing a paper mask on his face. Time and again, he points at Pooja whenever the 'I wanna make you mine' part of the song is played. The song progresses with thumping beats. The crowd is lost in hysteria. The dance too has caught a lot of speed. The dancer moves towards the amphitheater exit, swirling all the way and returns jumping around. The one who swirled away was Ayodhya and the one who returned was Kunj!

He too is wearing the same type of mask. The dance has almost ended. Kunj removes the mask like a hero and walks to Pooja, requesting her hand. She can't believe it. Her mouth opens wide, hands land on her cheeks. She gently walks, placing her hand on his and enters the stage. They dance the last few steps together!

As soon as Ayodhya had switched places with Kunj he had hurried to practice fencing. There is nobody in the badminton court...

Ayodhya waits on with the sword. The air is mysterious. Ayodhya stands still like a deer at a lake trying to sense some movements around.

"Swoosh... swoosh..."-he wields it twice to the front and moves back defensively. He gets a feeling that he is not alone. He always feels that but tonight, in the quietness of the tranquil court, he feels its presence strongly.

"Whhhip..."-someone attacks him at his face and vanishes! He ducks.

"Zooooom."-this time someone slices his chest. Ayodhya retracts in fear! He gently touches his chest with eyes carefully scanning around. He feels no pain.

He breathes deeply and crouches. He has readied himself for a fight- a fight with the imaginary opponent who is flickering, visible at times and disappearing almost in an instant. Ayodhya can see him as a pale featureless figure in white, holding a silvery sword.

"Swooosh."-the opponent strikes first. Ayodhya perturbs him with an aggressive and sudden charge to his right. The opponent withdraws. There is silence restored momentarily.

"Whiiiippp!"- in an instant he is back, cutting through silence. Ayodhya falls back and hits a pole. The opponent tries inflicting heavy blows on his body. Ayodhya is scared. The opponent is not fencing; he is no sport. Ayodhya slashes his sword randomly to neutralize the bloodcurdling blows with one hand while rests his other hand on the ground in an attempt to move back. The opponent is getting the better of him. Ayodhya closes his eyes. The figure is now visible without flickering. It stands in front of him dauntless and causes serious blows on his body. It is getting bigger and bigger in size.

Ayodhya suddenly hears his grandfather-"C'mon Appu... Last seven overs remain..." The memories of his school days, swoop down on him.

It was one of the precious moments when his grandpa had visited the grounds far away from school to watch his grandson in action... Ayodhya is badly hurt. His elbow, shoulder, left thigh... There are fiery blows imposed by the raging bowlers. Ayodhya's eyes have filled with tears, not able to even maintain a steady stance to face the deliveries.
"APPU!!"-his grandpa shouts.
"If you fear, you'll fear more. Look back at it... Look at the ball in his hand! You have a bat with you!!!"
"Chaaarge!!"
"You have a sword with you!!!!"
Ayodhya opens his eyes. The figure has assumed a humongous size. "Zzzzzippp"-it tries to break his head into two. But its sword hits empty space. Ayodhya stands behind it!!
He is quick to cut through its neck. Its size reduces!
He continues to charge at it. He is quick, not giving it a chance to counterattack. But it is easily defending by nullifying his actions. He has won only half the battle.
He suddenly remembers Asrar's words. He now focuses at the tip of its sword. It is moving fast but Ayodhya is able to follow its movements. The fight continues. Ayodhya is getting more and more confident. He quickly observes the trick. A pattern!!
The tip of the figure's sword is following a pattern. And Ayodhya has deciphered it. The next round of pattern begins. Ayodhya cuts through the negative space within it to pierce through the figure's tummy. It retreats! It has reduced its size further. Ayodhya strikes for the second time. The size reduces again. Now he resorts to a blitzkrieg! His feet, body, hands and eyesight have found coordination. They are operating in tandem. The figure has started to get bleaker and bleaker and its speed slower and slower. Ayodhya leaps high in the air and brings down his sword heavily on it. The final blow!!!
The figure vanishes!
The next evening Asrar is surprised to see Ayodhya charge at him continuously without giving him a chance to even return some blows. Asrar's eyes scan Ayodhya's feet, knees, hips, arms, shoulders, eyes and hands perform in perfect unison until a steel tip obstructs his eyes.

Ayodhya stands holding the sword at his face!
"Practice breeds familiarity, familiarity boosts confidence."-Asrar thinks about Ayodhya's level of confidence.
"You win!"-Asrar gets up, walking to the table to remove his head gear.
"When a student defeats his master, it is the master who wins."
Asrar turns. Ayodhya fuses in the darkness of the night.
Ayodhya and Kunj have managed to help each other for two years now. So, let us get back to fifth semester. Ayodhya is waiting in the college for Kunj. Mini project on his mind.
"So, Ayodhya... How are things?"-Kunj meets him. "Fine..."
"I'm fine, too... You know how awesome it feels to be in a relationship?"
Ayodhya remembers the three children of his grandfather. "Relations are like antibiotics."-he mumbles. "Look who I am talking to..."-Kunj frowns.
"Heyyy... Whoooo... Ha ha ha."-Pillu and group pass by. Ayodhya and Kunj turn to see what the commotion is about. "Don't look at them Ayodhya. They will come after you."-Kunj immediately looks elsewhere. Ayodhya turns back.
"So the 'Bihari' thing is stopped now? After you became famous... They might have started to see you with respect I hope."
"Habits Ayodhya, habits... If you've decided to trouble a person, you'll do it even if he achieves something great. After the shooting incident I became famous on BlueTube. You know what these guys said? They said that I am a gang member in Bihar who loots villagers. They started commenting that I was the head of the gangs of Phasseypur. You remember the singing competition I won last time?"
Ayodhya had sung the actual song standing behind the stage while Kunj had only moved his lips holding a switched off mic to win the singing competition. Ayodhya looks on. "They said I was a street singer. Now they say I am a street dancer too."
"They gave you what you did not desire. You grabbed what you did not deserve. You're even."-Ayodhya clarifies the balance in fortune. "You mean I did not deserve Pooja?"-Kunj is serious. "I meant the popularity."
"But I sometimes think I did not deserve Pooja too. She told me yesterday that she likes me because of my talent."

"Life is unfair, Kunj. If you're good, the balance tilts in favor of negative situations. The good ones come only occasionally. If you really care for her then her reasons don't matter. You're talented but not in extra-curricular activities like dance and music... may be... you're a good entrepreneur."

Kunj looks at Ayodhya in awe. "But Ayodhya, sometimes I fear. I've come this far. There is no way to return. I fear getting caught. What would happen then? What would she think of me then? What if she breaks up with me?"

"The biggest culprit that gets one caught is the fear of getting caught."

"Do I really deserve her? I mean, tell me honestly."-asks Kunj after a tinge of introspection.

"The world is full of choices. You either bring down your desires to what you deserve or raise your worth to what you desire."

Kunj feels better.

"The worst case might be that she might end up friend-zoning you."

"Break-up is better than friend-zone. Any day... Friend-zones are new forms of SEZs. Special Exploitation Zones..."

"... I will be getting married in less than five years after graduation. Hope it will be a perfect one now that I've found her."-he brings out more of his hidden thoughts.

"Perfect marriage is the one in which the couple knows that there is nothing called perfect marriage."

"Hiii..."-Pooja stands behind Kunj. Ayodhya turns to see her wait for Kunj. He takes leave. Kunj's eyes fall on the words printed on her top-"NOTHING IS ILLEGAL UNTIL YOU GET CAUGHT."

He breathes light. It is like a good omen for him that Pooja herself is endorsing against his fear.

"Pooja, one sec... HEY AYODHYA!!"-Kunj catches up. "What have you thought up for the mini project?"

Ayodhya is unsure. He doesn't bother much with the academics. He is learning and mastering newer aspects of life. Studies seem too insignificant a challenge for him. He does not respond.

"There is only one thing I know that interests you."-Kunj smiles. Ayodhya looks on waiting for his answer. "Guns!!"-Kunj pats Ayodhya

and leaves. “You have weird friends.”-Pooja whispers.
Ayodhya receives a call from his grandfather. Every time his phone flashes his grandfather’s number, Ayodhya becomes anxious... And prays that he is not in any sort of trouble from the trio...
“Grandpa?”-he speaks softly trying to gauge the mood on the other side.
“How are you, Appu?”
Ayodhya heaves a sigh of relief. “I’m fine. Just thinking about a mini-project.”
“Good to hear you are taking a lot of interest in studies.”
“I’m interested, yes I am. I am in the top five scorers in my class consistently. But grandpa this mini-project is out of compulsion. Just to negate the competition.”
“Whatever you do, make sure it is put to use. What have you thought of?”
“Ummm... Something to do with guns. I just love them. One pull and eternal peace.”
His grandfather is shocked. He had not expected such violence filled words from the small boy that he knows. “There is a difference between peace and silence, Appu.”
Ayodhya pauses to think.
“As you said, peace is eternal. And silence isn’t. Guns can only silence. They can’t bring peace.”
“Sorry grandpa. I didn’t mean to hurt you. I just... just got carried away.”-he looks at Kunj who is sitting silently listening to one of Pooja’s never ending anecdotes.
“Take care Appu.”
Ayodhya is back in the central library. He is on the weekend shift. There is nobody in the gigantic state-of-the-art library. He seems upset with himself that he has hurt his grandfather. But he has kept open a huge book on guns. Different types of guns, their specific uses, construction, design, features are all there in it.
He doesn’t like what he is doing but somehow he is unable to close the book. He looks as far as he can through the window. He can hear the leaves of the coconut trees making a typical noise that he loves. There is a security guard at the ATM. He is armed with a rifle and a small handgun.

Ayodhya closes the book immediately and walks out of the library. "Shravan, keep an eye on the ground floor. I'll be back in half an hour."-he yells to another employee in the first floor. "Okie."

He walks to the guard but doesn't know how to begin. The guard looks back. Ayodhya slips into the ATM. He opens his wallet and checks the account balance. He knows there is nothing other than a few hundred but still does it cursing his fate.

He walks out feeling rich. "The AC in the ATM is not working."-he strikes a conversation. "There is no AC yet. We'll get it next week."

"Oh I see... What is your name?"

"Shibulal... Working at ATM since ten years. I can deposit cash for you in the other machine. I can also do transactions in four different languages. If you face any trouble you can call me. Do you know a secret? I know about the ATM more than the bank manager does. But who gives respect to someone sitting outside?"

"Oh great... No, no... Respect is for knowledge. Not for the... location. And you know much more. For example, you know how to handle a gun."-Ayodhya brings in the topic. Shibulal moves a little and pats on the marble next to him, asking Ayodhya to sit. Ayodhya's acting classes are fruitful. Shibulal is bored sitting all alone throughout the day. Nobody thinks of him as a human. He is just the filler of a space that should not be left vacant. That's all. Back at home his two sons do not have time to display their supremacy to impress their wives, let alone caring for junk like him. He has been sitting at the ATM after retiring from the Army. His only companions have been the memories! The days his beautiful wife was alive and healthy, feeding the two kids at the temple, the moments he spent with his fellow soldiers in far flung borders, just yards away from the enemy waiting to fire at the fall of a hat.

"Yeah, I can shoot anything with guns. The gun should have proper range, that's all."

"See... Can the manager do that? Ha ha ha."

"He can't even lift a gun!"-Shibulal whispers before laughing aloud.

"Can I lift it?"-Ayodhya feels he has struck the cord too early.

Shibulal doesn't hesitate though. "Yeah, sure... Here."-he hands over the rifle. Ayodhya acts as though he has never seen a rifle before. He

struggles to hold it. The conversation continues for some time, about different models of guns available in the market, their price, applications etc. “What’s that?”
“Pistol...”
“Oh, how different is a pistol from a revolver?”
Shibulal shrugs at the mention of the word ‘revolver’.
“Pistols are safer to use. Revolvers can misfire. Everyone prefers a pistol. They are sure it never misfires. Even common man can handle it easily. Many households possess it. Recently the baby girl of my former colleague’s son shot herself with her grandpa’s pistol. You see... Even kids can use it.”
“What happened to her?”-Ayodhya feels uncomfortable with the incident. “Nothing... It had just grazed her head as her aim got disturbed when she pulled the trigger. Small girl, small hands... Ha ha ha.”
Ayodhya waits on. A strange thought suddenly comes in!
He is glad, relieved and what more? He is sure grandpa is going to love it!
“Shibulal ji, I need to go.”
“Yeah, see you later. I’m on night shift next week!!”
Ayodhya always gets friends who are nobody’s friends.
He starts off with the mini project- he considers the design of the most popular model of pistol. He goes through the sectional diagram and tries to understand the function of each component. It is not enough. He decides to make a thorough research. A week rolls by. He is satisfied with the information he has gathered but wants some physical feel of it.
It is raining heavily. If you see straight ahead from the skies, you can see the island faintly lit up in the hazy dark clouds. You need to wait for the occasional lightning to see it in full grandeur. It can be seen in the vast sea like a diamond lost by the Gods somewhere in the trash of the man’s earth.
“Shibulal ji, how are you?”-Ayodhya walks to Shibulal who is smoking beedi, a country made tobacco product, in his chair. “Hey sonny, how are you? Night shifts are particularly boring.”
“Yeah I know. Shibu ji, I have a small project to make in my college. I think you are the perfect person to help me.”
“What? I don’t know anything about studies. How can I...”

"Shibu ji, it is a small information. Actually my project is on this..."-Ayodhya displays the A0 size drawing sheet, spreading it across Shibulal's lap like a blanket. "This is the inside of a pistol!"-Shibulal immediately recognizes it.
"And you told you don't know anything..."
"But what project are you doing with this?"-for a moment he feels guilty of letting Ayodhya handle the rifle. He is saddened by the fact that Ayodhya is interested in a negative object. Negative entities grow stronger if they are not addressed. But usually you humans tend to shy away. Everyone can deal with good, positive entities. But the real value to life can be added only when negatives are resolved and eliminated. And Ayodhya is cognizant of it.
"Nothing to fear. I am not going to make it more lethal or something like that."-Ayodhya assures.
"Yeah, I know you won't."- Shibulal nods in agreement, recalling something. Ayodhya is pleasantly surprised. "When I was talking about pistols and quoted the girl who tried to shoot herself, as just a passing example, you interrupted and asked me what her fate was after. You have a touch of humanity in you. I've seen deaths, boy. Death is something that thrills you until you inflict it on someone. The very next moment kills you from within. Causing death is the biggest difference you can make to someone's life."
Ayodhya stands still, not realizing that he is getting drenched on the left side of his shoulder.
"Go ahead... What do you want to ask?"-Shibulal's immense faith in him makes him emotional, a rare thing for someone like him.
He explains his need to see the insides of a pistol and understand more. "If possible..."-he concludes- "I want to see the manufacturing of a pistol."
"My boy, I don't know how and where it gets manufactured ... and sometimes why..."-he sinks his head in the blanket. "But my comrade in the army- Birju Das has a servicing shop for arms. He stays in the downtown Rovat, about 15 miles from here. This Sasni area is suburb you know. One second..."-he takes out his old Nokia cell phone. "Hey Babloo, how are you? How are your son and daughter-in-law?"

"...What? Your daughter-in-law kicked you? Like the mule that we led into the Chinese border? Whose kick was harder? Ha ha ha..."-his brownish teeth show the negligence about his teeth over the years.

Ayodhya can't believe that soldiers can not only digest the bitter fact that their own family members treat them like dust but also take it as fun. "Ha ha ha... See Babloo... We are anyway going in less than ten years... Why do we... Yeah exactly... You know better than me, ha ha ha... They are kids. They'll learn it anyway."-he nods thrice, to show that he is in total agreement with Birju Das. "Ok, jokes aside, now I have a young friend... Very good boy... No, I don't know his name... Doesn't matter... He is a very good child. He wants to see some guns and make a study on it. No, no... For class marks... Ha ha ha... Yeah, these days class marks are important you know... Gone are the days when a morsel was important. We used to leave the studies behind and run home for a meal. These days, kids leave their food for studies. You've grown old, you ass! Wake up at least now! Face the fact... Ha ha ha"

Ayodhya spends the next few days in Birju Das' ARMS & AMUNATIONS SERVISE CENTR. Although it is a decaying old shop lost in me, the 'servise' is first-class. It is proven by the fact that most of the private bodyguards of top class politicians, film stars and businessmen utilize the skill of the five decades served, wrinkled, shaky but ingenious hands away from the glare of the public.

Ayodhya starts his tasks. In a matter of fifteen days he goes on to design from the existing one, a new type of pistol that leaves both Birju Das and Shibulal dazed!!

It is the mini-project evaluation day. Pillu and his gang of five have spent twenty thousand rupees to buy a robot from an industrial dealer and are now displaying its movements and actions to the panel. They get a comfortable 190/200 each.

"Ayodhya... Come in"

"Where is your team?"-one of them asks. "Do I look like I need one?"-he feels like asking. "Sir all the teams were already formed when I started with my project. So I was left alone."

"Why did you start late?"

"Sir I suffered from typhoid twice in the last two..."

"Ok... Show me the project report."-a second interrupts. He obeys. Their heads converge like the leaves of the touch-me-not plant when disturbed. They bounce back immediately after reading the title of the project!
First time in their lives they have seen a project on pistol. "What is this Ayodhya? You've made a pistol?"
"No, I've made a reverse-pistol. That's the technical name I've given it."
They calm down. "What made you decide upon a weapon?"
"If we can accept the negative objects in life and eliminate the negativity in them we end up bringing out a positive object."
"Explain us about the reverse-pistol of yours."
"Sir, turn to drawing number six. This is the most popular model- the one used by most of the people- servicemen and common men alike. Take a look at the path from the magazine to mouth. The bullet is pushed this way up into the firing area where the hammer propels it out of the mouth at high velocities."
The panel takes some time to understand the mechanism. They ask several questions on how he got hold of a manufacturing drawing of a pistol, how he was able to understand the technical part and... who helped him in it.
"Sir the drawing can be obtained from the internet."-he did not reveal the fact that the central library contained hundreds of such books with drawings. "I am an engineer. I am supposed to be self-reliant. Nobody helped me Sir. I searched on the net whenever I had difficulties."
"Who did you collaborate with?"
"I did it myself."
"Ha ha ha... It is ok. You know this is a college. It is ok to accept facts. Who helped you? A friend from the US? Israel? Russia?"
Ayodhya imagines Shibulal with his beedi and Birju Das with his tools. "Indians."-he smiles.
"Ok, please continue..."-another lecturer interrupts. He has seen more students gather outside.
"Sir, compare this with the reverse model which I have designed."-Ayodhya switches drawing sheets. "It has the same construction except at this place..."
"Yeah... We can see it... Yeah."

"When the bullet slips into the channel it follows a different path. It is loaded in the reverse direction and hence the name- reverse-pistol!"

They look at one another.

"The mouth of the pistol is left unaltered. The bullet has its sharp end pointing towards the rear of the pistol. The direction of pulling the trigger is also left untouched. It is all the same but... Have a look at the rear. There is a small opening in front of the bullet's nose, concealed within a wall of thin sheet metal."

"The section thickness is small... Yeah... Is it of a different material?"

"Yes Sir. It is just for optical illusion. People think that the same material and thickness is maintained."

"So the moment the trigger is pulled the bullet easily pierces across this sheet metal and emerges from the rear!!"-one of the panelists deduces with a lot of thrill.

"Yes Sir... It does not shoot the person it is pointing to. Rather it hurts the person who pulls the trigger!!"

"Hurts or kills?"

"Depends... The hammering is of the same magnitude. It imparts the same force but there is no mouth to add an initial velocity."

"And how does it kill a person standing, say, ten meters away...? Behind the shooter?"

"Highly improbable... For the same reason... It does not have the velocity to sustain long range flights. Ten meters is too long I think. I don't have the prototype yet. And moreover the purpose of this new design is not to kill a person in a different style. It is just to protect the person who is pointed at."

"You could've made a dummy gun rather. Why should a real pistol be modified?"

"Sir there are countless dummies in the market. People can easily identify them. But a real pistol, for that matter anything real, always brings out the true self of the person using it. If the person has decided to kill someone he won't use a dummy. He should be made to look like a dummy."

The biggest question was still itching to be asked- "Why did you make a reverse-pistol? I mean I've asked you already but I want the... the..."

"To give a chance!"-Ayodhya leans back.

One of the panelists folding the drawing sheet, satisfied with the design, pauses to listen to Ayodhya. The best part of the entire project is to come from Ayodhya's mind. The third panelist who is going through the report stops and looks at him. He knows that what Ayodhya wants to say cannot be found in the report.

"Sir many people kill others for whatever reasons they have. I mean, the common people. Recently we saw in NOT NOW the live footage at the highway toll booth. When the booth employee asked for the toll fare, the politician took out a pistol and shot him dead. We see news of warring street gangs all around Dweepa that go about exacting revenge by gunning down rivals. They also take innocent lives if they are not satisfied with the extortion amount."

"Most of the times people use a pistol. If the politician deems it right to shoot down the employee or if a gangster decides that a shopkeeper is to die, then there is no harm in their getting hurt, themselves. There is no harm..."-Ayodhya pauses for a while.

"Then there is another perspective too. If a small angel knows that a pistol kept in the dad's room can help her end her life because the teacher beat her up and asked her to die or if a college student who is not able to make it to the next semester prefers not to live to see his friends move up without him or if one wants to impose self-punishment to the most extreme levels because one loved a stone in the form of a human, they are ought to be given another chance. A second more... to think again before they take the extreme step... or rather, after."

"You know Sir; it is all in the mind. The tendency to end life of self is driven from within... Most of the times... External factors are never significant. Do you know why? Because they are not permanent! No external compulsion has remained forever. Never... But an internal one does until given some time. Time is the healer Sir... We need to give them time... Even if it is in minutes... If the small girl still wants to kill herself, she anyway will. Probably by some other means.... But then we can increase her lifespan by a few minutes or days before she figures out the next method if at all she could. Probably hearing the shots, the parents of the college student may come running and counsel him,

increasing the lifespan by another sixty years!"
"It is all about time, Sir. One second makes a lot of difference. And so does a second chance at life!"
This is the reason I love Ayodhya. He values me more than he does to anyone else.
"And you know what? People believe in omen. Especially Indians. If they understand that their attempt at suicide has failed, they consider it a message from God to live and fight on. As I told you, it is all in the mind."
He continues- "Many a time people change their minds after it is too late. For example, a person who has jumped off from a building may decide that he shouldn't have jumped, in the last few seconds of his life. A random thought... A feel of regret at the decision or a sudden confidence at facing the challenges, or a last fervent pleading to God to give another chance... may come as the ground seems closer and closer. Who can save him at that point of time? Duperman? Riderman? Or the local boy Trish? No, Sir... Not even God. But the same is not the case when someone fires a bullet at self. The person can be saved by a falsely designed gun. It wouldn't even make a scratch on his temple and rather moves in the opposite direction. The only casualty can be a person standing next to him, enjoying the scene!!"
"Ha ha ha..."-the panelists share a laugh. One of them is still serious. "Have you ever been attacked? Or have you ever tried to kill yourself? How could you understand the human factors so well?"
"For 200 marks... This need not be answered."-he reminds them that it is an academic evaluation.
"Sorry... But meet me later in the evening. We'll apply for a patent!"
Ayodhya smiles. He feels blessed.
"And be regular to class."-the machine design lecturer advises.
"I'll try."
"Ayodhya..."
"Yes Sir?"
"You call it a reverse-pistol technically. But what brand name would you give it if it is commercialized?"-a panelist asks with a smile. The others too seem curious.

Ayodhya looks outside to force his mind. He sees Kunj and Pooja clicking pictures of themselves with their cheeks touching ostensibly to reason to themselves that they are to squeeze into the photograph.
"I call it a Selfie!!"

11 A PROMISE UNFULFILLED

Ayodhya waits for Mr. Bunny at the Physical Training Center. He has exhausted all the leaflets in the attendance certificate. He now wants a new one.

Pillu and his friends are playing carrom with their supposed girlfriends that they have successfully managed to 'strike' a relation with. Ayodhya notices them. Some of them are his classmates.

"You guys are fit only for carrom."-he comments within himself and waits on. His classmates ignore him deliberately lest he snatch away their 'queens'.

They are not interested in playing. It is more about being there, with them. Ayodhya feels superior to them all of a sudden. And why is that?

He has submitted the Compact Disc containing the design of Selfie, the patent application, the write-up, and other documents to the lecturer.

"Sir don't we need the actual working model for patent?"

"No, the design is enough. Not even design. Just the concept and a basic drawing is enough. But since you already have a design I am insisting on including it. Patenting is done to protect intellectual property of a person or an organization. In your case it is of the college and you are the Inventor. If you want it for yourself then you'll have to manage expenses of filing a patent. It is difficult. Anyway, try and get a model ready just for a practical experience. I know it will take time. Probably you may get it ready after you complete the course. But still... Try manufacturing it."

Ayodhya sits feeling the sheer thrill of success.

"Isn't he your classmate?"-a girl asks Ayodhya's friend who is getting ready to strike. "Yeah..."-he is not willing to look at him. "Call him... Let him play too."-the queen orders.

"Leave him. He's a loser. Ha ha... He has lost so much that he has nothing more to lose."-he replies rather loudly to please Pillu so that he'll include him in the cricket team. Ayodhya doesn't like it although he is not immature to react. He, however, decides to poke the 'winner'. He waits and waits, hoping that Mr. Bunny would not return until he deals with the winner. One of the girls heads out. A second one follows. The third gets a call from someone about whom if Pillu gets to know he'll suffer a heart attack. She quietly slips away to attend it.

Ayodhya grabs the opportunity I've given him. I hope he gets a long window. Sometimes I play with him. And enjoy losing to him.

"So Pillu, how's it going?"-Ayodhya pats Pillu. "Hi Mr. University Player... Sorry, this is a local game."

"Then let me elevate it."

Ayodhya supplants the 'winner' on the chair but not before snatching his wallet peeping out of the pocket and the flashy sunglasses, beautifying his head. "Is this complimentary with Boost?"

"No, five grand."-replies he with a hint of anxiety. Ayodhya returns from the wallet, the credit card and every other thing than cash. Pillu signals the 'winner' to calm down and leave the matter to him. Ayodhya looks around over the carrom board. White pawns, black pawns and of course the queen are all scattered around. His eyes fall on the queen which is in the most difficult location to hit from Pillu's end. It is lying at the hole but has to be hit with a rebound, that too through two closely lying pawns. "Isn't it a bit difficult?"-Ayodhya asks Pillu. "Yeah but why the **** are you asking about that?"

"Oh God! Your words scare me Pillu..."-Ayodhya shivers in fear. "I'll hit that white one there."-he points at the pawn at the other end.

"after hitting the queen... Both from your end!"

"If both land in the hole, I'll keep these with me."-Ayodhya holds the sunglasses and the wallet full of cash.

"And what if you don't hit?"-Pillu demands.

"I don't have anything to lose. Right? My boy?'-he turns to his classmate.

Pillu gets up from his seat to let Ayodhya occupy it to play. Ayodhya turns the board around!

"Never leave your position. People snatch it away anyway!"-he gently places the wallet and sunglasses on the corner of the board near the hole to his left.

"But there is a minor change. You'll get only one strike to score both pawns. And you'll strike with your left hand."-Pillu beams with victory even before the challenge begins. Ayodhya waits for a moment, introspecting something. He takes a careful aim. He knows it is a one in a billion probability that everything will fall in place for him to score both. But at the moment he tries to believe that it is possible. It is all in a moment.

He tries drawing all his thoughts, senses and the last quantum of energy onto the task at hand. Focus and belief are the only two ingredients that make that favorable one-in-a- billionth outcome possible.

He lets go of his finger through the barrier offered by his thumb. The striker slides like soap on wet floor, rebounds at a corner, shoulders the white pawn into the hole, changes its direction to pass through the two closely lying pawns, rebounds again at another corner and stops after gently hitting head-on to the queen.

The queen slowly sails into oblivion like a spaceship into black hole.

Pillu's jaw drops! The 'winner' expresses a disastrous gaze and spares a worried look at Pillu. Pillu wants to somehow pick a quarrel with Ayodhya but he has still not come out of the trauma. Somewhere in the corner of his heart, he is admiring Ayodhya. Ego, once hurt, stops all the good feelings towards a person from surfacing.

Ayodhya's hand clutches the prize kept on the table- the wallet and the sunglasses. He turns to the loser and cleans the sides of the glasses using the end of the loser's shirt.

"When are you returning them?"-asks Pillu.

"Losers keep pawns, not currencies."-Ayodhya gently blows the powder sticking to his hand on his face. Mr. Bunny returns to the cabin. Ayodhya walks in for the certificate. "Hi, Ayodhya. Sit. So? You exhausted the booklet?"

"Yes Sir."

"There was a meeting with the Principal. The design department was praising you that you have developed something that is going to be patented. Good, keep it up."-he pulls out a booklet from the table drawer and tosses it on the table.

"Tomorrow is the selection for the inter collegiate T20 tournament. Be at the grounds on time. Else you'll be relegated to team C."-he starts signing on the blank sheets of the booklet.

Ayodhya sits hoping the leaflets were cheque leaves for an account full of money.

"Mr. Lonely... I'm Mr. Lonely..."

"Hello Kunj..."-Ayodhya answers the call.

"Ayodhya, I don't know how you'll manage but I want you here in fifteen minutes."-Kunj is upset with something.

"Where are you?"-Ayodhya asks calmly knowing that it is quite normal for Kunj to get emotional.

"In the closet."

"What?!!"

"I mean... I'm calling from Criminal Lifestyle mall. Right now I'm in the toilet... Sorry boss... Sorry... I didn't notice... Hey listen, Ayodhya. Pooja is with me... in the mall. I just told her I'm going to pee. Listen... Fifteen minutes. Please!"

Ayodhya collects his booklet and leaves immediately. He misses the direct bus to Criminal Lifestyle and starts walking to the next stop. A 'share auto' stops at him, teeming with passengers loaded beyond allowable numbers. Dense pungent odor from inside reaches Ayodhya's sensitive nostrils. Luckily he has a place to lock his right foot at the rear of the auto rickshaw. He hangs onto the vehicle like a periscope on a submarine. The heads of passengers inside the auto rickshaw are surfacing out, again and again, for fresh air, as someone inside has made a wrong dietary decision.

Criminal Lifestyle nears. He gently lands on the speed breaker on the road like an aircraft on a runway and walks off. He stands in front of the mall, looking around for Kunj.

Kunj has already spotted him from the Pizza shop. "Ayodhya, here..."

"Thank God you came. Listen, there were a few guys out there. They were playing at the nets. Pooja and I were watching one of them bat. After they played they started making rude remarks at me. They were also passing vulgar comments on Pooja. She's upset with that. One of those guys has played well and has set a record of 14 boundaries in three overs, by far the highest. His name is on the honor's board there."-Kunj points at a white board. The mall has a cricket practice net in the middle. A bowling machine is at one end to deliver tennis balls at the batsman.

"So each player gets three overs?"

"No. One over. 100 rupees for one over. If you manage to score five boundaries or three sixes in one over you'll get the next over free of cost. It is like that. He has missed only one boundary in the first two and two in the third."

"Where's Pooja?"

"She is watching movie in the fourth floor."

"Give me 100 rupees. I'll take care of the rest."

"I'll give 200... 300... Whatever it takes but I want to avenge the..."

"What kind of a specimen are you? You always talk about avenging, retaliating... Why can't you just drop the matter?"-Ayodhya gets irritated. "Sorry..."-Kunj looks elsewhere.

Ayodhya immediately understands that Kunj is highly reactive because he has only two true friends- Pooja and Ayodhya. He is miles... nautical miles... away from home, studying in the prestigious institute. He has somehow tolerated all the teasing and mockery by other students for years and is now eager to see changing times. He wants to make himself believe that he remains unbeaten in every challenge thrown at him.

"That guy in IPL cap. He is the one who has set the record. Seems to be good."-Kunj tries to instill some seriousness in the swagger that he sees in

Ayodhya.

"If everyone who wears a cap is a good player, even an umpire can be the man of the match."

"Shall we go to a movie later? After I drop Pooja home?"

"I rather watch the fair & homely fairness cream advertisement featuring that gorgeous actress a hundred times than watch one movie."

Kunj does not understand- "Oh, ok. I like the Pairtel 5G ad girl with that boyish hairstyle."

"Anyway, I'll play. But I need you to do me a favor."-Ayodhya accepts money, not able to understand what made him suddenly reveal his hidden feelings for the girl in the advertisement.

"Oh, I know. You want me to keep your love for that actress a secret? Done Sir!"

"No. Run around in the entire mall, floor by floor, until I'm done with the overs!"

"WHAT!!"

"Don't ask me why. I have no time."-Ayodhya walks to the man at the counter. "Listen..."-he stops half way. Kunj looks on. "No escalators."

"Next..."

It's Ayodhya's turn. "If you hit the ball full toss to the nets in front of you, it is considered a six. If it is not a full toss, it is a boundary. Side nets carry one r..."

"Let's start."-Ayodhya walks in, not interested in anything other than what is really needed. He knows his objective. If you're clear about your goals, you'll know what is necessary and hence what is unnecessary.

It is all set. “First over first ball... Ready...”

He looks into the darkness of the machine’s nozzle. ‘Sshottt!’-a ball flies at him. Ayodhya moves front and easily heaves it straight back at the machine. “Good shot... One ball, six runs... First over second ball, ready...”

Kunj, in the meantime, is jogging slowly. A security guard at the ATM stops him, signaling a gesture that is the same for a ‘why’, a ‘where’, a ‘what’ and a ‘what the ...’

“I... I... Ummm... I am looking for my friend.”-he turns in circles and jogs on.

“Second over third ball... 24 runs.”-the deliveries now look like fireballs out of a cannon. The bowling machine operator has gauged that Ayodhya is not just another player.

Kunj halts at the third floor to catch a bird’s view of the happening at the nets. There is a small crowd gathered around the nets, mesmerized by Ayodhya’s batting. Ayodhya turns at him for a fraction of a moment. Kunj circles himself around and resorts to jogging again until he finds the food court.

“Fourth over first ball... 72 runs... Ready?”

Ayodhya slams a delivery straight back to the bowler. “78!! Good!”

The crowd is euphoric. “Whooo...”

Kunj stops sipping milkshake at the food court on the fourth floor. He hears the noise, walks outside, leans against the balcony and stands shocked! For a moment he doubts whether he is in a mall or a cricket stadium. The entire mall, from ground floor to fourth, is immersed in watching Ayodhya. Some, as usual, are video-recording.

A while later the operator requests Ayodhya to give up batting as it would take a hit at his daily income. Kunj receives a call from Ayodhya.

"Job done... I'm leaving."-he doesn't even wait to hear from Kunj.

Kunj returns to the cinema hall with a smile that denotes more of admiration than success. Pooja's eyes are filled with tears. The movie has taken a sentimental turn after a comedy filled first half. She asks amidst sobs- "Why are you sweating so badly?"

"I... Will tell you later."

The movie is over even before Kunj has savored Pooja's endearing sad face. "You look so cute when you cry."-he remarks as they walk out, still immersed in the spell the movie has cast on them. Pooja gets annoyed. She walks fast like a seasoned commuter in Mumbai locals, without a word.

At the ground floor she spots the honors board and stands still!

"FOUR OVERS 108. KUNJ BIHARI YADAV."

She runs back at him and hugs him tight. Kunj, in the meantime, too has seen the board. Of course, why would he not?

"I am so rude. Am I not?"-she starts sobbing.

"You look cute when you cry."-he blurts again!

She suddenly starts chuckling. "So that's the reason you were sweating... You played four overs!"

"Oh!!"-Kunj now understands.

A week goes by. The class is bustling. "Hey, Ayodhya. Can you teach me batting? I want to bat like you... for Pooja"

"You can't"

"Why?"

"You play cricket for your girlfriend. To play like me, cricket should be your girlfriend."

"Please submit the assignments today... I won't accept if you delay."-the same old Machine Design lecturer yells at the top of his voice. Ayodhya is not even aware of the assignment let alone doing it. He just doesn't like doing what he has already studied on his own, for the sake of someone else. He turns to Kunj.

"Here... Submit it."-Kunj holds the file he has completed in Ayodhya's name. Ayodhya walks to the dais and places it gently among the stacks of files. The lecturer looks on as though Ayodhya is requesting for a big loan without proper credentials.

"So now, those who have not submitted, please stand up."-demands he. Some students grudgingly rise from their seats like a series of Diwali flower pots. One among them is Kunj!

Ayodhya expresses a mild surprise and turns away.

"Actually I was able to complete only one assignment. I decided to submit in your name. You have helped..."-Kunj follows Ayodhya to the cafeteria.

"Finish it off soon."-Ayodhya walks away hurriedly. "But I won't get any marks. The deadline is over."-Kunj runs behind him, trying to catch up. "It is not about timeline. It is about relativity, about how you stand out. This timeline drama is to categorize people. He wants to know who belongs to the Yes group and who to No. You belong to the wrong one. It is on you to get off from there. The lecturer doesn't think you'll complete the work. Surprise him and get out of there."

"What if he still doesn't agree?"-Kunj is apprehensive. "You need a stone-heart to condemn someone. A lecturer would never do that."

"How can you be so sure that he cannot be so?"

"He wouldn't have been a lecturer otherwise."

"What would he have been then?"-Kunj is curious. "Me!"-Ayodhya does not reveal what he thinks.

"Mr. Lonely... I'm Mr. Lonely...."-his cell phone rings. It is the lecturer who wants to patent Selfie. "Ayodhya your CD and patent documents are missing. Someone was here in the night. Come quick!"

Ayodhya's anger surges!

He is in the lecturer's cabin. The lecturer is busy searching. Ayodhya closes his eyes, recalling everyone's face that was involved in the events related to Selfie.

A scene opens up. The evaluation hall... "The lecturers? What would the poor souls get by pinching the design of something they freaked out knowing about?"

A second scene follows. The meeting between college Principal and the teaching staff. "Again... Same people. Mr. Bunny? No way. He is happy with the balls."

A third surfaces. Mr. Bunny's voice echoes!

"Meeting with the Principal... design department was praising you... going to be patented."-the words repeat. They get louder and louder. Ayodhya is nearing the answer!

He suddenly feels the loudest noise. Noise of carrom pawns getting hit.

"PILLU!!!"

"Sir, I'll be back with the documents tomorrow."

Ayodhya takes Kunj's help who in turn relies on Pooja's information that Pillu and his gang would take Pooja's classmates to a rave party at the beach that evening.

"But how will you manage to get them to reveal it? They are a bunch of tough guys. You are so weak."-Kunj is skeptic.

"I have a cousin."-Ayodhya walks on.

The evening is cool and the atmosphere is pristine. That's what nature provides you. But some in your kind spoil whatever they lay their hands on. The music begins slowly amidst fire and furor. Ayodhya lies in wait yet again, flat on his tummy in the sands of Dweepa, this time for Pillu. He has come in the same old attire- a hankie across his face, eyes covered by sunglasses and a funky skull cap on his head. The night falls. The rave rages...

Pillu is dancing to the tunes. Ayodhya sees a manifestation of Pony in him. There are more people tonight than there were the last time. Pillu is somewhere within the crowd, it is not easy to drag him away. Surprisingly, there are a few Bouncers-sturdy hulks who manage security in pubs. They are brought to the beach on rent from a local pub. Ayodhya is not sure about who they are and for what. He has never seen a Bouncer before and has never heard Asrar talk about them. Well, they are poor chaps rich in protein. And they are highly underrated since their potential goes unrecognized in the company of drunkards. "I don't know who you're but I know what to do with you."-Ayodhya thinks as he observes them keep an eye on the surroundings like CCTVs.

He moves in. The lights are dazzling every now and then on the participants. It is hard to keep track of Pillu but Ayodhya's eyes bear laser-like focus. It seems the lights are following Ayodhya's sight. Bit by bit he transfers his body weight on to his toes. His torso rises from the sands. His hands are buttressed deep. They are ready to spring any moment now. The Bouncers are circling the area. There is none but one gap in the cordon. As the gap turns in his direction, Ayodhya scrambles ahead!

His feet are accustomed to running on sand. The toes land at a forward angle, not giving enough time for his legs to sink in. The sand flies behind his feet, vanquished in its attempt to pull him in.

He breaks the cordon and heads straight at Pillu. A girl suddenly appears from nowhere, dancing in a trance. Ayodhya pushes her by the neck out of his way. The next neck is Pillu's!!

He drags him out from the middle and rushes out of the cordon again. The Bouncers are so busy looking around. Ayodhya has successfully managed to pull Pillu out in the dark, closer to the beach. It is now that they have spotted him!

"Hey!!"

Two of them run in the direction of Ayodhya.

"Just for a change."-Ayodhya bangs Pillu's head on the wet sand and starts digging out more sand. Pillu struggles to escape. Ayodhya hits Pillu on his shoulder and twists his arms. Pillu is in acute pain. His hands are tucked into his own trousers and the belt is tightened.

Ayodhya has dug deep enough, wide enough. He buries Pillu's head in the sand and cements the area around by stamping with his feet. Pillu's head is completely in the sand, the rest of the body mildly trying to recover it. The Bouncers are charging like a pair of wild rhinos. A drop of sweat leaves Ayodhya's forehead as he waits for the right moment. The feet of one of the Bouncers fly in the air, swept across by Ayodhya's. The giant body comes down with a thud along with the drop of sweat!

The other one almost lands a punch on Ayodhya's abdomen, that, if had been successful, would have sent him in coma. Ayodhya jumps high, propped by the sluggish shoulders, and brings him down by landing on his neck, locking it between his legs. By now two more Bouncers are seen heading towards the beach. Ayodhya quickly recovers Pillu's head- "Where are Ayodhya's documents?"

"In Ria's room."-Pillu gasps for breath.

The next morning Ayodhya gets back his documents from Kunj through

Pooja.

“Now I’m definitely going to manufacture it! Come what may.”-Ayodhya’s eyes well up for the first time in his so called life. He has skipped the selections and hence stands relegated as a captain of Team C which carries no hopes of qualifying for the knock outs let alone win the tournament. “I will try to include you in the main team. But as a substitute player.”-Mr. Bunny offers.

“Better to captain minnows than cheer for favorites... Thank you Sir.”

What is more important is the fact that the previous night he has taken down two strong men single-handedly in less than a minute. Asrar is happy although he has never approved of Ayodhya’s act, nor has he openly admitted to the record time. But Ayodhya knows... After all, it is Asrar who has taught him acting!

Yet another year rolls by in a matter of seconds. His college days are over. Ayodhya has learnt more than he had joined it for. It is the global recession time-a testing occasion for the net worth of a professional. Ayodhya has been miraculously selected by a software company called ‘Reinforces’-a giant company from the tiny Philippines, known for grueling training during initial days of joining. They believe in reinforcing coding concepts in the budding developers and mechanize them for the red ocean of dead dreams-the software world!

They have set up a sprawling campus in Dweepa. ‘Harvesting of souls’ is a term they have adopted from some European institutions as a part of their Global Research Program for Inner Peace; and coincidentally, the target country too. They have harvested a total of 350 souls from the locally available nursery despite a tail-spinning economy. They have all the reasons. The older employees are to be weeded out. Young blood is always tastier. The students too are on their toes for Reinforces so much so that many twelfth standard students plan to join Computer Science Engineering branch in college, get placed in Reinforces, undergo the dreadful training, obtain a certificate and jump to the competitor companies demanding superior salary and hence provide an edge to negotiate dowry. Believe me, all this in twelfth standard!

Ayodhya belongs to a kind which is like the 'Bubbles' screen saver-the ones that go wherever the crowd takes them to. It seems that the crowd and the HR have connived out of the universe to land him on the so called 'bench'. One is condemned on the bench if one is forced to accept lower salaries and kept as a 'man-in-waiting' for future projects and compensate for those rigorous planners of twelfth standard.

Ayodhya had given away his employee identity card to one of his colleagues to carry out the swiping formalities while he had returned to Sarovar Nagar and stayed with his grandfather. The betting incident involving the Killer XI and the Hunter XI happened in this period.

Now he is on his way back to Dweepa, walking along the bridge to board the ferry. He wants to escape police at Sarovar Nagar after the assault on Killer XI. His grandfather has managed to keep them at bay but at the cost of Ayodhya's beloved motorcycle-Yezdi- the last sign of his father.

He is not in touch with Asrar or Kunj- not even by phone. He wants to move on, not quite habituated with relationships, but relationships are like promises, like the one the ferry he is sailing in makes to the port before leaving for Dweepa, a promise of return!

12 THE END... BEGINS

"National Strength Front has skillfully managed the mammoth task of finding a Chief Minister from its ranks and Dweepa has finally heaved a sigh of relief, putting an end to all speculations. Soon after the swear-in ceremony, the CM occupied the official residence 'Swarga' and vowed in front of a euphoric crowd that he will not leave any stone unturned in punishing the brutal killers of the earlier CM candidate. The crowd, frenzied by the gripping speech, burst out into sloganeering 'NSF Zindabad (Hail NSF)!' and welcomed the new caretaker of the island. With cameraman Cherry, I'm Yummy... Er.. Yami... NOT NOW."

The media finish the news, wrap up and leave Street #2, Raj Tilak Road.

The Chief Minister's festive official residence beaming with bighearted party workers distributing sweets and VIPs indulged in vulgar talk, suddenly bears a creepy look. An ominous tone evaporates the excitement in the voice of the Police constable who is guarding the gate. It is a quirk of fate that when some men appear, dark clouds cast vicious shadows over earth.

"I have a last question... Can I go in?"

“Press meet is over. Go away. The CM is busy.”-the constable pushes the visitor.

The visitor signals ‘I am willing to pay you money’. “Wait near the police van.”-the constable’s voice softens; eyes roll around to see if he is being overheard.

A while later the policeman walks behind a tree within the residence where the rest of his colleagues are resting. The best time to commit a crime is when there are too many policemen.

“I think it is Babloo’s day today.”-one of them utters dejected at the loss of money in a card game. The constable signals a ‘nature’s call’ with his little finger before hurrying to the van parked outside the residence.

He reaches the van. Nobody seems to be around. He loiters, ostensibly to look for a place to urinate. He still can’t find anyone. He stands with legs apart, facing a newly built wall. But his head turns around on either side, eyes inspect the area, hands hesitantly converge. The wall expects a curing but in vain. He hears a whistle and grins from ear to ear. He immediately leaves from the wall in its direction. He is offered a five hundred rupee note by a stocky hand. He examines it against sunlight.

“Generally I do not accept gifts from media. They carry out sting operations, you know. But I knew you were genuine.”-his smile erodes again. There is no reply, only murderous stillness.

“Why are you still here? Go ask... You had a last question for the CM, right?”

“The question was your last!”-the visitor speaks with a smile. The policeman does not understand. The smile gives him a hope that everything is going to be all right. “Ha... ha... ha.”-he feigns courage.

The visitor locks his fingers in the constable’s mouth, grabbing the lower jaw from inside. The policeman is unable to complete his... last laugh!

He struggles to get rid of the hand like a cockroach nailed by a needle. He tries to bite hard. The grip tightens, clawing out flesh from the mouth. He growls in pain like an animal being slowly sawed across the neck. Another hand locks into the upper jaw. The lower jaw is mercilessly ripped away from the rest of the poor man's skull!!

Gharial hurls away the piece of jaw and starts wiping his hands on the inside of the cloak worn by one of his henchmen.

"And always add an 'even' before saying 'the CM is busy'... It is a good element of surprise."-he enters the residence, in police uniform.

The night casts its shadow on the CM's residence. There is still no wind... yet... about the policeman's death. The next morning, surprisingly though, there is storm in Sagar's office.

"ACP Sagar!!! How many more deaths do we have to see before we catch that... that..."-the commissioner hesitates to even take Gharial's name in his mouth. For some reasons, the picture of his wife and kids appear in front of his eyes.

"Gharial..."-Sagar's determined eyes assuage his feelings. Sagar's parents flash across his eyes before his eyeballs could catch up with them.

"Yeah... Whatever..."-he is still apprehensive.

"There were no surveillance cameras working yesterday at the official residence. I think we have a mole in the department, Sir."

"Look Sagar... I want no explanations and no excuses. We have got you here as a specialist. We need results. Nothing else... You will get whatever you want. Additional force, unlimited powers, you name it and I'll get it. If you want, I am ready to kick out anyone you suspect."

Sagar stands looking straight back at him, asking for the most precious of all.

"I need time. That's all..."

The commissioner leaves without a word, too atypical of him.

Sagar sets up Gharial's image across the city, developing the earlier CCTV footage of him. Prize money of one million Indian Rupees is going to be offered to anyone who catches him dead or alive. The image bears a tall, sturdy man with a hat across his face. The eyes are not clearly visible. It is a step Sagar has taken with least hope. He knows the image is not going to help much in identifying Gharial. But tenacious faith compels even a tenuous attempt.

The same evening Sagar's cell phone rings. It is Jackpot at the other end- "Sir, we have a situation at the South end of Raj Tilak Road... The popular cartoonist from THE MIMES OF DWEEPA has been murdered!"

"Have you informed Raj Tilak Road police station?"-Sagar tries his best to avert diversion from Gharial's case.

"No Sir..."- Jackpot is very anxious. "The murder is typical Gharial style!!"

It is eleven in the night and raining heavily. Sagar stands in front of a coffin. His heart thumps aloud to prepare itself for a grotesque sight.

They stand opposite to the legislative assembly near the swear-in area where the previous CM candidate was set to take charge the other day and the new CM took oath just the previous day. The coffin box is opened. The rest of the team carries out the formalities. The photographer clicks pictures with a lunatic glee. Certainly! His eyes have better lens than that of his DSLR camera. They see a lifetime opportunity in the horrid crime scene. He has moved from sensitivity to indifference, stopping inches short of sadism... all for one damn career.

Jackpot has got the day's copy of THE MIMES OF DWEEPA. "Sir, yesterday the new CM assumed office and today this cartoon has appeared in the paper. The murder too is of the same type, Sir."

Sagar takes a look into the paper-

The cartoon shows a caricature of the present Chief Minister in front of a chair bearing the label 'CM', addressing a jubilant crowd yelling 'NSF Zindabad', the Indian Flag flutters at half-mast behind him. He is standing on a dais that is shockingly the coffin of the previous CM candidate! It is so high that he can see the crowd in its entirety. The crowd is all across, in the shape of the map of Dweepa. The dais or rather the coffin is transparent at the side facing the reader and opaque at the side facing the crowd in the picture. The previous candidate's body is drawn to be lying in the coffin.

In summary, the cartoonist wants to convey to the reader that the present CM has cashed in on the chance provided by the death of previous candidate. And that the altitude with which he sees the crowd is actually the charisma and stature of the dead candidate. The flag at half-mast indicates that it has not been too long since the demise. The opacity of the coffin towards the crowd is to convey that the general public is unable to see through reality or has volatile memory.

Sagar observes the dead body of the cartoonist.

"Sir, the cartoonist has been boxed up alive and conscious in the coffin before being placed in front of the swear-in area. He has struggled inside the coffin for a few minutes before succumbing. We can see the scratches on the insides. It was kept here at about ten in the morning. A really heavy person seems to be sitting on the coffin. The cartoonist was not able to free himself. None in the huge crowd of workers remembers seeing anything when they came here to clean up the litter after yesterday's ceremony. They left at 09:50."

"But the gardener who was here at 10:05 in the morning has spotted it and immediately alerted me. We suspected bomb and after the bomb squad ruled out any such thing, our forensic experts were called in to examine the content. It did not take us much time to find out whose body it was."

"Good job, Jackpot! You're better than the circle inspectors."-Sagar means appreciation. But a frown appears on Jackpot's face.

"You're better than Tommy."-a voice echoes in Jackpot's ears. It is the voice of Shyamala's daughter when he had rushed to pick the ball for her every time she hurled it away in the Police Quarters Park. He always wanted a moment of happiness with her daughter who he thought, could soothe his pain. Now he feels that the daughter has not acquired the traits of her mother but of her father Purushottam!

Sagar carefully scans across the picture. He notices the eerie similarities!!

There is the coffin in which the cartoonist was boxed up. No chair can be seen in the vicinity. The lawn has been cut-shaped like the map of Dweepa. "Quick! Turn the search lights there!"-Sagar orders. Jackpot obeys. The Indian flag is surprisingly waving at half-mast in the middle of the night!!

Sagar stands in shock!

"Call the gardener! Right now!!"

The gardener is brought. "What are your duty timings?"-Sagar thunders.

"Sss... Sir, six in the morning..."

"Then why did you report at ten?"

"Sir, as I was about to leave in the early morning, a party worker offered me sweets. After a few minutes I fainted. When I woke up it was ten."

"Where is the CM's chair?"

"Sir?"

"The chair that was kept on the coffin. Where is it?"-Sagar is sure it was kept there.

"I... I... Sir... took it home. It was on the box and nobody was around."

"Can you recognize the party worker? Do you remember his face?"-Sagar is hopeful. "Sir his eyes were covered by the NSF party cap that he was wearing. But he was huge..."

Sagar frowns. He walks to the van and leans against it. "This man... He's so fearless, taking us for a ride every time with his fanciful ways. What business has he got with a cartoonist? Is he looking for some artistic crimes? To please himself?"-he presses his fingers against his forehead, not able to sustain the pressure created by the speed of Gharial's acts.

"MIMES OF DWEEPA belongs to the opposition party. Then... Is the ruling party using Gharial? No... Their own candidate is gone. His... son... too... is gone. That means... Oh my God!!"-Sagar's hands slowly retreats from his forehead, dripping water through his coat. His pupils enlarge as they do every time he gets a solid intuition.

"Yes... Yes, Sagar. You're right. The father and the son, both are gone. Their family literally ruled NSF for the last forty years. The last two scions are dead and gone. NSF is now open!!!"

"Sir..."-Jackpot rushes to him. "A call for you... Diverted from the control room. The person is anonymous and wants to talk only to you."

Sagar is surprised.

"Hello?"

"Gharial and his men are at number 617, Stallion Apartments, Gold Street. They are attempting the murder of a young man, probably in his early twenties. I've informed the local police already but time is ticking. I want to tell you I am going to interfere. I want to go for the kill."

"Who are you?"-Sagar hurries in his jeep.

"Someone who, if had been in your place, would have taken down the monster by now."

“No!! You’ll not enter the house... You are committing a blunder. Wait for us....”

“Bad decision is better than indecision, Sagar.”

“You don’t understand. You’ve informed his...”

“Bye.”

“Hello... Hello.”-Sagar speeds on with his men in the heavy rain.

The security guard at the apartment is asleep as usual but strange that he is not going to wake up ever again. The caller, meanwhile, passes by the guard surprised, walks behind the apartment, looks around and with an uncertain mind grips the drain pipe.

He is careful, not making even a faint noise as he makes his way in. He strains his eyes, trying hard to cut through the pale darkness and spots a few potential obstacles in the house. He knows he is going to take on the most dreaded man on Dweepa. His blood vessels are almost going to burst. His breath is hotter than usual. He tries to keep calm and enters the drawing area. A lone goldfish lurks aimlessly in a bowl of water. There is light behind the door to the kitchen- the only lit area in the whole of the sixth floor.

The caller crouches and scurries a few steps towards the kitchen. He arms himself with a few objects before gently bringing the ears to the door to determine any human activity. There is no noise except the continuous sound of the flickering bulb and occasional, desperate calls of a male lizard.

And then suddenly the entire drawing area is lit up!!

The caller turns back alarmed!!

“The Police are late. They have a reputation to care for.”-Gharial sits cozily on the sofa at the edge of the room.

"You know the best part of reputation? Do you think it is a... a... a disadvantage to care for reputation? A weakness? A negati... umm... drag?"

"It is an investment! A synergy! Yes. It shields you and helps you deceive on a much larger scale in future, than the cumulative magnitude all the non-reputed guys can ever manage... Because reputation brings faith in you... something you can always toy with."

The caller stands upright. Gharial's humongous appearance does not seem to shake his confidence, now that he sees Gharial. It is always the anticipation that is the scariest part.

"Do you know what the first thing I do is? When I go for game? I watch out for signals. Here..."-Gharial lifts the bowl containing the goldfish. "Being Gharial, I think I have a fair understanding of the behavior of a fish."-he holds it high up in the air.

"A fish always looks around for predators... and uninvited guests."-he turns scornfully at the caller. And as soon as it spots one, it makes the first dash opposite to the direction of the threat."-he inserts his stocky forefinger into the bowl. The fish tries to reach the farthest possible end in the bowl. Gharial slowly pulls it out on his palm. The beautiful goldfish wiggles desperately.

He looks on, enjoying the sight.

"It is a strange state. Do you think the fish is struggling for life? Huh?"-he pauses.

"It is only trying to get out of the state it is in. If it had a voice and I had asked a question- 'Is death ok for you?' It would have answered- YES."-he gulps it!

"Is death ok for you?"-he asks the caller. The caller is silent. One of Gharial's men walks forward towards the caller. He is approaching rather fast.

“Is death ok for you?”-Gharial asks again, more threateningly.

Suddenly, the caller hurls a paper weight with dead accuracy at the man and it hits him right on his eye. The man collapses.

“Ok and granted!”

Gharial is not moved. “Bravo!!”-he claps, taking care that the fingers touch gently.

The caller is sharp. He thinks quickly. He knows that Gharial has another plan up his sleeve. “I always like preys like you. The ordinary ones are too bland. They die even before I devour. I prefer some sport before food. Good for health, isn’t it?”

The caller is calm. He observes the rest of the men... three of them excluding Gharial. They understand that he cannot be distracted. They charge at him all at once! He escapes from two and attacks the third by bringing down his heavy foot on the chest. The third is badly hurt. He feels difficult to breathe. Somehow, he manages to get back. With Gharial, failure is death. Now the caller escapes the third and the second and kicks the first one brutally under his chin. The man loses his front teeth. His brain is cautioning a data overload, now that it is inundated with signals transmitted by nerves from multiples parts of the skull. He stands still, unable to think. The second one is in two minds. He has no backup. Both his comrades are hurt. He hesitates. Gharial twists the head of the second man violently. The neck makes a clicking sound. The second man drops down dead!

“A click in time saves mine.”-he turns his own neck in a jerky fashion and proceeds towards the caller in an intimidating walk. The caller is intrepid. He gauges the distance between them and the length of Gharial’s pillar-like legs. After a quick estimate, he allows Gharial for some distance, charges ahead, leaps and when Gharial tries to block him at chest height, he suddenly allows himself to lose altitude, slides along the floor and wedges Gharial about the abdomen to his back side with his feet. For the first time in life, the two-hundred-pound Gharial is felled!!

A loud thud is heard as Gharial's huge skull makes a meteoric impact on the floor. He is hurt on the neck, the rear portion of his skull and the back bone. But he is shockingly calm. He slowly sits with his legs stretched on the floor and jerks his neck once to his left and once to his right with a vicious smile. The caller wastes no time. He grips Gharial's neck in his heavily built arms and squeezes with a force that reminds me of an adult anaconda in the Amazon testing its strength on a caiman. Gharial too gets hold of the caller's neck and bends it over across his own shoulder. The classic case of an infinite loop sets in. The first one to lose patience loses life.

Gharial is poisonously shrewd. He knows that the only way to gain over a tough opponent is to make him lose his focus, distract him, shock him. He kicks open the bathroom door. The caller naturally turns his eyeballs towards the bathroom. He is left frozen!

Gharial cashes in on the chance, in a flash, wrecking his opponent's neck!!

He swiftly moves away using his hands. The caller lies on the floor, with eyes open. Gharial is not yet sure whether he has heard the clicking sound and if he has, whether it is convincing enough. He breathes heavily. For the first time in his life someone has taught him the value of a breath. He looks around for some wire or a rope to choke the caller once again... to get convinced. Nothing seems to be around. The house is newly occupied. He then removes his trousers, wraps across the caller's neck and tightens it with all his energy. His two surviving men notice something outside the window. Sagar and his Police party are approaching the apartment stealthily, armed with guns.

"The Police! They're here!!"

Gharial is quick to judge. "Oh so punctual..."

Sagar has the apartment covered thinly with the available men. The

Local Police arrives as a separate party. The noisy cars prompt Sagar to reconsider his assumption. "Are they really to catch him?"

His dubious stare puts in discomfort the policeman from the other party who hurries at him. "Sir, we're eighteen of us."

His men rush into the apartment without any orders from Sagar. "Stop!!!"-Sagar yells moderately. "We go in."

He knows it is foolish to venture in to nab a ghastly human with just three personnel. But his intuition favors the decision- "Three determined men are better than eighteen with a doubtful agenda."

Sagar scans the area. The apartment is all alone. Nobody can manage to escape from terrace. He drops the plans for terrace. The lift is out of order by order from Sagar. They start off.

They take turns, clearing the stairs and quickly gaining floors. Jackpot walks cautiously towards the partially opened door of flat number 617. He nods at Sagar. Sagar kicks open the door and barges into the house, ready with his pistol. There seems nobody in the house. They switch on the lights. The caller's body is lying with Gharial's trousers around his neck. Sagar inspects. There is no hope. He stands dejected at the situation, not able to respond quickly.

"Sir!!"-one of the policemen is aghast!

Sagar rushes to the bathroom.

Another body is found, the one of the occupant, the one Gharial came looking for. His head lies in the tub full of reddened water. It is evident to Sagar that he has been drowned. There are marks of water that has been splashed on the brightly colored walls multiple times. Each splash has made a bell curve-like pattern on the wall. The man's head has been banged into the tub over and over again.

Behind the curtains, it is written in blood- HE PLEADED 'KILL ME

OR LEAVE ME'. I KILLED HIM AND LEFT HIM. I REALISED I'M NOT GOOD AT LOGIC. SORRY.

Sagar is pained as well as extremely angered by the words. He grows impatient. The policemen stationed at the ground floor sense some movement. It is the only way out for Gharial. They immediately alert Jackpot.

"Sir, they have somehow managed to reach ground floor!!"-Jackpot turns. Sagar is already out of the flat. He has overheard the communication. The police party has fixed steel rope every time they cleared a floor. The rope is now at sixth. Sagar swiftly grabs hold of it and leaps! The descent is picturesque; it appears as though he is standing in the air and the floors are quickly moving upwards. He cuts through the space within the spiraling stairway and lands directly in front of Gharial!!

An injured Gharial is always more dangerous. He walks straight at Sagar. Sagar fires a shot!

The bullet hits Gharial on the chest. He is thrown back a few steps but not even a scratch can be seen.

He is infuriated. Sagar is unpleasantly surprised. "You... You... You..."-Gharial points his forefinger at Sagar and quickly starts approaching him. The other policemen resort to firing, only to be retaliated by Gharial's men with Kalashnikovs.

Sagar in the meantime fires another shot, this time at Gharial's head! Gharial lowers his head gently. The hat shields him from the bullet, diverting it.

Sagar is shell shocked!!

"You bring 1947 models. You need AK 47 ones."-Gharial grabs a rifle from a constable. "You dented my reputation, officer."- he smashes it against the constable's head. His walk reflects his hunger for blood.

Sagar retreats slowly. An adhesive sheet flies down from the sixth floor trapping Gharial in it!!

Gharial tries to set himself free but to no avail. The more he tries moving his arms, the stronger he gets stuck in the adhesive. The gel slowly solidifies on his body, literally arresting him.

“Well done, Jackpot!!”-Sagar is ecstatic.

“Never thought you’ll catch me with my pants down, did you?”-Gharial quips.

The other men make their escape, leaving Gharial behind. Sagar does not risk the lives of his men. He knows what a Kalashnikov is capable of. Two of the policemen are already hit.

The entire Police force surrounds Gharial, waiting for the solidification to complete. A few delicate minutes pass by. Gharial is immobile under the net.

“Ha.. Ha... Ha... How wrong was I!”-Gharial struggles to break free. “...Always thought that a conscious person cannot respond to a situation only under two occasions... When paralyzed or when... ha ha ha... you know when... ha... ha!”

Nobody except Sagar still has the guts to step even an inch closer to him.

Sagar removes Gharial’s hat. Gharial’s head is down. “I kill whoever looks into my eyes, ACP Sagar!”

Sagar is surprised at Gharial’s knowledge of him but does not display. But he can’t help the chill from running down his forehead as he takes a look at a hatless Gharial!!

“There you go. One more in the kitty.”-Gharial’s smile is abhorrent.

“You think we’re dumb? To fear you? To let you roam around after all you committed?”

Gharial is unable to move his head- “Dumb people are everywhere... even on Quora!”

“Who do you work for?”

“Ha..ha... ha... You call this work? So naive you’re. It pains me to know that I’m going to kill you someday.”

“...this is art, my cat-eyed, brown dyed friend- an art that caters to the need. Everyone needs some news to burn their lips on morning tea.”

Sagar slaps him!!

“Killing people is art?”-shouts Sagar. “A barbarian like you can only be found in the jungles.”

“Your slap reminds me of Shifali...”-Gharial licks a drop of blood oozing from his lower lip, enjoying the taste. “She had slapped me for no fault of mine. Then we compromised. She thought it was some Aamir Khan-Madhuri Dixit cine story. She fell for me. How I went forward to kiss her... and ended up pulling her tongue out. A woman’s tongue is indeed sharper than her teeth.”

Sagar stands still unable to bear his words.

“Everyone cheats... as per one’s capacity. Everything is a perspective, Sagar. We’re all children of perspective. I call it art. You call it savagery. You know how silk is made?”

“Silk worms are reared... They are protected from predators, provided shelter, fed some yummy mulberry leaves and allowed to thrive. They are given hope, shown dreams that they will, someday fledge to the fullest and live out their entire lifespan. Ah! How sly.”

“And one day... They are boiled alive. Their bodies are peeled and silk is made. You call it delicate, precious and glamorous. So inhumane you’re that you go a step ahead and call it art! An art form followed from ages. But if a man is killed, you call it barbaric act followed in the jungles?”

“Human life is more precious than a silk worm’s. That’s the hierarchy.”

“Did the worms approve it?”-Gharial smiles. “Everyone believes as per one’s comfort. There’s no one good, no one bad. Good is just absence of bad... And it doesn’t take too long to flip the noisy coin of a man’s mind.”

“Who were those men with you? How did you recruit them? Why are they with you?”-Sagar has no interest in the unruly talk of a frozen, incapacitated Gharial.

“Necessity is the mother of invention. Compulsion is the great grandmother of necessity.”-Gharial replies calmly, his eyes etched on Sagar’s.

“How did you compel them? Did you brainwash them? What reasons did you give them to join you?”

“Reasons... biblical or biological, don’t matter. Reason is for those who have time to decide. I play with time, Sagar. I give time to act. And only act. Time is my biggest trump card.”

“How about the rules? The laws? Ever heard of them?”-Sagar bends over, hands on his knees.

“Oh, yeah... Yeah... Yeah... I... um... know them. They are so gorgeous, aren’t they? To whomsoever it applies notwithstanding in lieu of thence including but not restricted to necessary but not sufficient ...”

“You guys... You make beautiful rules, so nice.”-Gharial pauses, giving a deep thought. Then he looks back at Sagar as though he has got a point.

“But sadly, the value of a thing is realized only when it is broken.”-he whispers. “Don’t you think the beautiful rules naturally warrant someone worthy enough to break them?”

Sagar stands up. Gharial continues- “And when will you put to use the rules meant to be used when the rules are broken?”

"Well, all the time."-Sagar rubs his pistol. "...even if the President accepts."-he winks. Gharial winks back!

Jackpot has come down the stairs, he's staring at Gharial. Gharial turns to him. Jackpot feels uneasy. He tries to overcome it. "Those rules are a deterrent."-he stutters. Sagar is not interested. He slowly starts walking to the lift door. He knows it is pointless talking to Gharial.

"Deterrent? Ha ha... Even detergents are far worthier than deterrents. They do clean up the mess."

Jackpot is still under fear. Gharial consoles- "Don't worry so much. I still love you. Your death will be easier."

His eyes fall on the police emblem on Jackpot's uniform- "Dweepa police is like the class teacher gone crazy with troublesome students on one hand and a scornful head master on the other."

Sagar, meanwhile, has reached the lift. He curiously looks at the oval hole that was made by Gharial and his men as they had emerged through and the Policemen had sensed their movements.

Sagar peeps in. "Oh God!"

Gharial's escape plan was impeccable!

Gharial and his men had a gas cutter. As soon as they noticed the Police, they hid themselves in the lift at sixth floor. Gharial knew that the lift would be disabled.

They had a rope tied to the metal suspender of the lift's ceiling, sliced open the lift's floor partially and descended to the ground floor using the rope. At the ground floor they had to cut open the door. Sagar runs his fingers down the oval cut.

"Take him away, Jackpot."-he leaves, trying to dig out lapses he might have committed... or might commit.

“We’ll take over from here.”-the Gold Street Police assert. “What’s your name?”-Sagar deliberately avoids the name plate. The officer looks on, perplexed. “Oh! You! The Home Minister once told me that you don’t carry even a Rubway parcel properly. This thing...”-he turns towards an unmoving Gharial. “...is a prized, tranquilized catch! Something more than pizza.”

Sagar directs the Police Party. They start towards the nearby Central Prison Road. Sagar’s cell phone rings. He receives a Shutapp message-

Come home urgently. Emergency!!-it is from his mother.

What’s the matter? I’m on my way.

Someone entered Maya’s house by breaking open the door. He is threatening to kill Maya.

Sagar instructs Jackpot to take care of the rest and dashes home. Maya is his neighbor and is to be saved as of now. Gharial is no longer a threat, he feels although his intuition does not support him.

A sudden surge in responsibility numbs Jackpot’s brain every now and then. His colleague is driving the vehicle while he is in command. He does not like being a part of action ever since the marriage debacle- the greatest action of his life. But Sagar’s faith in him is too much to refuse. He feels proud, he feels nervous. He feels all sorts of irony. At the moment he somehow wants to reach the prison as soon as possible and throw the devil off the back. His only solace is the armored vehicle-nobody can mess with it.

“It is not the machine but the man behind the machine that matters.”-Gharial yells from within the confines of the vehicle’s rear. Jackpot is stunned!

One of the policemen kicks Gharial’s face! Gharial laughs. “Your kick reminds me of my stepbrother. He used to kick me every day since I was his stepmother’s son. One day he broke his leg in an accident. It was lying severed from his body. I took it home, washed it and carved the femur out of it. The same night I served him his own boneless leg piece. After dinner I stabbed him with his femur."

The Policeman sweats!

Gharial leans towards another policeman, prompting the policeman to push him on the floor of the vehicle. "What's happening there?"-Jackpot roars with his newfound responsibility. He is at the moment proud that his colleagues are under his command.

Gharial lies down on the heated floor. The adhesive slowly melts!!!

Suddenly bullets are shot at the van. Gharial's men shoot with their Kalashnikovs. Jackpot's comrade misses a heartbeat, looking at the fiery bullets getting stopped just before his eyes, after hitting the bullet proof glass. He takes a frantic turn, not able to overcome the shock.

"Noooo!!!"-Jackpot yells as the vehicle topples.

"They did not run away to escape you but to confront you at a better location. Intelligence is following a group of fools without objections, waiting for the first opportunity to fall out."-Gharial explains to one of the policemen. The doors are forced open from inside. His men take the policemen captives. The driver is dead due to impact. Jackpot is injured but alive and conscious. He lies in the van hoping that he is not spotted. One of Gharial's men walks to the front of the vehicle. He inspects cautiously and spots Jackpot. He catches hold of Jackpot's collar and drags him out.

Jackpot shivers, eyes closed tight and hands folded, pleading at the man. The man doesn't seem to show mercy. Suddenly Jackpot takes out a small tube, consumes some of its content and drops motionless with froth-like matter oozing from his mouth!

The man looks at his prey meet a painless end. He feels dejected at such an easy death to Jackpot. He abandons Jackpot's body at the van and escapes.

Sagar, in the meantime, has managed to reach Maya's house. Everything seems normal. He sees Maya fine and unhurt!

"You're all right?"-Sagar is shocked. His eyes dilate.

"Your question and the expression on your face do not match."-Maya, the kind of indifferent neighbor he is, is upset.

"Which one is true?"-asks he.

Sagar dashes home. His mother, an ardent football fan, is watching a match between Real Madrid and Barcelona.

"What's the matter, Sagar?"

"Why did you send me a Shutapp message that Maya is in trouble?"

"Who? I didn't..."-his mother is surprised.

Sagar's intuition rings alarm bells!

He tries calling up Jackpot in vain. He dials the prison's number. "No, no... Our last contact with them was at the K-junction."

Sagar rushes back. Surprisingly, it is the rain that gets heavier as he steps up the gas. He reaches the spot near K-junction and looks at the toppled armored vehicle. Not able to believe the fact that Gharial has escaped killing all his men, Sagar walks in the torrents slowly. He has forgotten the raincoat.

He circles around the vehicle slowly. Here and there, he can see used bullets of Kalashnikovs. The vehicle is intact but the contents are missing.

He is heartbroken. He knows that curtains have almost been drawn to his career as a police officer.

Jackpot's dome-like stomach is visible in the fade street lights. Sagar walks like a dead man to see the body. He sits slowly near Jackpot's pale body. The tube Jackpot had used, lies nearby. The froth filled mouth says it all to Sagar.

"You were a true policeman, Jackpot. Forgive me for being so gullible."-he takes Jackpot's head in his hands.

"Sss... Sagar Sir? Is it you?"-Jackpot springs back to life!!

"Jackpot?!"-Sagar is shocked. He drops the head.

"Sir..."-Jackpot's head bangs on the ground but manages to get up. He hugs Sagar tightly.

"You are alive?"-Sagar's eyes dilate again.

"Yes Sir... But others are gone. They were dragged away just the way goats are dragged on Sunday mornings."

Sagar is happy and sad at the same time. "The... The... tube? It is shocking to know you carry such a thing with you to the field! Don't you have faith in your seniors? And how did you survive it?"

"No Sir... I wanted to deceive them. I generated a lot of saliva and allowed it to flow from my mouth after consuming from the tube."-Jackpot stands up with Sagar's help.

"What was it then? If not cyanide?"

"These are pills for constipation!!"

"What!?"

"Yes Sir... I got an idea at the last moment!"-they walk down to the road.

Day dawns over Dweepa.

Ayodhya nears the island on the ferry. Sun rays emerge, puncturing the clouds!

“One ticket to Reinforces South Campus, please.”-he buys a ticket at the Dweepa Metro. He sprawls his legs as he sinks on the bench at the South line. For a moment he remembers Asrar. Just for a moment. And this remembrance is a first of its sort-

“Sir, I have got placed in Reinforces. And I am taking up the job.”-Ayodhya does not have even a touch of shame informing Asrar that he is not interested in using his skills for the society. He feels it is quite absurd and rhetorical- ‘doing something for the society’.

“And yes, I’m doing something for the society. I’ll build codes.”-he adds.

“No, Ayodhya. After all that you’ve learnt... You’ll bring a code to the society.”-Asrar smiles, patting him.

“I am going today and I will not be meeting you again. I had told this even befo...”-Ayodhya interrupts to be in turn interrupted.

“You’ll meet me for sure.”-Asrar leaves the badminton court for the last time.

“No, I won’t meet him.”-Ayodhya thinks as he sits awaiting the metro. He wants to look at something to stop himself from remembering Asrar.

His eyes inadvertently fall on the TV screen, surprised at the sudden cease of non-ending advertisements. They generally break only for announcements. But today is different.

“Thank you, Gautam... In the yesterday’s grotesque Gharial act, the victims are just too many. Much has been covered about the killing of the popular cartoonist from THE MIMES OF DWEEPA.

In a fresh incident yesterday, a young man, who was the admin of the RAKING NEWS satire e-paper and also a popular Fakebook troller, has been killed in an interesting way. He was targeted because of the satire column- Govt mulls adopting Gharial’s model of death to attain birth control."

Ayodhya searches about the column through his 5G internet data pack. The content loads, loads, loads and finally opens-

The new NSF Government, taking exceptions from the policies of the previous government, has decided to make public, its plans for a cleaner, greener and beautiful Dweepa sparkling with sparse people. "Gharial is our icon."-the island's Health Minister was quoted as saying. "He has so far cleansed the island of scores of people. Why fear him? Why hate him? Why hunt him? Why don't we think out-of-the-box and start taking things a bit positively?"-the minister was reported as supporting the 'free service provider' in an era where the word 'service' is rarely separated from the word 'tax'. He also inaugurated The Gharial Slaughter Research Institute and Fundamental Studies in New Town. As a mark of departure from the traditional ribbon cutting, a man lucky enough to be chosen from the Island's Luckiest Man Contest was taken to the bathroom and drowned in the tub.

The inauguration was followed by cultural programs in which the participants demonstrated their psychological prowess on stage which involved various means of taking lives. A bust of Gharial was inaugurated and beheaded after the program. Overall, the health minister's visit was a phenomenal success, the audience turnout surpassing that of the Dweepa Common Health Games.

Carrying the momentum forward, the NSF party spokesperson, is said to have pitched in for the Noble Please Prize to be awarded to the 'Agent of Ultimate Peace'. "As you all know; the Noble Please Prize is awarded after a lot of pleading. We also know that pleading usually takes place in front of Gharial by his victims. And hence we are kickstarting a signature campaign for the ultimate cause. If not the Noble, at least the 'Dweepa Gem' should be conferred on the man of the hour, who is governed by down-to-earth attitude so much that it has taken him underground."-the spokesperson's statement was clear.

The opposition, though, has made scathing remarks at the statement. "Instead of limiting his expertise to population control and awards, the government has to ponder over his creativity in killing and safeguard his intellectual rights by patenting the processes. Dweepa has become the apple of the eye of the whole world and Gharial, the seed in that apple!"-the historical statement was made hinting at the fact that though the apple can be seen, the seed cannot be. This was followed by a demonstration marked by burning of effigies of the health minister, the home minister and the chief minister.

Hours later, the NSF spokesperson is said to have 'hit back with the Newton's apple' on the opposition's head by quoting the Gharial Institute's Objectives and also quoting that the opposition's desperation is all over their faces to be witnessed.

It is to be seen as to when further news rakes up.

Ayodhya gets a faint clue that the ruling party might be using Gharial; the same intuition that Sagar experienced. He closes the page and keeps back his phone. The news at the TV is on...

"Two policemen have been abducted and one Head Constable Jackpot has escaped the messenger of death. The biggest news that has just come in is that the person who had alerted the Police about Gharial and had taken on the beast is none other than the famous undercover cop; superman of the Indian Police- retired intelligence officer Mohammed Asrar!! Officer Asrar attained martyrdom yesterday, fighting the Gharial monster. He was a 1980 batch IPS officer..."

Ayodhya is shocked! He stands up slowly, looking at the photograph of Asrar. It is the first time that Ayodhya has seen a person he knew, die prematurely. For a moment, he turns human. For a moment he feels that he has lost a dear one after he was born. But only for a moment...

"... ACP Sagar has been suspended. The home minister has ordered a thorough enquiry in the matter, promising the islanders of severe action against the officer if found guilty. However, the minister is refusing a full-fledged RBI investigation, reposing faith in the Island Police. New Delhi is obviously worried with the developments. A special team has been proposed to be formed to hunt down the dreaded criminal but the government of the island is accusing of the Centre of exercising too much control over the union territory and curbing state powers. People have been voicing concern through Fakebook posts, Bitter tweets and Shutapp messages. What's in store for the islanders? What is going to happen to the bravehearts captured by Gharial and what is going on in the mind of ACP Sagar is a thing that can be answered only by time. With cameraman Yami, I'm Tommy; NOT NOW... Oops! With cameraman Tommy, I'm Yami; NOT NOW."

The advertisements resume.

Ayodhya is back at the counter- "One ticket to YIT please."

Ayodhya's train takes him to YIT Dweepa station. He is going to Asrar's house ostensibly to find out more but actually wishing to see his body. The neighbor is awakened in the wee hours of the morning by a new bird at the compound- Ayodhya.

"Sir... Sir... Sir."

"What is it? The police troubles in the night and people trouble in the day. I am fed up, I'm telling you."- a woman emerges wearing a night gown.

"I want to see Asrar Sir's..."

"Oh God! You media people... Now I have to give even interviews?"-her body language displays that she is extremely busy and has no time for interviews. She is not interested in knowing whether Ayodhya is from the media. She just wants to consider him so and herself as a celebrity. It is a natural feeling as she has been an unnoticed housewife for four decades. Now she is desperate to be like Kanaka Sundari- her favorite actress who is set to appear on the silver screen with her latest movie- 'How to kill a million'. What a name! The woman loves the title.

"His body is taken to the Freedom Grounds. Today his last rites will be carried out with state honors. Go to Freedom Grounds. I'll give your interview there."

Ayodhya walks away to a distance and turns back. She is back in her nest. Nobody is around. A cruel curiosity sets in on him. He wants to find some clues, know more about the incident. With a single leap he vanishes into Asrar's compound!

Asrar lived all alone. His job was his only companion. The house is old; the door is locked. Ayodhya walks to the backyard. The bathroom window is partly broken. He finds a rope coiled and slightly hanging from the roof above. He jumps high and grabs it. There is a mini truck parked just outside the compound. It is of the gas cylinder supplier. The man has gone to a nearby house with the cylinder. Ayodhya recalls the typical sound when the cylinders collide while taking out; the thud that a filled cylinder creates when it is dropped gently on the ground; the series of metallic noise when it is rolled on the road... It has been a few minutes since that sound. His subconscious has recorded it.

"I should be quick."-he ties the rope to the window frame and starts unrolling it. He hops out of the compound, ties the free end to the rear of the truck and waits patiently back in the compound and ready. The driver returns, wrapping a booklet in the pocket of his trouser, tucking a pen behind his ear and rolling an empty cylinder. He hops quickly in the truck. Ayodhya jumps out and waits just behind the truck. It starts and tries to move. The bathroom window is pulled. The driver senses some obstacle. He gets down. Ayodhya hears the sound made by the jump. He quickly guesses something and climbs on the bumper of the truck. The driver bends down to inspect if the rear wheels are obstructed by some stone or a wedge-like thing. Ayodhya's feet are out of his sight.

He tries starting it again. Ayodhya can see cracks being formed around the bathroom window. The window is almost out of the wall. The driver gets down again. He walks back to the rear and inspects. Nothing is wrong. He returns to the seat and this time the truck moves smoothly.

Ayodhya is back in the compound. He waits until it is evening. Most of Asrar's neighbors are out on a stroll with their dogs. Walks are the only occasions when dogs command more respect than men. Imagine going walk with your family member. Nobody cares. Everyone has a family member. But with dogs, it is a matter of prestige. You'll be seen as one who can not only feed oneself but also rear a dog. Ayodhya slowly pulls the window. It doesn't take much effort. He barges in!

He walks to the bedroom, trying to find things Asrar might have used recently. A few clothes lie on the table. The broken cot is decorated with a dirty blanket and a pillow. A laptop can be spotted partially covered by the blanket.

He slowly moves the blanket away. A data card is seen connected to the laptop.

He switches on the laptop. His eyes are on the screen but the other senses are alert, intensely scanning for intruders.

Asrar had shared all the passwords with him. The laptop 'welcome's him. The internet is connected. He promptly opens the 'search history' in Goggle. The contents flash. Ayodhya scrolls down to read from last to first to maintain the search chronology-

Gharial-Dweepa, NSF, THE MIMES OF DWEEPA, Cartoonist murder, Gharial.

The last Goggle search had yielded information different than the first one. It was more detailed. Ayodhya finds out that Asrar had gone deeper in to the search until he had hit upon the previous day's column in RAKING NEWS about Gharial!!

The next few searches read- RAKING NEWS administrator address, RAKING NEWS 'Contact Us'.

Asrar had then signed up for Raking News Community and sent a message to the website. But Ayodhya is not able to find out what message it was. His helplessness is slowly getting the better of him. He is slowly losing patience. There is no reply by Raking News in Asrar's e-mail either. Ayodhya feels the pain of failure. "If I could get the message, it could turn out to be a game changer."-he thinks.

There is no lead yet. He closes the browser and moves the cursor to shut down the computer. Suddenly, he spots a text file stored on the desktop area. He slowly moves the cursor and double clicks it with a rush of adrenaline. The file opens up. Asrar had requested the administrator's residence and office addresses. Asrar had warned the admin that his life was in danger and he was vulnerable to a Gharial attack. The words were first typed in a text file before copying in to the website. Asrar had earlier suffered internet connection loss when he had typed a lot of words online and clicked 'Submit'. So this was his solution.

Ayodhya feels that Gharial kills anyone who speaks of him negatively, perhaps even positively. He closes the laptop and walks around the house, examining things. A lonely Asrar had maintained a diary that Ayodhya finds on the TV cabinet. He flips pages about Asrar's personal life until he finds-

"... and his name is Ayodhya. He is such a puzzle that it is impossible for an 'intelligent' officer like me to understand his thoughts. He's just like a stone turned human. No, literally... Hard to imagine, isn't it? He said to me clearly that he would not take up the task of protecting the society. He hates the very word... 'Society'. But I still hope that one day, he does.

I have trained many officers in my tenure, seen many brilliant and bright students pass by but Ayodhya stands right out there in front of me. Everything stands frozen when he walks to take on his opponents. Every time I look at his beaten body rise from the floor of the badminton court, his eyes assure me of a defeat I will face in the next round. He falls in every round only to get up with a greater conviction, a greater resolve.

Enough for now, getting sleepy..."

Ayodhya is still indifferent. In fact, he just doesn't like his mentioning in the diary. He passes over the diary on the cot and turns to leave. He starts walking to the window he entered from.

“Stop Ayodhya!!”-a fearful voice is heard.

He stands still.

“Go back!!”-it orders thunderously.

“Go back to the book. Open it!”

He resumes his walk. “Stop Ayodhya... Go back to the book. Open it!”

“Stop Ayodhya... GO BACK TO THE BOOK. OPEN IT!!”-the voice gets louder. He has kept his left foot on the grill of the window to leap out. In the last moment he retracts!

He walks fast impatiently and flips the pages with heart full of hate.

“Enough for now, getting sleepy...”

“... Hey, one more thing! I didn’t have anyone to wish good night. But from tonight, I consider him my family, I can wish him... Good night Ayodhya, good night son.”

Ayodhya drops down on the cot!!!

He reads it again- “Good night Ayodhya, good night son.”

The human in him resurrects! The emotions tide from nothingness!!

The diary suddenly feels warm. The house suddenly smells good. He sits feeling an unusually contented heart. He feels like talking to people, laughing with them, letting loose the reins he thinks he holds his existence with. He feels the dawn of love as the night swoops down on Dweepa.

13 B2, 26

Ayodhya walks in to the building he has just rented a flat in. It is located near his office that is in the famous tech park-The Pungent Dungeon. As in a dungeon where those who go inside cease to exist, the park has a reputation. Men who enter it cease to be men and become robots.

The brighter side is that Ayodhya is more open to interactions than he was before. He has carried Asrar's diary with him. He has obtained the flat key from the owner. He has refused a roommate against usual practice and has negotiated well for the '1BHK'- a flat with one bedroom, one hall and one kitchen. Most of his colleagues stay in the same building. The rest stay in the same township.

As usual, today too, there is no power. Load shedding is rampant on the island.

"Hello..."-a colleague of his, who has earned a name for his software testing abilities and abhorrent precision, smiles at him. What precision, you ask? Just wait...

Have a look at him. He has big eyes, bush-like hair, wide nose and stiff, receptive ears like those of the elephants. He combs his hair every hour in order to give shapes to it. But even after two and a half decades his extremely sensitive senses and crazily brilliant brain fail to detect the error in judgment- his hair can never be set!

"Hi..."-Ayodhya opens the lock to his flat, turning back at him.

"I'm your new neighbor!"-he walks to Ayodhya offering a handshake, his fused eyebrows reminding Ayodhya of an adult albatross with fledged wings.

"Nice to meet you."-Ayodhya completes it.

"I'm staying here since one year and two months. You came today-o?"-asks he.

"Yes, I know."-he himself answers in the same breath. Ayodhya keeps his half-open mouth half open.

"You know my name-o? Hmm?"-he asks again.

"No."

"My name is Tintu."-he answers again. "Your name actually?"-he awaits Ayodhya.

"Ayodhya."

The power supply is restored! The building glows!

"Nice name... Hmmm..."-whenever Tintu exclaims "Hmmm..." he means he is doubly sure of his statement. And when he doesn't, well, he is still sure. Doubly!

Ayodhya brings some luggage inside. "You know my native-o?"-Tintu asks again, helping Ayodhya with the rest of the items.

And of course, he himself answers- "I come from Pathanam Thitta. Hmmm..."

"In Kerala."

"Pathanam Thitta... you have heard of the exact place-o?"

"It is in Adoor. Hmmm..."

"You know my father's occupation-o?"

"Bank employee."

"You know his hobby-o?"

"Member of Clarkist Feminist Party."

"You know my brothers and sisters-o?"

"One younger sister... Baby Jojo... No brothers..."

"You know my best friend-o? Pheno... Pheno Menon. Girl... Hmmm."-he reaffirms. All the while Ayodhya is silent. Mmm...

"You joined newly, I think so."-Tintu continues with his strange accent of English. Ayodhya shakes his head- "No, I was on the bench. Just returned after personal leave."

"Oh, then ok. I didn't know. That's the problem, actually."

Some miracles of nature happen only once in every millennium; only when the elements on earth-fire, water, wind hatch a plot and execute perfectly in unison. It happened today when someone like Ayodhya and someone like Tintu became neighbors. I don't foresee any such convergence for another thousand years.

"Come to my room... Hmmm."-Tintu is sure of the invitation. He means it.

"I'll show you my awards. I won after successful coding testing. I developed new methods of testing, actually. I received the award from Mr. Howdie Codie ... CEO... You know, CEO... He came down to India from Philippines... To give the award to me actually..."

"Hmmm..."-Tintu pushes his chin backwards stressing on the last point. He also raises his eyebrows in a look that indicates the seriousness with which he worked for the success and the extent of truth in his conclusion. Ayodhya looks on.

"Great! Congratulations!! I'll come sometime."-a moment later Ayodhya realizes the delay in complimenting him. "I'm tired now. Can I see you later? If it is ok with you...?"- he walks in to the kitchen. "What time will you come, actually?"

"Nine?"-Ayodhya requests. "Come at nine twenty... Hmmm... I'll be busy up to eight. Then I'll watch a small movie. That's the problem, actually."-Tintu scratches his head.

"Please come at nine twenty... three. Nine twenty-three."

"Done."

"Ok... Tata."-Tintu leaves for his door, keeping his steps in extremely divergent directions.

"Which is the best LED TV in the market for twenty thousand, actually?"-he turns.

"I don't know."

"Ok, tata."

A colleague of Ayodhya has just returned from the gym. Ayodhya overhears from the kitchen, Tintu telling her about him. "I became a new neighbor... Again... Hmmm."

"His name is Ayodhya, actually. He is very good. Speaks very less, actually... Two... two point three percent of how much I speak."

Ayodhya can't help smiling mildly. It is the first time ever... A mild precursor...

The next day, Ayodhya walks to the office. The campus is full of people whose class and caliber are honed in the US. "Dude, why is there no flavored water in India? Shucks!!"

He walks to the fourth floor. He has been assigned to a Team Leader or a TL in short.

"Good morning, Sir."-Ayodhya wishes his team leader. The TL turns.

Ayodhya is unpleasantly surprised. The TL is rudely shocked!!

It is Pony!!!

"Oh! Ha ha... Oh God! Why God why!"-Pony breaks into uncontrolled laughter. "This is the ultimate coincidence that could happen to anyone!"

Ayodhya stands timidly looking at the ground. "How are you, Sir?"-he asks politely. "How is your relative?"-Pony comes to the matter straightaway.

"He is working in Debacle Software Limited. But I am not in touch with him."

"What's his name?"-Pony is dangerously curious. "He generally doesn't interact even with his cousins. I don't yet know his real name."

"You must be kidding. The other day you told- 'Sir I don't have anyone other than him. Please spare him'..."-Pony enacts. Ayodhya maintains a timid look.

"Where does he stay? How does he look?"

Fear is all written on Ayodhya's face. He shivers as he tries to make an eye contact with Pony. His sight naturally falls on Pony's jaw-the scar that was made when Pony had fallen down from the stool on that night in Gaanja Park still remains.

"He doesn't leave identity... Only impressions."

Pony mildly slaps Ayodhya, hard enough to be painful, soft enough to be unheard by others. Ayodhya bears it without a word. "He can't bother me. He can at best bother himself. What did I say?"-he pushes Ayodhya by pressing his palm against his cheek. "He can at best bother himself."-Ayodhya replies slowly like a child.

"Go, your team leader is on leave today. Mine is a different team. Go; listen to your briefing from your team mates. I'll find out about your relative anyway."

More than half of YIT Dweepa has been recruited by Reinforces. So, it is no surprise that Pony is a TL there. And no surprise again, that Pillu too is in the same office!

"Hey, university player!!"-he walks to Ayodhya. Ayodhya had guessed it right- "If Pony is there, Pillu is sure there. It is a connivance of time!"

Ayodhya doesn't turn. But someone else does!

Long, partly curled hair makes way for a bright, shiny face. The eyelashes beat slowly in admiration. The lips curve up gently. The ID card hangs like a lemon tied to the gorgeous truck by its loving owner to keep evil spirits away. She doesn't talk to him but stands nearby, ostensibly going through a file. But Ayodhya knows.

"What a surprise... Hey someone get a chair. Our university player has hurt his *** sitting on a wooden bench throughout a year."-Pillu turns to another colleague of his. The girl looks on at Ayodhya, unperturbed, with wide eyes.

"This is your seat, Ayodhya."-she speaks. Her voice is not quite sweet as is generally expected. It doesn't suit her appearance. And if you are dying to know of her complexion, she is moderately fair with an extremely clean face.

Ayodhya's seat is next to hers. The cubicle is quite a dream for those engineers. They have, many a time, cited one reason or the other, to change their cubicle- too close to AC duct, too far from the duct, too close to the entrance, deep, deep down the aisle... But a stroke of luck had played such a game that their demands had complemented one another and their seats were interchanged mutually without needing the golden one.

After sitting on the bench for months, Ayodhya finally occupies the golden cubicle!

As he descends on the soft cushion of the chair, the rest of the engineers feel pricked. It seems like his coronation ceremony!

Pillu is disappointed. He walks away, utterly dejected.

"Hi, I'm Anca."-she smiles. Ayodhya feels the gentle perfume from her hair. Her family photo adorns the monitor screen like a shield against any wrong moves, all set to take on anyone for a gang-war. The photo of her trekking trip decorates the coffee mug. Many tiny, sparkling, unidentifiable but beautiful things dangle here and there marking the 32-yard circle for her. The rest of the cubicle is to be understood as belonging to him.

"Hi, I'm Ayodhya."

"Yeah, I know. You occupied the flat yesterday, didn't you?"

Tintu is the only person who can surprise Ayodhya.

"You played cricket for your university, right?"-she asks offering a chocolate. "How do you say it was cricket?"-Ayodhya asks even though he knows how she knows. "Tintu helped you with the cricket kit and Pillu called you a university player."

Ayodhya nods. "What are you? Batsman, bowler..."-she keeps her palm on her glowing cheek. Her cheek presses against her eye, making it look differently beautiful.

"Water!"-Ayodhya answers in his mind. "I can be everything and nothing. I can take shapes, I can flow, I can evaporate and become invisible at the first sign of trouble. I can condense and return when the time is right. No force in the world can compress me. No object can bind me. I escape, I besiege. I am water!"

"Batsman-wicket keeper"-he displays nervousness, trying to make her understand it.

"Oh, Dhoni?"-she exclaims a bit loudly, sintering the broken hearts few cubicles away. Ayodhya doesn't react.

"Anyway, I'm your team mate. Let me explain you about the new project. Here... This client is based in..."-she moves closer pushing her chair with her toes. He can feel her breath. A few strands of her silken hair trouble her eyes from focusing on the file. They are twisted along their lengths and crescent shaped at the ends.

Ayodhya sits looking in to the turning pages of the project file. They flip even before he reads the content completely. "That is the best shot I can take at life. Live as happy as possible until each day passes by you even before you realize..."

Elsewhere, a queer coincidence can be seen. Just as Ayodhya had sat on the chair of the golden cubicle, Sagar too occupied, for the first time, the seat in front of an inquiry team. There was not even a moment's difference.

He is being questioned by the team of seniors sitting in front of the curtainless window. The sun is right above. Intense light from the window blinds Sagar's eyes. Helplessness, dejection and worry have occupied his mind like waterweeds carpeting a lake. Just like the lake is choked to death, Sagar's mind has slowly started to succumb.

"Tell me, Sagar. We know you fired a shot at his chest and head. And he escaped..."

"He, who?"-Sagar bends forward. The officer's mouth dries. He looks at the other members and continues- "So, he escaped. Probably it was Kevlar. But you did not fire a third at him. You could have easily shot at his knees which were bare and exposed. We could have nabbed him. Why didn't you?"

"Jackpot had guessed it right. He had understood that Gharial was heading towards me and my shots were ineffective. So Jackpot had let go of the adhesive net from the sixth floor and I was directly under it. So I moved backwards immediately and Gharial, in my pursuit, got stuck."

"You still could have fired..."

"Yes Sir... But I thought it was needless since he was already captured. Shooting at his knees would have made me sit in front of another team of inquiry. He would have been hospitalized and the delay in producing him at the court could have allowed his escape..."

"And we get a feeling that you're using the adhesive net just too often. Is it because it is your invention and you want people not to forget it? Sorry, Sagar. This is department. Not an avenue to satisfy ego."

"No Sir. I had no idea Jackpot had brought it in the car. I was looking into the murder of that policeman at Swarga-and then Jackpot called me to the cartoonist scene."

"He seems to have too much of admiration towards you. Is he a part of your plan?"

"He was almost caught and barely escaped death from the hands of the one you hesitate to even take name of."

There is no hope. He is sure it is going to be a never ending probe.

He struggles to face the obvious fact that he has been suspended. After the inquiry he returns home, goes to his bedroom and sits on the chair, looking at his old uniform sway in the cupboard from the hanger. It reminds him of his thorny past-

He has completed his Engineering from a distinguished college in Meghpur, a cosmopolitan and a twin city to Delhi, developed to reduce the burden on the national capital and its associated regions. 'I'm not from Delhi or NCR' is a sentence often used in Meghpur to strangely keep them away from being linked with the capital. But the epidemic doesn't spare Meghpur.

Sagar has a family, a job and a desire. He wants to join the Indian Police Service. His parents are one of the few extremely pious people in a promiscuous city. They are against it.

He has always fantasized seeing himself in the uniform and going around beating up goons, helping people. A young Sagar runs home on a cold Meghpur evening. "Mother, get my charger. I have to go for the classes."

"You didn't even have your snacks, son."

"I had it in the office!"

"Hi, Sagar."-his uncle comes home on a visit from a faraway city. He is the source of inspiration to Sagar on surprise raids.

"Hi Uncle... Will meet you later... Got to go for classes."-he wears shoes impatiently forcing his heels in.

"Which class?"

"UPSC coaching!!"-his father answers. "Oh! So you want to become an IAS officer. Good, good!!"

"IPS."-Sagar wears his helmet and leaves. Even in the hurry, he notices his father's upset face.

It has been two rigorous years of preparation. The previous attempts had ended in failure. In the first attempt he was not able to clear the first round. In the second attempt he was rejected in the second round. In a few days' time he will be attempting for the third time.

But this year is different. In the first round, the aptitude section 'CSAT' is only a qualifier. General Science 'GS' is crucial now. Earlier, candidates used to score high in CSAT- 170/200, 180/200 and just manage a 60 to70 marks in GS to clear the cutoff of 220/400, 240/400.

He halts at the traffic signal and gets immersed in thought-

"Now prelims round has become more unpredictable. I never had fear of exam. Now it has slowly started creeping in. But Kartika Shukla... the topper... her speech was encouraging."-he puffs a hot breath in the closed space of the helmet. "That red signal seems to tell me that I'm not going to make it."

The signal instantly turns green!

That night, his father summons him. "Why did you say to uncle that you are aiming for IPS?"

"Leave it now... Dinner is ready."-his mother wants to stop another of those high pitched arguments the father and the son drag through fateful nights. "No, Parvati... His madness is increasing day by day. Today he has the temerity to talk about it. Tomorrow? What if he pursues it?"

"Father, it is a farfetched thought. Even the prelims have not begun and you are talking about becoming an IPS."

"I don't care!! You will either be an IAS or IFS. If at all you crack the exam. That filthy job of the police is for others."

"Others? Who?"-Sagar locks his brows. "Sagar, even you?"-his mother is irritated. She expects either of them to be silent.

"Let us know of it mother. Who, father?"

"... those who are willing to surrender self-respect."

"Did you get it? For whom? Now go, have your dinner. I don't mind you continue working as an engineer. But I don't want to hear the word Police again. I don't want their sinful shadows to spoil the sanctity of my home."

Sagar is adamant. He captures the point his father has put across against IPS- "Even IAS and IFS can be so, father."

"Don't argue with me!!"-shouts his father.

"Parvati!!!"-he turns to Sagar's mother who is serving rice on his platter.

"Take this knucklehead away."-he pushes the platter in utter disgust. She stands shocked.

"Stop involving mother in the argument, father. Reply on the points alone."-Sagar is calm.

"Are you interrogating me? Have you started rehearsing that wretched job with me? Huh?"-he crunches his stomach, losing breath due to excessive shouting.

"Father... Please don't say such words... I just want to fulfill my dream."

"So now you are emotionally blackmailing me? I'm your father. If you become a police officer against my wish, you don't have a place in my home."

"Trrring"-a call on Sagar's phone brings him back to present.

His past haunts him occasionally. But after being suspended, he has started to think about it almost every day. "Hello?"

"Sir, you want food? I'll get some Biryani."-it is Jackpot. "No, Jackpot. I'll call you if I need. Thank you."

"Ok Sir."-Jackpot's voice slowly diminishes. The past is back with Sagar.

The Fancy Dress Competition of Class Two...

"Sagar! Here's your diary."-his teacher hands it over to him. He impatiently opens the last page. His eyes are looking for the writing in red.

'DOCTOR-Please bring a fancy stethoscope, a pair of spectacles, a white apron and an empty syringe.'-he reads it. His eyes fill with tears. The Physical Training (PT) master's son has been given the role of POLICE OFFICER.

He walks to the staff room. The class teacher is seen talking to the PT master. He waits for a moment. "Should I go after the PT master leaves?"

"No... if I fear him, how will I get courage to catch criminals?"

"Teacher!"-he approaches her. "Yes Sagar?"

"I don't want POLICE. I want DOCTOR."

"Yeah, you're a doctor. Aren't you?"-she is confused.

"Oh... I'm sorry. I want POLICE, not DOCTOR."-he gently pats his forehead. She smiles. "You see there?"-she points at the PT master's son, who is Sagar's classmate. "He looks stronger and he is taller. So he makes a better candidate, doesn't he?"

"Let us then have a fight competition!!"-Sagar suggests. "Or a general knowledge quiz about POLICE."

The PT master's ego is pricked, twisted, peeled and burnt in front of his gorgeous colleague. "You little brat!!"-he slaps Sagar. Sagar's lips bleed. "I'll disqualify you from the competition!!"

Sagar's possessiveness doesn't allow fear to even come closer. His insane obsession brings a smile on his face- "Your son is physically unfit for an officer, Sir!!"

"You swine!!"-he slaps again. Sagar's teacher shields him from the master, hugging him. Sagar can feel her nervous breathing and the strong series of pulse along her neck. "Leave him, Sir. I'll take care."-he feels her wind box as she utters.

The master turns and starts walking away. "I'll remember you, Sir. After twenty years when I become a Police Officer, I'll take care of you!!"-he shouts from the safe confines of his teacher's arms. She presses her fingers gently on his lips. "Mind your words, son."

She takes him to her seat, offers him a chocolate, kisses his reddened cheek and wipes off blood from his lips. "It is so hurtful and it was unnecessary!"

"If this hurts me, then what do you say for the injuries I'll sustain fighting criminals?"-he asks, licking his chocolate laden finger. "It has hurt me!"-she brushes his hair.

"See, this is only a stage event. It is only for ten minutes. Nobody is forcing you not to become a Police officer in reality."

"You were wrong, teacher!"-Sagar comes out of the past memories and walks to the cupboard and feels the ironed sleeve of his shirt.

"Life too is a stage event. Time is limited and there are players."-he regrets even to this day, after twenty years. "You are directed, opposed, supported, judged, applauded, and criticized. It all depends on how much of each of it you would receive."

"Teacher, I can't think of anything other than a Police Officer even for a minute. I'll be the best officer, on stage and off stage, you'll see it."

"Do you remember you were warned last month against wearing the lapels on your uniform?"-she smiles, impressed with his reply. She brings out another topic of discussion, pulling his lapel with her finger. "And I got special permission for that."

Sagar had opted out of the event. But in reality, he was in.

He had qualified for the Union Public Service Commission or UPSC exam's third and final round-the interview.

"So Mr. Sagar, you said you want to pursue IPS. Why not IAS or IFS?"

"It is my ambition to become a police officer, Sir. We see every day that the word Police has become synonymous with corruption, violence, misuse of power and injustice. People feel nervous with Police around. This mindset has to change. I want to be that change."

"You mean to say that so far there has not been a single officer who has strived for it? And you want to be the first one?"

"No Sir, take for instance Officer Singh who passed away last year. He was the most popular cop in Meghpur. He tried his best to restore law and order. But it has been talked that some who wielded extreme power silenced him and the case too."

"Ok, let us not go deeper in to the controversy. But what if the same happens to you?"

"That will happen to anyone who is honest and sincere. Meghpur has a history of such acts in its short period of existence. And it can happen even if I am IAS or IFS. But it is a cycle, Sir. Whenever righteousness is silenced it takes form in another manifestation. Someone else will carry the mantle."

"No doubt, your optional subject is Philosophy, Sagar. Well said."-one of the interview panelists smiles.

"What is wrong with the Police System, Sagar? According to you?"

"Sir, the first and the foremost point is that the whole set of procedures and Police Laws. We still follow the British rules from the pre-independence era. We are so lethargic to even take a look. The system should be upgraded with changing times. Statistical data shows that as populations grow, crime rates grow. But the policing methods, the speed of processing remain same. This mounts huge pressure on the establishment. Corruption sets in and people lose faith in it. We need to change the..."

"Give me one idea... Yeah, sorry. Go ahead."

Sagar wipes his forehead. "We need to change the policies holistically. Sir there has been tremendous pressure on the policymakers that the Police setup be more efficient. I have a concept. Just like there is a separate branch for traffic police, there has to be a branch for investigative police and active police. While the active police maintain law and order and attends distress calls, investigative police takes up the task of dealing with the mountains of pending cases and fresh cases too."

"Is this your own idea?"-an interviewer asks, looking suspiciously.

"No, Sir. We discuss these topics in our study circle."

A few weeks after the interview, he anxiously opens the website for the results. The internet service is down due to heavy traffic. Tens of thousands of candidates too are feeling the heat of anxiety on the tips of their forefingers. He spends a sleepless night. The web page opens the next day. He is in!!

It is his father's turn to be sleepless. Sagar leaves for Mussourie for training. His father becomes weaker and weaker day by day but not for too long in fast paced, changing lives. These days he sleeps peacefully... in grave number 20, Sector number 4, Meghpur.

Sagar and his mother now stay in Dweepa.

"Sagar!"-his mother calls him out of his past. "Have you booked the train tickets?"

"Yeah... Check the SMS on the phone."

"Ok... Get my chappals out. I'm done."-she hurries with her handbag. The clock strikes seven. Sagar walks with his mother to the bus stop. "Sorry mother, no car today."-he apologizes within himself that he is unable to drop her to the railway station in the Police car. "You're apologizing as though you have always dropped me by car."-he thinks about her probable reaction. He smiles. He has always used public transport whenever he is off duty. "And they have slapped a case against an officer like you."-he feels she would conclude.

Sagar admires the take-it-easy attitude in his mother all though he has never spoken about it. He loves the craze she has for football. She is a die-hard Barcelona fan. Whenever she's in trouble or feels sad, she just watches one of those recorded matches between Barcelona and Real Madrid.

Anyway, he doesn't speak to her unless really needed. There is a reason for that.

They reach Dweepa Railway Station. "Here, check the berth number."-she thrusts her phone in his hands. He opens the SMS and mumbles- "B2, 26... Side lower."

He raises his head and spares a quick look at the LED display. "This is A2. We need to..."-he looks in either direction. "...go this way."-he turns back to lift the luggage. The LED with the 'B2' display nears.

B2, 26. He takes another look into the ticket and smiles at the sheer coincidence. The recent past after his father's demise opens up-

"Mother, we need to shift from Meghpur to Kolkata. A new case has come up. It might take a few months to solve it."-he is booking a guest house in Kolkata over the internet.

"Are you the only one who has to work? Why are others earning money?"-she kisses his forehead as he turns. "Only those who work can earn money. And those who don't are busy making it. It is a complicated case. I have so far solved three difficult ones. They have faith in me."

"But how about your wedding? Panditji has brought a proposal, you remember?"-she keeps the bowl of corn flakes. "Yeah, we'll see about it later."-he stands carefully on the cot and pulls down a suitcase. The phone rings. "Hello, Panditji? What happened?"-she starts with a smile. Slowly her smile vanishes as Panditji speaks. "Ok... But make sure you explain well to the next alliance proposal."-she is upset. Sagar doesn't enquire. He calls up Panditji later in the day. "Yes, Sagar. The girl is good in every respect. I had sent her bio-data to you last week. I had gone through your application form. I even remember it. Your mother had specific requirements right? Education as Engineer/Doctor only... That is option 'B', complexion as 'very fair' that is option '2' and age as 26."

"B2, 26... She falls in that bracket... She is a software engineer. I feared she would demand a groom who is a software engineer too. But she wants a snake charmer and insists on someone who knows handling a python. I could not get anything. I didn't ask much. What does a python do?"

"What!? A python? I... I... don't know. It coils around and suffocates its prey. What else? Umm... It eats too much and rests too much."-he is totally perplexed. It is only after browsing on Goggle that he found out about it. Python is computer coding software popularly used in the IT industry. She wanted not a software engineer but a software engineer with 'a good grip on Python' as mentioned in her response.

Sagar's mother gets to board B2, 26 in time but still awaits the other B2, 26. Sagar stuffs the luggage under the seat in the compartment. "Bye, mother. Take care. Call me up once you reach Kochi."-he takes leave in his mind after he has left from the station!

The train has arrived to Dweepa from Mangaluru in Karnataka, along the Arabian Sea. The Sea Rail operates on the bridges across the Arabian Sea. Sea Rail is a profit making company listed in the stock markets. It was started under Public Private Partnership between the Government of Dweepa led by the NSF and the elite business class of India. Owing to the better Commuter Delight Index as compared to its counterpart on land, the IRCTC, Sea Rail was fully privatized. NSF party members hold quite a number of shares and are unofficial partners in the business.

The island of Dweepa connects Lakshadweep, Minicoy and Karnataka by a series of sea rails. A rail line from Minicoy joins Kochi through the south wing of the Arabian Bridge through Dweepa junction. It is the same train his mother has boarded.

He walks back from the station, rekindling more of those recent memories.

... Of the incident that took place a month ago-

He has just killed a dreaded criminal on the streets of Nadir- the most notorious slum in mainland India. He is concerned with the violence that could erupt anytime in the hot-blooded slum dwellers. His mother calls him up. He is so involved in making precautionary arrangements that he ignores her call. He has been avoiding talking to her after his father's death. She has never raised a finger at him or held him responsible for the demise but he feels guilty. Her silence stokes further.

And the guilt has slowly transformed into a peculiar hate he has developed towards him. No doubt it is my gift.

This hate is a hate that he can inflict on himself only if he shows it on his mother. It is a strange punishment. He shouts at her to hurt himself. He goes to her to apologize but shouts at her again. It hurts him again. She bears it. She is like that infinite sink that takes up every caustic word from Sagar. He hopes she scolds him back, but it is never to happen. She is his mother!

She has been busy dealing with the tenant at their Meghpur residence since four years. He does not pay the rent properly. He ignores his owner's phone calls. He has money for everything else than rent. She talks about it to Sagar often. Sagar shies away.

"You take care of it, mother."-he runs away from the problems... and her. He is happy with his profession, or at least thinks so. She has been making regular trips all the way from Dweepa to Meghpur every month!

Last month she had waited at her own residence in rain, in vain. Sagar is aware of it. On one of the rare occasions he had reluctantly received her call, she had a made a hidden request in her mild, feeble voice. She wanted him to take over the responsibility or at least lend a hand. "Please don't call me when I'm at work!! How many times should I tell you? If it is raining, go stand in shade!!"-he had shouted at her and disconnected the call. The very next moment he had wept badly... like a child.

It repeated... the shouting and the immediate weeping... a few days ago. He could not hide tears in front of a sympathetic Jackpot and the opportunistic fraudster locked up in the cell.

He doesn't know why he feels so desperate to tell her he is not what he is behaving like. He wants to tell her he is the same boy she used to take to school holding him in her arms. He is the same baby she used to shield in her sari against hot sun. He is still the same boy who depended on her for everything. He still depends on her smile. His throat chokes every time he thinks about her. He wants to relieve her of all burdens.

So strange that he also believes he is her biggest burden. "Mother, one day I'll end it all."-he promises her in his mind. But when he receives her call, a peculiar hatred surfaces from his inside and sinks into her heart through the tip of his tongue. He feels he'll get another chance to tell her everything. But then he doesn't realize... I am after all, I!

"Why did you call up again?"

"Sagar, I am sorry. Can you just tell me what I could do if the tenant does not heed to pay rent? Should I send a notice?"

"Do I look like a lawyer to you?"

"No Sagar, I just thought you may know."

"No! Answer me!! Do I look like a lawyer to you? Don't you have the sense whom to ask about it?"

"I am sorry, Sagar. I was just... Did you have lunch, son?"

"You know what the time is now? Six thirty. Is it a time to enquire about lunch?"

"No... Sometimes you don't get time to have food. So I..."

"Mother, enough!"

"Don't call unnecessarily and spoil my day. I know how much you love to talk over phone!!"-he slams his cell phone down on the table. He imagines her slowly placing back the receiver, probably questioning God as to why He gave her a son like him or probably still worrying that he is not taking enough care of his health. Only the second one is true.

He crosses the main road and enters the lane that leads to his house. He has to walk three kilometers straight. He doesn't mind. He was jogging more than that distance during his IPS preparations. At the moment he is recollecting the incident at the matrimony office in Dweepa, shortly after assuming charge to track down Gharial-

The office is small yet neatly arranged. An incense stick spreads its aroma all around. A dancing doll is swaying its neck and waist slowly. There is also another family waiting for Panditji. The father of the boy holds a big fat folder containing details of prospective brides 'engineered' for his son. He looks at Sagar and makes a mental calculation about how his son fares against him. And smiles secretively, ably shielded by the rich harvest of his moustache.

Sagar's mother had zeroed down on the B2, 26 of her choice, this time a doctor. She holds the file to him allowing him to go through it for a few seconds before nodding in question. Sagar nods back in an affirming manner.

The father of the other guy is fatally curious. His eyes assume a belligerent look. They seem to convey to Sagar that Sagar is eligible to search only after his much superior son selects a bride, akin to a less worthy mongrel finishing off the crumbs after the big bad dog has eaten.

The father tries to peep into the file by slowly leaning to his left, reposing his torso and faith on his giant circular base that could even support a trade center. Sagar, nevertheless, makes the objective easier by displaying it openly in front of his face. The father reverts.

It is human nature. You take more interest in what others try to find. Even if they are trying for something you already have. And the tendency increases when you have more... when the more you know that they are looking for things you already have. You are strange beings, really. The other guy's father has a bigger folder than that small file Sagar's mother has with her.

Sagar, on the other hand, knows that B2, 26 is not right but he agrees to his mother than objecting to it, hoping that everything will be fine.

You humans, you are embodiments of irony. You do exactly opposite of what is needed for a happy life and hope for a miracle to bring to you that happiness.

Panditji enters, cursing the hot weather. "Namaste!!"-he wishes both the families. He calls the other family first as they had been waiting longer. Sagar sits looking at the photo of B2, 26. Sagar's mother leans over his shoulder, scans through the photo again and immediately concludes- "The girl looks quite good and seems very well behaving. We shall meet her this week."

A week later the family of the girl meets them at Panditji's office. An exchange of pleasantries signals a 'Here, have it. Enjoy it quickly and get prepared.' It seems to portend the high-pressure informal interview.

"The boy's eyes are attractive... Errr..."-the father of the girl hesitates. Sagar's mother waits on.

"In the bio-data it has been mentioned that he is a Central Government employee. I know the salary will be low but it is quite good. Ha ha... He seems to be matured enough to understand how to work in a government job. But we don't know which department he works in. Umm..."-he wants her to pick the blip and respond. "He is a...

a civil servant."-she smiles, looking at Panditji.

Panditji nods, smiling sheepishly. Sagar gets the wind. He doesn't like hiding facts. Sagar replies calmly-"Uncle, I am a Police officer. Assistant Commissioner of Police, Dweepa."

The father begins to pant for breath. The girl looks on at her father in amusement. "My daughter is actually going for higher studies. We cannot commit anything about her marriage. We just thought of meeting some families to start the groom searching process. We are actually not quite serious about it right now. Thank you."

"Father, I want to talk to him. I'll do higher studies after marriage."-she wants to see her father's reaction. He drags her out of office, whispering into her ears- "Goons of same color flock together. And it is called a Police Station!!"

Sagar bows down his head. He doesn't like it. He would have accepted personal remarks but not a dig at his department. "Nobody opts for Police job. Could you see now?"-he feels his mother asking him with her eyes, sitting still.

After a few days he had met that very girl in a mall.

"Hi, Sagar. I'm Soor. You remember? I had come to meet you at Panditji's office?"

"Yeah... Soor, I remember."

"I've got two tickets for the movie. My friend did not turn up. Are you interested?"-she rubs the tickets in her fingers. Sagar is off duty. It has been years since he last watched a movie. He doesn't think twice. "Yes."-he steps behind her on the escalator. It looks as though he is in a trance she has cast on him and he is slowly ascending to a paradise.

The interactions have increased of late. Strangely, Sagar doesn't find Soor's calls annoying unlike his mother's. Soor, these days frequents Sagar's house. She works in Heaven Seven Group of Hospitals. It is the same group of hospitals that the three murderous children of Ram Prakash have built with sweat and 'blood'. It is making profits at an unprecedented rate.

Sagar is so overwhelmed by Soor that these days he can't wait for her calls. Today, after his suspension, he is more than eager to speak his heart out to her.

"Hey Sagar! So? Where are you?"-she calls him up just as he reaches home. "Suspended and separated."-he lies down on the bed.

"Where's auntie?"

"She left for Kochi. My cousin is arriving from the US. I had told you, right? ...my younger cousin whose parents passed away when he was a kid?"

"Yeah... Yeah... He was studying in the US, wasn't he?"

"Yes. He completed his management course from Michigan and is coming to Dweepa"

"Great! Is he an engineer?"

"No. He studied law. After practicing for five years he applied for Michigan. He is now looking for a job in India."-he changes sides on the pillow, leaning to his left.

"Um.. Hmm? What's his name?"

"Ayush."

Four days pass by. Ayush has arrived from Kochi to Sagar's home in Dweepa with his mother. He is so excited about the new island that he has been touring the entire place since three days.

Sagar's case is gaining heat thanks to the media. He has shifted his stay from his own house to the south of Dweepa near the Pungent Dungeon so that Ayush's job searching activities don't get disturbed.

This time the calls for the Center's intervention in pinning down Gharial have increased multifold. But the island government has been stubborn. "Please refrain from curbing the island government's powers."-NSF gives out a joint statement after an all India meeting with other NSF chief ministers. The NSF resorts to the tried and tested method of silencing the outcry- setting up of an enquiry team. "The team is looking into it. We will start taking action when the enquiry is complete."-the spokesperson in front of the Legislative Assembly building merges into the eternal void in his shiny white Ambassador, among the white-in-white politicians. He is confident that the enquiry will take another ten years. Probably by then either Gharial or Sagar or his own government might have vanished from the scene. Either one is fine.

Down in South Dweepa, a parallel development has put Sagar in deeper worry. Ayush is more interested in watching Game of Bones- a series that shows a lot of skin, than look for a job.

Sagar's mother tries her best to motivate him. But nothing seems to work out. She can't force him much as he can feel that she is discriminating him for not being her own son.

Sagar is elsewhere in his rented house. She leaves him a Shutapp message about Ayush's indifference. He simply deletes the message.

His case is due to be heard in Dweepa High court the next day. His lawyer is their family friend, his father's classmate in school. He has been consoling Sagar that there is nothing to worry. But Sagar knows. The ministers at the highest level in Dweepa are involved in throwing him out of Gharial's case... or rather from the department. They need Gharial. "But why? Can't they understand he is a threat for them too? He is such a criminal. He has killed one of their own partymen."-he stares at the blank wall, creating images of the slain CM candidate, the current CM, the cartoonist and Gharial.

"In politics, it is not parties that matter but partners."-he answers himself. "And the best partner for a politician is he, himself."

A sudden disturbance in the tranquility of his house shocks him! He runs straight to his garden. It is Jackpot, trying to scale in to his compound.

"Hey Jackpot!!"-Sagar is happy to see someone who makes him feel at ease. His dedication, sharp wit and more importantly the name-JACKPOT- makes Sagar hopeful about life; that there is a jackpot to be hit somewhere, sometime. Even the poorest of the poor, the weakest of the weak carry on with life holding on to the piece of log called hope in the flooded river of misery.

But at the moment, Jackpot is holding on to the compound in a strange position. His rest of the body is towards the inner side of the wall while his belly is amazingly compensating on the outer side. Sagar rushes at once. "Hey, wait on."-he yells as he goes out of the compound to push the belly inside. Jackpot is mentally preparing for the imminent fall by estimating the height, looking at the ground. Sagar tries to push him and suddenly remembers something. He goes back into the house and brings out a matress. He keeps it at Jackpot's projection on ground. He slowly tries retrieving Jackpot from the wall. It is futile. Sagar hops out to the outer side in a flash, much to the awe of a stranded Jackpot. He gently pushes his belly inside.

"No Sir, no!"

"Why? I've kept a matress under you. Don't worry."

"No Sir. My belly doesn't like it!"

"WHAT!!?"

"It has its own feelings. It really doesn't like being treated as a burden. It considers itself as the mark of Jackpot. I know it is a bit crazy to talk like that but it is a fact. If it is offended, I get stomach pain and suffer from indigestion, diarrhea..."

"Ok, ok. What do you want me to do now?"- Sagar retreats.

"Nothing!"

"And then?"

"Then nothing."

"Then how will you get down?"

"Shhh..."-Jackpot silences Sagar. "Come down, there is nothing to worry, just come down with me..."-he starts talking as though there is a child nearby. Sagar understands it after a few seconds. Jackpot's belly falls for the pampering and slowly starts slipping down with him. Sagar walks slowly to support Jackpot from below. The belly locks itself again!

"Sir, please move away!"

The belly reverts to the slipping act. Finally, he lands on the matress!

Sagar, for a moment, forgets all his worries and loses himself into an unstoppable smile.

"Hey Jackpot, you are supposed to be in Dweepa North aren't you?"- Sagar walks inside, holding Jackpot's injured shoulder.

"Sir..." Jackpot dusts his hat and wears it. "I've come here secretly to tell you something. I met a guy called Kunj Bihari Yadav. He says he has studied in YIT Dweepa and is currently unemployed. He and his friend want to help us catch Gharial!!"

"Now why are these guys so interested?"

"Sir, Kunj Bihari is unemployed. I don't know about the other guy. They had decided in their college days that they will pursue Entrepreneurship in social service. After hearing about Gharial's case, they have decided to open a detective agency. They don't have a license or training. They are completely out of the records and Sir... They have ideas!!"

"What idea?"-Sagar sits down unable to believe that Jackpot has fallen for the words of a couple of engineers. "Sir I knew you would ask me this. So I have brought Kunj Bihari Yadav with me!!"-Jackpot starts moving his index finger, in a way that indicates 'I knew this before'.

"WHAT!!?"-Sagar is shocked again. "How do you manage to shock me, Jackpot?"

"Sir..."-Jackpot blushes, taking it for a compliment. When things are ambiguous, it is better to take positively. "Sir, can I call him inside?"

"Call him now."-Sagar shows his despair. He thinks he could at least guide them to proper career than suck them in the dirty game.

"Hey, Bihari!!"-Jackpot claps and waves at someone outside. A few minutes later Sagar sees a man with pointed hair and different looks stand at his door. I have the power to change persons. I have changed Kunj from that Romeo looking for revenge for Pooja to a volunteer in fighting crime.

"Bihari, this is ACP Sagar."-Jackpot stares with eyes threatening to carry out the required formalities. Kunj bends down with right hand in front of the chest, positioned in a half-Namaste and the left hand folded to his back. Sagar doesn't like it.

Jackpot understands Sagar's feeling and immediately switches over- "Tell him about the clue you gave me."

He tries to make Sagar eager. Sagar looks at Jackpot and turns to Kunj. "Sir, myself Kunj Bihari Yadav. My friend and I were classmates in YIT Dweepa. We studied well but could not get placed due to recession. He, however, was on the bench in a software company and eventually got a project. But I am still jobless. In order to start a detective agency, we are trying to find some cases. Gharial case is very interesting, Sir... So..."

"What is your idea?"-Sagar cuts Kunj's words. He is curious. The ACP in him still has the urge to perform his duties. It doesn't matter even with a couple of foolish men. "They could be double agents too. Someone sent from Gharial and his NSF gang. But there is no harm in testing the waters."

"Sir, we can establish Gharial's identity. We have his trousers. He had strangled Asrar Sir with it, right?"

"His trousers have been checked. There is no clue. We cannot determine fingerprints on cloth and there is no hair on it either."-Sagar shows reluctance although he is mildly interested in Kunj's words.

"Sir, yesterday... When I was returning from the urinal to the sink, I noticed drops of my urine on my fingers."

Sagar waits on.

"I pulled up my trouser zip back and washed my hands at the sink."-Kunj's words fall on Sagar's ears like first drops of rain on drought-hit soil!

"So..." Kunj's face turns serious. Sagar's too is serious. Jackpot's? No, not really. Sagar gets up slowly and waits for a moment before patting Kunj.

"So... Gharial's trouser zip might also have traces of urine. And we can extract his DNA!!"-Sagar completes the rest.

"But there is a problem."-Kunj adds. "Sir, you're suspended as of now. And as far as I know, you're on their radar. So it is better that my friend takes care of the field."

"I'm on their radar. Who are they?"-Sagar is curious to know. "Sir, it is an open secret for anyone with some common sense that people at very high levels are involved in getting you trapped. Gharial is not alone!"

"How can you say that? And what will they get by supporting him? What is the 'high levels' you are talking about?"

Kunj is calm- "Sir the ruling party, opposition party and don't know who else... But they are all involved. Gharial cannot escape the authorities otherwise. What they get... well, Gharial will reveal once he is caught!"

Sagar admires his temperament and intense thinking. "How old are you Kunj?"

"Almost your age Sir... One or two years older or younger."-Kunj smiles, looks at Jackpot. "You and your friend are in!"

"What is your friend's name? Why didn't he accompany you?"

"Sir, he is a bit umm... strange... He does not know social etiquette.

He is good at solving problems though."

"Your mission starts. The program is initiated, Kunj."-Jackpot pats him.

"Thank you for inciting this pogrom."-Kunj deeply thanks Sagar. "What are you talking?"-Sagar looks at him and Jackpot. "Sir, Kunj is attending Spoken English classes. He is from Bihar. So, understandably..."

"But till now his words were quite fine."-Sagar is astonished. "Sir, his English goes for a toss when he gets too emotional. Not all the time!"

"Amazing!! So what is the plan?"-Sagar turns to Kunj and Jackpot. There is silence. Sagar folds his hands in front of his nose and alternates his sight between Jackpot and Kunj.

"We find Gharial's trousers. We were carrying it to the prison from Gold Street when his men attacked us. After that, the Gold Street Police took it into their custody and carried out Forensic tests for namesake. If I'm right they might have burnt it by now."

"Might or might not!"-Kunj opines. Sagar nods, approving of his thought. "Yes, might or might not. But how do you say 'might not'? What reason would they have to retain a potential proof?"

"See, the Gold Street Police might have got info from the ministry to destroy any proof against Gharial. But if they are least sensible, they'll retain harmless evidence. Such as the trousers... For the public and the media. If a time comes when their sincerity is challenged, they will show these things as proof that some work has been done. If all the things are destroyed, they will end up in trouble."-Kunj answers.

"It is decided then. Jackpot, you're the best man for this job."

Jackpot has a strange fate. It makes him sad every time Sagar compliments him. The moment he heard 'best man' Jackpot felt sad about Shyamala again. It was Valentine day celebration and all the participants in the Wing B of the Police Township had assembled for the best couple fancy dress contest. Shyamala and Purushottam had dressed as a wedding couple in Christian attire. They were declared the winners. At the photo event, the photographer had made Jackpot stand next to Purushottam as the 'best man'. Purushottam had passed a painful comment-"Don't worry. If there was a Best Man contest, you would have been first!"

"What happened?"-Kunj shakes his shoulder.

"I'll get the trousers. But Kunj, you have to keep a watch at the station storage area. They might have stored it there."

"No, no, no. I am a background supporter. Ayodhya will be there with you. He is very sharp."

"Ayodhya? We would like to meet him sometime."-Sagar suggests. "I did call him but he insists that we must never meet three kinds of people until it is really needed."

"Which kinds?"-Jackpot is upset.

"Lawyer, doctor and... police."

"Oh yeah? But he is ready to meet criminals? Are they so dear to him?"-Jackpot raises his voice. "Sir, you know what? We think alike. I asked him the same question."

Jackpot shrugs at Bihari. "How can a Bihari...?"-he doesn't say it.

"What was his answer?"-Sagar is calm yet it reminds him of someone. "He asked me not to speak so lowly of criminals. They are the reason police earn their salaries! And sometimes medals!"

"Sometimes posthumously. Tell him the next time you meet him."-Sagar smiles.

Two days pass by. The night of action, chosen nicely by Jackpot, arrives. A jacketed Jackpot walks like a scheming jackal up to the station and waits like jockey ready to race at the sound of the pistol, to jack up Sagar's efforts.

The policemen are relieved that Gharial's case has settled down the records without a sound. They are having a cake-cutting ceremony in the station. "Hey who is there to take care outside?"-the sub-inspector asks casually amidst smiles. "Sir nobody will loot the station if nobody is there for a minute."-the one supposed to be outside, responds. The sub-inspector, almost cutting the cake, pauses- "Nobody will loot even if the gate is left unguarded permanently. This is my station!"

"An empty station!"-the man replies. "Hey, cut the cake quickly. I can't stand it."-another policeman is desperate. Jackpot has stealthily moved in to the station. He slowly keeps a box of large bottles under the table, next to the packs of Chicken Biryani and pinches one pack for himself!

About half-an-hour later, one of them bends down the table and tries retrieving the Biryani packs. He is shocked to see the bottles!

"Who is that great man who got us these?"-he raises two of them, one in each hand. Jackpot is overwhelmed with pride that he wants to answer him. But he is bound. No, it is not duty consciousness. The leg piece!

The sub-inspector is amazed- "I never knew I have so many secret admirers! Who is it?"

There is no answer. "Sir, did Full 2 Caterers send it along with Biryani? They always seek to impress their customers by sending extra items."

"Don't worry. We have not asked them liquor. It is not there in our order. So enjoy it and forget about the money. Some people need to drink to remain sober."-the sub-inspector replies.

"Open the bottles!!!"

The celebration begins. Jackpot scurries in to the stores. He finds Gharial's trousers kept as a waste cloth under the water dispenser to wipe the wet floor. He tries to make his escape through the backyard in the darkness. He stumbles across a pipe and yells mildly. A constable who has come to dispose the empty bottles, spots him.

"Hey, who are you? STOPPP!!!"

Jackpot realizes that there is no hope hiding. He dashes to the front gate!!

The response by the rest of the personnel is late, slow. But the number is overwhelming for Jackpot. They run across, cutting in to his path. Jackpot seems to have been caught.

A savior leaps high above the compound!!

It is Ayodhya!!

His face is wrapped in handkerchief, eyes are shielded by sunglasses, head is covered with a cap and a jacket adorns his shoulders.

He swirls about his right toe again and again, kicking the jaws of each one of the policemen. He gauges the right distance to spin from and height he has to raise his extended foot to reach their jaws. The spinning and kicking continues in quick succession. Within a few minutes the station bears a deserted look except for a couple of stray dogs disturbed by the noise and a few scattered, unconscious men.

The next morning, Sagar's residence has a wondering Kunj and a thunderstruck Jackpot!!

"What was that thing that destroyed six men in a matter of seconds?"-Jackpot asks Kunj. "It was my friend Ayodhya."

"I want to meet him."-this time Jackpot requests.

Sagar too is in disbelief at Jackpot's description. "Sir, he refused to meet anyone, stating that it jeopardizes his..."

"No, Kunj. We will not try to meet him. His thoughts are correct."-Sagar backs Kunj.

Late in the previous night when Jackpot had brought the trousers, Sagar had already approached Abhilash, the forensic expert in the HQ, unofficially, for the DNA traces on the zip and Gharial's identity through official records.

Years ago, amidst much furor and controversy, the Chaadar Card Scheme was passed. It was a protective blanket scheme covering all details of a person and his family members, the details including the retina, fingerprints and DNA.

Abhilash has compiled the report. As it is a high profile case, Sagar had requested Jackpot to collect it personally to not leave any clue. Jackpot has brought it.

It lies on the table. The DNA report, the identity report.

Kunj opens the packet slowly and reads out the details of Gharial!!

Well, the report does not give Gharial's background but certainly points out at his address. Jackpot has just risked his career for the trousers. Sagar does not want to send him again. He turns to Kunj. Kunj nods affirmatively.

The moment I have always been waiting for has finally arrived.

It is Ayodhya's turn!!

14 SIMMERING HOPE, LOOMING THREAT

Sagar has continued to stay away from home. The search for Ayush's job is getting tougher and tougher. Sagar receives calls from his mother almost every day about it. Of late, he has started to feel depressed. But there is a ray of hope!

Ayodhya's efforts to track Gharial have begun and... Ayush has taken up Sagar's defence at the court. He is doing a splendid job.

It is late evening. Ayodhya stands at the stairs of his flat, while almost everyone is flat after dinner. He spots a few girls getting down the stairs, looking at him. A cooker from a mysterious kitchen whistles in vain.

"We devour with our eyes."-the girls seem to convey. They are heading for a night club for the weekend, wearing glittering new clothing designed to optimum. Most boys would not recognize them, if, the very next moment, the boys were shown passport sized photographs of the faces of the very girls.

Ayodhya, though, thinks about the sudden decision he has taken to help nab a criminal although he still hates the term 'social service'. It is not a decision taken in haste or under emotional impulsion. He had spoken to his grandfather about it before Kunj's meeting with Sagar.

"Appu, don't vie to avenge Asrar's death but continue his work. We know it is never too early to make a beginning. But we fail to notice that it is never too late to leave a legacy either."

"Asrar could not complete the task. But he is not too late for it. He left you behind. If you were just my grandson, I would have stopped you. But you said he thought you as a son. Go ahead."

There was a pause. "... and cover your face... every time you venture out into the shadow of apathy. To show your true self, it is best to be anonymous."

Ayodhya was overwhelmed. He had already been practicing the habit of covering his face right from college. Genes they were that were responsible. "Grandpa, ACP Sagar has given me a gun... for protection."- he had brought out a new matter.

There was a long silence.

The grandpa had started after a puff of uneasy breath- "No, Appu. Don't keep it. It all starts with one bad reason... such as the one you're giving now. If you don't keep a weapon, if you don't have an offensive with you, you'll try your best to escape a confrontation. Most people keep weapons stating self-protection. But they will never know that the cognizance of it secretly attracts them to a confrontation. It is human tendency to use resources that are available. The evolution of species has brought in this tendency. Unused things get vestigial. The nervous system of every species hence prompts them to use their resources at the slightest opportunity. Humans are no exception."

"If you believe in Asrar's training, if you trust his competence; return the gun to the ACP."

Ayodhya had gripped it tighter- "You know they were a part of my childhood. And I don't mean Diwali."

"I know how much you love them."

"...and Appu, one more thing. Save money for yourself. If you spend on what you want, you can't spend on what you need."

Ayodhya had thrown a piece of bread at the dog on the street, walking down the road, not heeding much to his grandpa's words. He had seen the dog promptly take it away and bury it in sand!

"Sss.. Sss.. me"-one among the girls walking down, disturbs his thoughts. He looks on figuring out who hissed and why.

"Sss the time?"-the girl to the extreme right, asks. "Ten"-he replies, looking at her wrinkled clothes and neatly ironed long hair. They walk away, looking at him. Ever since Anca has spoken to him, the attitude of his colleagues has changed. He remembers these girls who made fun of him when he first entered the office. The trademark hiss... Tonight, they had a question in their eyes. "How did you end up with Anca?"

He stands at the stairs, planning out the next course of action to trace Gharial. The address is there on the paper. Gharial's home is in mainland India. Gharial's original name too, is available in the Chaadar Card details. How and when to strike is all he has to decide on.

"The time is ten."-he suddenly thinks about Tintu. There is no wind yet, of Tintu, who usually meets him after dinner. And Ayodhya is surprised that Tintu has been strangely avoiding him since a week now. He walks slowly to get back to his room when Tintu appears before him suddenly. Ayodhya smiles. Tintu doesn't respond. Ayodhya doesn't care.

"When I walk away like that, people generally ask me if I'm all right. Hmm..."-Tintu turns around to point at the lapse in responsibility.

"Sorry, Tintu. I missed it. How are you? Is everything ok?"

"No, nothing is ok actually."-Tintu turns sideways, raising eyebrows and looking down, implying 'tell me, how can anything be ok if you behave this way' to Ayodhya.

"What happened?"

"Come to my room."-Tintu invites in a complaining tone that seemed less like an invitation and more like an order. Ayodhya follows him. Tintu opens the door to his flat. A sharp smell of sweaty clothes uniformly mixed with that of a room freshener, hits hard on Ayodhya's nose. His sight blinds for a moment.

"There is something rotting."

"Nothing, that's the room freshener. Some perfumes are worse than odor, hmmm..."

There are a lot of brochures and printed papers of various models of LED TVs.

"So, when are you buying?"-Ayodhya flashes a paper.

"For now I'm just searching... Anyway, see, these movie DVDs. You remember you took them to your room to watch?"

"Yeah, and I've returned to you."-Ayodhya points at them, signaling to Tintu that Tintu already has them.

"And why did you side with Vijith fans?"-Tintu questions with his trademark gesture of raising brows and looking down, adding more strength to his query.

"Who is Vijith?"

"This hero is Vijith"-he holds a DVD with a picture of an actor emerging from flames, bleeding at the leftmost corner of his forehead. "This one is Ajay"-a different actor is seen on the other DVD, saluting the fans.

"I am an Ajay fan. And I am against Vijith fans. Ajay is the best Malayali actor. He has original muscles. Vijith is a crappy hero. He is a burden to the Malayali film industry. But after watching the movies from my DVDs you said Vijith acts better than Ajay."

"Why at all do you keep Vijith DVDs?"

"To tell others how bad an actor he is!!"

"... Only Ajay is a true hero. And... and... Mallu Arjun of Kannada industry is also a true hero... But definitely not Vijith."

Ayodhya does not oppose. "I'm sorry."

"Not only that."-he dances his head. It looks like a swaying cauliflower. He seems to ask Ayodhya as to why he is apologizing so soon. There is more to complain.

"You also gave wrong review for Tamil heroes too."-he holds out a different set of DVDs this time. On one, a bottom angle view shows an actor holding the ends of his spread lungi to tie them up and get ready for a fight while on the other, a different actor is trying to woo the lead lady quarter his age and half his size.

"This is Mammolal. Awesome hero. You said he acts badly. And this is Mohanty. Very bad actor."-he squeezes his face.

"And you have kept the Mohanty DVD to tell others how bad he too is?"

"Yes."-Tintu asks with his expressions as what is wrong in it.

"Sorry, I am a bad reviewer. Is that why you avoided me for a week now?"

Tintu nods confidently. "This is the only judgment you have made correctly."-he conveys with his body language.

Ayodhya shakes his head and walks towards Tintu's restroom.

"Why don't you flush your commode?"-he comes out.

"I've heard that Dengue mosquitoes thrive in clean water."-Tintu answers.

"You could just flush and keep the lid closed."

Tintu blinks. "Oh! I had forgotten about the lid."

"Tintu Sir..."-a boy, about eight, stands at his door. Tintu swiftly pays him a hundred rupees and takes a USB pen drive from his hand.

"Why are you so early?"-he asks, inserting the drive in his laptop. "I have to go home quickly today."-the boy replies. The pen drive takes time to get detected.

Tintu brings out a filthy towel. Ayodhya stands gazing in astonishment. He just doesn't understand what is happening around. "This is Ayodhya Sir, actually."-Tintu introduces him to the kid, showing his hand as though Ayodhya does not deserve a 'Sir' if not for his age... the boy's age.

The boy looks timidly at Ayodhya and stands scratching his left heel with his right toe, holding a chair.

"What's your name?"

"Sonu..."-he smiles cutely, exposing the window between his upper front teeth created by the shedding of two milk teeth.

"Which class?"

"First standard. Government school."-the boy raises his hand behind his shoulder, gesturing a 'yes, you are right; that same old, godforsaken one'.

Ayodhya turns to Tintu. "What's that? Why are you turning your parents' photo around and covering it with that filthy towel?"

"It is not filthy. It is clean. Hmm..."

He has the holy book too, wrapped in a filthy cloth and kept in the drawer. He copies the content into his hard disk and returns the pen drive to the boy. The boy hurries away unable to bear the strange odor. Ayodhya had many times felt that he should have asked Tintu about it. "Don't you bathe?"-he finally does.

"I do."-Tintu turns his eyes scornfully, indicating that Ayodhya's question is outright rejectable.

"But I never hear the splashing sound from your bathroom?"-Ayodhya involuntarily brings out the clues that support his doubt.

"I bathe, hmm... In the night. At two!"-Tintu closes the door and draws the window curtains to avoid people peeping in.

"Why at two?"

"Pch... My wish, actually."-he is irritated.

"Why are you making the room dark? Are you going to watch a movie?"

"Yes... The Dark Night."-he replies, eyes full of desire. "Oh, great! Why did you pay the boy?"

"For the movie..."-Tintu answers turning his face in his trademark 'why else'. "You should have just asked me. I had downloaded the movie long ago. I still have it."-Ayodhya wants Tintu to regret.

"You do?"-Tintu expresses a weird surprise. "Yes"-Ayodhya doesn't understand why he is so shocked about it.

"It is an epic movie by Nolan!"-Ayodhya credits the movie director. "No, no..."-Tintu hits his own forehead real hard!

"This is not Batman's Dark Knight. This is The Dark Night. N-I-G-H-T"-he smiles.

Ayodhya gets the meaning!!

The sequence of jumping to his feet to grab the USB drive, paying the boy instantly, copying the contents and quickly sending the boy away, the act of turning his parents' picture around, covering the holy book, closing the door and drawing the curtains...

"I'm leaving, Tintu. I am sorry for disturbing you..."-Ayodhya walks to the door, although a strange pull tries to draw him to the movie. He stands still at the door. Tintu feels glad, thinking that Ayodhya has changed his mind.

"You... You... made that small kid supply you the movie? What if that kid goes on to watch it at home? Have you ever thought about it? You may end up spoiling that poor boy."

"What are you talking actually? He approached me to buy these movies. Hmm... Twenty rupees for 2GB full."-Tintu slowly moves his palm twice, facing Ayodhya, to denote how much he has invested.

"That boy looks so innocent. I saw it in his eyes. You don't care for the child."-Ayodhya murmurs to himself. Tintu overhears it.

"How does he get these movies?"-Ayodhya is now louder.

"He works in a Cyber Café run by his neighbor who downloads them and sends the boy to supply and collect money. That boy is already spoilt! Hmmm..."

Ayodhya thinks deeply. A strange voice buttresses his feeling that gets stronger and stronger.

"Those eyes, Tintu... They screamed at me... asking me what we do with them... What they contain that everyone is so mad about them. I saw it in his eyes, Tintu... when you introduced me to him. His eyes were asking me- 'at least can you answer me?'"

"If you're not interested you may not watch. But you can't advise me actually. You want the movie-o?"

Ayodhya leaves. He sees Sonu play on the mosaic tiles of the ground floor, trying to hit pebbles, sliding the USB drive! He hasn't gone home.

Ayodhya enters his house and closes the door behind him. The cool breeze from the air conditioner soothes the heat. He walks to the table and picks up the laptop. He opens the file containing Gharial's details and slowly sits on the cushion chair.

Suddenly, alarm bells ring in his ears. His eyes, though, seem calm. His blood starts rushing madly through his body. He can feel the presence. "Someone is there in my room."-he understands. He slowly closes the laptop and the front door. His shaving kit is lying on the floor, with things scattered. He takes out his razor, mounts the blade on it and slowly proceeds to the kitchen. The kitchen, as usual, is teeming with cockroaches.

Ayodhya senses movement behind the refrigerator. "Is it Gharial?"-he thinks as he slowly moves towards it. There is some water lying spilled on the floor. He spots the reflection of a human figure waiting for him to make the first move!

He can't make out the features but there it is! A mysterious being, lying in wait.

Ayodhya turns his body sideward. The waiting game begins...

Ayodhya has raised the razor to slice open the neck the moment the intruder shows up. The intruder on the other hand, is waiting with incredible patience behind the refrigerator. None of the two is giving up. It looks as though a magician has cast a spell on both of them and has frozen them to eternity. The droplet of sweat on Ayodhya's neck follows the folded skin and trickles down his chest. His hand, though, is steady. Patience is not waiting. There is a reason the two have been given different names. Patience is waiting with focus. Focus, concentration... these are extremely rare. They are the ones that make a well endured wait fruitful.

Ayodhya focuses on the dark figure that is not showing even the slightest intention of giving in. His cell phone rings in the hall!

He just can't afford to hear it. His eyes seem to be in a pursuit to hole through the opacity of the refrigerator. His feet seem to have vowed not to move. His breathing is like sand escaping a clenched fist.

Two hours pass by.

He feels the uneasy urge to urinate. He has had too much water after dinner. He just doesn't care, nor does the figure.

Another hour goes.

The figure is rock solid. He can only see the end of its cloth moving in air. He waits... It waits... One side of his mind focuses on the task at hand while the other reminds him of that hot afternoon. He is playing a cricket match. A tough match... A really tough match...

His grandpa is watching him from the stands. Most of Ayodhya's team mates have succumbed to the pressure. They have got out trying to slog, unable to bear the conditions-quickies firing cannons, spinners delivering magic and fielders caving in with their dark shadows. The coach's shouting to rotate strike, the next batsman's already lost patience making him loiter around the boundary, the heat, the humidity, the pain in the feet, the hurtful words of the opponents and the ruthless, cadaveric look on the umpire's face. They have all succumbed to it.

Ayodhya is trying to survive the overs yet again. It is drinks time. His grandpa walks to him. "Great going, Appu. You have shown you are different. Don't mind the words of your coach. Hang on. Just hang on... Do you know about patience? It is no ordinary quality..."

He bends down and looks into his grandson's eyes through the depths of the helmet.

"Do you know what patience is? When your stomach feels like throwing up immediately because you're up to something continuously, when your limbs start showing signs of opposing what your mind is commanding them to do, when the copious sweat dancing on your forehead tempts you to wipe it off, when you ignite anger and bitter hatred for you in the minds of your companions, when you bear the constant mouthing of foul language being showered on you, when smiles appear on the faces of your opponents knowing that your own people are against you, if you still hold that tenacious grip on your actions and of others, if one small voice from within suppresses all the noise and clamor outside and one mind rules over thousand others to keep the light on, then that is called patience!!!"

It is two. There is no change in the position except that a mosquito has landed on Ayodhya's right arm, sucking life out of his skin. He waits on without moving a muscle.

There is sound of Tintu entering his bathroom. Ayodhya can hear it through the walls.

So Tintu seemed truthful when he said he took bath at two. But there is no sound of water flowing from the tap or shower. There is no splashing, no nothing. Just pristine silence and fifteen minutes... Tintu's bathroom door opens again with a shriek. And silence conquers again.

There is movement behind the refrigerator! Finally!! The figure has given in!!

Ayodhya is ready to take on.

"Aaahhh!!!"-it emerges with a loud cry!!!

It heads directly at him. He stands amazed! The razor drops!

It hugs him tight!!

It is Anca!

"Cockroach! There is a cockroach!!"-she points to the place she was hiding at.

"Wait Anca..."-he is still. He looks at the walls. The mosquito that had bitten him flies past the curtains. He closes the door to the kitchen. His eyes follow its path of flight. It teases him, coming low down and suddenly gaining height. He attempts thrice to squeeze it in his palm but all he has done is pump up some blood through his veins.

"Ayodhya, are you crazy? Leave it."-Anca gulps some water and stands absorbed in his crazy act.

"No, it sucked my blood, tested my patience..."-he finally lands his hand thunderously on the wall. The wall vibrates!

The mosquito is smashed. His blood that was sucked has made a patch on the neatly painted wall of the newly constructed apartment.

"Even I tested your patience, Ayodhya. What will you do to me?"

"It wasn't you!!"

"What made you find out there was someone?"-she sits on the couch.

"The aroma of your charisma."-he goes to the bathroom, latching the door behind him.

Anca stares perplexed.

As he landed on the chair with his laptop, he had felt a warm cushion in the air conditioned hall. He had immediately found out that someone was sitting on the chair.

A loud flush is heard.

"Won't you ask what I was doing here?"-she places her chin on his shoulder, hugging him from behind as he emerges. "No."-he switches off his laptop.

"You are so strange."

She walks around, scanning through things- "I came here to visit you. I've never been to your room, have I? Just thought of surprising you."

She pulls out his cricket kit lying in a mess. A pair of wicket keeping gloves catches her sight. She tries them on. Ayodhya is busy preparing his bed- accumulating things on the floor so that his body does not touch the floor when he sleeps. The things can be anything.

"You might have played many matches, haven't you? How many have you lost?"-she asks, dropping her head sideways to imply that it is a strange question.

"None."

"Don't bluff."-she nudges him by her shoulder. "You lose when you play to win. For me playing is winning. It is all about playing."

"That means you are not competitive. You're happy just to play."

"No. Being competitive is a part of playing. I just think that there is a bigger victory than winning the game. You win when you learn from your mistakes. You win when you introspect and evaluate even in a triumph. You win when you maintain a high morale even in an utter loss. You win when you accept the end result with your heart. And more importantly you win when you apply your learning in a sport to your real life. Because a sport is a life within a life... that you have created to know more about yourself..."

"How do you take dive catches? Can you teach me?"-she tosses a can of deodorant from the left hand and catches with her right, not really interested in his talk.

"Make a commitment that you are not going to drop it."-he starts brushing his teeth.

She removes the gloves and walks to him, admiring his routine. Her eyes fall on the sink. "Why do people buy brownish sink? We can't make out if it is dirty."

"Some people prefer that."-he replies calmly.

"Tomorrow is off anyway. I'll help you clean your room. When did you last do it?"

"Navratri!"-he replies with froth-filled mouth.

"Oh God!!"-she startles and runs away laughing loudly. "Ok fine. Get all the things tomorrow. Crapic, toilet brush, mop, broom, plate, dustbin and scrubber.

"What is a scrubber?"-he washes his mouth, letting out a jet of frothy water.

"How do you clean utensils?"-she asks surprised. "I use a handful of coconut fiber."

Her face squeezes more than the squeezed coconut fiber her eyes find at the sink half-dead by mutilation. "And how do you clean the sink?"

"Are they to be?"-he wipes his lips. His eyes drag him to sleep. He leaves for his bed.

The next day Ayodhya starts his travel to mainland India. The Sea Rail station of Dweepa to Minicoy is at the tip of Pungent Dungeon. Despite his team leader's instructions, he has decided not to work that weekend. "What do you mean? What is the mantra?"-his team leader had warned.

"Be sure of your objectives with respect to the project. Know your mantra."-the team leader had bent his thumb, forefinger and middle finger in front of Ayodhya's face and rotated them about his forearm to indicate a concise form of a circular imaginary object called 'mantra' that Ayodhya has to have in his mind.

"This project is going to be your baby, Ayodhya. Take good care of it."

"Consider it my Paternity Leave!"

The team leader had stuck to his stance- "I want the second milestone completion report first thing on Saturday."

Ayodhya had to rely on Anca. Anca was always helped by others. For the first time, she had to help. And she had accepted it.

Ayodhya is traveling to Kochi over the bridge. The ride is as smooth as the sliding of a bullet in the pocket of a well lubricated pistol. He walks to the door of the bogie to savor the touch of the ride. He hates the confinement of the second class AC compartment.

He opens the bogie door.

The magnificent view of the majestic sea on either side fills his lungs with newfound energy! The droplets of the moist winds kiss his face. The sea, though, roars in his ears warning him that he is passing through its territory without paying obeisance. The whistling train soothes him by reminding him that he is in its safe custody and there is no need for anxiety. The sea feels indignation. It roars louder!! The train taunts it with a shrill whistle. The sea roars again, almost rattling his eardrums. He stands firm at the foot board, undaunted!

The train to Gharial's address is on the next day from Kochi. Tintu should have booked the Akal ticket by now. Akal tickets are available only one day before the journey date and are fast exhausting ones. A train on a busy route is to be booked within the first few opening seconds after ten o'clock in the morning. Sometimes even after the payment is done, the website regrets the booking due to jammed services.

Tintu, though, is a master in Akal booking. He keeps the passenger details in the Master List. He logs in at 9:55 and keeps hovering around in the website to avoid auto-logout due to idling. At 9:59 sharp, he submits travel details and as soon as it loads, completes the payment in a master stroke!!

He has never failed in Akal booking and it is a record!! Hmmm...

Ayodhya, as of now, can barely make a phone call, let alone book an online ticket. All the hype about 5G network is not a thing in seas.

He reaches Kochi that very evening and calls up Tintu immediately.

"I am busy actually, hmmm."

"You mean you did not book the ticket?"

"I booked yours first. You did not get the message-o?"

Ayodhya notices a message from IRCTC lying unopened in his inbox. "Yeah, got it now. Thank you Tintu."

"One minute, one minute. Hello, hello... HELLO..."

"Yeah, I'm there. Calm down."

"I want to go on a toy train journey in Darjeeling when I visit Gangtok office next week. But I am clueless. That's the problem, actually."

"You'll get the toy train ride, don't worry. The Siliguri route is closed but high up in Darjeeling they still operate. Anything else?"

"But I want the ride on 26th of this month at morning seven O'clock. Hmmm."

"Ok, just check the timings once you go there."

"Pch... What is this you are talking actually? I don't want last minute rush. That's why I have opened IRCTC, actually."

"You mean you want to book a toy train ticket in IRCTC?"

"Hmmm..."

"I guess that's not possible."

"Are you sure-o?"

"Hmmm..."

"Hey man. Don't tease me like that. Are you sure-o?"

"Yup."

"That's the problem with IRCTC actually. Sea Rail is better. Hmmm."

Ayodhya shakes his head at the irony of life.

Anyway, returning to the booking of Ayodhya's ticket, when Tintu had submitted the payment, the page that was loading was facing an obstruction from incoming traffic from other bookers. But it was I who intervened on Ayodhya's behalf!

Yes, you got it right. I actually interfered in human world. I did that many times before and I will keep doing that. I have a name for not heeding to people's needs. Most of the time, I'll have it my way. But in some rare cases I'm forced to.

Ayodhya's is one of those cases. The reason this time, is simple-

Sometimes people make choices and I just go with them because they invest their soul into it. It is the only entity that is beyond my control. Do you know why? Because your soul is not you. I cannot control a thing in you that is not you. You're a mortal, your soul is eternal. If you do something at the command of your soul I'm helpless...

Ayodhya's soul craved for the ticket. He had his only chance. He is not rich enough to visit that distant land yet again. He lacks me. He definitely is not rich enough!

And how did I interfere?

Two thousand one hundred years ago, a squirrel was about to die of grave injuries inflicted upon by the tom cat in the nearby bushes. It was dragging its feet to the water. I hastened its death near the foothills. It decayed in a matter of days. The soil was enriched with its remains. The seeds of a large tree sailed to the place in the fast winds. All but one dried in the arid soil. The seed that had fallen on the nutrient soil at the squirrel's place of death found life. The seed grew into a large tree over the centuries. And then came, after many more centuries, the telecom revolution. Network towers were planted across India. The place where the tree stood was the ideal location for the Sodaphone tower but as it was a worshipped tree, the tower was located elsewhere.

Mr. Dholu, who was one of the contenders in booking Akal ticket was at such a location that the tower failed to catch his signal because it was yards away from the limit of the transmission waves. If it were at the tree's location, Tintu's record would have been broken for sure.

Tintu won by a slender opening.

Yes, it seems impossible. I wouldn't disagree. I am a force beyond you. I am the only one whom you have not been able to master. I slip away. And as I always say, it is all about the right moment and who could utilize it better?

Come humans, out of your confines and appreciate my prowess at interference.

Give me a chance. That is all I ask. When someone angers you, smile at them, give me a chance. When something does not go according to your need, stop making it worse, give me a chance. When you are not able to choose one thing over the other, stop thinking and give me a chance.

Give me a chance and I'll set things right. Believe me!

Ayodhya undertakes a tiring journey for two days and a night from Kochi to Gharial's house. The railway station exit is swarmed by the auto rickshaw and cab drivers. Ayodhya is successfully baited by one of them.

"This one"-Ayodhya shows him the address to Gharial's house. "Ok, two fifty rupees."-the driver displays his palm to convey to Ayodhya 'I am telling you right now. I won't listen to you later'.

"Ok"-Ayodhya has no clue about how things work there. All he cares is to get to the house.

The driver turns the fare meter on!!

"You just said 250..."

"This is to fool the traffic police that I'm following the mandatory meter rate. You just pay 250."-he zooms past a busy fish market and a shopping mall crammed with visitors. It stops at a signal.

"Hi darling!"-a manly voice is heard with a loud clap. Ayodhya turns startled!

No, it is not Gharial.

"How about giving ten rupees to Kajal baby? I will keep you forever in here."-a strange person moves the sari at the chest.

Ayodhya looks elsewhere. "Oh my Ranbir Kapoor, offering ten rupees will not make you any poorer. Why so grim? You want a kiss?"-

there are many of them, thronging his vehicle. The signal has turned green. The driver starts. "Hey, don't be so hasty."-one of them squeezes the driver's cheek and pushes it. "What are you going to do going home so early? I will be there, don't worry."

Ayodhya reluctantly hands over a ten rupee note. "Long live my hero."-the taker circles the note around his head and they all leave.

"Why did you give them, Sir?"-the driver looks at him through the circular mirror at the left. "This place is known for them."

"What do you mean?"

"Sir, this place is infamous for men dressing up as third gender and tormenting people for money by touching them here and there, squeezing their body parts and sometimes assaulting them. You will find them at every signal. By now they might have informed their comrades at the next signal about you... that you are a weak-hearted chicken and should not be missed."

"Why do they do that? Why don't they just work?"

"They are all fugitives. This is one way to be among the public and still be unseen. The Police do not harm them for any reasons. And they cannot catch a random person to check for gender."

The next signal arrives after a minute. "You see there? They are all men!!"

The men arrive staring at Ayodhya without beating an eyelid like a pack of hungry wolves prowling at a young deer from all directions. Ayodhya slowly pulls his cap over his head, ties his hankie across his face and wears his sunglasses.

"Hey cutie!"-one of them claps.

Ayodhya kicks him brutally on his chest. The man falls at the road divider. False breasts get dislodged!

"Say again?"

The man fails to even get up.

The rest of the men get enraged and pull Ayodhya out of the vehicle. Ayodhya falls on one of the bikes but gets back quickly. He bangs against his knee the head of the man who had pulled him out. He drags a third out to the zebra crossing and slaps on the cheek violently thrice in quick succession, holding the neck with his right hand. Three of them try to pin him down on the road. He wedges one of them over to the other side by pivoting against his waist on the ground. One man escapes!

The traffic policeman stands watching the actions in fear. Some people record the video but none interfere. It is India, you see. For a moment it all appears queer before it gets back to normal.

Ayodhya resumes his journey. He asks the driver to stop a few meters away and waits until the driver has left after accepting the money.

Gharial's house is empty as he had expected. It is a two storey mansion with a once-beautiful garden.

The door is locked and the lock is dusty. A few newspapers scattering here and there decorate the entrance. Ayodhya walks around the building a couple of times and of course is being observed!

Well, not by Gharial's men but the lady in the opposite house. She stands seemingly watering the basil plant in her verandah but her whole body is transformed into invisible eyes and Ayodhya can sense it. I sometimes feel she is the best person to keep vigil on the porous Lines of Control of the world.

Ayodhya wants to appear genuine. He walks to her casually. She is eager to talk to him but somehow manages to turn away with only her right ear in his direction.

"Excuse me, madam!"

She turns back immediately lest anyone else snatch away the chance. "What do you want?"-she climbs down the stairs and walks to him aggressively to check the transgressor at the gate and impress the neighboring ladies that under distress she does not get stressed but presses her way forward.

"I wanted to meet the person who stayed... um... stays in that mansion."-he speaks softly.

"That house? Well, there was a strange man staying there from the last five years. I don't know where he came from and where he left for. Come inside, I'll tell you everything."-she opens the latch.

Ayodhya walks in. This is his best chance. The greatest spy in the world can never give a better account.

"What will you have, son?"-she grins.

"A glass of water please."-he is surprised that some ladies risk their safety for gossip, by letting strangers in.

She goes into the kitchen. "That man never spoke to anyone. He was always holed up in his room on the first floor, scribbling things on paper. I could see that from my window even though there was a mosquito mesh in his window!"

"Where did he work?"

Her answer shakes the ground beneath his feet!!

"He was a writer!"

"Writer? How do know that?"

"As I told you, he never spoke to anyone. He used to sit scribbling things. And occasionally venture out. I have also seen the postman bringing him some letters. He used to rush at once to receive them. They were from publishing houses and agents. I had enquired about it with the postman once."

Ayodhya turns to get back to his house and collect those letters. "Who has got the keys to his house?"

"His back door was always open."

"Thank you, madam."-Ayodhya gets up to leave. "What's the hurry, son?"

"I have booked my return ticket in the evening."

"By the way, where do you come from?"

"Dweepa."

"Why do you want to meet him?"

"He is my business partner."

"Oh, is it so? It is so cute of you that you have started business at this young age. If you have any money to be handed over to him you may leave it here, I'll hand it to him over when he returns. We too are a business family. We have garment business."-she wipes her palm against her night gown.

"If we don't mind our own business, we lose it."

"Lose what? Mind?"

Ayodhya walks to the house, collects the letters from the box and enters the house through the back door. The kitchen stinks badly. He walks straight to the room on the first floor. He is amazed by the sight inside!

Heaps of papers lie on the floor. But what shakes him is that a few gharials are looking on at him!

Ayodhya backs off for a second. "How the hell have they been surviving on their own in an empty house?"

He knows very well that the gharial species are masters of deceit. They lay in wait like corpses and any unwitting move by the prey ignoring them, meets a certain death. Ayodhya picks up a bamboo staff and moves it around the head of a smaller gharial. The animal does not respond. He knows their ways. They are the best actors for dead. He pokes it in its eye. There is no reaction yet. He brings it down heavily on its tail. There is no movement. He flips it over with a lot of energy. The gharial stays in an inclined position, resting on the sides of its legs. Ayodhya is slowly getting convinced that it is dead. But gharials just don't give up until the most opportune moment. I sometimes feel they are next only to me to seize opportunity!

Ayodhya walks to the kitchen and searches frantically for something, kicking things around. There! He finds a can of kerosene. And a match box is right next to the stove. He pockets the box, fills up a bucket of water and carries the can and the bucket to the room on the first floor. The gharials still lie as they were when he had left.

He sprinkles kerosene on their skin and throws a lit match stick on them. They start burning instantly!

He is now convinced that they are actually dead!!

He pours water and puts off the fire. The smoke and the stench combine to form an aroma!

He slowly lifts the smallest one. They are the rarest species of crocodiles and are highly endangered. But in Gharial's house they are aplenty.

He observes them one by one. They are all stuffed with some materials inside their bodies.

Taxidermy it is!!

Gharial has a taste for taxidermy-the art of stuffing carcass to make them look alive. Ayodhya gathers some of the papers lying on the floor. They are a part of chapters of a novel. He collects them all, glances over them one by one and segregates them based on his best judgment.

He opens the envelopes of the letters. They are indeed from various publishers and literary agents. Ayodhya finds Gharial's email address in the letters. He wants Kunj to get in touch with Jackpot and get it hacked. He takes out his phone and explains everything.

Jackpot asks for a couple of minutes to get in touch with Abhilash and hack the account. Ayodhya goes through Gharial's chapters. They look interesting. The letters... They are replies of rejection from the publishers who do not want to publish his novel and agents who do not want to represent. A total of 122 rejections.

He gets Gharial's email account password through Shutapp. He wastes no time in logging in. The account loads...

The day is getting over. There is no electricity as the supply has been cut off due to non-payment of bills. Mosquitoes are creating a lot of havoc. He lights his torch and places it away. He knows. Mosquitoes are attracted by light. There is some respite now.

The account is finally open. Gharial has not accessed it since years. Unread mails in bold letters have filled his inbox and there is not even a single personal mail in it. Same is the case in his sent mails. There are only mail communications between him and various publishing houses and agencies.

In some, his tone is the one of pleading. In some, he has abused them knowing that they are not going to heed anymore. For example, check this out-

You dumb***, you don't think twice to publish Kanaka Sundari's shit on 'WARDROBE MALFUNCTION' while reject a masterpiece written by an unsolicited writer like me!!

There is no reply to that abuse anyway. Ayodhya looks at his watch. It is eight. He has to leave now. The one thing he could not trace is Gharial's link with the top politicians of Dweepa. "How does he know them? Why is he being patronized even when he has killed a CM candidate? What is his background? Where did he stay before he moved to this house?"

The house has no further answers. His return starts in some time. He has to hurry.

As he sits by the window in the cruising city-bus, he notices a strange phenomenon happening by the riverside. A lot of motorbikes in all their splendor and glamour wait in passion all along the road dotting the river bank, for their owners to return. There are people dotting the far away river bank sitting around with what appears to be bottles. They are waving their hands to bid happy journey to the passengers in the bus. Ayodhya feels that they are probably drinking. But why are they sitting away from one another?

"Their owners are not in a state to attend to their bikes."-an old man notices a puzzled Ayodhya.

"Oh, are they... high?"

The old man nods away – "No, they are defecating."

Ayodhya is shocked!! He looks again at the bikes that seem to be waiting like avengers of the owners who have been pulled away by thunderbirds.

"But those people seem to be quite well-to-do to afford toilets...?"-Ayodhya brings out his confusion.

"Well, yes. But they cannot succeed within the confines of four walls. They love freedom. They shit in the lap of nature."

A few minutes later, Ayodhya reaches the railway station. The train is delayed by an hour. A beggar comes to him on a wooden slab fitted with small wheels. He is squatting on the slab and pushing against the ground with his hands to move ahead. His legs seem to have been incapacitated. He begs with both hands. Ayodhya ignores him. He moves ahead. "Samosa... Hot Samosa... One for ten rupees, samosa."-a vendor passes by. Nobody seems to buy. Ayodhya starts walking around. A while later he notices the samosa vendor quarreling with the beggar for money. He feels sorry for the beggar. He feels like intervening for him. The beggar struggles to keep grip on the currency notes he is holding. The vendor is trying to snatch it with all his might. The vendor can stand and it has an unfair advantage. He kicks the beggar repeatedly on the arm while the beggar holds it to his chest.

Ayodhya starts towards the beggar, while, at the same time, keeping an eye on the belongings. But before he could do anything, he is cruelly surprised!

The beggar stands up, kicks the vendor and runs away with an unmatchable speed.

The vendor gives up. His basket of samosas is dearer. He destroys the beggar's wooden slab instead!

He is joined by his friend. Ayodhya walks closer to listen to the conversation.

"Leave him... He is gone..."-his friend pacifies.

"Slimy rat!! I'll see how you will go for your rounds now!"-he is enraged.

"That mongrel earns more than us."-he doesn't stop.

"Leave him. There is no use feeling jealous. Even you could have learnt yoga!"

"I don't want sinful money. I don't want to cheat."

"Look who is talking!"-his friend lifts the basket on his head. "What rate did you call today?"

The vendor is still fuming, looking in the direction the beggar had vanished. "I'm asking you!"

"Huh? One for ten rupees."-he turns.

"Ok, meet me at Menaka Bar at twelve. Samosas... Hot samosas... Two for fifteen!"

"Five years in this place is enough to make one a dangerous cheat."-Ayodhya leaves. His journey to Kochi begins. He starts reading the manuscript written by Gharial on sheets of papers. He finds it quite engrossing. "Ice cream, tasty ice cream..."-a vendor walks past his berth. Ayodhya is suddenly brought out of the story. He tries clicking a space bar to stop the VLC player from running the story and to buy ice cream.

He gets two cups of it and gets back to reading. A footnote written by Gharial catches his attention-

When you are distracted while reading a novel and you feel like clicking an imaginary space bar, take it for granted that the novel is a masterpiece.

"And sure it is."

"Look at the hypocrisy. Last week our actress Kanaka Sundari accepted on a talk show that her boldness in appearance and filthiness in words were setting a wrong example to the younger generation and she promised to behave responsibly. Yesterday, this is how she appeared to the media interaction and these were her words."-an elderly man holds the newspaper to Ayodhya. Ayodhya is not bothered. He gets back with the book.

"You can't miss it!!"

Ayodhya gets angry at the man. "Why is he disturbing me?"

But the man is silent, his head buried deep in the paper. "You can't miss it!!"-the voice gets bolder. Ayodhya's pulse shoots up. He holds his temple and closes his eyes.

"You want some water, son?"-the man's voice interferes with the strange one.

"You can't miss it!!"

"Are you alright?"

"You can't miss it!!"

"I suggest you take a pain killer."

"You can't miss it!!"

"GIVE ME THAT NEWSPAPER, FOR GOD'S SAKE!!"

"Here!"

'Kanaka Sundari, with her bewitching beauty, is sure an asset to Khaaliwood- the director opined. Her next movie is going to be released this Friday under BIG BANNER productions. Not only that... Reports have started to pour in that the sun tan beauty is going to launch her long awaited book- WARDROBE MALFUNCTION. It has been rated as the top reference for upcoming models as a confidence booster!'

Ayodhya sinks!!

"This is a chance Gharial is not going to miss. It is a sure threat!"

15 ... COMES AROUND

Ayodhya is back in office and Anca has done his work. The rest of the colleagues are awed. How on earth is it possible that Anca, the queen that she is, has been made to work by Ayodhya? Oh, so cruel of him.

"Hi, Ayodhya, seems like you had gone to meet a distant relative in mainland... Who is he?"

"My cousin... Thank you for your help. I could now show it to TL."

"Hey, come on! You need to repay! How about dining with me this weekend?"

"Sure."

Ayodhya could see others burn within. He settles down. "Hey Ayodhya, check this out."-Anca has opened a BlueTube video on her cell phone. "It is a man beating up three others at a signal at the same place you had gone to... and at the same day and time. Did you witness it?"

Ayodhya sees his video. He is beating up with face covered. It has been recorded and uploaded by a motorcyclist.

The comment section is full of praises for him. "No, I didn't see it."

He turns back. "If it is on air, then Gharial too might have watched it. Or would be watching it soon. He can't just ignore something like that in his own hometown. And definitely there are similarities between my moves and Asrar's."-he thinks.

"Then should I attack him before he gets alert or should I wait? Should I attack before he gets to Kanaka Sundari? How will I gain entry among celebrities? He has good contacts among politicians. He can make it. This dilemma is similar to the one I keep facing all the time. As a keeper, should I stay close to the stumps for stumping or stay a bit behind for the edges? Kunj has to talk to Jackpot about it. No, not the keeper thing."

A few days later Kunj and Jackpot meet up at the restaurant and Kunj explains to him everything that Ayodhya has uncovered. "So she is releasing her book this Friday after judging the Miss India contest."-Kunj speaks fluent English.

"You are speaking well for a Bihari. Good! Which classes do you attend?"

"Please don't remind me. I speak wrong only when I become conscious of it."

"Well, leave it. Hey, you know what? Sagar Sir is going to be restored as ACP again! In a few days... His cousin Ayush has been amazing in his preparations and defence at court. But one thing is for sure. Whether he is an ACP or a common man, he has no ego. He is such an amazing simple man... What say?"

"Yeah, you're right. He's such an amusing simpleton."

"Oh, not again."

"See, I have a plan. My friend goes inside the hall and stays near the ramp. Kanaka Sundari is the judge. So she will be sitting close to it. You and Sagar stay outside. If I fail to nab him inside, I'll splash red ink on his body. You may nab him when he comes out"

"The plan is ok. But why should your friend be at the ramp? I can be too. I know how much you wish to see the models walk nearby."

"See, Jackpot..."

"Sir..."

"Ok, Jackpot Sir... It has its own pros and cons. He'll be directly in the line of action and will be vulnerable. If it is ok for you, even you can..."

"I was just kidding."-Jackpot receives the Rs. 60/- bill and his glass of juice from the waitress. He takes out a 100 rupee note to keep in the booklet.

"I'll pay, don't worry."-Kunj takes the booklet and the note from Jackpot's hand.

He hands over the note to the waitress, keeping in the booklet. "That is my money. You said you'll pay."-Jackpot gets confused. "And so did I."-Kunj smiles.

"What else can a Bihari do than that?"-Jackpot mumbles.

"Excuse me, madam!"-Kunj calls her. She turns.

"Keep the change."

She smiles.

"Much more!"-Kunj whispers to Jackpot. Jackpot gets irritated. He leaves his juice untouched and walks away in anger. Kunj promptly lifts Jackpot's glass of juice. Jackpot waits on his motorcycle for Kunj, still upset. Kunj finishes it and shows the empty glass to Jackpot. He now puts water and shakes well before drinking it again.

Jackpot starts off his bike and leaves without Kunj. Kunj gets up slowly, grabs a handful of mouthfreshener at the cashier and exits the restaurant. He walks some distance in the same direction as Jackpot and manages to sit on the bike at the signal!

"Why don't you buy a bike?"-Jackpot is upset with his futile attempt to leave Kunj back.

"I don't know how to ride bikes."

"Oh I get it. Biharis only know how to ride a bicycle!!"-he consoles himself.

"Short people should burn calories. They look very obese otherwise."-Kunj passes a comment looking at a short woman on the roadside. But he indirectly wants to mock Jackpot.

"And tall people should clean their nostrils."-Jackpot hits back.

It is evening. Ayodhya has prepared a sweet dish made of pure ghee, studded with cashew nuts and dried grapes. He has opened the BlueTube video of his thrashing of the men at signal.

Tintu barges in.

"Do you know about the latest resolution in LED TVs these days actually? I am planning to buy the most advanced. Hmmm."

"No."

"Your flat owner was here, actually."-he spills the biggest secret with protruded lips and popping eyeballs in broadened eyes.

"He went inside and saw the mess you have made of his flat. He was shouting that he will expel you, actually!!"

Ayodhya hardly cared about housekeeping. And after getting into the Gharial business, he gave up even thinking about it. Thinking doesn't make a difference anyway.

"He didn't enter the flat. He might have peeped in through the window."

"Yeah, you are right actually. I wanted to scare you, nothing more. Hmmm."-Tintu smiles sheepishly.

"But man, how did you say that correctly actually?"

"If he had entered the house, he would have fainted at the stench!"

"Ha ha ha... That is why Gosain of Crapic Ad does not enter a bachelor's house... But yours is cleaner than mine, actually!"

"...but tomorrow he will come. I heard him talk over phone!! Hmmm..."

"Who? Gosain?"

"The owner!!!"

"Oh no!"

"Tintu, your maid servant! Ask her to clean my flat too! I'll pay her the same amount as you do."

Tintu gets into deep thought. Ayodhya makes it out observing Tintu's forefinger plunge into the infinite depths of his nostrils and dig out a healthy mass of mucus at the bent tip of his finger. He can see Tintu's shrunk eyes running a complex program of pros and cons. Tintu's rolling of the thumb against the mass on his forefinger indicates that it is still under progress.

It loads and loads, rolls and rolls before the thumb resorts to detaching the ball of mucus which is then dropped on the floor. Before you judge me, humans, these actions seem gross only when others do it.

A second attempt into the nostrils brings out yet another mass. Tintu's eyes shrink further. The ball gets finer and finer into a crystal.

Ayodhya waits on...

Tintu finally nods in the affirmative and leaves. Ayodhya too returns relieved. On the floor the sizes of the fine crystal lying next to the bigger ball are of the same ratio as those of the earth and the moon.

Ayodhya reopens the BlueTube video.

Viewers have hailed his as a superhero. But as he scrolls down the comments, the tone is of confusion, query and at the end... of caution!

There is a comment many others are unable to make out. The person has a random username 'G'. His comment reads- "If you try to help those who are compelled not to avail it, you would be compelling yourself to be helpless."

Ayodhya immediately makes out!

It is Gharial!!!

He has given a veiled warning to Ayodhya by observing the fight similarities between him and Asrar, as expected.

Ayodhya recalls his grandpa's words on one of those childhood days when he had come to see Ayodhya play. Ayodhya had helped his teammate get his hundred while sacrificing his own because on a previous occasion his friend had sacrificed his wicket for him.

"I don't know why I am so happy today, grandpa..."

"To be happy you should remember the help others do unto you and forget those you do unto others because while the former action motivates you to help others the latter saves you from expectations-just or unjust."

He sits back, thinking deeply.

Finally, he contacts Abhilash through Kunj and Jackpot and posts an untraceable reply- "Then help yourself!"

The next day, he is woken up by bangs on the door at six.

"Thud... Thud... Thud..."

The things in his head wobble due to the sudden jerk. They are not prepared.

"Coming."-he falters and hits the end of the chair as he walks with sleepy eyes.

It is the maid servant. He allows her in, cursing the owner. She looks at the mess and starts at once. As she brooms, she finds a dead lizard right under his 'bed'.

"Oh, so that was the root of all stench!!"-he understands.

She walks back, exhausting her enthusiasm- "Sir, I'll clean up Tintu Sir's room first. Yours will take a lot of time!"

"Ok."-he feels overjoyed!

"And Sir, today's charges are double!"

It is evening.

Ayodhya has got an additional latch fixed to his flat door. He calls Tintu.

"Tintu... Could you do me a favor? When I return in the night, I want you to lock this door with this padlock and keep the key with you."

"Hey man, are you nuts or what? You will be inside and I lock it from outside-o?"

"Yes. I can't bear the disturbance the maid causes every morning. I want good sleep. I want her to clean my room after she is done with the others."

"She comes very late, actually. At six in the morning. Hmmm"

"Don't argue Tintu, please help."-he offers the padlock fitted with key. Tintu accepts it.

He goes back. The TV shows breaking news!

"Today was a day of relief and joy for Sagar. Or should I call ACP Sagar! You can see him coming from the court. The citizens of Dweepa are jubilant! You can see behind him, his cousin Ayush who has successfully defended him in the temple of justice. With cameraman Yami, I'm Swami, NOT NOW... No, with cameraman Swami, I'm Yami, NOT NOW."

There is a video of Sagar's receiving the order from a superior officer. His face shows a relieved smile. But deep down, his woes continue. Ayush has won him the case. Yes, the same cousin he had disliked. He has been too casual with his job search.

Ayush is Sagar's paternal cousin. Sagar's father and Ayush's mother were siblings.

Although Sagar disliked Ayush's lethargic attitude that despite being talented Ayush hadn't attempted to get a full-time job, he hadn't quite talked about it. During the course of the case, he spent some time with Ayushand talked about childhood, school, TV shows... In the few days they interacted, the two cousins got to know about each other more than what they knew all the years. It was a catharctic experience for Sagar.

But he still hates Ayush. Because Ayush succeeds in getting Sagar's mother scold him!

Sagar's mother, in a bid to make Ayush understand the importance of getting a job at the right age, sometimes ends up scolding Ayush. Sagar wants her to scold him too, or slap him for the death of his father. Her stone-like silence on the matter stones his delicate psyche every day.

Nevertheless, Ayodhya is happy about Sagar being the ACP again.

Ups and downs are my gifts to you. And do you know what is special about them? You can't reject them.

It is weekend and Ayodhya is getting ready to leave for dinner with Anca.

His grandpa was pleased the previous day. He had asked- "Have you made any friends in office? Do your colleagues even know you?"

"They know me but don't really know me."

"And there is a girl. Anca."

As Ayodhya wears his shoes recalling that conversation with his grandpa, his cell phone rings...

"Mr. Lonely..."

Co-incidentally, it is his grandpa. Every time when he receives the call from his grandpa, his heart fears the news of the trio returning. But today he is happy. His heart has mustered some courage.

"Appu, the trio was here this morning. They have returned from abroad. They have beaten me up badly to tell them about The Blue Bell Villa. I am a bit hurt on my head but the doctor says it is ok."

Ayodhya is in shock!! He fails to keep pace with his grandpa's words. His heart batters against his chest!

"I'm coming there!!"

"No, Appu! Don't behave like everyone else! You don't have to come here. They are not after me. Listen..."

There is a lull. Ayodhya's eyes have reddened. "Are you ready?"-Anca is standing at the door in her beautiful red dress. Ayodhya shows her his palm and squeezes his eyes to denote that he needs a bit more time, walks in his bedroom and locks himself up.

"Is that Anca?"-his grandfather asks amidst cough.

"Leave it! You were saying something."

"Tell her that her voice is differently sweet."

"Grandpa, you were saying..."

"Listen carefully. I... I... could not hold up against the pressure. My own daughter was pressing my neck with her knee and my son was kicking my stomach. I... I... gave in... I told them your name, work location and designation. They know about you now!!"

Ayodhya bites his towel in grief. Tears flow for the first time!! He has imagined the horrendous scene.

"I... I... am sorry, Appu. More the wealth you make, less the value your life carries. You are in danger now!!"-the voice is feeble, suppressing sobs.

"It is alright, grandpa. You did nothing wrong. You... It is ok."

"But you could have given them whatever they wanted. That Blue Bell Villa... Where is it? Is it more important than our lives?"

"It is the only reason I am living. And want you to live..."

"What are you talking? You are surviving for some piece of real estate?"

"No, not just real estate. It has a treasure buried under it, seven generations ago. The whole city knows it. The trio knows it too. My grandfather had made the fact public. Since then, many have tried locating the villa to break in. But nobody has been successful yet."

"Why haven't you told me that? And why tell now? Where is it? How does it look?"

"Ah, the villa! It was once a beautiful mansion. But just like the old house we live in now, the Blue Bell Villa too has borne years of neglect. We have never been to the villa over the years and have at times forgotten that it is there somewhere. It's the daily struggle for livelihood, you know! But just like any other vestigial thing, the villa has been fading from our memory... Ummm... My memory."

"What? Grandpa? You mean... What?"

"You heard it right. Now don't act like a child. Don't make her wait... And one more thing. No calls from now. I came to know they have political connect. Very deep. With NSF. So much that the eldest daughter knows the Chief Minister personally. Even Soman does. They have grown extremely rich. Do you know Heaven Seven Group of Hospitals is owned by Soman?"

"Yeah, I know. Then why are they after a piece of property? The Blue Bell Villa?"

"I told you... The treasure... that is buried under it."

"It is all about habits, Appu. People reach positions, attain power, and change attitudes. But the only entity they can be pulled down with is their habit. Do you know what makes us weak and vulnerable in front of our foes, Appu?... Being predictable. And what makes us predictable? Habits! Information cannot be more accurate than habit!"

"Nothing can beat information, Appu. Enmity is a mind game. And confidence is a game changer. If the enemy is aware about you, you are losing your strength. And of all things on the planet, habit is the only permanent information!"

"So the trio is under the habit of gobbling up property. A small villa doesn't matter. They want it."

"So, no calls?"-Ayodhya is calmed down.

"No, try finding an alternative. They'll surely tap my phone."

"I'll try. Just see if you can open a new email account with some obscure name. I'll think over."

"Ok, Appu. Take care. Don't make her wait."

Ayodhya walks out of his door.

He is with Anca but he is just not there. He tries his best not to make her find out about his state of mind. But Anca finds out.

"Something seems to bother you. What is it?"-she holds his hand. "Nothing."-he retracts.

"After that phone call, I guess."-she walks down the road. A few passersby stare at her with lecherous eyes. A few look at her wholly. Ayodhya gets a strange feeling. He wants to beat them to death. He had never felt like that before.

He stares at those staring at her. They don't care. It is not their brains commanding their eyes.

She walks along with him, almost touching his arm. Her eyes fall on his, every now and then. She understands that he is not able to get out of his emotions.

As they walk to the restaurant, she notices a huge crowd hurrying here and there. There is a temple up the road and it is an auspicious full moon day.

"Ayodhya, shall we go to the temple first?"-she suggests.

"I don't go to temples."

"What?"

Ayodhya is silent. She locks her fingers into his and pulls him in the direction of the temple. "Hey, I've never been to a temple before. I feel extremely uncomfortable. I'm already riddled with problems. Please don't add to it."-he holds her wrist with the other hand and pulls back.

"See, since history, temples have been easy targets... soft targets... We have been made to believe that going to temples is too old-fashioned. Something to be abhorred... You need to come with me or I will not help you with projects."

Ayodhya walks in. As soon as they near the entrance, a man sitting at a shop starts walking at them briskly. "Leave your chappals there... It would be safer."

Anca doesn't care. They leave them at the entrance where everyone else too has. The man murmurs something. They enter inside.

"Here, pray to this God first. You cannot enter inside to meet the presiding deity until you seek the blessings of this mini God. He is very powerful."-the man suggests. He has followed them in. He is pointing at a makeshift room within the premises of the temple.

A priest in that room calls them frantically, ringing the bells tied to the ceiling. Anca holds Ayodhya's arms and moves away. "He'll make you sit there and won't leave you until you pay him a hefty amount."-she warns.

"Turn this way."-the man appears again. Both of them turn surprised.

He sprinkles water on their heads and chants a hymn. Anca shows on her face that she is not happy with that at all. "Can't you mind your work? Why are you after us?"

"Hey, look at you!"-the man exclaims in quite an animated manner. "I sprinkled holy water on you to wash your sins away and instead of expressing gratitude by offering some money, you are blaming me?"

"Look... You washed away my sin? Fine, I'm pure now. But if you don't leave, I'll commit a new one and forget washing sins you'll never able to wash your..."-Ayodhya stops at the wrong interval. Sometimes stopping at the wrong point serves better than complete sentences. Sometimes...

The man stands dazed!

"We don't want your help. We can manage ourselves."-she interrupts before walking to the center of the temple and bending down at the water body.

She touches the pristine water and jerks her shoulders at the chillness. She holds her palms in a cup-shape, prays for a while and pours it on her and Ayodhya's heads.

Ayodhya feels a queer sense of touch as water flows down his forehead. It feels as though someone unknown, unidentifiable, has given him an assurance that he is not alone in his quests. Some supreme, watchful eyes seem to be protecting him. He has never felt such a presence before.

They leave to the main area. The man now walks ahead of them. "Look, the right direction to enter the area is from here. You are walking in the wrong direction."

"Look, my cousin is a very dangerous person. If I make one phone call, he'll come down to thrash you."

Anca ignores the stranger and walks in the queue, pulling Ayodhya with her. An old man standing in front of Ayodhya turns back and smiles- "Your cousin seems to be hot-blooded. He better visit temples. Anyway, temples these days have lost the value they were built for. Do you know that there is a lot of science involved in the location, construction, rituals and hymns? They were centers of spirituality, knowledge and wisdom. They used to allay fears in the minds of citizens."

"They still do."-Ayodhya speaks involuntarily. The queue is moving slowly as devotees have started departing after their prayers, one by one.

"Yes, but alas... Look at the situation now. You'll find more crooks in and around temples than on railway platforms and bus stands. That man found out that you are newcomers."

They are now very close to the heart of the temple. The devotees have started to chant the hymns. The bells ring incessantly. Anca pats Ayodhya gently and asks him to fall back. She wants to lead him so that he could know about the rituals. He obeys.

They are just steps away. He wants to see what others travel miles to have a look at, what kings and emperors laid down their lives for, what cities were named after and what lit the light of hope in the trampled lives of common people. His slow, short steps make him more anxious. He has never felt this anxious before. He feels that someone stronger than him is waiting for him. The chant has reached a high pitch. The ringing of bells rages. Anca tries saying something. He bends down to listen to her.

"Fold your hands, pray to God."

He reluctantly folds his hands. She makes way for him to see...

There it is!!!

The idol decorated with flowers and leaves. The dim glow of the oil lamps around it casts a thin light. He feels he is submitting to an entity that knows everything about him. Suddenly he remembers the imagined scenes of his parents getting killed, his grandpa getting thrashed, Asrar being strangled and he himself being alone all the years. And then suddenly... He feels calm. There is a flow of coldness in his rattling mind.

A priest offers a pinch of sacred ash and vermillion. Ayodhya takes it in his hands and looks at Anca. She smiles, applies faint strokes of both on his forehead and closes her eyes tightly for a moment.

They walk towards the exit. Ayodhya is filled with a strange confidence, a peculiar strength and a strong urge- to come back to the temple.

He spares a look at Anca. She stands in the queue to collect the holy offerings. She appears more beautiful than before. On one hand his eyes admire her looks and on the other his mind feels guilty of not going to a temple and calling names to the deity.

He looks at the sky- "God, I apologize for everything I have done to you... by my actions and thoughts."

He closes his eyes for a while. A supernatural feeling flows in him, comforting him. He opens his eyes and looks around.

A few old ladies are bending over something and are doing nothing. They just seem to stay that way for a minute and then leave. There are many of them. He waits on.

Anca returns with handfuls of offerings. Her waist-long hair blows in the breeze of the wide spacious precincts of the temple. The breeze gets wilder. Her clothes tighten up on one side, making her toned body prominent. "If she were a fast bowler, even her Yorkers would've struck at my heart!"- Ayodhya gets mysteriously attracted. He regrets not noticing her beautiful build ever before- "There she was, sent by God as a beautiful attachment and extracted in the next cubicle. And I was needlessly downloading images of Apna Vyas Patel."

She gives him some of the offerings as they sit at a corner. "Are you feeling ok now?"-asks she. He smiles. She has seen it for the first time. "See, there are things we don't feel like telling others. That's ok but we should at least share them with God."

A thought comes up in his mind. Why not tell Anca that about his reality? That he has no secret cousin? About the two lives he is living-one as an IT professional and the other as a... whatever that is? That he was the one who had beaten up the thugs at the signal? If someone too can know about him, it helps him throw the burden of pain off his mind... He can be free of the stress he undergoes as a lone combatant...

"Anca I want to tell you something... About me..."

She looks at him with eyes full of expectations, conveying to him that she already knows what he wants to tell her.

"Yeah? Go ahead."

"I am actually not everything that I am.... I mean... There is something more about me."-he struggles. He is not in the habit of sharing his thoughts

Anca giggles. "Take your time and make it more graspable. These words are going to be the most memorable ones in your life. And there are shorter ways of putting them across."

He agrees with her in his mind. "How do I start? With my

childhood?"-he looks across.

"What's happening there?"-he remembers he wanted to ask her about the ladies bending over.

Anca looks along his arm in the direction he points to. "Oh that? That is the idol of Nandi-the bull. There is a saying that if you make a wish in his ears he will help you fulfill them."

Ayodhya smiles. "Go tell him in his ears about the thing that was bothering you after the phone call."

Ayodhya's smile vanishes!

He gets up at once. "Bend over at his ears."-she yells as he walks. He washes his soiled hands at the tap and proceeds to the bull.

The old ladies wait for their last companion who is whispering in the stone ears of the idol- "It has been six months since my son has left for America. Make sure he is fine and getting enough to eat."

She leaves as soon as she sees him wait for her to finish. He bends down at its ears. He feels stupid, foolish. But he wants to give it a try.

"Help me save grandpa."-he whispers and leaves immediately, hoping that nobody takes him for a crazy lunatic.

He returns to Anca. She has not yet finished eating the offerings. She feels strangely full. She can't eat more. Her hands are soiled. She struggles to reach out to her purse.

"I just want to keep this remaining food in a paper and take home. Can you see if there is any paper in my purse?"

He sits down next to her and takes out a paper. It is a printed ticket of Indian Railways from Mangaluru to her hometown.

"Yeah, that will be fine. That's my last week's journey ticket."-she puts the contents in the paper and walks to wash her hand. Ayodhya waits for her, searching for words to start with about his secret life. A small boy dashes against him and falls down crying. Ayodhya lifts the boy and apologizes in a kid's style. He gently rubs his hands on the boy's yellow colored shirt. The shirt has words written in black-IF YOU CAN'T KEEP YOUR OWN SECRETS, DON'T EXPECT OTHERS TO."

Anca returns and takes the purse and the offerings from him.

"So you were saying something."-she looks at him coaxingly.

"Nothing. I'll tell you later."

She shakes her head, smiling about a futile expectation- "Shall we leave?"

They walk out. A few ladies who were sitting chatting and talking casually at the entrance when Ayodhya and Anca had entered, are still sitting down there. They spot Anca and Ayodhya exiting. The woman at the extreme end towards the entrance gets up slowly as though she had an urgent task of welcoming someone.

She stares at an approaching Anca. Anca feels uncomfortable. Ayodhya feels that something is about to go wrong. The woman bends forward, holds her hands out and shrinks her face.

"Oh dear mother, have mercy on me and my children. Give me a hundred rupees as alms. The Lord will bless you and your children."-she walks behind Anca. Anca tries walking faster.

Ayodhya turns back to see the woman's companion remark- "She still hasn't learnt yet. One should walk in front of the person. Not behind!!"

The woman too ramps up her speed. Anca starts running mildly. The woman takes to her feet and comes right in front of Anca. Anca finally yields and offers her ten rupees. The woman leaves. She walks back and takes up the last position in the sequence. " Had you failed this time, we wouldn't have given you a second chance!!"-another one gets up as another devotee makes his exit!

"Oh hello, now give me my 501 rupees."-the man who was tormenting them earlier reappears.

"Even Gods in the teleserials don't appear as quickly as he does."-Ayodhya thinks.

"What? Are you nuts? I'll hand you over to the Police."-Anca shouts threateningly.

"What nuts? I have guided you in the temple. The temple is full of thieves and I assured that you don't fall in their traps."

Ayodhya holds his shoulders and takes him along. "Show me the ATM."

"Ayodhya, are you mad? He is fooling you."

"Wait for me at the bus stop."-he vanishes in the crowd. The man walks along gleefully. Ayodhya walks in, draws some cash and walks out, without sparing a look at him. He stops Ayodhya-"My money?"

"I have worked hard with crooked bosses, in critical situations, under pressure... to earn this money. And you have the temerity to call it yours?"

The man signals his comrades who are sitting at the tea shop.

"If I want to, I will even call that girlfriend of yours as mine!!"-he gets encouraged at Ayodhya's weak appearance.

Ayodhya keeps the money in his pocket. The other men walk towards him, arrogantly. Ayodhya tries to leave. The man catches hold of his collar. Ayodhya's anger rockets up!

He holds the man's head firmly and elbows his neck hard!!

The man coughs blood!

The others stand stunned... wherever they are!

He collapses on his knees. Others back off!

One young lad still charges on... not on his feet but tongue- "Bro, we are three. Let's take him down!!"

The leader, the fat, cute, chubby guy standing in the middle, resists- "Sir, I am sorry. You may go..."

"Bro, what the heck? Let's cut him!"

"Please don't mind his words, Sir. He is new to our gang."

"Put him on the bench for a few months and under probation for a year."

Anca is waiting for him at the bus stop.

"Why did you give him money?"

"I didn't. I just drew some cash"-he replies.

"And some blood"-he tells himself!

The bus arrives. "I'm not hungry. You?"-Anca asks.

"Yeah, a little bit."

"Why don't you finish off the offerings? We need not go for dinner."- she holds the paper at him. Coincidentally, they both get seats as two people get up to get down at the next stop.

He finishes off in a jiffy, wipes his fingers on the paper, crushes it and keeps it in his pocket. Anca signals him to hurl it away out of the window. He refuses- "I'll find a dustbin."

He spots a sweeper on the road. She looks very ugly.

The road in front of her is full of debris and carelessly disposed waste. But the road behind her is spick and span. He looks at Anca's mesmerizingly lovely face. A strange thought comes in his mind- "Who is more beautiful?"

They get down at The Pungent Dungeon stop and return to their flats. Ayodhya enters his flat, scans around cautiously and relaxes when he finds no intruders. He removes his shirt and throws it away. A crushed paper pops out of it and rolls along the floor. It is Anca's train ticket. Ayodhya gets an idea. He wants to find out her age!!

He opens the paper and sits on the chair. She is a year younger than him!

He ponders over her ticket. It is booked under the Akal quota. The address of the account holder who has booked the ticket catches his attention like gunpowder catching fire!!

The address is of Pony!!

Ayodhya specifically remembers Pony's address because Pony was one of the threats Asrar had warned him about!

"Threat type number 2: Someone who relentlessly tries to gather information about you or your family or your things. It is an exceptional behavior. You need to collect whatever information possible about such a person."-Asrar had trained him during one of those theory classes in 5th semester. Ayodhya had promptly followed Pony's details in Reinforces. But the Anca connection was well hidden by Pony. Ayodhya had got a clue on the night Anca was found snooping into his flat, hiding behind the refrigerator with extraordinary patience!

He had felt that she was not as innocent as she looked. And her constant questions about his cousin!

That was another factor that had reasoned against her naivety. A far more convincing fact was that she became instant friends with him, and was being too close to him. For a person with such a disgusting appearance and ordinary academic and professional records, it was a bit too far.

But it was my gift that he had slowly started getting rid of wrong thoughts about her. He is human too. He already had many people to be wary of. He wanted one support... for a lifetime.

But now he knows the bitter truth. He spits into the sink. And thinks deep...

Akal booking is so critical that anyone would go to a very close, trusted person. And hence... he understands... Anca is a closed chapter.

He gets up and leaves towards Pony's wing in the apartment. As he nears his flat, he crouches and hides behind a tall show tree. The surveillance camera is pointing at the other side. He is safe.

"I think he was going to tell me something about his cousin. But he backed out at the last moment."-Anca sits at Pony's desk while he stands smoking at the balcony. "You should have persuaded him somehow."-he is upset. "Nobody has ever dared to touch me till now and that cousin of that mouse... he assaulted me, humiliated me. I could've gone to dad but later decided to deal with him on my own."

The bull has shown Ayodhya the way!

As he returns, he finds Tintu in a jovial mood. He seems highly elated with something. He walks into Ayodhya's room, licking cream from his wrist. "I am so happy, hmmm."

"Yeah, tonight even I'm happy. But not as much as you."-Ayodhya opens the door lock and gives Tintu the padlock.

"I know... You are point zero-zero-five-three percent as happy as me. But you know one fact-o? The world's greatest happiness lies in smooth and complete pooping!! Hmmm."

"Now, where did that come from?"- Ayodhya laughs loudly although he feels disgusted at the response. He laughs so loudly that Tintu stands amazed at an experience, first of its kind!!

"Hey and one more thing, actually!"

"Someone was here yesterday and the day before, looking for you!"

Ayodhya's laugh vanishes!

"Who?"

"I don't know, actually. There was a man who came to see you the day before yesterday. It was two in the night and I was bathing. He had called up someone and told that you were not in your flat, hmmm."

"But I was here..."-Ayodhya is perplexed.

"Yeah, but I had locked your door from outside, you remember-o?"

"He came yesterday also!"

"He may come tonight then."

"Hmmm."

Ayodhya requests Tintu to lock the door as usual and keep an eye on the man. "But what if I fall asleep by two, hmmm?"

"I know you won't!!"

It is two.

A fleet of short footsteps can be heard in the serene night. A man can be seen in the bright moonlight, approaching from the stairs to Ayodhya's flat. He is well-built, wearing a leather jacket. He is tall, sturdy and armed with a pistol!

Ayodhya and Tintu keep an eye from Tintu's house. Tintu is unconcerned. Ayodhya understands that Tintu's mind is craving for a bath to such an extent that he wouldn't care even if the man had come for him!

"He can't be Gharial."-Ayodhya tells himself. Gharial never uses conventional methods of killing.

The man looks at the locked door, brings his pistol at the lock to blow it off. Ayodhya waits on without any expressions on his face. Tintu broadens his eyes.

The man pauses, his finger on the trigger. Ayodhya stands looking at the man's shivering finger.

"Heck!"-he kicks the door and leaves. "He is weak."-Ayodhya looks at Tintu. "Ok... Leave now..."-Tintu is scared to death but has enough courage for a late night bath.

Ayodhya walks soundlessly out of the house and follows the man. The man walks down the Beach Road. Chilly wind from the sea makes Ayodhya shiver. He follows, nevertheless, holding back the chattering of his teeth, trying to broaden his shrinking shoulders.

The man heads to a hotel. Ayodhya follows him, maintaining a safe distance from him. The man is talking to the receptionist at the hotel. Ayodhya is stopped by the guard.

"I'm a doctor!"

He is in. "Doctors are never questioned in India. They like that and expect that."

The man is getting into the elevator. Ayodhya does not know what to do. He hurries up the stairs, keeping an eye on the elevator level indicator at each floor. The man goes for a good four floors. Ayodhya reaches the floor in time to see the man's faint reflection vanish through a shiny walled passageway.

He runs on his heels, dampening the noise as much as he can. A string of shouts is heard from an open door down the hallway.

"What do you want me to do?"-the man shouts!!

Ayodhya stands at the door, not trying to peep in. He just wants to listen.

"That brat seems to have moved out of the flat. The oldie might have warned him. I would have holed his head by now. I will enquire with some people in the flat tomorrow. Someone might give clues. Now stop shouting at me. What?"

"Hello, hello... What?"

"Fine... I'll book a room with three beds. You both may come over here. And bring that knife I killed that ass with."

There is silence.

"Hello, I'm calling from 401. Is there a vacant room with three beds from tomorrow? 202? Great... Book it."

The door is closed. Ayodhya leaves. It is the brother of Ayodhya's father. The murderer!

Ayodhya understands that the knife that was used to slice open his father's stomach will be brought to be used on him!

He had desisted against harming the trio, hoping that such a moment never comes. He had attempted nothing in order to honor his grandpa's words. But now it is too much to ignore. "I tried my best to save you but you seem to have a confirmed departure."

He walks down the hotel floors, knowingly not using the elevator. As he walks to the gate, the guard looks up at him with eyes full of respect.

"I tried my best to save him."-Ayodhya pats him, dejected. The respect shoots up tenfold!

The next day he sits in his cubicle, thinking deeply while his hands get busy working in Casual Basic software. Anca brushes his hair slowly. Pillu stands envying him.

"You were saying something."-she whispers in his ears.

Her touch, her voice and her presence feels so abhorrent to him now.

"I'll tell you mine Anca, but how about you? Do you have any secret?"

"Are you not on Fakebook?"-she asks, implying that there was no need to ask her had he been a member of a social networking site.

"No."

"My 'about me' reads- 'I am an open book. Only needed to be seen'. I've no secrets, Ayodhya."

"Thank God I'm not on Fakebook."

"Well, anyway. My secret is quite simple."-he begins.

"I have a small family. I stay with my aunts and my uncle in Sarovar Nagar. I have a cousin who is so protective of me that he used to pick up fights with bullies for me when I was young."

"Where is he now?"

"He is in the US. But his mother, aunt and uncle are here. I have made arrangements for their stay in Hotel Izu, room 202. My flat is too dirty, isn't it?"

As soon as he finishes saying it, he gets a phone call from his house owner- "I'm coming over today. I have something to talk to you."

Ayodhya gets it. His expulsion is inevitable. The maid never got a chance to clean the room. "Isn't your cousin coming over?"-Anca's eyes shine.

"No, not as yet. He is busy working for Debacle Software. He'll join later."

The very next moment he becomes worried. The owner!!

He sits scrolling through the phone numbers. All of a sudden, he gets a brilliant idea!

The owner hails from Kerala. So does Tintu. Ayodhya swipes through the contact list on his phone.

He dashes home that evening to meet Tintu. Tintu's door and windows are closed, curtains drawn.

Ayodhya knows it is useless to call him now. It will work against. He waits for a couple of hours and a fifteen-minute extra time. Tintu finally opens the curtains and comes out like a gladiator ready to take on any beast in the arena.

"Tintu..."-Ayodhya approaches from behind.

"Tell me. I was busy, hmmm."

"I know. That's why I didn't disturb you. I came about two hours ago."

"Two hours and sixty-three seconds, actually. I heard you open your door, hmmm."

"You can say two hours, one minute and three seconds right? Why sixty-three seconds?"

"I'll save three words and three seconds, man. It's called optimization, hmmm."

"Ok..."-Ayodhya pauses for a moment. "Tintu, you have to help me from the owner. He is coming tomorrow."

"So what can I do actually?"

"He's from Kerala."

Tintu raises his hand and shakes his head assuring Ayodhya- "Kerala bond is stronger than Fevicol Bond!"

"Make sure you keep the door open and go out of sight before he comes tomorrow. Have no fear when Tintu is here... Hmmm."

"Thanks, Tintu."

The next morning Ayodhya faces a hard day at office. His project is getting delayed. The team leader is upset. "If the project does not get over within the extended deadline you will be kicked out!!"

Ayodhya is in serious trouble. He walks home. As he reaches the flat, he hears the voices of Tintu and the owner!

He looks around. He wants to hide somewhere. But it is too late.

"Kozhapilla, ungle (No problem, uncle)"-Tintu comes out. "Madhi, madhi, madhi... Athra madhi (Enough, enough, enough... That much is enough)"-the owner is glad.

" Hey Ayodhya, you did not tell me you are Tintu's neighbor? I would not have come here. Don't worry, he'll take care of your flat."

Ayodhya is relieved. He does not want to know how Tintu managed to convince him. Ignorance is bliss, especially when you're overburdened.

It is evening. The breeze is gaining speed and losing heat.

He starts out to Hotel Izu.

The Hotel is teeming with policemen. An ambulance and a police van grace the entrance. In India, police vans are seen as harbingers of ill-fate.

People have thronged to savor some action, some suspense stories.

Ayodhya walks to the person who collects parking toll from visitors. "What happened?"

"Three people died in an accident today."

Ayodhya is shocked!

"Who were they?"

"I don't know. They had probably come today. They went out at three in the afternoon and were knocked out from the bridge by a truck, I guess. I don't know. The Police are waiting for their relatives. But I think they are quite a cash-rich party. The CEO of Heaven Seven Group of Hospitals is flying down here in a few hours. I don't know how he is related to them."

"Heaven Seven? That hospital at North Dweepa?"-asks Ayodhya as though he doesn't know.

"Yeah... He is traveling from the main hospital in Delhi to the Dweepa branch."

Ayodhya slowly moves step by step to the ambulance. The doors are closed; the windows are dark. He can't see a thing.

"How old were they?"-he gets back to the man.

"They were about fifty-sixty. The male body was huge. The other two were women."

Ayodhya slowly walks away. He can't believe a person as ordinary as Pony can pull off such a perfect murder. "It has to be him. Who else?"-he brushes away the thought that he too is responsible.

The deaths were indeed orchestrated. When you humans kill, it is called a murder. When I do it, it is called an accident.

You use tools to kill. I use myself.

He watches the policemen bring out things belonging to the trio. Ayodhya's eyes well up unexpectedly. He can't believe it!

One of the policemen stands inspecting a knife!!

16 THE PAYING GUEST

Ayodhya is playing rock music loudly, quite uncharacteristic of him.

He lies cringed on the floor in his flat, dejected and heartbroken. His mind is bringing in front of him, what he has seen yesterday...

The knife...

Its brownish, sleek, wooden handle and curvy, toothed edge might have been one of the last objects his father might have seen, he thinks.

He has drawn his jaw backwards, his cheeks are wrinkled and his eyes are tucked inside the depths of his skull. He breathes in deeply and moans aloud!

"Haaaaaah!!"

"Uhh..."-he breathes in again.

His hands hug imaginary persons in the space between his body and the knees. He moves his knees closer to support their backs and hug them closer with his forearms.

It has been more than two decades. He has never cried. But in twenty hours he has moaned, groaned and rolled, struggled to breathe and beaten his palms on the floor. That is the power of sight. It can dig out lesions healed by me. It is my greatest enemy.

"FATHER!! MOTHER!!"

"FATHER!!!"

"MOTHER!!!"

"FA... AAA"-he shrinks his body further. He bangs his head against the floor. His ears long to listen to someone. All the incidents that he had seen about parental love, brush by his face. There is no voice heard. He yearns for a symbolic sound-probably a phone call from a stranger, the sound of the lift opening... something... nothing!

He turns his head left and right, his forehead hinged against the ground. His tears that have touched the floor through the end of his nose have been spreading like blotting of ink. They shine in the silvery moonlight that is cascading in through the window.

It reminds me of one of the glummest moments in history-

The fate of one of the mightiest emperors of the world-

Jayapala!

The capital city bears poignant silence. The royal palace that once looked like a bride, envying travelers across the land, turning traders magically into poets and making them sing verses in its praise, invoking unkind curiosities in the minds of distant inhabitants who listened to them, has almost turned into a rubble. It has fallen to the eyes of the coldblooded tyrant of the nearby Ghazni.

The blackened bricks of the mammoth pillars have been exposed after the burning of plasters of lime. The gigantic doors are stripped of the golden railings. The chandeliers have been smashed to the ground. The sharp, aqua blue pieces of glass are still scattered. Some have just been painted red by a pair of feet getting dragged towards the exit...

The feet that were accustomed to the velvet carpets of glory, the feet that were washed by the soft waters of Peshawar, the feet that stood firm against the face of oppression and waves of violent attacks, the feet that refused to step back even after witnessing the gory sight of atrocities at a scale unprecedented, now make a quiet move in tandem into the deep shambles of history.

They support an emperor whose colossal build is testimony to an unbreakable body. But alas! His spirit has been wrecked.

A sheet of white cloth is wrapped around his waist and drawn across his chest. But it has failed... failed miserably to hide the marks of battle axes and arrows on his skin, cut deeply at some places and deeper at some other. Of spears and javelins, of daggers and swords and finally the marks of abuses, ridicule and laughter... on his heart!

The emperor walks with folded hands chanting the name of the divine. His head is shaven bare, his eyebrows etched away clean. His sight is glued to the distant flag at the mast of the royal entrance- the flag of the Shahi Empire!

He knows, like his breath, it is the last of the few flutters the flag is going to dance with in the affectionate streams of the dry winds.

He has instated the bravest of his sons-the ablest of all- Anandapala- on the throne that he knows is about to bite dust and lay buried for at least a thousand years in the soil that it rose from.

His resolve to check the advances of the barbarians of Ghazni has been commendable. The series of wars he fought against Ghazni after the fall of Zabul have delayed the inevitable to an extent that a generation has peacefully closed its eyes. The last one that he has fought a few weeks ago has been particularly terrible, turning not only tables and tides around but a whole civilization upside down!

The battle of Peshawar was lost and all the royal family members taken captive. The citizens lost faith in their emperor.

Jayapala was paraded on the streets of Ghazni, bare and bent. He was made to walk on hot coal, fight with monkeys imported from the east and bear the raining spits on his face by the courtiers of the Sultan. After he agreed to pay a huge indemnity, his family was returned.

He has been sent back on a filthy donkey to the gates of Peshawar, to send a message... of an impending final assault!

"My Lord!"-the voice he had lost his heart to, thirty-five years ago, has successfully paused his walk to the gates from the royal abode.

It is his queen. "For weeks, I spent my moments in the enemy's den, immersed in humiliation. And now, I want to immerse myself along with you in the holy fire."

Jayapala does not turn to see her virtuous face- "You have a duty to support your son, the new emperor of Peshawar, in his administration and warfare. I am a lost drop in the ruthless ocean of time."

He continues his walk to the pyre. The whole city stands around the palace walls, not knowing if their admonishing of the emperor was correct, now that he has heeded to their wishes.

"My Lord... I want to die a queen!"-she follows him, finally fusing into the golden flames of mine.

Anandapala slowly removes his crown, places on the empty throne and observes it standing a step away. A newly crowned emperor is not supposed to witness the end of his predecessor.

He walks out of the durbar hall. The blood on his body is still young; the scar in his heart is raw. He walks behind the pillars, away from the sight of his courtiers and kneels down on the ground.

"FATHER!! MOTHER!!"

Ayodhya is fast asleep, a supernatural beam of moonlight mysteriously caressing him!

On the other hand, Sagar feels that his fortune has come alive.

There is an unmistakable lead in Gharial's case. Gharial's next potential victim is Kanaka Sundari, at the ramp show. Kunj's plan is just perfect, with a tiny, trustworthy team of three. Kunj has decided not to participate in field operations.

Sagar has donned the uniform yet again, raring to go. He knows it is stupid but it has been a long, long wait. Ayush and Soor have become good friends too. Sagar's mother is forcing him to decide on the date of his engagement. These days he receives his mother's calls as quickly as he can. Sometimes, he even expects eagerly.

It is evening. Soor and her father have come to Sagar's home. No, not the home he had rented near The Pungent Dungeon. It is his previous house where Ayush and his mother stayed.

"Hope the engagement date is not too far. We are ready anytime you wish for. We'll have the wedding ceremony soon."-Soor's father looks at her, implying to her that he has obeyed her, and spares a stare at Sagar.

"Yeah, next month?"-Sagar turns to his mother. "Sagar, why next month? We'll have it as soon as we can. You are only getting engaged."

Sagar's face crumbles. He had different ideas, not exactly in line with his mother's guess.

He, nevertheless, is glad at the series of turnarounds.

"Yeah Jackpot?"-he receives a call, walking out of the house.

"Sir, the Fashion event is going to be held in the sea, aboard a cruise-ship owned by Chimpu, the famous director of Khaaliwood. It will sail from Dweepa to Karwar next week."

"Great news, Jackpot. Hope nobody else knows about our scheme..."-he is ready and willing. He just can't wait for the week.

"No Sir. But we are not sure if Gharial has planned to attack her at all, let alone his boarding the ship."

"He will. He has to... now that I have returned!"

He turns around. Soor stands with her hands folded. She raises her brows, in a gesture to indicate what he is up to.

"Who has to do what? Now that you've returned?"

Sagar lifts her, sweeping her feet from the ground and almost walks into the house.

"Put me down. What are you doing?"

"Just answering you."

"I got it!"

He drops her feet gently. "Actually it is my subordinate, Jackpot. We are going to nail that wretched Gharial this time."-he holds her closer across her shoulder.

"That dreaded criminal? That guy who is all over the news? That guy?"-she turns at him in a serious look. "Yeah, that same beast... We are going to hunt him down on a cruise-ship."

"He is a beast. And as far as I know, when he hunts his victims become history."-she delivers her apprehension, in a punchy style.

"When beasts are hunted, it creates history too."-he replies.

"Sagar... Listen to me. I can't see you risk your life for a gangster. Were you the only one available for the department to assign this task? We're getting married, remember?"

"See, I am a Police officer. It is my duty to nab criminals. I don't think what others do as officers but I will do my duty. And moreover, I'm not the only one selected. Jackpot too is a member. And there are two more people... Civilians... Probably moderately literate... I can feel from the name. Kunj Bihari Yadav... That poor chap is not even employed. His friend is working for a meager salary in that notorious tech park- Pungent Dungeon. That too in Reinforces... What can you say about their fate? They don't even have pistols for self-defense."

"See, Sagar. I don't want to argue."-she shakes her head in short, quick sideward movements.

"I am giving you two options. Either you get engaged to me and quit this job or continue with your passion and say goodbye to me. Good that you brought the matter up before engagement."

Sagar is aghast!

Soor is not joking. Not at all.

"What do you want me to do after I resign?"

"Dad will find a job for you."-she sets his collar right. He moves her wrist away. "Soor, I... I... just... I've already lost a dear one to this job. I don't... I can't lose another."

"See, Sagar. I will convince my dad that after you get married to me you will either quit the job or take up some desk job in the department. I'm making a compromise here. I don't want to, but still... for our future..."

"There can't be a post for me to just carry out paper work. We are selected to face danger. What would you do if you dial 100, ask for help and the person says- 'Sorry, our officer is busy with his desk job?"

"Ok, fine... What about low risk jobs? Like nabbing a small-time thief?"

"I'm an Assistant Commissioner of Police!"

"I don't care. Go to Dweepa junction. There are a lot of small thieves."

"And one of them is right here."-he gently bangs her forehead. "The one who stole my heart!"

"I should not take you to movies."-she complains, pushing him away. "Then I'll arrest the entire Khaaliwood!"

"And make them act in the cell!!"-he hops back.

A week goes by.

Ayodhya is ready to board the cruise-ship. It looks amazing with all the lights and all the glass furniture. He can see it from outside. Jackpot has arranged a green-pass for him through Kunj.

Ayodhya is wearing a grand suiting for the night. It costs twenty thousand rupees. The money was given to Kunj by Jackpot. Ayodhya had picked up the suit that he was eyeing since two months in the window of the store across The Pungent Dungeon. Every day he used to stand facing it and raise his heels so that the reflection of his neck aligned against the black bow-tie. And he could attempt a trial without actually wearing it. Tonight... His dream has come true.

"How much does this belt cost?"-he had asked the salesman. "That one is cheap, Sir..."-the man had answered. How could a customer spending twenty thousand on a suit opt for a synthetic belt? "This one is pure leather, Sir. It gives good life."-he had pitched in for its durability.

"It has already taken one."-Ayodhya had refused. The man had stood perplexed.

Ayodhya too has fallen for the fashion that suiting is. In a tropical country like India, it is trendy to wear suiting and buy air-conditioners to cool off.

That's why I sometimes say- Luxury is irony accepted.

"The department will work with more enthusiasm if such liberal funds are approved."-Kunj had thanked Jackpot as he had received such huge sum all at once. Jackpot hadn't replied but felt the flesh of his chest ripped by the knife of his words. It had reminded him of his leave application for his wedding that was not approved even when he had saved enough of the leaves because his superior Purushottam wanted to go on a budget honeymoon to Manali with Shyamala.

Ayodhya walks in to the ship, the sentry dares not to stop him. Great clothes open the doors. The deck ushers him in!

The peak of wealth, success and glory opens up its arms over the pits of stinking superficiality.

He sees the famed, ruthless and callous movie industry of Dweepa- Khaaliwood- and its family. Literally... The family is so big that the members seem to have forgotten who is married to whom. Men and women alike, display their class by sounding loutish.

Ayodhya can see Chimpu, the director who makes it to Scar awards every year, only to return scarred with rejection each time. Chimpu's wife walks next to him, making sure that the glassware kept at the edges of the tables is not crashed with her bulging waist. Their daughter, in a two-pieced indescribable cloth walks with her own three-year-old daughter.

She has lost her market recently and wants to get back to news under the 'FROM OOMPH TO OOPS!!' column of The Mimes of Dweepa, hoping for a little publicity.

Her daughter stands in front of a small aquarium full of colorful fish and turtles, looking beautiful in that expression of curiosity. She probably feels the irony that the poor creatures are confined in glass over a boat sailing on top of their natural abode.

Anyway... Ayodhya can see Jackpot and Sagar too, disguised as some wealthy businessmen- meek-looking chaps with marauding tastes.

"The guest, the judge and the brightest star of tonight's show... Kanaka Sundari!"-the announcement is made.

A posh suite of the grand cruise-ship bears a gloomy look. Tears that have reached beyond the capacity of broad, black eyes tapering to the fine eye lashes, are threatening to wash away the tint of pink beneath.

Kanaka Sundari it is. The most celebrated actress in Khaaliwood. She waits for a call from the show coordinator. It is going to be a promotional appearance for her next flick.

Her slender hands caress the cushion of the soft couch she sits on. The touch is of loathe. The feel is of pain.

She recalls the last decade or so, that has been stolen from her life. She had landed on Dweepa with a dream-a dream to rule the country- from posh cosmopolitans to unheard places like the Teen Paiyya village near Patna.

She now feels abhorrent of what she wanted then. She wants me to take her back. Sorry girl, you have no choice... You have no choice now because somewhere in the past you made a wrong choice.

It hurts me though. It hurts me to see lonely pairs of eyes yelling of repent, hearts imploring me to turn back and souls burning inside the stillness of tied hands, pleading me of another chance. But I am helpless...

Kanaka Sundari remembers her innocent childhood. She had no thoughts of being an actress. She always wanted to study. And study well. But that was the only thing she was miserable at. And a day came when a wrong nod at a split second changed the rest of the course of her life.

She looks away. The huge TV running an animal show fails to draw her attention. Years have passed by and she is amazed with the fact.

The same director who had introduced her to the industry has cast her again and tonight is the night of fashion. She has to judge the winners. The new batch of dreamers...

She knows her days a counting. The peak is after all a point. All that remains after that is descent... a series of introspection, a revisit to the paths taken to glory, an act of self-evaluation and a forced kneeling at the command of conscience.

Her struggle, however, is from within. There is no way she could go out without touching up her face. It is no more the same. She fears to touch it after what she thinks I have done to it. Well, girl, I'm not the only one responsible.

She knows her turn to doom will come sooner or later. "Ma'am, your time has come."

She nods and reaches to the remote control of the TV to switch it off. She aims at the TV but stops to see the footage of a stray dog in one of Indian cities trying to woo its mate. "How sad that I compared him to a dog... He is only Satan."-she thinks about Chimpu, the director, who had given her the break she had longed for.

She looks at the dog again, considerately. "Every animal has a human in it."-she concludes in her mind and switches off the TV.

"And every human has an animal in him!!"-Gharial's reflection portentously falls on the TV screen!

She turns slowly, admiringly. Someone, for the first time, has shared a thought of hers. He walks towards her, pumping his knees up and down, keeping his steps crossed and clicking his fingers-

"You're a Barbie girl...

In a barbaric world..."

She agrees with every word of his. I'm not sure if she is scared. Her mind is hidden in the many roles she dons. So deep that it is unfathomable even for me!

But she is surprised for sure. She tries looking into his eyes well covered under the darkness of his hat's shadow. He slowly lifts her feet and places them on the couch. She doesn't oppose. She is lost in thought.

His hand struggles in his pocket- "Deepest pockets are those that have the right thing at the right time."

He takes out a rope!

She keeps watching him unwind and start binding her to the couch from the end of her legs.

Gharial winds eight quick turns. She takes me eight years back.

With every turn now, she forces me forward by a year...

"Kesha Sundari and Kanaka Sundari!!"-the judge at the auditions declares. She just can't believe it!! Her first break!!

Everyone applauds. Some are sobbing, though. They have come from various places with the same dreams as her. They don't mind losing out on the auditions. But they can't accept that two girls who were with them till now are going to make a leap of their life right in front of their craving eyes.

But it is not all that great for the two of them and the others don't know. You humans have a bad habit of exaggerated imagination of facts than the facts really are.

They are asked to meet the director separately for some 'mentoring' and 'counseling'. It is only after that that he will decide who leads in the first movie and who does in the second.

They look at each other. The competitor in both of them rushes back in their minds. "Miss Kesha Sundari... You are to meet him first. The date and time will be informed later."

"Madam, is it an interview? It was not on the list."-a naïve Kesha Sundari is anxious. The judge-coordinator-whatever gives out a wicked smile.

"Yes, informal."

A week later, Kanaka Sundari had seen a cryptic change in Kesha Sundari's conduct. Kesha had become very quiet and spoke only when she saw Kanaka.

"Kanaka, go away. This informal interview is not... a..."-she had collapsed on Kanaka Sundari's lap, weeping bitterly.

She had sat caressing her childhood friend, feeling strange.

Gharial winds two more rounds.

Both of them are seen laughing like witches in a success party.

They have descended down their dignity. They have hacked their conscience at the altar of ambitions. They have paid the price. While Kanaka Sundari's project has taken off with her in the lead role, Kesha Sundari has made way for the daughter of one of the Khaaliwood superstars. Kanaka Sundari is cast while Kesha Sundari is outcast. She, however, has gone on to become a renowned dancer, appearing for situational dances such as when the hero has a plan up his sleeve and the villain is enjoying her dance in his haven. Her role for five to six minutes has earned various movies in a few years. And she has earned so much that she has to weigh her money to measure it.

Kanaka Sundari has attained unmatched stardom... so much that she brought the reigning, middle aged queen of Khaaliwood down crashing. The glass doors and windows of beauty salons and spa, the desktop wallpapers, the restricted pockets in the wallets, the profile pictures and of course the shiny interiors of auto rickshaws indicate the end of an era and the dawn of a new one.

Gharial's slow yet strong winding has reached her shoulders.

Kesha Sundari is in a spot of bother. She faces severe competition from foreign actresses too. These days though, things are slightly better. Chimpu has conducted so many interviews that he is not interested any longer.

She decides to diversify her income. She invests heavily to open her brand of clothing stores, jewelry store, an aerobic gym and the 'Kesha' chain of restaurants. She is also considering endorsing a cheap product in an immortal TV advertisement. She has bought a flat in the poshest locality of mainland India. But it doesn't seem to pacify her. She is hoping to make a comeback after a liposuction therapy- a process of sucking out excess fat from her mind.

She wants the good old times back again.

Kanaka Sundari's case is no different either. Newer talent has taken Khaaliwood by storm. The generation has come of age. She is slowly but surely being pushed out. She has finally understood that the turns that I take bind the best in the business to mediocrity.

She has started to appear as a judge in reality shows and fashion events to keep herself alive in the media.

She has also set up her own Production House and is profited by a string of super-hit movies. But nothing can beat the rosiness of youth. She has lost her glowing skin, her natural, unfazed complexion. She also feels the nauseate monotony of color and glamour of the pitiless industry.

She is at a promotion party of the biopic of the star footballer from Portugal. It is a Hollywood movie and the star is in India for the event. Kanaka Sundari looks at his girlfriend who is holding two mugfuls of beer. She is young and gorgeous. Kanaka Sundari is trying her best to ensure that the media does not capture a snap of her and the girl together. The stark contrast can have nullifying effect on all the attention she has given to her face. Kanaka Sundari is patted gently on her arm. She turns around. It is the once-leading actress she had supplanted. They hug each other gently but the eyes of the actress yell at her- "Look at you!"

The girlfriend is roaming around. "Hi..."-she greets Kanaka Sundari casually and passes by.

Kanaka Sundari smiles and hopes earnestly that the media get to inhale the girl's breath.

Gharial singlehandedly lifts the couch with her strapped on it and walks to the window.

"It's all about biological accidents."

Ayodhya is at the ramp, waiting for her to turn up. Sagar and Jackpot have mixed discreetly with the business class, admiring the occupation. The show is about to begin. The anchor bends into the microphone and expresses something with creased brows. They are meant for that, to show their wrinkles with every small damned deviation.

"Sir!!"-the head of the makeup team for the actress, comes out in grief!

"Ma'am is not to be seen!!!"

Ayodhya, Sagar and Jackpot slowly but cautiously walk to the cabin with the rest of the crew.

There is no sign of her. The cruise-ship cuts through the waves and makes it towards the nearest landmass. The fishing town of Dweepa-

Matsyali...

The trip to Karwar has been abandoned!!

The Dweepa Police is called in again. Kesha Sundari cries in Chimpu's arms.

"Jackpot, call up Kunj. We need to talk to his friend. He has to be somewhere around."

"Hello, Kunj... We have a problem. The actress has vanished. Can you tell me the ways to meet your friend? How could he fail? We need to talk to him right now."

"Sir, he is not good at talking."

"So what next?"

"He had called me. He said he has spotted a heavy object tied to the railing on the ship's balcony and suspended into the sea."

Sagar and Jackpot rush to the balcony. The crowd has gathered, trying to pull the rope and bring the object to the surface. They stand with thumping heart and eyes full of toxic curiosity.

Up comes, from the sea, her couch!!

The Police reach the spot and cordons off the ship.

"No one leaves!"

Sagar and Jackpot are already on their escape route under the sea wearing scuba suits. They can't afford being caught in disguise. It will only complicate the case. They see in the grim light of the sub-surface of the Arabian Sea, another man making his way ahead of them. They try catching up in vain. Ayodhya reaches the shore and merges into the darkness of the coconut farm!

It is noon! Ayodhya is watching the video of the news on his computer in office- "Yesterday's chilling disappearance of the queen of Khaaliwood has opened a new mystery. The Police interrogated the entire crew on the ship except three who seem to have escaped underwater. And surprisingly, the makeup staff of the actress were not to be seen either! The lift operator said that he had felt there was something wrong when he had a group of people in his lift, wanting to go to the deck. He says they were murderously silent. But unfortunately the operator is blind and hence cannot identify suspects. The magnanimous director Chimpu has employed him as a part of his philanthropy."

"The head of the staff who informed the gathering of the disappearance also has disappeared with her team. To the police, already embroiled in the Gharial case, it comes as a double Yami. With cameraman Warren Whammy, I am Sammy, NOT NOW."

"Oh no! To the police it comes as a double whammy. With cameraman Warren Sammy, I am Yami, NOT NOW."

Ayodhya feels let down. It was a golden chance.

He is unwell too, after the swim in the cold waters last night. He has started to think extremely negative. He closes his eyes.

"Hello, Sir. We don't pay for sleep."-his team leader has spotted him at the wrong moment. "I wasn't sleeping. I was just..."

"I need the report of your project by Monday. It has to take off and that too, smoothly. The clients will be here next week."

He is tired. He brushes his hair and gets back to work.

"Hey!"-it's Anca.

"Hi"-that's Ayodhya.

"You never initiate a talk. I've never seen you responding positively. Anything wrong?"

"My uncle and aunts passed away."

"Oh God! I am sorry!"-she keeps her chin on his shoulder.

"It is ok."

She gets back, surprised!

"Your cousin? He knows about it? He is returning from abroad, isn't he?"-she is getting comfy at her share of the cubicle.

"Yeah, but his flight is cancelled."

It is evening. Tintu is flaunting his new Royal Enfield Bullet. He has even got its silencer changed. "I'll buy the LED TV later, hmmm."-he replies to a friend of his.

Ayodhya watches it from high above, at his apartment. For some reason, his beloved Yezdi comes to his mind. "I am going to get Kunj to talk about it with Sagar and get it back."

As of now, he is weary and cold. He writes a long mail to his grandpa who bears an obscure mail address as was decided-

'Dear Grandpa,

Hope you are doing fine. I just want to tell you that you are now free of the three children you thought were yours. You need not worry now. They passed away! Yeah, they died in an accident. But we will still continue this chat through mail as there is Soman still left. He may harm you. So it is better to continue. You know very well that I am not in a habit of sharing my feelings or writing long mails. But I still want to tell you that I'm feeling suffocated with my situation... our situation. Gharial escaped. I don't know how he figured out but he was clever. He came in, disguised, and killed the makeup crew of the actress first before killing her. He drowned her by casting her on her couch in to the sea. I was a failure there. ACP Sagar and Jackpot had hopes on me. I shattered them all. I came to know that Sagar was happy. His engagement was fixed. Now it seems he has postponed it. All because of me... And I am struggling for food. Office takes a long time in the night. The mess gets closed. I eat outside, that masala stuff... I... I don't know... I am failing at work too. Client meeting is scheduled and my project is getting nowhere. I am struggling with the juggling of many things that I am doing. I am stressed out. Grandpa, you

Yours lovingly,

Ayodhya.'

He doesn't know what more to write. He walks down the apartment and catches a glimpse of school kids playing cricket. "It's been so long."-he proceeds to play with them.

"This is a bet match. Are you a good player?"-a boy asks him.

"I think so."

He gets to bat at the end of the match as the last batsman. "Last over, one run to win, yaay."-his team mates are happy. "Hey, get the money ready. Today's treat is in Farishta."-the boy tells to the losing side.

The bowler hurls a full toss.

Clanck!!!

The stumps are rolled!

The opposite team celebrates. Ayodhya has missed a dummy delivery!

His captain is furious. He snatches the bat from him- "I thought this guy can bat. My mistake..."

"He was not even sure if he was a good player."-another boy remarks.

Ayodhya leaves. He can't believe it. Suddenly he remembers the incident in which he had hit two pawns on the carrom board in a single strike. It was such a rare feat. He had felt he was on top of the world. But today, he could not even play an easy delivery. He thinks about me and smiles. He smiles at the wily mirage of patronage I flaunt on your kind.

On the other side, Sagar is being questioned. "Look Sagar, we don't know whether it was Gharial. But if it isn't him, it is even more dangerous. We can say he has set a bad precedent to other criminals."

"Sir, in one month, Gharial won't be a name. I give you my word!"

"We expect action, Sagar."

He arrives home late in the night. Ayush is in his room, watching TV. He looks at Ayush and gets even more tired. His mother comes with hot tea. "Hope you didn't get drenched. Was it raining at your station too?"

"Yeah, a rain of words. And it is continuing here too."-he looks at his mother deridingly, grabbing the cup. She walks back without a word.

Ayush holds a packet of chips at him.

"When will you grow up, Ayush?!!!"-he shouts all of a sudden. Ayush's ears beep for a moment. His mother rushes back and takes him away.

Sagar gulps tea and walks into his room. "I don't want dinner, I'm sleepy."

"Have one roti, son. Just one small..."

"Get lost!!!"- he slams the door. His mother retracts her finger from the hinge just in time!

Sagar has seen it. He hits his forehead, knowing what would have happened had she failed. He feels sorry. He wants to hug her and apologize. He walks back to the door, holds the latch to open it, and lets it be... His eyes moisten.

Trring...

"Jackpot what's up?"-he always gets a call from Jackpot whenever he is down.

"Sir, Kesha Sundari has made a public remark over Kanaka Sundari's disappearance. She has used swear words and has vowed to fight against Gharial. Sir, her comments are trending all over Bitter, Fakebook and news channels. Check out the #Keshakrosh in NOT NOW!"

Sagar wipes his tears and switches on the laptop. "Yes... Yeah, Jackpot."

"Sir, I think she is next!!"

It has been a hectic week for Ayodhya and Sagar both. Ayodhya, on his part, is busy getting the things moving for the client from the US while Sagar and Jackpot have worked out a plan to pin Gharial whenever he is going to attack Kesha Sundari. They are sure he is after her. Sagar has decided not to avail Kunj's help. Kunj is held back by Ayodhya against approaching Jackpot, out of guilt.

"Dude, can you open this-o?"-Tintu is shirtless. He offers him the box of chocolates his brother has brought from the US. He is not able to open the pack.

Ayodhya is shocked! Tintu has bathed. "You bathe at two, don't you?"-he points at his wet body.

"Dude, it is sweat. Not water. Just came out to let the air evaporate it. Hmmm."-he stretches his arms wide. "While others waste water, I help bring rain."

"I'm no dude."-Ayodhya smiles as he unlocks his door.

"I know. But I like the word, dooode!!"

"Why did you change the silencer of your bike?"

"All that make sound are not bikes. Hmmm."

Ayodhya opens the pack for him. And Tintu happily takes it back in his room!

Ayodhya picks up his laptop and is surprised to find a reply mail by his grandpa. He looks around if Tintu is there. He hadn't said 'Hmmm' when he left.

'Dear Appu,

I never felt that they were my children. Neither would I enquire where their rites were conducted. But I can only hope you are not involved in it in anyway.

And about Gharial, I have seen on TV. I am not an expert but can only say that he has a habit of lurking in disguise. Be careful and don't let anyone know about you. Sagar's personal life is his own castle. Don't invite hard feelings. They come uninvited, anyway. So don't invite.

We are humans- creatures with unlimited usage plans. We use one another in different ways. So, it is very much possible that Sagar can be using you for his work. Don't overthink.

Eat more fruits, don't consume the masala stuff on roadside. Learn cooking. Believe me, that's how I impressed your grandma. Learn it.

As far as getting stressed out is concerned, I have an advice. Being stressed is akin to drowning. Some people know how to swim. Some are newcomers like you. You have two options. Submit and go down in its depths or beat your limbs and do something to overcome it. Try resurfacing from the depths if you are not able to stay afloat. And do you know the best part? You can lift yourself up to the surface. It is not difficult. Buoyancy supports you. But to come out of it completely you need your own energy. Your family and friends are like the buoyant forces. They can only bring you up to the surface. But it is your own ability beyond!

Don't worry about work. Just keep trying. Don't miss me. Have no attachments. We are all here to go. Easier said than done... But doing is not impossible. Spend time with Anca.

With a lot of do's & don'ts but doing nothing,

Your grandpa,

Ram Prakash.

Ayodhya smiles and opens BlueTube for some cooking videos.

"Learning cooking-o? Hmmm..."-Tintu makes his way in, offering his I-phone 5, rotating his head as though he has caught Ayodhya stealing. He has got new looks...French beard, extended hair down his ears and face laden with talc, giving a weird, ashy look. It is evident that he has tried his best to spike his hairline. The hair is getting back to normal, furling and curling. He hasn't bathed, though.

"Yeah."

"How do I look?"-he stands sideways, giving the best look that he can. He smiles weakly, with self-conscious eyes and folded hands. "Hmmm?"

"Mammoolal and Ajay... They are no match for you!"-Ayodhya means it.

"Hey man!"-he blushes out from his portrait stance.

"No, seriously. Hmmm."

"Will you take my pic-o?"-he requests, thrusting the phone and looking for a place to pose in.

He finally settles at the sink.

"I guessed it."

"Hey man. This mirror at the sink will show my other side of the face. So only... Hmmm."-he stands with face inclined in all the three dimensions.

It reminds Ayodhya of the passport-sized lined up pictures in the local hair salon of Sarovar Nagar. The men showcased the styling options like comatose bodies looking for spark somewhere down.

Ayodhya clicks a couple of quick snaps. “Why suddenly? Pics?”

“You are not on Fakebook-o?”-he turns, taking back the phone, as though Ayodhya has evaded tax.

“No.”

“My engagement!!! With Pheno Menon. Hmmm.”-he walks to the door. “When are you getting married actually?”

“I am looking for eligible brides on corporate websites of top companies.”-Ayodhya wants to stump Tintu.

“Why don’t you try on Tinder, actually?”

17 UNMASKED

The video of Ayodhya thrashing the bad guys at the traffic signal has a new comment by 'G'.

'When I turn up, some have to leave...'

Ayodhya feels no surprise.

'You should probably bathe.'

A third random commenter is not at all happy. He is one of those who are always itchy to involve in the famous 'comment war' fought online. He is 'IndiaRockzzz'.

'Hello, lissen. Wassa madr about? If u ve any personnel enemety jes don't use BlueTube plzzz.'

He doesn't understand that it is between Gharial and Ayodhya.

Ayodhya walks back to kitchen. He has brought beans for curry tonight. But he hates kneading the dough. He hates it from the bottom of his heart.

But there is no other option. Feeding your stomach is the sole undeniable obligation.

He starts kneading, thinking about ways to get to Gharial.

“What has he planned? Kanaka Sundari is gone. He may attack the publisher next. Or Kesha Sundari who has made extreme remarks at him. But he is always a step ahead. He knows I’ll be there for him and he plans his kills excellently. How do I find him? He’s so unpredictable.”

The wheat flour he is kneading is not sufficient. He can make about three rotis with it. He needs more flour. He gets to the kitchen shelf and finds that he needs to cut open another pack of flour. He searches for a pair of scissors. It is nowhere in sight. He searches for five minutes. Nope... It is still not there. “I can’t even find a simple object. How can I find Gharial? Huh!! Forget it!”

He gives up the search and lights the stove to boil milk. As he lifts the pail of milk to place it on the burner, he finds the scissors beneath it.

He gets back to kneading.

“Ayodhya, you’re missing it!”-a scary voice makes a threatening remark from somewhere around!

He turns. The curtains blow in the mild wind. There is no one in the flat. He gets back.

“You are missing it!”

“Ayodhya!”

The voice is creepier than before!

He stops.

“Your’e missing it” “Don’t miss” “Ayodhya” “Don’t” “issing it.”

“yodhya” “you’re” “don’t” ...

The words reverberate. He presses his eyelids into his eyes.

“You’re” “Ayodh” “Don’t.”- the voice seems to consume him!

He feels someone nearing him. Someone unseen! He can only feel the presence. He isn’t alone!!

It is gaining on him. He gets on his feet and stands against the table. The voice is beating his ear drums. “Ayodhya...” “Don’t” “You’re” ...

He turns around... ducks...

And looks!!

The scissors!!!

“Yes!”

The voice leaves him alone. There is no one now. He can feel his sweet breath!

“I found the scissors when I stopped searching for it and started doing something else... Is it one of those simple lessons I tend to overlook in the race against time? I won’t go after Gharial. If the voice wasn’t right, it wouldn’t have forced me. I’ll find him when the time is right! For now,

I'll focus on someone else."

He starts kneading with rejuvenated feelings! It is an accomplishment. A silent one...

"So what is next?"

"Grandpa has to be secured. Anca is with Pony. And Pony is waiting for my cousin. So?"-he finishes kneading the flour into a fine, smooth ball.

"Soman!!!"

Sagar and Jackpot have worked out a plan to save Kesha Sundari. They are going to shoot to kill and shoot at the heads. A plan as simple as that... Every day, they are keeping vigil at her flat in the posh South Dweepa. They know that the publisher too is under Gharial's radar but feel that she is more vulnerable.

As days slip by, Ayodhya has become more and more exhausted after working in the office during day and cooking at home in the night. And he hasn't mastered the art yet.

Today is a special day for him. He has been reprimanded in front of all his colleagues by the team leader. His project evaluation is due this weekend and it is going at a snail's pace. The shadow of the Dungeon's gallows has consumed him partially.

He has returned home. Tintu has gone to Pattanam Thitta to get engaged. He had sent the invitation to Ayodhya as an image file in Shutapp. Ayodhya had aptly replied him with the image of a thousand rupee note and a one-rupee coin.

"He might shout at me for that."-Ayodhya opens the lock to his house.

He leaves his bag on the table and switches on the water heater for bathing. He wants to go out for food but can't face his colleagues in the apartment after the insult in the morning. He decides to cook...

As he bathes, he thinks of the dream he has seen the previous night. Or a nightmare... that he is in front of Gharial and is going to fight to the finish. He had woken up as soon as he had seen Gharial get a hold of his neck. He hadn't brooded over it as it was getting late to office. But private moments bring about hidden thoughts to the fore.

He is worried even as he feels the comfortable soothing by warm water in the chilly evening. He has seen himself in front of a gigantic Gharial. He knows Gharial is unrivaled in brute strength. "How Asrar might have fared against him? He might have been crazy to take on the monster. But wait a minute... Asrar had muscular arms like a pair of maces."-he looks at his lean arms in the mirror. It feels so shameful. "Even Anca is stronger."-he feels down as he brushes the mirror off the steam to see his reflection.

With eyes still on the mirror, he reaches out to the bottle of shampoo. All of a sudden a cockroach hops out of it and jumps on the wet floor. He drops the bottle as he shudders. He attempts to stomp it. It escapes behind a bucket. He raises the handle slowly and lifts the bucket abruptly. The cockroach, surprisingly, is prepared. It makes a dash at his foot in a flash!!

He retracts his foot jerkily, slips on the floor and falls with a bang! The bucket lies tumbled next to him!!

He sits down unmoving. The shower is still on. A trail of water drips from his head as he engages in his thought...

"A small insect, not even the size of my toe, has felled me with such ease."-he gets up.

"I am more than half of Gharial!!"

He stands still looking into the mirror. A moment of solace blows over his mind. He turns around and walks to the corner.

Pichchkk!

The cockroach is dead!

Sagar and Jackpot are braving the cold night in front of Holy Lady Street, South Dweepa. They are lying in wait for Gharial with AK 47. The actress is holed up in her flat. She has probably understood the gravity of her comments.

Sagar closes his eyes and bends his head down on his arm. It has been a long wait... For Gharial... It has been longer for Ayush and his mother. He just doesn't know how to handle responsibilities, all of them requiring his immediate attention. "Had I not been foolish on that night after catching him, it would've been a closed case by now. Had Ayush applied to one of the jobs, we would've been much lighter in our hearts. Had mother slapped me once I would've been..."-he keeps his painful eyes on the cold, sleek metal body of the killing machine, not able to think much. The foggy air his nostrils blow, settles on the gun in a hush.

Jackpot dwells in the memory of Shyamala at times and at times thinks about his son who is aspiring to go abroad for higher studies. He had never thought about it. "The younger generation has changed."-he sits, hiding at the other side with his weapon against the natural damping setup of his belly.

The lights in the actress's flat go off. Sagar and Jackpot get suspicious.

Gharial hasn't come for her yet. Is it the publisher he is after?

Not far away, another light glows. Ayodhya has lit the stove. He has placed the pan with oil in it and allowed it to warm up. He has even chopped chillies and onions. The next job is to put in the pan some mustard, turmeric, the paste of ginger and garlic and the chopped items.

He proceeds to locate turmeric. It is not in sight. And so is the paste. He somehow gathers the things and hastily adds them in the pan. The oil bursts as soon as they are added. The items are charred beyond hope. He had taken too long to get the input ready.

He slams his forehead, turns off the burner and empties the pan in the bin. "Ayodhya!"-the same, mysterious voice tries to draw attention. This time he doesn't need to be coerced.

His eyes shine!

He attempts again. But this time, there is a difference. He has kept the items ready in correct quantities in the lids of their respective containers.

As the oil heats, he adds them. It has work out smoothly and more importantly, quickly!

"This is why my project is getting delayed!!"

He returns the office next morning and spends the whole day getting the input ready instead of following the routine. The change in his working style earns him returns after four more days. He comes to office and opens the folder to see that everything has been worked to minute details and the project is ready for take-off.

The client arrives in the forenoon session. Ayodhya produces the documents related to the project. The client is happy, the team is happy,

Ayodhya himself is happy and more importantly the team leader is happy!

"What is your mantra? Can you tell me the clear cut idea in your mind about the schedule?"-he rotates his fingers for mantra and slides his palm from his forehead like a knife to stress on 'clear cut'. Ayodhya always knew that his team leader and the Project Head were at loggerheads and disliked each other immensely.

It is a light moment and he brings out the Project Head's equivalent of mantra called 'funda'.

"Sir, the funda is..."-he tries to poke the team leader.

"Don't tell me the whole funda..."-the team leader interrupts by rotating his arms, thereby making Ayodhya visualize a huge ball of... err... something.

"Give me just the mantra!"-he closes his left eye indicating the need for sharpness in sight essential to view the microscopic size of 'mantra' and rotates his fingers. Anything that tries to occupy minimum space is spherical in shape. And hence the rotation of fingers...

He also implies that mantra is more concise than funda and thus the Project Leader doesn't know about the core.

Ayodhya only smiles...

It is night. He has returned home. Another comment by Gharial catches his attention-

'You're weak.'

The same IndiaRockzzz who had earlier replied to their comments notices the new one. He is fed up with the comment war with the random Pakistani guy 'PakiTaakat', after the mundane remembrances of the innocent women folk in their families and the distinctiveness with which both of them were given birth.

He finds a harmless, naïve newcomer in 'G'... someone who can't even type about specific parts of human body and the adjoining areas.

'U r also week. I mean whoz not week? A polotician izz week in election tym, conmam man izz week afterelection tym, I am week in exam tym and u r week in night tym. Lolzzz.'

Ayodhya finds it extremely hilarious. He sprinkles one of those precious smiles, in solitude.

He nevertheless leaves a reply to Gharial-

I know and that had made me stronger.

The scene at the office is smooth. The mantra is clear. It is weekend again and he has the time, energy, will and of course reason to start to Heaven Seven Hospital of Dweepa where Soman is staying after the demise of his dear ones. Ayodhya has seen Soman on TV and Goggled out about him.

He waits at Pungent Dungeon stop for the direct local train to Heaven Seven station. There is no platform and one has to 'climb' into the train. He feels for the ladies, the elderly and the kids waiting nearby. A small boy looks at him pitifully.

The train arrives. The people slowly get up from their seats. Ayodhya senses competition. He walks to the edge of the station and hops in to the coach. A window seat lies in wait and he grabs it.

As he turns his face sideways to utilize the narrow view the grilled window is offering him, he sees the same poor boy fold the sleeve of his shirt looking at the coaches like a matador expecting a raging bull.

Ayodhya is curious to know what the boy is up to. The train slows down. A sign of quietness passes by. Something big is about to come. Ayodhya gets back in anticipation.

And suddenly it rains!

Handkerchiefs!!

They rocket past the walls of the coach, into the grills and on to the seats. A couple of them land on his lap. He throws them away. The kids are scampered by their guardians. The mission is clear- 1. To reserve as many seats as possible with the hankies 2. To reserve as many window seats as possible.

They rush eagerly to share the spoils. A tall man on the platform, unconcerned with the seats getting filled, smokes the last bit of beedi and takes up a position far away from the coach. He slowly removes his backpack and eyes the emergency exit. One of the kids too spots it at the same instance. The boy runs to reserve it. The man hurls the backpack through the emergency window!

Three-pointer!!!

The thing occupies the seat even before the boy takes the leap!

Ayodhya is crammed on all sides with the small family that has almost fully occupied one whole coach. The Lady of the Coach is all guns at Ayodhya-

"Why don't you go occupy the next bogie?"

Ayodhya doesn't answer her. She murmurs some curses. He leans against the window. She murmurs them again. Others look at him scornfully. The same actions continue for a long time.

He learns a very important lesson. One who grumbles is not always the victim and one who doesn't is not always the offender.

She is next to him with her son at the aisle and daughter at the window opposite Ayodhya. Her husband is at the aisle on the other end, not too far. Ayodhya is feigning sleep, hoping that she doesn't bother him.

She jabs him with her elbow in his ribs, indicating that she has never spared even the dead, ever in her life, whenever she wanted anything out of them.

"Why don't you switch places with my husband?"

"Why?"

"We are a family. All of us get to sit together."

"Then I'll switch with your daughter."-he opens up an alternative such that he still gets the window seat. She starts cursing him again-"blah... blah...blah... as though he is going to settle permanently... blah...blah... blah" Her mantra is clear-the family should sit together. Who calls it a family otherwise? And the window seats that are more sacrosanct than the family bond, cannot be compromised.

"Thank God I don't understand her language."-he thinks. "Else, she would be in trouble!"

"Why don't you stand for a while? I need to keep the basket to serve food for my children."-she strikes another of her missiles. Others too have joined in cursing him. "Look how stubborn he is. Looks like a kid...

nah, brat!"

Ayodhya could easily walk away. But he doesn't. He still maintains his stance than stand. He doesn't want to be counted as inferior to a non-living basket.

"How can I give in for mild pressure? I am yet to brave the storms."

It is the Heaven Seven stop. He reaches the hospital through the subway. The building is majestic. The beautiful hoarding advertising about the hospital assures him that it is not a mall he is entering in. The advertisement shows gorgeous models as doctors and nurses. Even the patients are quite good-looking and cheerful. The photo snaps display various state-of-the-art facilities available and the extent the staff goes to treat the inmates. A creative slogan urges people to turn patients to avail the 'once in a lifetime' facilities.

"The advertisement is well thought."-Ayodhya admires the creativity. "Nobody wants anything until somebody wants them to want something."

The road opposite the hospital is lined with vendors of tender coconut and sugarcane juice.

A mild quarrel seems to be taking place between one of the sugarcane vendors and his customer. Suddenly the customer slaps the vendor hard under his ear and crashes the glass on the road. The other vendors gather around. The situation is very tense. Ayodhya stands at the end of the road, witnessing silently.

A war of words begins. It is slowly raging into a fight. Collars are being held. Tongues are getting bent over the teeth. Eyes are getting redder. Fists are getting clenched...

Ayodhya asks one of the men awestruck with the action.

"What's going on?"

"Don't drink the juice!"-the man doesn't look at him to show that he is a treasure of information.

"Why? What happened?"

"The ice is of low quality."-he points at one of the gunny bags.

Ayodhya is baffled. "How can ice have quality? Is it the quality of water?"-he thinks. The quarreling customer swiftly uncovers one of the gunny bags.

Ayodhya is surprised to see that the ice has a mild, reddish appearance.

He takes a closer look. Some tiny particles seem to have been frozen and trapped in the ice.

He walks around. Pieces of ice have scattered on the road. He slowly picks up a few samples, empties his water bottle and forces the pieces in to it. Others are busy savoring the scene. He slowly walks to a sugarcane vendor.

"If he doesn't want to drink the juice, he shouldn't! He has no rights to shout at the poor vendors."-he tries to gain trust of the vendor. The vendor looks at him with locked brows, indicating that he is in full agreement with him.

"So far, nobody has complained to us about our juice or our ice."-he strikes the air with his index finger. "Yeah, I know. You're earning money through hard work. These people do not complain about the politicians and bureaucrats about the misdeeds. They target only poor chaps."-Ayodhya strikes twice. The man seems pleased. "Leave them, Sir. You want juice?"

"No I just had some."-Ayodhya turns away. The vendor wants to talk more-"Sir, do you know a fact?"

"No. What fact? Don't tell me if it is scary. I am a very sissy fellow."

"Not scary. It is about corruption as you just mentioned."-the vendor's voice is dramatically low.

"Corruption? Oh God."-Ayodhya expresses interest.

"The chief of this hospital is a good friend of the Chief Minister, Home Minister and even the opposition party leaders. He has good influence with the Police and the bureaucrats too."

"What's the big deal? Every rich guy does that."

"Hey!! Hey, hey, hey!"-the vendor waves his hand indicating that Ayodhya is too hasty in conclusions.

"This guy is just too much."-he winks slowly.

"Really? But the VIPs may be visiting for a health checkup too."-Ayodhya whispers.

The vendor points his hand at him and stands still for a few seconds, each second conveying the magnitude of jolt he is experiencing at Ayodhya's naivety.

"See, I'll give you an inside story. But you should promise confidentiality."

"I am a forgetful guy. There is no use narrating stories to me."-Ayodhya looks disinterested. The vendor bends over.

"I know."

Ayodhya is shocked!!

"I know... You filled your bottle with ice and forgot to keep it in your bag!!"

Ayodhya touches his bag and turns to see that he has kept the bottle on a cart. "Oh, thank you."

"I understand that you want to taste chill water and hence you filled it. But I suggest you don't drink it. You seem to be a nice fellow."

"Why shouldn't I drink it?"

"That ice is not made. It is brought."-the vendor gives it away!!

"Brought? So what's the big deal?"

"Hey, which world are you in? Do you know we bring ice free of cost from the hospital?"

Ayodhya's head reels!!

"WHA..t?"

"Yes. The hospital provides us with ice recovered after the cadavers are disposed. After the kin of the dead claim the bodies, the ice has to be discharged. But the hospital gives us for free."

"But why?"

"Corporate Social Responsibility..."

“They retrieve certain parts from the bodies and sell them as transplants.”-he continues.

“How can you say that?”

“The ice bears reddish marks. That means they have cut open the bodies after operating on them!!”

“Oh, ok. Thank you.”- he leaves. His body feels numb!

He takes out his cell phone and dials a number. “It is the right time to let Kunj contact them.”

A while later Jackpot receives Kunj’s call.

“Sir, the samples have to be given for Forensic tests quickly.”

Jackpot is not interested in anything except Gharial. But Sagar is curious. Within minutes, Jackpot arrives to accept the samples. “You think you are a great detective?”-he is unhappy with Kunj.

“With your blessings.”

“I can bet it isn’t you who found about the samples.”-Jackpot wants not to give any credit to Kunj. “I am a Bihari. How do you expect me to be brainy, Sir? My friend was in the field. He gave me these samples.”

It is twilight.

Abhilash from the forensic lab has updated Sagar with the ghastly discovery. Ayodhya feels the chillness of fear after hearing the news through Kunj.

The ice indeed contains the flesh of human body!!!

In the two ice pieces he had collected, there was presence of flesh from the digestive tract and flesh from under the skin. "That means the hospital is really selling transplants! The vendor was right!"

This is the one clue that is going to turn the whole plot around. The information by an ordinary street vendor...

It happened centuries ago too. A similar incident I am not able to help but recall.

It is the closing years of the 15th century... 1498 C E

The sun takes another peek in to the city of Lisbon, Portugal. The preparations had started when news had come that the sea route Christopher Columbus had claimed to have discovered to the Indian sub-continent is false. Today it is the culmination.

The court of King Manuel is brimming with courtiers on this special day.

All eyes are on Vasco Da Gama, attired in the finest of clothes, with the typical hat tucked at his waist.

"It is a new opportunity bestowed by God to fulfill our ambitions."-one of the clergymen in the whitest of coats stands in the center of the hallway. "The time has come to set sail on an adventure never ever been successful since time immemorial."

Vasco Da Gama feels his throat getting dry. "...We proclaim the first of our men of the early 16th century to show the light to the Golden Bird!!"

The court reverberates with applauses. Vasco Da Gama spares a minute amidst his forceful smiles to know what exactly made the man exclaim 'first' of the voyagers. "What the hell is in his mind?"

"Thence we take up the expansion of this holy Portuguese Kingdom across the sea and spread the message of God!"-the man raises his arms.

"Should he fail in this campaign, we pray to Thee to take Vasco Da Gama and his brave men into the bosoms of heaven and grant him eternal bliss!!"

The court turns hysterical!

"Enough!"-Vasco Da Gama curses as he bows to the king. "I'll make a recommendation to the King to take this man along."

They proceed to the Port of Lisbon after the customary rituals.

The ship is all set to sail. The crew is beaming with joy. It is the biggest and the most expensive ship ever in the history of Europe. People from far, far lands have flocked to have a glimpse of the giant. It is made of the finest of timber and the strongest of designs. The deck is full of state-of-the-art equipment for smoother sail. The steer is provided with a belt and pulley arrangement, the first of its kind.

Vasco Da Gama is escorted with all the precious gifts and presents that could befit the Kings of the Golden Bird. His brother is on the other ship.

"May you succeed."-the king wishes him luck as he bows down.

"May?"

The journey begins!

Portugal can be seen fading from sight. "Which way, skipper?"-Guerrero, the second-in-command wants to know. "Just a little longer along the coast and we'll see."-Vasco acts as though he is in complete knowledge of the route.

"Aye."

They sail along African continent. A month has gone by. Vasco, not knowing the next plan, strides on the deck, feigning deep thought. The voice echoes-"Should he fail in this campaign, we pray to Thee to take Vasco Da Gama and his brave men into the bosoms of heaven and grant him eternal bliss."

"I won't fail, I won't die. Because I won't try."

"I'll remain close to land all the time."

"Land!!! Land!!"-Guerrero exults!

Vasco hopes they have made it to the Golden Bird. "Nay."-Guerrero turns his head as soon as he understands that it just a cape- The Cape of Good Hope has just been discovered!

Vasco gets confident. The African continent is tapering down. "Skipper, shall we change the course now?"-Guerrero is fed up.

"No, I mean yes but make sure you don't lose the coast. There has to be land in sight all the time."

Guerrero is surprised. He stands looking at Vasco.

"The Golden Bird is a land!"

"Aye."

Three weeks pass by. It is a bright, sunny morning at the port of Zanzibar. "Skipper! Look!!"-Guerrero is shell shocked.

The light on the biggest ship in the whole of Europe is being turned to darkness!

Vasco's jaw drops!!

It is the shadow of just another ordinary merchant ship from Gujarat!

The ship is modest but humongous. The captain of the ship is courteous. He enquires about the voyage and assures him that he'll take him to the Golden Bird safely. "But take me along the coast."-Vasco requests.

"It is not I to decide."-the captain points at the mother ship.

Vasco turns and gazes through the telescope!

A mountain seems to be approaching them!

The skipper of the mother ship is Chandan Bhai. Vasco is brought aboard. He feels that he is seeing another Lisbon in the middle of the sea.

He looks at the steersman effortlessly toying with the wheel. The compass and the other equipment are way advanced than the latest ones in Europe. The goods on board are costlier than the costliest gift he is taking to the Golden Bird.

"You have to take me along the coast."-he repeats.

Chandan Bhai laughs it off- "As you wish."

The course is changed. Vasco's ship is flanked in all directions by the Gujarati merchant vessels. The mother ship leads the way. A few weeks pass by. Vasco wakes up. His steps make the hollow wooden stairs to the deck vibrate, raising dust. The sharp rays of the sun hit his eyes. He turns back, tightly blinks for a minute and looks around.

There is a small break between two vessels. He, though, can't see land. He walks to the eastern side of the deck and looks to the farthest end between the minimum spaces between two vessels. No land!

"No land?"

"NO LAND!!!"

Chandan Bhai invites him for breakfast. Vasco is more than eager. "Chandan Bhai!!! We're out of land!"

Chandan Bhai offers him a dish made of grain. "Calm down, Sir. We are traveling in the middle of the Arabian Sea, far away from land, since six weeks now. I knew you would get scared and hence made my vessels flank you from all directions!!"

Vasco is surprised, scared, awed, embarrassed and finally calmed. "I was told that your people make spicy food. Yours is so sweet!"

"Welcome to Gujarat, Sir."

As I sail by the lofty masts of the ships into the future, I can see how a horde of seafarers from Europe juiced out whatever was possible over centuries; in men, material and moments of glory.

All that is because, on one fateful day, in the middle of a sea, a generous, broad-minded heart of an ordinary merchant gave a bunch of opportunists the lifeline of India.

Ayodhya is restless. He writes another mail to his grandfather.

'Grandpa,

I just found that Soman is running a transplant trade in his hospital. I had gone to Heaven Seven Hospital here in Dweepa. And found out from there.

He is stealing organs from cadavers before handing over to the kin. This has been confirmed forensically. ACP Sagar wanted to raid the hospital but I felt we should gather more information before that. If it is a mere transplant trade, it wouldn't attract the attention of political top brass. I have heard about his contacts with them. There is something more. We need time.

As of now I am not pursuing Gharial. I feel exhausted with working on multiple fronts. So I'm doing things one by one. Office work is easing out. Of late, whatever I cook has become swallowable. Hope you are doing fine.

Yours lovingly,

Ayodhya

"Soor, we need to meet right now!"-Sagar calls up.

An hour later, Soor meets him at his house. He narrates her about Heaven Seven's transplant scandal. Her eyes remain open in disbelief!

"Anyway, I'll try to find out tomorrow."-she gets up slowly. She is in deep shock. "Soor, it is a very sensitive issue. Do it carefully. Nobody knows it other than the five of us."

"Five?"

"Yeah... We two, Jackpot, Kunj Bihari Yadav and his friend who collected the information... If you face any problem, just call any of us."

"Can you give me the number of that Kunj Bihari Yadav? Is he trustworthy?"

"I'll text you. He and his friend are doing a wonderful job."

She leaves.

Kunj receives a call from Soor requesting him to be at the hospital in the evening along with his friend. She wants them to plan out a method to get to the bottom of the matter.

"I have access and you guys have resources. Let's plan."

Kunj agrees- "Sure, Soor."

But Ayodhya is skeptic. He does not want to share the field.

"Plans only help you fail unsurprised."

Kunj nevertheless sets out to Heaven Seven all alone.

The local train is not even half full. A lot of seats are vacant. He sees two small kids look at each other. A perfect reflection of curiosity...

One of the kids touches the cheek of the other. The other smiles. He can see that the two families belong to two different faiths. They are cuddling and encouraging the kids to play with each other. There are smiles everywhere. But there is one fact only I know about.

After thirty-five years, after the last of the parents has passed away, there will be a nationwide friction of some sort. The same kid will make a scar on the same cheek... Thirty-five years later... Mark my words!

Humans, you are so sensitive to communities and insensitive to humanity to which they point. It is not entirely your mistake, anyway. Innocence is a godly quality I rob you of.

Heaven Seven stop arrives. Kunj uses the subway to the building. There are many patients waiting at the lounge. It is bustling.

Kunj is unable to reach Soor through phone call. He decides to meet her at her cabin.

The entrance to the doctors' private cabin area has a sign- 'Entry Restricted'. There is a lady at the pathway, sitting in a closed chamber near the access panel. Visitors have to have proper reason for the visit, wait till they get due appointments and only then enter the private cabins.

It is only after she types the password that the doors will open.

Kunj cannot take chances. He observes that she is busy with snacks. "Please have some."-she offers. "Thank you, madam. So sweet you are."-Kunj tries to gauge if she is talkative.

"No problem Sir... Actually, these snacks are made by me for the festival and..."-she goes on.

She is!

He pinches her cell phone and wants to unlock it. He has to draw a pattern on the screen. "I need to use the wash room."

He locks himself in the toilet and takes out his cellphone. He flashes torchlight on her phone and observes the glass screen held horizontally in front of his eyes. The finger marks show sliding of her thumb in a particular pattern-a Z with two vertical lines. It is a difficult one in terms of start point, the path and the end point. He resorts to trials hoping that she does not get a chance to use her phone as long as he keeps it. A minute passes by. He has eliminated a few combinations. The next one is right! He immediately calls his number from her phone.

He accepts the call and returns to her cabin with her phone on call!

He waits until the she has finished her snacks and talks. "Madam, can I go in?"-he gives no reason. She feels good that so far he is the only one who has listened to her patiently and expressed no disinterest. "Please..."-she types the password, whispering the code to herself. Although he cannot hear it directly, he is able to pick it up through her phone!

'264ROHIT143'

He walks in to Soor's cabin. She isn't there. He gets a call from her almost immediately.

"Hey, Kunj. Where are you guys? I am at the entrance."

"I'm just coming."

"Hi. I was waiting at the lounge with the patients."-he meets her at the entrance.

"Where is your friend?"

"He is not well."

"What's his name?"

"What's in a name?"

"Ha ha ha... I meet a lot of jolly guys from Bihar."-she takes him to the cabin.

"So? How do we start?"-she rubs her palm like an anchor at the cookery program on TV.

"It should start from you. You have the access. Just give me the working schedule of the hospital and the routine of the staff."

"And then you have to try and gather information carefully, especially about Soman."

"Dr. Soman is a very reserved person. It is hard to talk to him."

"You don't have to talk. Just observe him. And try to have a look at the mortuary where the bodies are kept. We'll plan the rest later."

"I'll leave now."

"It is drizzling outside. Why don't you wait till I finish my shift? I'll drop you by my car."-she offers.

"No, it is ok."

Kunj takes leave. It is cold. The roads are deserted. A gang of toads has wreaked havoc in the bushes with incessant croaking.

As he walks down the subway he feels somewhat uneasy. Something seems to have gone wrong. He is missing the presence of someone. He feels Ayodhya should have been there. He sends Sagar an SMS that he is feeling insecure. "Will be there."-the reply is quick.

"When you don't find what you're missing, turn around."- a deathly voice eases his thoughts.

Kunj turns around!

Gharial it is!!

Kunj bolts!

Gharial's men cover up from the exit. He is trapped below the quiet roads!! "This is a classic case of getting holed up!"

"Please, I am just a poor guy looking for employment. Please!"-he falls to

Gharial's feet. Gharial relieves his leg. Kunj is thrown away!

He lies flat on the ground. Gharial holds his neck- "Kunj Bihari Yadav. What's your BMI?"

Kunj holds his wrist with both hands. Gharial lifts him abruptly. Kunj is in the air! He looks like a hen in the hands of a butcher. "Whoa! Whoa! Whoa! You're poor indeed!"

Gharial drags him along the subway. Kunj's feet resist in vain. He screams!

"Who else is with you? Who is the... the... guy at the signal? Who is uploading comments on BlueTube?"

"He is Ayodhya from Sarovar Nagar."-Kunj gives away the secret.

"Um... Hmmm."

"He is good at everything. He can dance, sing, shoot... I...Aarghh!"-he feels the tightness of Gharial's fury. "I... don't know where he stays in Dweepa. But I have his number...Ppp... Pp... Please spare me."

One of Gharial's men notes down Ayodhya's number. They take him to a nearby ATM. The guard recognizes Gharial. He can't believe that the man all over the news is right in front of him. All of a sudden he remembers the ways Gharial employs to kill his victims.

He covers himself up immediately and feigns sleep. The blanket provides him faith that he is not being watched. Gharial thumps Kunj on the ATM. His men tie up Kunj's hands at his back. They bring his face in front of the air conditioner and secure his neck to the ceiling with a rope. Gharial increases the air flow of the AC to maximum. The stream beats Kunj's nostrils with extreme force. He struggles to inhale breath.

If Kunj tries to get down from the ATM, he'll be hanged and if he doesn't, he'll suffocate.

"Let's see who wins."-Gharial takes off his hat, remarks on the two deaths competing for Kunj. Kunj can see Gharial's noxious eyes. The sound of siren rises from the glary horizons of the empty roads

Sagar drives on!!

Gharial takes the guard with him as though carrying a parcel. "Let's find your worth online. But pray to God that I don't get too creative."

Kunj is unable to inhale. The flow of air is too much to take. His lips are deformed. They deform in a different way when he turns his head. He tries to move his head where the flow is lesser but no. He can't really move that much.

It is too cold and Sagar has passed by, not noticing the ATM. Kunj can see death from close by. He has to choose. The other one tries to beckon him away from the one approaching. His face is getting numb... The skin is getting discolored. He is almost... there... when I play a spoilsport!!

Yes, it's I... Again...

About forty years ago, one of the forested areas in mainland India had a muddy pathway. The clouds were sailing towards the eastern side and I diverted the path to the south east. As the clouds continued their journey they were intercepted by a mountain range. There was heavy precipitation that week. Due to constant footfall, the pathway was slightly deeper in the soil than the level of adjoining grasses. This led to water accumulation on the pathway and the path was closed. A survey team to set up a power plant was supposed to cross the forest through that path to enter the village but since it was closed, the villagers took them around the forest. The team felt that going around the forest was hectic and hence moved on to some other location, citing accessibility as the obstacle in their final report.

The other location is the one that provides electricity to Dweepa through transmission lines along the Arabian Bridge. Had it been the original location, the transmission would have been smoother given that the current location has a lot of friction between villagers and authorities.

So tonight in Dweepa, there is the culmination of ordeals. Villagers have assembled in front of the plant, blocking operations. And hence...

There is power cut!!

The Island Bank of Dweepa has removed the uninterrupted power supply from the ATM as one of the cost-cutting measures. So, the air conditioner is SWITCHED OFF!!

Kunj's body temperature returns to normal. The numbness recedes. He rests his head against the vent and closes his eyes. He falls fast asleep.

It is the next dawn. Kunj shouts aloud for help. He is heeded to by the milkman.

He returns home, shivering with cold, quivering with fear.

Ayodhya is in the office. He is shocked with what has happened to Kunj.

Anca brings him coffee. He does not sip it, ostensibly looking busy. He bows down his head and presses his brows against the angle at the elbow. Somehow, his memories as a child pass by him-

It is winter.

The ball is swinging like a piece of magnet getting repelled by an invisible one of the same pole. He has dropped three catches despite the new pair of wicketkeeping gloves. He misses another one and it goes for four. The captain doesn't say a word despite the team mates' immediate provocative gazes. "Wicketkeeping is the most thankless job. You take a great catch and it is your duty. You drop it and you're in for it. What do I do now? Where am I going wrong?"-Ayodhya crouches for the next. The batsman attempts to cut it square. Ayodhya estimates the bounce to be chest high and readies himself. It takes an edge and flies past his hands that are fixed in front of his chest. His eyes helplessly gape at the half shiny ball sail like a balloon.

"Come on Ayodhya, what's this?"-the captain swings his head in despair. Ayodhya looks at the ground apologetically. He shows that he is in deep introspection. But in reality he is just waiting for the captain to look elsewhere. "Should I check if he is still looking at me?"

The next ball is bowled. There is an edge again. Ayodhya is ready and waiting for it this time. He takes a flying catch, almost getting carried away by the force. As he descends on the ground, the idea strikes!!

He, uncompromisingly, has to expect a chance off every delivery. He has to assume that the batsman is there to give him catch-practice and is missing it most of the times.

"Hey, Ayodhya. Not feeling well?"-Anca caresses his hair. He gets up.

He has opened the internet. The NOT NOW video displays the lifeless body of the ATM guard hanging on the electric transmission wire lines!!

Ayodhya is prepared! He walks out of office and calls up his grandpa- "Grandpa, Ayodhya here... Quick... You need to pack up!"

"Appu!! My baby! How are you?"-his grandpa is happy to hear his grandson. "Grandpa, it's about you. Gharial has got to know that I am from Sarovar Nagar and the people around will definitely help him get to our house. You need to move to a safe location."

His grandpa is stunned! The infamous Gharial has got his attention on Ayodhya. "Grandpa, are you listening?"

"Yeah..."-his grandpa replies mechanically. "I know a place, grandpa."

Sagar and Jackpot have now turned their focus on the publisher. His office is in West Dweepa.

KINGPIN PUBLISHERS-the board at the posh office dazzles. 'In a quest for new revolution'-the punch line summarizes the archaic objective of supporting new authors. The publisher has made a lot of money by publishing the works of some handpicked new authors- the celebrities. So the tag line still holds good.

Jackpot walks in to the office full of people immersed in computers and sailing through MS Word and PDFs. The Afro-haired, French-bearded, Indian boss with an Italian snack, sits, editing the work of Paneer Kahn- the superstar actor contemplating retirement. He is too busy to be disturbed. Kanaka Sundari's book has topped the market sales after her disappearance. The editor is secretly happy with that.

One of the young editors stops Jackpot, parroting a series of standard instructions- "We do not entertain appointments. Whatever you got to get published is to be sent by email. Please do not visit if not invited. And if you don't hear from us in three months please consider it a regretful 'no'."

"Uninvited guests always leave a mark. And a mark can be a scar too."-

Sagar enters behind him. The young lady recognizes him- “ACP Sagar!”

“Can I meet your boss?”

“He is on video conference with Paneer Kahn on his upcoming novel. Anyway, I’ll try.”-she shows them the waiting lounge.

“Sir, you may meet him now.”-the lady offers after a good twenty minutes. The publisher, Mr. Mama, welcomes them with a tinge of suspicion. He is just another Indian who considers policemen a bad omen. Sagar strangely is reminded of his father.

As they settle down, Jackpot begins- “Mr. Mama, you’re going to die.” “WHAT!!”-Mama almost gets a heart stroke.

“Jackpot, that’s not how you put it.”-Sagar intervenes.

“Mr. Mama, your life is in danger.”

“Oh, is it so?”-he leans confidently as though it is all routine and he is bargaining with the literary agent on royalty- “Oh, is it so? The debutant, unheard, unsolicited, unworthy author wants more than 5%?”

“Mr. Mama. Recall that you had rejected Gharial’s manuscript and later went on to publish Kanaka Sundari’s colorful book.”

“I know we have published her book but who is Gharial? The same guy on TV?”

“Yeah, the one who killed her. He will turn to you now.”-Sagar explains.

“There are many other editors in the office. Why not them? We are specialists in rejections anyway.”

“Because it was you who sent him the rejection mail!!”-Jackpot shakes his head with raised brows indicating that he knows all about it and Mama is going to pay for it.

"Jackpot, please."-Sagar is as calm as an ocean. "Mr. Mama, we will be on vigil at your house day and night. You need not worry. This is my number. Please call me if anything seems unusual at home."

Mama agrees in silence. Sagar gets a call from Kunj- "Sir, is Soor ok?"

"Yeah, she is fine. I spoke to her in the morning. She told me about the discussion you had. We are with Mr. Mama of Kingpin Publishers now."

"All right."

Something tells Ayodhya that the next attack in going to come too early. He is at home. A reply has come from his grandfather.

Dear Appu,

I am fine with the new 'home' you have chosen for me.

Do you know that younger scorpions are more venomous than the older ones?

Do as you please. But remember- intelligent defense and measured aggression is the key when you wade through unknown adversities. Emotions blind your thinking ability.

Sagar is an officer with authority to take actions. You don't possess it. But it is all right. As long as you're nothing, you can be anything. You may have to break laws as a common citizen fighting gangsters. It is fine. But don't break justice. Laws are man-made, subject to amendments. Justice is eternal. It is the law of nature. In fact, I am flouting a law by encouraging you.

And about multi-tasking, I'm sure cooking will teach you. Good that you're learning it. We should be experts in at least one thing others are bad at.

With expertise in advising,

Yours loving Grandpa,

Ram Prakash

Ayodhya opens the BlueTube video. The comment section has a new statement by 'G'.

2 wickets- clean bowled.

Ayodhya is quick to reply- One was a no ball!

IndiaRockzzz doesn't keep quiet-

Gimme batting, gimme batting. Plzzzzzzzzzz.

Ayodhya has had his dinner. He had cooked tomatoes. They were still raw. He fears stomach ache. He lies down on the floor, thinking of Kunj's encounter with Gharial. Hours pass by. He doesn't get sleepy. So strange... Every night he would sink in to sleep as soon as he lies down but tonight, no... Not a wink.

He walks out to the balcony. Tintu is seen returning with his luggage after paying the fare to the rickshaw. He has just bequeathed his free living to eternity and got betrothed. Ayodhya gets down to ground floor to help him with luggage.

"Hey man!!"-Tintu waves at an approaching Ayodhya lest he miss his presence. Ayodhya doesn't respond. He just picks up the luggage and starts walking back to lift. "Congratulations Tintu!"-he remembers as the lift moves up.

“Thank you, hmmm. Pheno Menon is such a phenomenal girl. I was stalking her matrimonial biodata. She had written that she wanted to work after marriage. I did not want to work after marriage. So it worked actually.”-Tintu flaunts a picture of him with Pheno, the picture displaying the couple, with robotic accuracy, stopping just short of hugging each other.

“Tomorrow I have to get a certificate from that NGO, actually.”

“What NGO and what certificate?”

“I was doing part-time teaching, actually, in a famous NGO. But now I need to get a certificate and leave the job, hmmm.”

“Oh! Work pressure?”

“Pch, not work pressure, not work pressure actually. For my MBA application profile. You know-o?”

“Our profile gets strengthened in US and UK B-schools if we submit service certificates by NGOs. Many MBA aspirants are forced to take up the task for this purpose. Otherwise who will join NGO, correct-o? UK and US schools are so dumb, ummm... point-eight-five percent dumber than us, hmmm.”

“Oh.”

“You seem a bit sad.”-He stresses on ‘bit’. “No, I’m not sad. I’m angry about my situation.”-Ayodhya follows Tintu to the flat. “Here, crush this bottle if you’re angry. It makes you feel better.”-Tintu offers the water bottle he has purchased from Sea Rail. Ayodhya takes it and throws it in the dust bin. “Why don’t you crush it?”

“It brings down anger.”-Ayodhya replies as he exits.

It has suddenly started raining from nowhere. Ayodhya wants to do something to stay ahead of Gharial. "The only way is to think like him."-he thinks as he witnesses some violent thunder right in front of him. "The thunder outside is no match to a spark inside."-he trusts his instincts to give him an idea. He has two options- either to pick up the thread from where he had paused the Soman's trail or somehow go after Gharial so that another Kunj episode is avoided. He prefers to follow the hospital one. "Let Kunj stay out for a while."

He sets out in the noisy torrents towards the local train station. He waits at the platform. He feels some discomfort with moist, heavy and itchy jeans. The sunglasses, the cap and the hankie are safe and dry in his backpack. He feels the night is going to be big. The train arrives at quarter past twelve. A silent journey seems to herald a night of chaos, a night of horror.

He does not debark at the Heaven Seven station. He does not want to risk the subway. He walks back from the next station. Heaven Seven hospital looks like a beacon in the moonless night. He pauses at the sugarcane kiosk to gear up with the cap, sunglasses and the hankie. The stink caused by the perennial urination at the compound makes him uncomfortable. He spills red ink on his left arm to fake bleeding. Heaving a sigh, he walks straight in to the outpatients' section and waits at the lobby. Nobody seems to be available except the nurse at the counter who rushes to bring some first aid.

Ayodhya vanishes!

"The restricted areas are restricted because every business needs something to be hidden."

He heads straight. The hospital looks empty, strange!

264ROHIT143 works! He is in!

He walks towards Soor's cabin slowly, trying to gauge activity inside. It is lit but she isn't there. Her apron adorns the armchair. He takes off his cap and hankie, wears her apron and a mouth mask. He places the stethoscope evenly on his shoulders and walks deeper into the restricted area.

A few wardboys are seen moving wheeled cots in a hurry to a dark entrance. Ayodhya follows them as though he is quite familiar with the activities. One of the wardboys stops at the entrance and gives way to Ayodhya. Ayodhya walks casually and notices more such cots lined up at the corner of the huge hall. He lifts the white sheet of cloth and finds an abnormally bulged cadaver beneath. He can see men at the end of the hall. He slips in to the darkness of the loosely lit end and proceeds cautiously. He can't see a thing. "They are probably transferring the cadavers in to the ambulance. But why? And how can they accommodate so many?"

There is not one but many of those vehicles and there is a dimly lit cement-road through a tunnel, straight out of the hospital. "How many more?"-a voice enquires quite haughtily. Ayodhya figures out by looking from behind. It is Soman!!

"Another two to three."

Ayodhya slowly crawls under a table and reaches quite close to Soman and his men.

"Make sure you reach on time. The doctor will be there at one o'clock sharp."-Soman leaves. The remaining cots are stashed quickly and the vehicles exit. The tunnel seems unending. The men inside cannot feel the thunderstorms. About quarter an hour elapses.

There is sudden gush of wind across the vehicles. The rain batters the ceiling. The thunder booms as though it was waiting for them to emerge out of the tunnel. They part ways, honking sirens.

The Police deployed by the central government to check illegal movements in and out of the island give way. Ambulances are signs of emergency. The vehicles meet again after a distance.

The journey continues in muddy paths, away from the luxury of neat roads. They come to a halt at a far, far location. The engines are switched off. The peculiarly attractive warm scent of diesel fills the insides of the vehicles.

The men dismount swiftly and start unloading the cots. Three vans are quickly emptied. The door of the fourth van is opened and the cots are lined up. The bodies are carried by two men who drop them at more people waiting for them with umbrellas, torches and lanterns. The torrents are getting only worse. Nothing much can be heard in the storm. The two men come back for the next cot.

“This body is too heavy to carry.”-one of them guesses, looking at the bed sheet spread over a huge cadaver.

“Let me help you!!”-Ayodhya springs from under the sheet, pushing away the cadaver over him! The two are taken by surprise. Ayodhya overpowers them in no time, kicking under the chin of one and smashing the other’s head against the wheel of the ambulance. He ties them up, drags them away out of sight and walks along the parked vehicles on the opposite side, to get as close as possible to the team of people working on the bodies. There are eight to ten of them, including the ones who have reached by the ambulances. Ayodhya stealthily crawls on the wet soil, his chest touching the ground and head flat, like a crocodile. The voices can be faintly heard-

“It doesn’t work... way... We... out... time.”

“He needs...urry up.”

Ayodhya tries his best, cleaning his soaked ears to listen well. “The CM is upset... There is still... lot... heaped... He... casual...”

The water level on the ground has risen. Ayodhya holds his chin up. He slouches closer, making sure that he stays out of light. His mouth mask is sucked in cold and blown out hot as he breathes controllably. Although he is irritated with the itching in the wet jeans, he cannot afford to make any relieving move. Correcting himself is a luxury he can afford at the cost of his life. He bears with it. Only his shoes, elbows and his head are visible. The rest of him is submerged in the pool of water. He is just behind them, dangerously behind them.

“Killing once in a week will not get us anywhere. I can’t afford to come here every night. I want to finish it once for all.”- one of the men with a white apron expresses, as he rips a cadaver along its abdomen. Ayodhya hears clearly. Another one holds a wide sheet of plastic over his head. A third keeps open a bag. The rest of the men guard the other cadavers. The first man keeps the knife aside, shoves his hands inside the dead body and brings out bundles of cash wrapped in polythene!! He hands over the bundles to another man who arranges the money in the bag. Money gets drawn from all parts of the cadaver, filling the bag to the brim. They dispose the empty cadaver into a ditch. “Next one, quick.”

“His job is to supply the bodies. And to do that faster, we need more Gharials.”

Ayodhya feels an intense rush of cold along his spine!

"The stock is getting over. And this time Dr. Soman is planning big! I heard he is going to bring down a building. Till it works, Gharial will be diverting the attention of the public to himself. He was very upset that the bodies of the ATM guard and the guy tied at the ATM were not collected. He was told that it was way too small but he wanted it. He says he can't afford to lose even a baby's body."-the man rips a second cadaver.

"He's correct. We cannot keep doing this forever. How long can we keep working this way for just two percent? It will take a lifetime to empty the CM's share of black money alone. Then there is the home minister, the opposition party, the bureaucrats, whew!"

"This is just a pilot project. If everything goes smoothly, the implementation will be on a... large scale."

"Do you know? This time we are shipping these bags to the eastern port. The coast guard has become very suspicious after one of our ships outran them into international waters on the way to Europe. This time Dr. Soman has made arrangements somewhere in South East Asia while the CM is ensuring the coast guard will be engaged in the west. The men of The Global Bank of Blitzerland will take care of it from there."

"You know too many things for a wardboy!"

The wardboy continues- "The Central Government is going to flush out the current notes and issue newer ones by the end of the year. NSF and the Dweepa Party have united to pull out as many notes as possible and exchange at Indian banks outside India."

"Oh, come on. What can a bank outside India do with Indian currency?"

"You said I know too much for a wardboy. And I say you're right."- the wardboy gives away a mean smile.

The muddy water of the graveyard touches Ayodhya's lips. But he is more concerned with what has touched his heart. Soman, Gharial and the politicians of Dweepa have been murdering innocent citizens and using their bodies as carriers to the graveyard at the outskirts of Dweepa. The black money is smuggled out to various countries in privately owned ships and deposited in Europe.

The next cadaver is drawn.

Zzzippp...

18 BLITZKRIEG

"Sagar, can you tell me when you will be shifting back? It would help me plan when to prepare the sweet dish for you."-Sagar's mother enquires when he would be getting back from the rented house in South Dweepa.

"I have decided to stay here for some more time, mother."-he replies without a thought. "Oh, ok... Ok."-his mother doesn't question him.

"Ayush has got rejected in another interview. It is getting tougher and tougher for me. Can you help me with contacting some consultants? His resume needs some professional help. I don't believe in online consultancy sites."-she seeks his help, taking care that she doesn't hurt him.

Sagar's dreamworld in which everything was fine and normal comes down crashing to the new reality. He feels an unusual fear that there could be no job left for Ayush if he takes things so carelessly. Ayush on the other hand is happy watching series after series in the Game of Bones. Sagar is worried. It is natural. You humans, you have a tendency to take things more seriously than they can actually get, after taking them more casually than they actually were.

"Ok mother. What should I do now?"-for the first time, his reply is soft. She takes away a moment to savor the rare occasion. "Nothing, son. Just go to Gold Street. There is an office that I saw. I felt we can talk to them on strengthening his CV."

"Ok, mother. Where is it exactly?"

"Opposite to the petrol station."

"Fine."-he hopes he remembers. He has come to Soor's house to meet her but she is still on her way. He, nevertheless, has got the spare key of her flat. She is his only means of solace. He forgets, at least for a moment, the pain and the pressure, when he puts his head on her lap for the comforting running down of her fingers through his hair.

As of now, he is in a dilemma. Gharial has put the best of the officers in deep trouble. The media has again intervened in the game of snake-and-ladder that he is losing, calling him a disgrace to the department and stirring a debate on whether he should be sacked as per the old rule- out of form, out of uniform.

He drops his head on the chair, gazing at the fan. Its every rotation seems to convey to him that life is a cycle.

Trrring! The door bell rings.

"Jackpot?"-he yells loud enough to reach the door.

"Sir?"-Jackpot stands at the door scaling the unusually high level of worry Sagar is in. "Come in. Any idea how to go ahead with Gharial? Sometimes..."-he starts off in a hurry, looking at the face of the ever faithful Jackpot.

Jackpot opens his mouth to say something but withholds to let him complete. "Nothing, go ahead."

"It is ok, Sir. Tell me what it is."-Jackpot offers. "No, no, nothing. Sometimes I feel I should resign from the service and go back to Meghpur."

"Sir then who else can deal with Gharial?"

Trrring!!

The door bell rings again. There is a visitor.

"I think he arrived."-Jackpot walks to the door.

"Sir, Kunj Bihari Yadav has come to meet you."-Jackpot returns to

Sagar's drawing hall. Sagar is not bothered with Jackpot bringing Kunj uninformed, and that too, to Soor's flat. He is grateful to Kunj that, as common citizens, Kunj and his friend are working towards a social cause. "They will definitely open the detective agency."-Sagar is happy.

"Yeah, Kunj."

"Sir, my friend has updated me from the field..."-Kunj explains everything to the last detail. Sagar can't believe it. "He has also informed me that it is better to get Dr. Soor out of the hospital as soon as possible. Her life will be in danger if she tries to attempt any fact-finding."

As luck would have it, Soor comes home. She has worn the gold chain Sagar's mother has gifted her. But she is missing the most precious of all jewelry... A smile... Exhausted, she brushes her brows. Sagar feels like hugging her and hiding her from everyone's sight. He is in a strange mix of feelings!!

On one hand he has got a breakthrough and on the other, there is a possibility he may lose Soor forever. "Hi guys!"-she walks to her bedroom. Jackpot and Kunj look at Sagar hoping that he would convince her to quit the job and apply elsewhere. Sagar doesn't know how to begin.

"Soor..."-he walks in the bedroom, closing the door behind him. "Yeah?"-she looks on, unpacking her purse. Sagar starts unfurling the truth about Heaven Seven. He looks at her hoping that she does not get too scared with the facts. But her face states clearly that she is devastated! She drops herself on the bed and presses her forehead. Sagar comforts her with his arm around her shoulders.

"Soor, you need to quit the job."

"So shall you. We will go to Meghpur. I can't see you suffer at the hands of the merciless news channels. I knew this day would come. That the world around us would crumble."-she starts sobbing. "Ok, Soor. Listen. Today I am going to raid the hospital. And after that the case will be solved. Once this is over, I promise I'll quit this job."

"Raid the hospital? What about the patients?"

"Nothing will happen to them. I know where exactly I have to raid. Kunj's friend is well informed."-he leaves.

"Kunj."-Soor comes out of the bedroom. Sagar and Jackpot look on.

"Please make sure Sagar is safe. I can't afford to lose him."-she thrusts his palm. "Don't worry, my friend will be there."

It is night. Sagar and Jackpot have arrived at the end of the tunnel. Ayodhya is at the other end-the main entrance. The activities are going on as usual. Sagar and Jackpot run through the tunnel and emerge into the restricted area with guns!

"Stay wherever you are!!"-Jackpot shouts. There is commotion all around. The morgue is raided and so are other private areas. Sagar is disillusioned!!

There is nothing surprising. There is not even a slight clue of any illegal organ trade, let alone using bodies as carriers. They return empty-handed. But there is a silver lining. A huge consignment carrying crores of Indian currency is seized at the north western harbor near Matsyali.

"Although ACP Sagar has to take moral responsibility of raiding Heaven Seven Hospital unnecessarily, causing disruption and panic among the inmates, he has got a minor breakthrough after his timely warning to the Coast Guards succeeded in preventing loads of money getting shipped out of India. With cameraman Jamie, I yam Amy, NOT NOW... Ummm... With cameraman Jamie I am Yami, NOT NOW."

"ACP Sagar! I just don't understand this whole thing. What are you up to?"

"Only time has the answer, Sir. Even I am in dark."-he knows he is under the scanner by his own department. He feels no surprise, if, even his senior officer is a part of the liaison. He has cleverly avoided any activity in Gharial's case, leaving everything to Kunj and Ayodhya. He has decided to only spring up suddenly at the vulnerable points of the case and seize the moment. And Jackpot is there after all. They have nicely worked it out!

"Ok, go ahead. You're a hero as of now. On Fakebook, Bitter, BlueTube, everywhere..."

It is the next day and is drizzling. "Sagar, I have quit the job! Now I am applying at Go Healthy Hospitals. But before that, I need to attend a medical conference in Singapore."-Soor updates him of her plan as he enters her flat. "You didn't tell about this before?"-he is saddened. "You told me about the problem only yesterday."-she arranges her passport and other documents in her bag.

"I'll meet mother before I leave. Are you not coming?"-she doubts his willingness to meet his own mother. "You go ahead."-he stands at the window as the drizzles settle on his face.

Ayodhya's arms are aching. He had dragged two men in the night at the graveyard. He has applied a coat of turmeric powder to ease his pain.

He feels something is seriously wrong with his actions. They are being foiled by someone right under his nose. "Who could it be?"

He opens the BlueTube video for comments from 'G'-

"Do you know grave yard is a place where someone lucky enough to survive me can go to?"

Ayodhya replies immediately-

"It is also a place where someone too lucky to finish you can be born in."

But 'IndiaRockzzz' has still not given up his demand for batting- "I can play wid any bat. Right-bat, left-bat, middle-bat... Gimme batting... Hey G... You ball any bowling... I not hit sixxxer. I push in gaps."

Ayodhya, bored, closes the laptop and settles down on the floor. The faces of Kesha Sundari and the editor of Kingpin publisher hover above, the blades of the ceiling fan wiping across them. "Who is first?"

"Jackpot, any news from Kunj?"-Sagar asks as he returns to his South Dweepa residence. "No Sir, no contact. Shall we secure Mr. Mama? I think Kesha Sundari's comments have become rotten news. Media is not interested, public is not interested... Gharial too may not be interested."

"Ok."

Ayodhya has closed his eyes, resting his back on the wall. Strange that he feels sleepy when he sits and doesn't when he lies down. His mind is running a series of faces and words in his charged up nerves. He knows he has to do something before Gharial does. "Where can he foment trouble now? Has the publisher been warned? Will Gharial attack him or he'll shock us by getting to Kesha Sundari first? He's unpredictable. That means?"

His eyes open suddenly to the glare of the tube light!

He jumps to his feet, grabs his cap, hankie and sunglasses and rushes out. "It's about time Kunj call Jackpot."-he takes out his phone. A few moments later Kunj calls up Jackpot hastily, giving him a lead to extract the address.

"Jackpot Sir, I want to locate this address urgently. My friend is already on his way to field without informing me beforehand."

"As far as we know, Gharial will head directly to the publisher- Mr. Mama. Kesha is out of question. By now he would know we are shielding her."-Jackpot tries his best to prove Kunj wrong. He wants to believe he is superior in deductions to a graduate of yesteryears, that too, from Bihar. "Jackpot Sir, you are making a grave mistake-Kunj warns. "No, no. We are sure Gharial is coming for the publisher now or later. If you want the other address, I'll locate it and message the contact number for you. Give me some time. I need to call Abhilash."

Ayodhya runs to the local train station. He gets the address as SMS from Jackpot through Kunj. "West Dweepa!"-Ayodhya request at the ticket counter.

"Hey Kunj, this is the mobile number."-Jackpot has received an update from Abhilash.

"Yeah?"-Kunj takes out a pen and stiffens his other palm.

"Hope I need not remind you that +19 is for Dweepa and +91 is for the rest of India... But the phone is not reachable... +19 48626 57199"

Kunj puts back his pen- "I need not write that down."

Sagar and Jackpot are patrolling the publisher's office discreetly in the guise of two tourists lost on the island with a paper map. People are trying to help them but they don't want it.

"Don't push your balls in others' courts."-Gharial stands in the most secretive part of the world. A teenager's bedroom! The boy's parents are out for a family get-together that the boy's age has refused to accept. They have snatched his cell phone away so that he can prepare for the exams. The landline is not working.

"Wh... Who.... Uh?"-the boy gasps at the moving mountain that Gharial is. The shadow of death curtains the boy's body slowly. He shudders in fear!

"The phone is out of order. It is a part of the world you know."-Gharial catches hold of his nape and runs his palm over his neck to feel the smoothness of the young prey's wind pipe.

"So you're IndiaRockzzz and you want batting huh?"-he bends the boy's neck backwards slowly. The boy can't believe he is facing 'G'.

"You see I am a better parent. They always made you sleep so that they could sleep. But I have no such motives. I'll put you to sleep forever."

"Please leave m.."-the boy can't speak. His head is bent backwards to such an extent that a mere strike with a finger can burst out blood. Gharial bends it further, taking care to keep it slow. He savors the peaking bone. "People bend rules. I only provide the final thrust to break it so that everyone hears. And you know what? The one who picks up the last banana from the basket isn't always the one who ate the most."

The boy almost collapses. Gharial raises his hand to smash the boy's neck. But in the nick of time, Gharial's neck is jerked backwards strongly with a rude pain!

Gharial releases the boy instantly and falls down.

"So you weren't aware of free-hit?"-Ayodhya stands on the table, crouched for the next move!!

"Is it over?"-Gharial stands up brushing his neck.

"It's another no-ball!!"-Ayodhya attacks with such an alacrity that Gharial feels the pain in his shin only after Ayodhya has slid to the opposite end. He can barely stand now. His men bring out Kalashnikovs. "Only the man. I kill the boy."-Gharial instructs. Ayodhya escapes outside through the grill-less window. He had seen the boy make a quick dash through it. After all, it is his house.

The men can't squeeze out. They have to use the main entrance. Gharial walks out slowly. Ayodhya attacks the first man out with a bamboo stick and snatches the gun. He swirls up in the air so high that he can muster enough energy with hands fully stretched up to bring the gun down on the man's head!

The next man's gun is hit by the bullet fired by Ayodhya! And his kneecaps are burst open.

The man collapses in pain. Gharial stands witnessing the fight. "A great man once said there is a very thin line between self-respect and ego. And we should always be careful with thin lines in our lives."-he suddenly talks philosophy in the midst of violence. The boy running out of the house is caught in a thin string across his neck. It slivers his throat as he continues to run. He feels a sudden spring of blood around. His eyes become blurred. "And Newton said that a body continues to be in a state of rest or motion until acted upon by an external force."

The boy is caught in another string that locks itself in his throat, arresting his movement. He drops dead!

"Run-out on a no ball!"

Ayodhya rushes at the boy to no avail. He pulls the string out. It is the one typically used to fly kites!!

Gharial has vanished. His men are not seen either.

Ayodhya understands that his presence there can bring the blame on him. He hops over the compound and escapes, leaving the gun behind.

Sagar is at the young boy's house the very next morning, investigating the murder. "ACP Sagar can be seen in the background. The ghastly killing of a young student in West Dweepa is understood to be the handiwork of Gharial. Exhausted bullets of the Kalashnikov were found in the premises, leading to believe that there was a massive gunfight. ACP Sagar himself seems to have fought with the gangster and his men. But the modest officer is refusing to provide any insight on the incident. Unfortunately, he could not save the boy. Has ACP Sagar, the supercop of Dweepa, inched closer to a startling arrest of the most infamous criminal in the world? Has he obtained secret supernatural powers hidden in the secluded mountains of Himalayas? Only time will answer. With cameraman Shami, I am Miami, NOT NOW... Not Miami, Yami... NOT NOW

"Sagar, could you go to the consultant office?"-he receives his mother's call as he returns home. "Yeah... No... Will go."

It is evening. Dweepa dazzles in the preparations for the upcoming festival. Sagar hops on his bike and rides on the busy streets in the cover of his helmet. He has become a familiar face now. Soon he is in Gold Street, opposite the petrol station. The office is closed as of now. The last thing he wants to see after a time-off from his busy schedule is the shutters slapped down mockingly.

There is a photo studio next to the consultant's office. "When does the office open?"-he asks the man at the studio. "In about half an hour.

You may wait here."-the man offers courteously. "Thank you."

The beauty of a photo studio is that there will be creativity at display. Different poses of the customers, their levels of self-consciousness, the occasions, the lighting in the background and the skill of the photographer will all be evident.

Sagar is deep in thought. He still hasn't got an answer for the failure in the hospital raid. He can't doubt the duo of Kunj and his friend. They have done a splendid job of taking on Gharial fearlessly despite the heavy odds against them. Jackpot was with him all the time. So what went wrong? How did Soman and Gharial get a scent of...

Blood rushes on his face unexpectedly! His thoughts come to an abrupt halt! In front of him lies a display of a framed photograph in the studio's show case that shakes the earth beneath his feet!

It is of Soor and Soman showing off their engagement rings!!!

Sagar blinks twice. Yes, it is Soor. He removes his helmet and walks closer. The man at the studio is pleasantly surprised. "ACP Sagar!?"

Sagar stares at it. Memories of time spent with Soor start tormenting him. "Can you give me details of the couple in this photo?"-he doesn't turn to the person he is talking to.

"Sure Sir."

"This photo was taken two months ago by Mr. Soman and his fiancée- Soon? Or..."

"Soor... Soor it is."

"Oh, yeah. It is an 'r'"- the man is pleased that his customers are Sagar's friends.

"But how did you say so correctly without even seeing the register? Do you know her?"

"I do now."-he leaves heartbroken. The shutter of the consultant's office opens just as his eyes open to reality. He hands over Ayush's details to them and rides back home with moist eyes-"How gullible I am. All that was needed was presence of mind and absence of heart."

But is it too late?

He tries calling her up. The only beautiful voice that brings about a frown is the automated one that informs that the person is not reachable. Soman too is in the hiding. Sagar is restless. He has given in to emotions, banging the desk at the office. Jackpot stands quietly, witnessing. "Jackpot, update Kunj Bihari Yadav that his life is in double danger. Gharial knows about him."

"Yes Sir..."

"... and his friend too."

"Yes Sir..."

It has been five hours now. Sagar, Kunj and Jackpot are all awake in the dark, ghastly hour. They squat on the floor, planning Gharial's hunt. "One thing is for sure."-Sagar looks at them both. He shows them that he has come out of the trauma and is focusing on the case. "After so many things have become clear to us as well as to them, Gharial will only hunt faster. In a way it is a Blitzkrieg! So I have an idea..."

The other two do not disturb. "We split!"

"I will be at the opera that the publisher is going to attend while you Jackpot... go with Kunj's friend and patrol outside the studio where Kesha Sundari's show is going to start tomorrow evening." "Sir, my friend operates alone. He is better suited at the publisher's opera."-Kunj is apprehensive.

"Why? He can have some fun at the actress's show. Do you know which show it is? Comedy by Chintu, of Chintu and for Chintu"-Jackpot objects.

"I am sure he'll turn down."-Kunj shakes his head in despair.

"Your friend can attend the show as a part of audience! You'll get to dance with the lady. The requests are all preplanned and scripted you know? I'll arrange for your friend's call on stage."-Jackpot tries his best to reason.

"No Sir. My friend has a niche category. He makes others dance."-Kunj sticks to his stand.

"And he hates comedy."

"Ok, I and Jackpot at the opera."-Sagar raises his hands to signal end of discussion.

"Fine, my friend at the publisher."

"But he wants the blind lift operator too to join him."-Kunj has another demand. "What the hell can a blind man do?"-Jackpot is irritated with the Bihari. The demanding Bihari is further intolerable to him.

"He can help identify Gharial."

"Done!"-Sagar trusts Ayodhya's idea.

Jackpot fumes within.

The next evening Sagar and Jackpot leave for Comedy by Chintu, of Chintu and for Chintu dressed as foreign tourists with the trademark half-pants and flowery shirts. Ayodhya is not very far from them. The opera house is brimming with artists in variously eccentric appearances and obsession with standard gestures used in acting and play.

Ayodhya has occupied a seat three rows front of Mama. He has brought the blind lift operator of the cruise-ship along with him, hoping for a chance discovery of Gharial among the crowd. The unique scent of the cushion seats and various brands of perfumes worn by the guests have filled the hall. The chandeliers are up above like big, bright stars.

It has been a long wait for the singer. Her flight from Kochi is delayed due to bad weather. Everyone has given in to hunger. Tea, snacks and soda is being served. Mama has had too much of soda. He rushes to the restroom. Ayodhya waits at the hall but sees a chance to call him over phone...

He warns him of the attack- "Mr. Mama, it is better you remain indoors in your home or office. Visiting a crowded place like opera will make it difficult to spot him."

"I am already in the opera. And you guys said he is unpredictable. Then how can you be sure he'll attack me if it is already expected?"

"Obsession kills unpredictability. Mr. Mama, he has a taste for blood."

"How about Kesha Sundari?"-Mama is an editor after all. The more he makes it difficult for others to convince him, the prouder he feels with the profession. "She could not be warned as there was no time."

"I'm at the opera. The lady is a rare gem."-he falls for his obsession. Inevitability delayed will only boost immunity. Warnings do not seem to have the intended effect on Mama. "No gem dearer than life, Mr. Mama."

"If he had come, the security would have taken care of him. Don't worry, if he makes it, I'll break his bones."

"Let's see if you can break wind!!"

Mama looks into the mirror. He loses the grip on his phone!

A strange being stands right behind him in a gown. Mama almost faints!!

"Do you know what the problem is with you? You are like the educated cockroach- if a pack of sugar is open at the bottom, an educated cockroach sees the uncut alphabets at the unopened top and returns hungry.

"Hello, hello! Mr. Mama?"

"On his way to his mamma, Ayodhya!"-Gharial answers as he starts throwing booklets in the air. "All that glitters is not gold..."-Gharial continues as he receives from his men, another handful of booklets to throw around. "... but all that litters is human."

Ayodhya dashes to the restroom and finds nobody there. He runs around the hall like a mad man, covering his face. Mama is nowhere in sight. People have started to suspect that something is wrong. "Mama! Mama!"

The security attends the situation. "Hey, what's wrong with you?"

"Mr. Mama is missing!"

One of the guests is shocked- "There is Gharial out there!!"

The people take to their heels, fearing death! It looks like the escape of an army of ants disturbed from a lump of sugar.

"This is the truth about people in frenzy. All they can do is to follow one another."-Gharial is glad.

Ayodhya knows Gharial will not leave without Mama. Dead or alive... A body that can carry loads of money in a single go cannot be let gone. This was the reason Ayodhya had rejected Kesha Sundari's venue.

He waits at the narrow exit with the lift operator. People are leaving in a hurry. Gharial's trademark overcoat and hat are not seen anywhere.

The lift operator stands with his head bowed down. There are intense activities happening in the brain behind the cover of dark glasses... He is holding Ayodhya's wrist. Both are still! Moments are slipping by... just like a stag receding in its position before gathering the force to strike the finishing blow.

And then, the moment comes!

The man presses Ayodhya's wrist with a grip that screams of the arrival of the Satan!!

Ayodhya feels a surreal shock!

"This man!"-the operator confirms. There is a thing about the blind man. His power of sight is taken away and... invested in his sense of smell!!

When Ayodhya had visited him to request his help, he had readily agreed. "Sir, there is something unique in his smell. On the other day, I had sensed that they were carrying someone tied to the couch. While the rest of the men had nothing unusual, there was this one man whose scent was strange. A never before one."

"Sir, the man is gone!"-the operator shakes Ayodhya's arm. "The... the... woman!!"-Ayodhya replies softly.

The opera is getting emptied. The 'woman', surprisingly, does not wait for Mama's body. She disappears! Ayodhya can't understand. "Can you please wait here? I'll have to look for Mama. Gharial is gone. There is no danger."-Ayodhya explains to the operator and runs against the crowd like a beast into wildfire.

"Answer the call, Mama!"-he whispers to himself, unable to bear the ringing. A few attempts later, Mama finally does!

"Please help me out of here! Please!!"-he pleads. "Where are you?"-Ayodhya stops running.

"In... in... this... back stage hall!"

"Oh, where else!"-Ayodhya dashes. "I have been locked up here and...."-Ayodhya can't hear him in the chaos. But he knows that Mama has been locked up.

He reaches the locked door. "Mr. Mama!!"-Ayodhya yells. There is no answer.

"Hey Mama!"

Now there is. "Help me ACP, help me Jackpot... I am here."-Mama bangs against the door. "That Gharial has brought the rejected manuscript copies from the office and dumped them here. He has also brought some snakes and scattered them around. Says that the key to the door is in the safe whose password is the name of one of the characters in... in... one of the manuscripts in.. in... this heap of manuscripts!"

"And when he left, he turned back and told that all letters are lowercase!!"

Ayodhya thinks hard. “Are those snakes venomous?”

“What do you mean? I’m not a damned snake charmer!!”

“How do they look?”

“Green

“Then yes!”

“Oh my God!!!”

Ayodhya looks around. There is nothing that can break the door. And the door is sturdy, artistically sturdy.

“Start off with the first one. Pick up the manuscript closer to you.”

“What the ****? Please get someone to... Oww!!”

“What happened?”

“One snake was close!!”

“They don’t harm unless you do. Pick up the first one!”

“You’re crazy!! Utterly crazy!! Hoooo...”-Mama’s bellowing can be heard amidst the nervous turning of papers. “Mama, it is ok. He wants you to prove that we cry over the situation rather than act even when things are not entirely out of control. Don’t worry, search for the names.”

“Pintu pees in the pants and hence he is thrown out of the class. Boooo...”-Mama wails as he notes down the name of the first character.

“Poppy beats her husband and the mother-in-law beats him further... Hoooo.”

“I had personally rejected this shit of a manuscript last year... Boooo!”

“Mama, it is ok. It is not your fault. Just keep on noting.”

Mama has noted down three to four names. Ayodhya is at the other side of the door. “Mama, now enter the first name- ‘pintu’. Check if the safe opens.”

“What are you talking? Should I get instructions from a fool?”

“When the time isn’t right, you have to.”

“There are hundreds of manuscripts still left.”-Mama looks at the heap. “This is exactly why Gharial is sure you won’t make it.”

“He knows the human tendency of spending time accumulating things than utilizing the available ones.”

Mama enters it. It mismatches. “No!”

“Next”

"No"

"Next"

"Yes!!!"

Gharial had deliberately thrown the manuscript containing the password closer to Mama, separated from the heap. He wanted to thrill himself to such an extent!

While Mama was going through the tortuous exercise, Ayodhya had alerted Sagar of the next attack-Kesha Sundari!!

"Welcome to Comedy by Chintu, of Chintu and for Chintu!"

The show has started. Kesha Sundari is waiting at the passageway to the stage. Sagar and Jackpot are among the audience, looking out for 'women'. There are a few jokes being cracked. "Please put your hands together to the sizzling star of Khaaliwood-Kesha Sundari!!"

She appears on stage. The director has agreed to let Jackpot dance with the actress. Chintu continues with his banter, requesting her to leave her legs with him and introducing her to his eccentric family members.

"Madam, tell me about your journey to stardom... From modest beginnings to reaching the coveted sets of Comedy by Chintu, of Chintu and for Chintu"

She laughs- "Well, I have come so high in my career that if I look down, I don't see anything."

"Madam, when contestants win the Miss India title, we see that they struggle to balance the misfit crown on their heads. Why don't we make elastic crowns for them?"

"Ha, ha, ha..."-she laughs according to her payment. So does the judge. His payment is fixed every season.

Sagar scans through the audience but doesn't see anyone potential of attacking her.

The act continues. She has to enact a politician since it is the election season. She stands behind the mic stand. It is too high. "Chintu, I can't reach the mic. What do I do?"

"Drink Complain"-Jackpot replies enthusiastically but softly. "Drink Complain, be a Complain girl."-Chintu replies. "Heck, I can be a comedian too."-Jackpot frowns.

"Now, from the audience, is anyone, my friends, intending to ask her questions...?"

Jackpot raises his hand. "Yes Sir... Please go ahead. Where are your eyes? Oh there! I am sorry, your belly is so prominent that my attention does not go to your eyes. Heard rumors that Gharial is using bodies as carriers... Mind you, you might be next. Your belly alone can carry all the cash in the Preserve Bank of India."

The audience burst into laughter. Jackpot burns. He feels so offended but can't help it in the line of duty.

"Why aren't you laughing, Sir? Have you taken up the mice bucket challenge?"-Chintu pulls his leg. "Laughter is like excreting. You can laugh only when it comes on its own."-Jackpot overtakes Chintu in comedy. A whole country laughs with him...

Sagar is not interested. He looks around. No threat. "Where are you hiding?"

"Ok, now. What is your question?"

"Madam, I would like to dance with you on the Rainy Dance song."-Jackpot's request is accepted.

He walks to stage. "First time I am seeing a balloon volunteer to get pricked by a needle."-Chintu remarks on the body shapes of Jackpot and Kesha Sundari. The dance begins. Everyone except Sagar is immersed in joy. And then suddenly!

There is chaos all around. The guitarist has beaten Kesha Sundari with his instrument!

"I don't know how to play cards but I am very good at hiding them."

Chintu runs to the upper storey of his makeshift house. Jackpot freezes in his place. Gharial removes his fake beard and grips Kesha with her hair. "When you go high up you must look far, not down."

His men spray bullets on the audience. But there is retaliation! Gharial's men are gunned down one by one.

It is Sagar under the shield of the judge's seat!

Kalashnikovs lie on the ground with dead Gharial's men. Jackpot has the golden chance to shoot down Gharial with one of the guns. But his fear seems to have consumed him, seeing Gharial right there. "I hate losers! And those who escape me."-Gharial leaves Kesha and proceeds towards Jackpot. Sagar runs to the rescue. Gharial lifts Jackpot at his back, holding the neck, while the rest of the body suspended. Jackpot's feet struggle in the air, with Jackpot and Gharial facing opposite directions. Gharial locks Jackpot's hanging feet between his knees and Jackpot's neck in his elbow. He bends in short jerks a couple of times, gathers enough strength and... with all his might pulls out Jackpot's head from the rest of the body!

"Out pops the head!"

Kesha Sundari's face is sprayed with blood.

Sagar fires at Gharial's face. Gharial ducks his head, allowing the hat to take the bullets. He is thrown back near Kesha Sundari. Sagar picks up another gun while Gharial picks up Kesha Sundari. "It the age old game, Sagar... Before you and I were born. The bad guy always has an edge."-he shows the glittering edge of the sharp knife he holds.

"Who asked you to be bad?"-Sagar still has his aim on Gharial. Gharial flashes his knife in front of her throat. "You see, the world full of good guys is so bland. Bad guys are the other set of ingredients that makes it tasty. And someone like me is a topping."

Sagar's sight falls on dead Jackpot for a moment. His eyes fill with tears. "Hope you're playing dead this time, too."-he thinks.

"No, how can he? By the way, which part are you talking to?"-Gharial replies. The deadlock is on. Sagar knows he can't take action right away. The actress is to be saved. "You guys, you two... are not good enough to be policemen."-Gharial points his knife at Sagar and Jackpot's severed head. "You are like a goldsmith doing the job of a blacksmith."-he slowly rests his chin on the actress's shoulder.

Sagar has his aim at Gharial. "The... the... other guy... Umm... Ayodhya... is better!"

He is felled by Ayodhya swooping down under his feet!!

"Think of the devil!"-Ayodhya thunders as he returns with another blow on Gharial's head, pulling off his hat. Sagar fires!! Gharial runs covering his head with his coat, out of the passageway. Ayodhya chases him like a leopard. Gharial picks up another stray gun and points it behind. Ayodhya hides behind a pillar. The actress hugs Sagar. He tries to free himself and join Ayodhya but she falls to his feet, gripping his knee tightly. "Please don't go. I want to live. He'll come back. I know he'll not spare me!"-she starts shuddering.

Sagar sees sense in her words. Saving her is more important than nabbing him. He takes her out of studio.

It has been a long wait for Ayodhya. He can see the hazy reflection of Gharial's heavy overcoat in the metallic finish of the wall. He sees Chintu, hiding near furniture and looking around. "How can he miss Gharial?"-he gets surprised that Gharial's position is clearly in Chintu's sight and Chintu seems to be missing him. He swiftly passes by Gharial's hiding, covering himself with a probable rain of bullets. Gharial's overcoat is still there but Gharial isn't!

Sagar joins Ayodhya outside the studio- "Hi, I'm ACP Sagar."

Ayodhya doesn't respond. "Hi, Ayodhya! Good work, man."

Ayodhya leaves. He walks down the road, removing his hankie, cap and the sunglasses. He has seen Jackpot's dead body and is disturbed with that. Sagar, on the other hand, drops Kesha Sundari at her residence. "Please walk with me up to the flat."-she requests. Sagar agrees.

"What floor?"-Sagar looks up above the towering building. He can see a random man standing at the terrace. "Don't worry, I'm at ground floor."-she replies.

Sagar feels surprised. He and Jackpot had kept an eye on the 12th floor all these days. "But madam, we had thought that your residence is in the 12th floor."

He feels bad at her saddened face. "That flat is of director Chimpu!"-she hesitates for an eye contact.

"Oh, I am sorry."-he walks around to check for intruders in the garden.

She bends a little to unlock the door. A faint laser light dances on her head. Sagar turns. He spots it! His eyes shine! Someone is going to shoot her.

"Ma'am!!!"-he runs to her. She turns her head. Sagar has almost made it to her when his eyes are sprinkled with blood!!

He wipes his eyes only to find her dead at the door!! The mystery man on the terrace is gone!

A few hours later, Abhilash gives a startling update- "She wasn't shot in the head. The laser was only to see if she was directly below the man on the terrace. And then a coin was dropped on her head!"

"A coin?"

"Yes Sir. A five-rupee coin has been recovered from her cranium. It had punctured her skull bone after been dropped from that height. Any object even with a few grams of mass at such an altitude can gather enough potential energy to pierce through the skull. Classic example... A used bullet fired in the air can come down and kill only with its sheer weight."

"It is obvious that after confirming she was directly below, the person had held the coin under the light of laser and just dropped it! Wind movement is generally low in confined areas like her apartment to deviate the object."

"Who else could do that other than Gharial!!"-Sagar replies coldly.

Ayodhya is at home, nursing his wounds. There is a glimmer of hope after saving Mama and Kesha Sundari that Gharial can go wrong too. But Jackpot is gone!

He feels tired and sleepy, yet strangely restless. Something serious, something immediate seems to approach him.

"Hey man, you took a dive catch-o?"-Tintu enters and crunches his face at the wound, like a cook opening the cooker to find over-boiled rice. "Yeah..."

"You are a bit sad-o?"-Tintu again stresses on 'bit'. "Yeah. Want to scold somebody. Really badly!"-he wants Tintu to leave him alone. "Then scold someone you hate."

"I need a reason. A subject."

"You need a subject-o? To scold-o?"-he stands like a teacher in front of a student who has scored low in a class test. Ayodhya laughs amidst pain.

"You saw the news-o? Kesha Sundari has been killed by Gharial-hmmm."

"No, she was saved."-Ayodhya answers spontaneously before he realizes Tintu's impeccable precision in everything. "Oh, I am sorry. So when are you buying LED TV?"

"I am checking the price, actually. They say 19999 only but why do they want to earn one rupee less? Hmmm?"

"ACP Sagar."-Kunj walks in the night to Sagar's residence. Sagar is in a state of mind that is stabbing him every moment. Jackpot, his trusted friend, is suddenly no more. He could not save the actress. Soor turned out to be a backstabber. Ayush is still as casual as before. And his mother hasn't forgiven him yet. His thoughts are so intense that he can feel the pulse at the temple battering against his skin.

"Kunj! Jackpot is gone, Kunj."-Sagar stands facing the sea as though Jackpot has sailed away in it. "I know, Sir. But when we come close to a major success, the price of sacrifice goes up."

"Sacrifices? How many? How many have I still to make? Sometimes I feel like strangling myself and escaping the loop."

"Sir, you are not a coward."

"That's what I used to think about me. But we are not what we think we are. We are just what we think."

"Sir, we saved Mama."-Kunj brings out good news. "He has been sent into hiding. He won't be seen around anymore."

Sagar nods. His heated palms slowly run along the sides of the cool wooden window frame. It feels good. "Sir, our next move? We are the only two left."

"No, your friend is there too. I just don't know him but looking at his moves I felt he is quite accustomed to fighting. Ayodhya! How was he in college?"

Kunj smiles recollecting how Ayodhya used to be unheard, unseen. "Sir, when we left college I knew him just as much as I did when we had joined."

"And now? How do you interact?"

"Sir, I have given him my word that I will never discuss him."

It is the next morning. Ayodhya, has received a fresh mail-

'Dear Ayodhya,

I haven't received a reply mail from you since so many days. Hope you still remember me.

I think everything is fine with your work now because otherwise you would have written to me.

Heard that the publisher Mama was saved and Gharial was inflicted a severe blow in his ambitions. Good going, son. Things will fall in place soon.

Don't worry.

Anyway, next Sunday is your parents' wedding anniversary. I just wanted to know if you can come down to Sarovar Nagar. It has been a long time since we celebrated anything.

Waiting for you,
your grandpa
Ram Prakash

Ayodhya wants to go home to his grandpa immediately and see how he is doing. But at the same time he wants to end everything soon. He sits scratching his forehead with the back of the pencil in his office. "Hi..."-Anca waves at him as she enters. He smiles. "I think you have not yet come out of the shock after the death of your uncle and aunts."-she speaks softly. "Yeah, true. But more than me, my cousin Soman is suffering."

"True, I saw in the TV that day. He was crying uncontrollably."-she bends down to switch on the computer. "And he says they were killed."-Ayodhya turns to see her reaction. She keeps her eyes still at the screen, presses the eyelids against her eyes for a moment before returning to her usual look. "How can he say that? Why doesn't he complain then?"

"He says he'll avenge their death. He is already on it."-Ayodhya walks to the printer. Her left shoulder shudders for a second. Ayodhya walks back.

"Where is he now?"-she asks softly.

"Sarovar Nagar!"

19 THE DEVIL'S ACCOMPLICES

A firm hand strikes Ayodhya! He yells in pain. He tries escaping from between the legs but Gharial has got him for good. Ayodhya punches hard on Gharial's stomach. But his stomach stomachs it. Ayodhya kicks his back with whatever force he can gather but it is as good as the kick of a hare.

Gharial brings down the mortal punch on Ayodhya's head!!

"Huhh!!"-Ayodhya wakes up.

It is a bright sunny morning after a torrential night. The trees are sparkling clean. The birds, as usual, are flying in a formation for a mission to gather food for life.

He walks to the bathroom, recovering from one of those haunting nightmares... of encounters with Gharial. Of late, they have become more frequent. "Is it a sign?"-he looks in the mirror, frothing his mouth with paste. His reddened eyes are a testimony to some of the goriest sights one can't ever imagine.

He doesn't know that he is preparing himself for the impending clash, making himself immune by running simulated versions of encounters, sub-consciously. He doesn't know he is doing it so well. It is similar to the Blue Bell Villa that exists but not known.

Well, there is one thing he is concerned with, more than the nightmares. About Soman's next move. He remembers the talk... "The stock is getting over. And this time Dr. Soman is planning big! I heard he is going to bring down a building."

"Which one?"- he asks himself. "And how?"

The questions he asks are to me. And he knows I will answer them whenever I wish to."

He starts preparing his breakfast. He notices the waste pieces parted away from the rest of the chopped vegetables. He feels upset with the flour he has spilled on the slab. He hates looking at the oil trickled at the end of the stove. He hates to clean up as usual, wash his hands as usual, continue cooking as usual and end up preparing late... as usual.

This time he decides to tolerate the mess until the main objective at hand, cooking, is done. And he ends up cooking fast.... unusually fast.

He picks up the remote and switches on the TV with the back of his left palm. There is a documentary being telecast on the contest between the ants and the termites. The ants want to get to the termite queen and conquer the colony while the worker termites try their best to save her. The ants have an advantage- the termite body is soft except at the head. So they sting over and over again. The termites seem to be losing. Ayodhya's eyes are on the TV screen although his hands are at cooking. The termites have a marginal hope in the fact that the necks of the ants are vulnerable to their teeth. A few ants are killed but they are just too many. The casualty rate of termites is way higher. Ayodhya feels that it is all over when suddenly, there is a change in battle plan. The termites have regrouped and resorted to tunnel warfare!

The entrance to the queen's chamber is through a tunnel and the termites have started to take on the ants singly at the mouth. The ants have begun to lose. Soon, the ants lift siege and retreat! Ayodhya smiles.

Sagar is at the office. He has been allotted a new team of officers for the mission, temporarily, until the final decision. He sits recalling the scenes at Jackpot's funeral. The tummy had burnt, taking away the first and the last sign of Jackpot. Gun salutes were offered for 'the martyr who fought valiantly in the highest traditions of Dweepa Police'. Sagar feels that Jackpot had escaped... escaped the cordons of society, the norms of life and the tragedies that were lying in wait for future.

"Purushottam!"-he calls the new officer under him. A person he cannot help but distrust. He feels sad about it. Lack of faith cripples inquisition.

"Yes Sir."

"What is the decision?"-he asks about the final call the superiors are going to take about his continuation.

"Sir, there is a raging debate. It is getting hotter. Some are in favor and some are against it."

Sagar walks to the window. The rain drops on the leaves of the Ashoka trees catch his eye. For a moment his mind deviates- "A drop seems so insignificant. But it is big enough to reflect the rest of the world around it."

"When is the meeting going to get over?"-he asks.

"When the debate gets over."-Purushottam replies. Sagar turns scornfully. "Are they not debating in the meeting?"

"No Sir. They are watching the debate on NOT NOW. They'll take a call based on the outcome of the debate."

"Then I'm in."

"How can you say that, Sir?"

"They can remove me only when the debate concludes."

"Hey, Tintu. I did not get the SMS of the Akal ticket. Did you enter my number or yours?"-Ayodhya asks about the responsibility he had entrusted Tintu with- to book the ticket to Sarovar Nagar from Dweepa.

"My record is broken, actually-Tintu bows down his head! Ayodhya can't believe his ears. The King of Akal has accepted defeat in the race of thirty seconds. "What can I do actually? Tell me? Hmmm?"-Tintu raises his voice sharply to indicate the end of apology and the start of excuse.

"I entered correct credentials in the login at nine-fifty-nine and twenty-two seconds, ok-o?"-he raises his hand and retrieves it in slow motion. He suddenly throws his hand in the air- "But the computer only made things worse. Hmmm... Hmmm. It took 28 seconds to load and opened at ten but..."

"It said wrong Captcha. Oh ho? Wrong Captcha, my foot-o?"-he feels for the broken streak. "Why did you ask me to book your ticket, actually? Why couldn't you have book it by yourself, actually? You have missed the Akal and your record is broken, hmmm. Not mine ok-o? Ok-o?"

"Ok. By the way I did not have a record. I think a new record has begun- of losing Akal bookings."

"That's ok, actually. A record broken is a record made, hmmm."-Tintu looks elsewhere, indicating that he has pardoned Ayodhya and Ayodhya is free now. "Next time don't ask me to book, Ok-o?"

"Fine. Calm down."

"Why should I calm down, actually? I can get angry and remain angry as long as I want. Anyway, my record is intact, hmmm."

Ayodhya walks back in his flat. He goes through the train schedule and bingo!!

"Hey, Tintu!"

"You record is not broken! The Akal booking was to be done yesterday morning! Not today! The train departs from Gold Street Station tomorrow dawn but its origin is tonight at eleven fifty from Minicoy! So we should have booked it yesterday!!"

"I told you, my record is not broken. Hmmm."-Tintu runs his forefinger in the air as though he is tightening an imaginary screw with the bolt that his finger is!

Ayodhya is still concerned. He has told Anca that he is going to Sarovar Nagar. He has even applied leave stating that his mantra of visit was clear. He just doesn't want to go to office now.

"Should I still try going to Sarovar Nagar?"-he knows something will unfold there.

The night in Sarovar Nagar is moonless.

Ayodhya's house looks haunted... The crickets, eagerly awaiting someone, show their restlessness. The trees have bowed down, unable to bear the ominous ticking of the century old clock tower in the next lane.

A human form walks slowly inside, opening the rusty gate. The owls howl foul play.

All of a sudden, bullets are fired! The man collapses, breathing heavily for some time before going quiet.

The next morning, there is no sign of the body or the blood. The owls have gone into hiding, the crickets have gone numb and the trees have woken up to null.

Sarovar Nagar goes down to the days of oblivion again.

Back in Dweepa, the chief minister is angry with the fact that his portion of money has been confiscated after Sagar's informing to the Coast Guard. He holds the Home Minister responsible for the lapse. He was always against Sagar's appointment to deal with Gharial. He wanted a puppet. But the Home Minister had insisted that such a move would engender suspicion. "You said the ACP will not even get a scent of it! Now he has even tasted it."-the Chief Minister thuds his fist on the table.

"Sir, most of your money has already been dispatched to the Blitz Banks. It was only the last consignment. And it is still lying in Dweepa. Although it is in the custody of the special team, we can fetch it."-the Home Minister assures.

"How will you recover? I need my money before we start shipping yours. If you skip mine, I'll make sure your turn will come only after that of the opposition party and other petty bureaucrats."

"No worries. We have Gharial!!"

"After the martyrdom of Head Constable Jackpot, the entire island is angry. Incidents of stone pelting at government offices and arson of public transport vehicles have been reported in Matsyali and South Dweepa respectively. There has been one incident of setting fire to a petrol station at Gold Street. The Petrol Station Owners' Association has decided to shut down all their stations until normalcy is restored.

People have gathered in large numbers in front of the Police Headquarters, demanding that the incapable ACP be removed. You can see placards such as SACK ACP SAGAR and ACP DOWN DOWN being held by several protestors. The Police force has resorted to water jet and tear gas to disperse the crowd but the Dweepites have shown that their spirit is strong. The ACP's residence where his family stays, has been provided protection. The ACP himself is not to be seen even in his rented mansion near the Pungent Dungeon. In a daring attempt, the money that was confiscated from the cargo ship has been stolen after the reserve forces were dispatched to maintain law and order on the island. With camerawoman Yamella, I am Pami, NOT NOW... One sec... With camerawoman Pamella, I am Yami, NOT NOW... Not again!"

The Chief Minister is glad to know that his money is back. "You know? When I was a kid, I had never seen money. We used to be so poor."

"Why not see it now? You might never have seen so much money at one place. It looks monstrous."-the Home Minister suggests. "My money is moved already. I can see yours. After Gharial's breathtaking success in the swear-in ceremony, we have hit a jackpot."

"That was the second success... Jackpot..."

The Chief Minister visits the violence hit areas, promising various actions against the culprits and wraps up the obligation in half-a-day. His bullet proof car races along the muddy soil. The Home Minister's car is not very far away.

They come to a screeching halt at a dilapidated farmhouse. The Chief Minister gets out of the car, looks at the house and turns back interrogatively at the Home Minister emerging out of his car. The other three party members, who are close confidantes of the Chief Minister, escort him into the house. "It is my house, don't worry."-the Home Minister assures as they walk in. The doors are closed from inside.

The house smells months of undisturbed dust. The furniture is covered by sheets of cloth that were white in color when spread. The spiders move about luring their prey into the attractive webs spun across the corners. It looks symbolic, analogous.

The Home Minister and the bodyguards surround the Chief Minister. "What?"-the Minister flashes his hands.

"You are about to die, you moron!!"-the Home Minister slaps him. The Chief Minister falls down on the floor. He wets his pants, sliding along the floor. A coat of sweat washes down from his forehead. He is angry but helpless. There is nothing he can do but die. He gives way to loose stools, out of fear of death. "He is stinking... Finish him off."-the Home Minister orders. The Chief Minister's bodyguards drag him to a corner, behind a wardrobe. Bullets are fired. Blood flows out from under the furniture. It is nothing new to me. The cycle is bound to infinity. The Chief Minister had hatched the plot of covering up the previous CM candidate's murder and protected Gharial. He paid for it dearly this time and the Home Minister is going to be the next CM.

There are many such incidents in the history of Golden Bird... The most notable of all is the chilling case of Tailapa III...

The southern region of the sub-continent is in tumultuous spells. The authority of the Chalukyan Empire of Kalyani has been waning...

Blood clotted fingers run down the iron bars of the cell. Mosquitoes have made the place more miserable. There is a small opening near the west side of the cell. Swollen eyes try hard to look through it... into the glorious past they have been the last sign of.

The end of Chalukyas has dawned. They have been, for centuries, a force to reckon with. They ruled from Badami, an awe inspiring city of the bygone era. Its prosperity was such that the Pallavas, their bitter enemies, had enough treasuries to survive for a whole decade solely on the plunder, after the Pallava king Narasimha Varma executed Pulakesin II and sacked Badami.

Chalukyas were once so powerful that they withstood the repeated onslaughts of the Cholas who were at the zenith of power subduing South East Asia. But after the Chalukyas had been consumed by one of their own generals who began the Rashtrakuta Empire, they remained subordinate to them for about two centuries.

Tailapa I, the Chalukyan vassal of the Rashtrakutas, unable to bear the humiliation of offering tributes to his overlords who, once upon a time, were under his ancestors, waited for the opportunity. The Rashtrakutas were declining in power. The other vassals were gaining strength day by day. Tailapa I had sensed that the moment to bring back the glory of the Chalukyas was ripe, lest the other feudatories snatch it, and declared war on the Rashtrakutas.

He won battle after battle, exterminated the last of the scions of Rashtrakutas and finally managed to establish the might of Chalukyas again after centuries!

The glory was restored but the capital wasn't. It was Kalyani!

The lineage of Chalukyas of Kalyani passed from descendant to descendant until today, the days of the last of the emperors- Tailapa III.

The swollen eyes turn to see down through the cellar, a faint light in the night. The head turns to see from the corner of the eye which is less swollen.

"Listen, soldier!"

"Your Majesty?"-the soldier responds, bending to pay obeisance to the Emperor defeated by his own feudatory.

Tailapa III notices the uniform worn by the soldier. It was the same design he had approved two years ago to Prolla II, his Kakatiya vassal who, today, has defeated and dragged him behind the back of his horse from the battlefield. Tailapa III had demanded death at the hands of the victor, in the traditions of an Emperor but secretly hoped for freedom in the traditions of a human.

"I no longer take orders from you!"-Prolla had dragged him on and imprisoned him in his fort.

"Can I get some water?"-Tailapa III asks the soldier. The soldier bows and departs, walking backwards to a distance.

Prolla is in deep discussion with the other courtiers. "Newness occupies space only after the old is washed away."-the Prime Minister opines.

"Death to Tailapa!"-the commander-in-chief raises his sword. Prolla notices the Prime Minister's face which does not approve of it. "I said the old should depart. There need not be an execution."

Prolla looks at his feet. The gem studded footwear display the reflection of his worried face. "He will be set free."-he dismisses the court.

The soldier brings water to the cell. It is an earthen pot. "Your Highness is going to be free."-he breaks the news. The Emperor gulps the water to his contended heart's content.

The doors of his cell open with a clang of released chain. His wrists are freed. Prolla stands with hands folded at his back, keeping his right foot on Tailapa's war helmet.

The Emperor walks to the vassal. "Go, I've offered you your life as charity. Your helmet is my war trophy."-he kicks the helmet.

It is not over yet. The Chalukyan cult is going to be coalesced with the new power center... The Hoysalas!

Tailapa III has been captured again, this time by another vassal- the Hoysala king Vira Narasimha. He and his generals stand around the fallen Emperor on the battlefield. The king pulls the hair of the Emperor and slaps him! The generals are awestruck at the treatment! Tailapa falls down and tries to crawl away. Vira Narasimha asks his son to drag the Emperor to a spot. Tailapa can see his knees bleeding to lifelessness. He can't stand. He is totally at the mercy of the Hoysala subordinate. He can feel the wound of the arrow on the left side of the abdomen being deliberately pressed by Vira Narasimha's son. Vira Narasimha pushes the emperor against a rock. Tailapa is lying on the warm surface of the rock. The back of his neck can feel the touch of the tip of the sword. He sees a gecko looking on from under a stone...

Whackk!

An empire comes to an end! "Hail Raja Vira Narasimha!!"-his soldiers roar in front of the torso of Tailapa III.

If only Vira Narasimha foreknew the kind of death meted out to his descendant Vira Ballala III...

The Home Minister has successfully purported a story of the Chief Minister getting killed by Gharial. Dweepa finds it hard to believe but accept him as the new man-in-charge.

"Instruct Gharial to fetch new bodies to transport the money recovered. And how long is this pilot project got to go? Why not at a large scale yet?"-his first orders as a Chief Minister is firm and clear.

Sagar is going to be retained as the ACP. "It is to show him how worthless he is in front of people and how helpless he is in front of us."-the new chief minister explains to the new home minister.

The dead body at Ayodhya's house in Sarovar Nagar has been brought to Heaven Seven Hospital Dweepa to hand over to the relatives as a failed heart transplant case.

Sagar and Kunj are back, planning the next move. Sagar receives a Shutapp message from his mother- 'The consultant at the Gold Street Office has given us an appointment. We are going. It would be better if you and Soor can make it too. The situation is tense; the people are against you but I know you can make it.'

He doesn't respond but it hurts him for reasons unknown to him. "Sir, if we could somehow locate Soor or Soman, we will be able to get to the bottom of everything. We need to stop pursuing Gharial for the moment."-Kunj wants Sagar to consider.

"But it is not possible. She has left the country. Probably Soman too has left. So the only way is to rely on Gharial's trail."

"We better chase mirage."

Sagar's phone rings. It is Soor!!!

Sagar can't believe it!! He accepts at once.... Just the way he does every time.

"Sagar! Soor here. Listen! Ayodhya has been killed and they have brought the body here."

"What are you blabbering?"

"Yeah, Sagar. I was with Soman all these days but these people seem to have no accomplices. I will meet you tomorrow evening at my flat and explain everything."

Sagar feels that the game is lost. Ayodhya has been silenced. "Kunj! Call up Ayodhya."

"What happened?"

"Call him, God damn it!!"-Sagar loses his cool. Kunj dials Ayodhya's number frantically. "Sir, his number is not reachable."

Sagar is brushing his eyelids nervously. He continues the act for a minute before hitting his thighs and walking to the bed room. He pushes the curtains away and tucks his pistol. "Kunj, let's go. We have a job to finish. Ayodhya has been murdered."

"No, wait! Wait! Sir, please listen to me!"-Kunj holds him back. "We need to tolerate! Ayodhya's death should not perturb us from pursuing our objective. His sacrifice would go waste."

"What shall we do now?"-Sagar throws the pistol on the cot.

"Sit down."

"... and plan."

"Why is Soor trying to help us? Have they faked his killing to trap us?"

"Sir, Ayodhya cannot be dead to the best of my belief. We need to verify."

"Kunj, I'll go to Heaven Seven, disguised as a sales rep. You have to keep a watch outside and alert me by phone if something goes wrong."

"Sir, with a person like me with you, everything will go wrong. That's why Ayodhya always kept me out of field."

"Don't worry. If something goes wrong, let it happen again. They'll get neutralized."

It is morning. The head doctor is away. Soor's cabin is closed. Sagar is in the hospital waiting lobby, trying to get some sleep. "I should have got really admitted for sleeplessness."

He senses an opportunity to break in to the restricted area. He gets the password as a Shutapp message from Kunj, in time.

He walks in carefully. Kunj has briefed him everything about what Ayodhya had seen. Sagar himself has an experience of raiding the area once already. There is a body lying at the edge of the hall. He rushes swiftly yet soundlessly. As he opens the sheet, he is stunned to see a body riddled with bullets. He thinks that it is of Ayodhya. He takes a snap and sends the image file to Kunj for verification.

Kunj does not reply. "Is he in shock?"-Sagar walks towards the exit through the tunnel. "If it is confirmed as Ayodhya, I'll keep Kunj out for good."

He calls up Kunj.

"Is it him?"

"Who is who?"

"I had sent you a Shutapp message!"

"I didn't receive any."

Sagar's impatience rises. He runs out of the tunnel and keeps on until he meets Kunj. "This body."-he displays.

"This... this... is of our college senior Pony!!!"

"What? Now who is this new entrant? How did he end up at Sarovar Nagar?"-Sagar is in a dilemma. "I don't know but he always targeted Ayodhya."

"Did Ayodhya kill him then?"

"He always talked about neutralizing the enemy. Does that include killing?"

"Yes. Where is he now? Has he started to flout laws?"

"Only he knows where he is."

Sagar will never know why Pony went to Sarovar Nagar and who killed him. Pony's incident is just a petty by-product of Ayodhya's intense planning. When Ayodhya had received the mail asking him to visit Sarovar Nagar, he had quickly judged that it did not come from his grandpa!

His grandfather had never asked him to visit home throughout the past, even when the urge to meet his grandson was getting heavier by the years. He was not so weak-minded. Had he been so, Ayodhya wouldn't have survived. And the second and the biggest reason was that the mail started as 'Dear Ayodhya' while his grandfather always started the mails as 'Dear Appu'. In fact, he never had called him Ayodhya.

Ayodhya knew that the mail was the creation of none other than Soman! He was desperate to kill him. Ayodhya had moved his grandfather to a location other than his home. But Soman had accessed Ram Prakash's mail address and through it, Ayodhya's. Soman knew that a person as clever as Ayodhya cannot be chased. He was to be made to fall in the trap.
Ayodhya did not fall for the emotions. He cleverly let the message reach Pony through Anca. He wanted Pony to be the test specimen. And he had risked the chance of Pony and Soman joining hands. It was a calculated risk, but very much essential like his trademark inside-out shot.

Ayodhya is at his office. He knows that Soman and his gang are relaxed. Nobody is going to bother them from now on. But Soman has a trump card not known to Ayodhya. He has located his grandfather through the Sarovar Nagar Police and sent him a word that Ayodhya had been killed. Ram Prakash had run all the way from the storage shed of the playground at Sarovar Nagar where he had been hiding. As soon as he had reached the Police Station, he had seen Soman sipping tea with the sub-inspector. "Hey, grandsy!! Great to see alive."-Soman had hugged him. Ram Prakash had borne it. "Where is the body?"

"Chill old man! This is a Police Station. Let's have a walk to the hospital!"-he had brought Ram Prakash to Heaven Seven of Sarovar

Nagar.

Ram Prakash was shown the dead body. The body was mutilated and hence was a bit difficult to identify but Ram Prakash's heart had jumped! He had felt that it wasn't his grandson. He had slowly held the body's right hand, sobbing and wailing. He had gently tried to bend the thumb. Ayodhya's right thumb was dislocated in childhood when he shot the man at school holding the gun backwards. But that of the body was fine. Ram Prakash had broken into tears, admiring his grandson's intelligence. Soman was convinced that Ayodhya was dead.

These days Ram Prakash stays at home, without a chance of contacting his grandson. Soman has spared him for now- "Live out your life until I come back again from Dweepa. Next time, it will be for the Blue Bell Villa."

Soman is back in Dweepa. "We need to kickstart the process again. Ayodhya is no more."-he explains to the new CM. "What about the grand plan of demolishing a building? And which building have you chosen for that?"

"You'll know, eventually."

The new CM pauses to measure the depth of his words. "Ok, get the body ready by tonight. I will be in New Delhi in the evening."-he departs.

It is evening. Kunj is at Sagar's residence. He has been asked by Sagar to remain in touch with him and Abhilash.

"Keep your phone switched on. Make sure you attend it when I call and keep it live. I may also send Shutapp messages."

"Sir, I have a maple phone. It can catch signals anywhere... Even in the tunnel. Why don't we swap phones? You use mine... And keep it live on call. It is a postpaid connection anyway."

"Great!"-Sagar agrees. "Sir, what if Ayodhya wants to enter?"

Sagar doesn't like the assistance of Ayodhya, someone who has killed a person, someone who has flouted the law of the land. "Ayodhya is not the right man... He is the best! Give the phone to him and ask him to get to the restricted area if I fail to make contact."-he makes an unusual decision, quite contrary of what he thinks.

He goes in again in the guise of a sales rep. He has decided not to wait for Soor or the evening she has requested. "I am from the Chief Minister's side."-he introduces himself to the head doctor with a radiance of enigma on his face, indicating that he is an insider. He enters the restricted area with ease. He calls up Kunj. Kunj listens to the discussion keenly. "So, did you bring the hardener?"-the head doctor inquires. Sagar is in a dilemma. He recovers, looking at the doctor as though the doctor is asking for something without fulfilling an obligation. "Yeah, yeah... The payment is due."-the doctor frowns mildly.

"There is no business that is never incomplete."-Sagar reasons to himself.

"But... you know, there is nothing called a completed business. Only transactions can be complete. Business is... vast."-the doctor leans, patting Sagar's palm. "Tell him, we are going to pay even in advance. We are bringing down a building and crushing people under it. The bodies will be damaged beyond imagination. We need more hardener to stiffen them and you know... make them into carriers. So, we'll pay by the end of this month and we want urgently. Tell him we'll transport his share in bulk... in one go! If you believe Dr. Soman, the demolition day is quite close."

"But the hardeners are now getting difficult to supply... Some glitch."-Sagar fires a salvo. "Don't talk foolish! I know your people have synthesized a lot of it... I know it is a brainchild of ACP Sagar... the adhesive! We stopped the use of adhesive nets to nab criminals by stating that it causes irreversible skin damage... You know that right? And how many gallons have been prepared since then?"

Sagar's heart crumbles!!

This comes as the last straw in his demoralized mind. He sinks!!

"So difficult to engineer, so very easy to doctor... Right?"-the doctor continues.

"We'll wait, anyway... But ask the CM to get them to hurry up!"

"Yyy... Yes doctor!"-he takes leave and a left turn!

His face reddens. He rests behind a pillar to recuperate. "Sir, it's ok."-Kunj whispers over the phone, trying to instill some presence of mind.

Sagar recovers and heads directly towards the tunnel. To his astonishment, he finds Gharial and Soman inspect a cadaver. He stands still... not by his acumen but in sheer shock at the scene!

"What made you choose this body?"-Soman smiles, patting Gharial. "Because you are too big for the sum."

"Ha..ha..ha."-Soman leads Gharial out of the hall into a closed, secret chamber.

Sagar looks around to hide himself. A chemist emerges out of it and starts walking towards a hiding Sagar. Sagar appears, pointing a pistol at him!

The man is stunned!

"You shout and I'll clean your skull! Probably it can be used to carry a few paise."

The chemist surrenders. "Now, strip!"

The man hesitates. "You either strip yourself or get your skin flogged."

The chemist takes off his clothes. Sagar locks him up in an abandoned operation theater and dons his clothes. He walks casually towards the secret chamber but stops short of the entrance. The body at the end of the hall seems to beckon him. He feels that some life is still left in it.

He returns, goes close to the body... closer... and closer... His hand slowly moves the sheet and... He drops down next to the cot!

It is of Soor!!

When Gharial was informed to arrange for a body immediately, he had seen a five-foot-four-inch Soor all alone in her cabin.

"Since you were a trusted... ummm"-Gharial had brought his fist to his chin. "... sleeping partner..."-he had signaled double quotes. "... of Soman, I... offer you a discount."

"I am committed to him. I am engaged to..."-she had whispered under her breath.

"Ah! Yes. How can I forget the shoving of earthen metals through those feeble bones of upper appendages..."-he had breathed out a cold puff on her forehead.

"He is sure committed to you. But he is obsessed with hoarding. Humans, we are... We are compulsive hoarders."-he had rubbed her sweaty palms.

"You may pick to die in a second... It won't hurt you... my personal guarantee... you know; I am... a professional. But since time is the only scarce resource with us, I provide you a window of... ten... seconds... to decide a fast one or a slow one, beginning now!"

"... and by default, your choice is... my favorite!"-he had whispered.

"One... two... three..."

Soor's eyes had welled up, recapturing her past. "... four... five... six..."

She had regurgitated hidden memories of Sagar, the promises made by Soman, and the kiss Sagar's mother had pinned on her forehead after giving her the gold chain. "... seven... eight... nine..."

"Fast!"

A punch that would have dented even the foreheads of the strongest of elephants had landed on her stomach! Blood had gushed from her mouth and nose like a river inundated.

Sagar sobs, holding her stiff hand, and begs for forgiveness... for being soft, vulnerable and ordinary!

He continues to sob for a few more minutes.. "Sir, what happened?"-Kunj whispers over the phone, not disturbing Sagar's sobs.

"What happ... Sir? Hello?"

Sagar disconnects. Kunj knows something is wrong and Ayodhya needs to enter.

On the other end in Dweepa, the protests against Sagar have gained more steam. The disappearance of Pony has shaken the software world. A number of Bits have been beaten on Bitter, countless Roasts have been roasted on Fakebook and angry videos have been uploaded on BlueTube even in mainland India, against the inaction of the ruling NSF.

The online emotion has spread like wildfire. A candle march has been decided to be held on Dweepa on the same night.

"Hey Ayodhya! How many times I should call you actually? You have a girlfriend-o?"-Tintu asks Ayodhya when he finally gets to speak to Ayodhya over phone.

"What's the matter?"-Ayodhya asks impatiently. He is extremely concerned with Sagar's security that he can't afford not to ignore it after learning all about it from Kunj. But he doesn't have even the slightest idea of Soor's death.

"You know about Pony's disappearance-o? A candle march from The Pungent Dungeon to Raj Tilak Road is scheduled tonight, hmmm. Via Gold Street. Can you join-o?"

"No, Tintu. I am busy. Are you joining it?"

"Hey, man... I keep waiting for these opportunities actually. In Kerala, we celebrate Bandh, protest and hartals more than we celebrate Onam, Vishu and Christmas. As a child I used to enjoy holidays on hartals actually. Candle marches are more... exx... ex...exciting than candle light dinners, actually."

"Have fun."-Ayodhya has to make it to Heaven Seven.

The protest has huge support. The local trains are cancelled. The petrol stations are closed. The roads are ghastly vacant. But there is an unusual rider on a smoking motorcycle, the road's king. It is Ayodhya!

And he zips along, on his father's Yezdi!!

If you remember, Yezdi is a motorbike that runs smoothly even on kerosene!! Superfast!!

It is midnight. The protestors have slowly started to gather at the Pungent Dungeon. Men, women, children, the elderly... everyone has come out with gleaming candles. Some are also holding placards with Pony's pictures on them. Tintu lights up the candle of a small boy. The light brushes away the darkness, revealing the boy's face. It is Sonu! "Hey man, you didn't give me any new ones, actually...?"

"I'll get them for you after the candle march! I thought you were busy buying the LED TV."

As you move well above the island and look down from a sufficient height, you can see an ocean of golden yellow sailing along the streets.

The march begins! The media grabs the chance. The telecast is in full flow.

"Let's paint the city naked!"-Gharial remarks.

Soman is shocked to see the news!

"The name of the person killed in Sarovar Nagar is Pony!!"-he whispers. "Then where is Ayodhya?"

He instructs the chief security guard to tighten the vigil at the entry points to the hospital, especially the secret chamber.

The secret chamber has much more than just a TV. There are stacks of bodies filled with cash. "That whole batch of bodies is of the guys at the bar with the CM candidate's son, isn't it?"-he turns to Gharial. "And these ones are of your own men."

Gharial is quiet.

Soman walks down the chambers and enters a circular area at an altitude lower than ground floor. "So there are hundreds of carriers still available. I unnecessarily hurried with more bodies. Sorry about it."-Soman frowns. He looks above. The ceiling is marked by a number of sluices opening inwards to the circular area he stands on.

"The day you apologize you'll fall in to mercy of the pardoners."-Gharial pulls a lever. A cadaver filled with cash slides down from the height and falls next to Soman with a thud. Soman slowly moves away. "You didn't get scared, no surprise you're Ayodhya's cousin!"

Soman looks at the fallen body. "Oops, sorry mom."

"I fear only death. And the bodies are dead themselves."-he clarifies.

Suddenly he senses all the sluices shake with some things sliding along. A body flies down behind him! He moves away. Another one bangs him hard from the side, almost flooring him. "Stop it Gharial!!!"-he shouts!

Another one drops right on his shoulder and he falls, bleeding from his nose. He stands up, looking sneeringly at Gharial. More bodies swoop down, burying him under them! Their positions are disturbed by him invisibly struggling to surface out. A while later, the disturbance ends...

"And you said the dead can't kill."

Gharial's men get back to work, clearing the mess.

The TV is on. There is live coverage of the protests being put down forcefully. "As you can see for yourselves, the protestors have reached Swarga, the Chief Minister's residence. They are trying to uproot the barricades. The police have resorted to the use of tear gas and assaults on the protestors. There are a few casualties reported. The ambulance is not able to make way out of the melee. You can see on my right, the effigy of ACP Sagar being burnt. The sloganeering is on and there is a lot of chaos around here. Oh my God! It's horrific!! The stampede... It's getting out of control!! You can see the man at the corner of the road getting all trampled up but he is shielding a small boy under him. The small boy! There! He is crying but is safe but I'm not quite sure of the man! There he is... lifeless, one among many, on this fateful night in Dweepa. Here, we have recovered the small boy. "Hey what's your name?"

"Sonu."

"Sonu, how old are you, Sonu?"

"Eight!!"-Sonu shows four fingers, sobbing badly. The reporter wraps his head with a scarf. "What are you doing here, Sonu?"

"I don't know."-Sonu answers obediently. The reporter now turns around the body of the man who had shielded Sonu. It is of Tintu!!

"The number of people lost in the stampede is just too many and the violence on the island does not seem to end any sooner. With cameraman Romie, I am Yami, NOT NOW."-she stands astounded!

Sagar enters the secret chamber. There is a lava of detestation spurting inside him. His father's demise, his mother's silence, Ayush's unconcern, Soor's betrayal, her death, the department's indifference, Jackpot's killing, Ayodhya's lawlessness, the disappearances of islanders, the media's ruthlessness...Sagar's cap of patience is blown away!

He takes a rough aim at Gharial and fires mindlessly! Gharial is thrown away but the bullets are wasted. His men stop the work and head to take up the positions. There are eight of them and Sagar shoots down three in quick succession. "Sagar, Sagar, Sagar..."-Gharial does not turn around. "How sad! I'll have to kill a sparrow like you. It is not up to my diet, you know! I need ummm... wildebeests like Ayodhya."

"Gharials are too small for them!"-a deep voice disturbs Gharial as he feels intense pain in his ears!

"Just because the pace is slow, do you think the snail does not know where it goes?"- Ayodhya has kicked him on the ear and escaped out of the chamber.

Gharial follows him while two of the men fire at Sagar with their Kalashnikovs. Sagar is behind the pillar while they lay in wait behind the bodies. Sagar has only his pistol and a grenade. Gharial allows the rest of his men to go after Ayodhya.

Ayodhya makes his escape to a narrow portion in the hall, denying them the advantage of an all-out attack. The first man hurls a hammer at him. He holds a jute cloth in its way, in full tension, by pulling its ends vertically. The hammer falls neutralized. The man charges at him bare handed, encouraged by his slim looks. Ayodhya uses the same hammer to knock him under the chin.

The second man enters the area, looking around cautiously. He sees a fallen Ayodhya and fires a round. "Clothes maketh a man. And eyes, a turkey!!"-Ayodhya has switched clothes... He has donned the first man's jacket.

The man leaps to knock him out with a kick. Ayodhya too leaps, plants his left foot on the man's lifted thigh, presses against it to attain the right height and kicks the neck with his right foot. The man descends with a crash. Ayodhya jerks the man's neck.

Firing continues inside the chamber. One of the men scoots towards Sagar while the other offers him cover by spraying bullets. Sagar senses the gravity. He fires at the man charging at him. The man's head springs out blood and he falls down a couple of steps later. The other man approaches Sagar with the gun continuously spewing deathly capsules at him. Sagar hurls the grenade! The hall thunders! The man dies but Sagar is hurt too. The chamber is too small to dissipate the energy released by the grenade.

Gharial halts his walk towards Ayodhya who is dealing with the last man. He changes his mind and walks in to the chamber. An injured Sagar inches slowly towards the dead man's gun but remains a few paces short of it as Gharial kicks it away.

At the other end, Gharial's last man is pointing his gun at the area Ayodhya is believed to be hiding. The waiting game is on.

"You know, Sagar! I sometimes do not understand why you and I should act this way. You and I are both cleansing Dweepa of the bad guys. You catch thieves while I remove some of the citizens..."

"How good is murdering people?"-Sagar coughs as Gharial lifts him with the collar. "Oh, yes! It is quintessential! You see, I killed a chief ministerial candidate, thus cleaning a potential... umm... corrupter!"-Gharial drags Sagar slowly towards the entrance. "It doesn't matter. Many more will crop up."

"That's exactly why I kill others too. You think a common man, honest and sincere, will remain so even at the position of power? No... You give people power and they'll show you their true colors. The only thing that binds men to civilization is lack of authority."

"Nobody has absolute authority in a democracy. Nobody is allowed to go against the society."

"It is only in the books. Books rule the world of knowledge. Minds rule the world of wisdom. If men knowledgeable of the rules pay servile obeisance to one individual, would the books slap them from the shelves?"

"Then who should run the government? You?"

"Well, I don't know. But if I do, I'll at least save you the jolt, you know!"-Gharial drags Sagar out of the chamber, grinning wide. The breach between his teeth on the upper jaw caused by the knocking of the golden tooth by the thugs of Sarovar Nagar is glaringly visible.

The last man opposing Ayodhya at the hall is shot down dead by Gharial and the bullets are emptied in the man's body! "Hey Ayodhya! Look at him! Your beloved ACP Sagar! Now, did you think I would come unprepared?"- Gharial poses a question aloud. Ayodhya does not move a muscle.

"I only wanted you to come."-he answers in his mind.

"You only wanted me to come?"

Ayodhya has even normalized his breathing to avoid any visible movement. He is just behind the pillar and the cupboard, shielded against bullets by the two unconscious men of Gharial. He can see Gharial toy around with Sagar's neck, pushing him here and there. Gharial grips Sagar's elbow and turns it backwards violently. Sagar screams in pain! Gharial thrusts his hand in Sagar's mouth and pulls out his tongue! Sagar wails, tuning to either side. His eyes redden with tears. Ayodhya's heart wrenches! Gharial looks around. There is no sign yet of Ayodhya. "Look at him, Ayodhya! I have killed many. But if he dies tonight..."-Gharial pauses to have a look at Sagar's watch. "... today... then it would be your responsibility. How many have you killed before?"

Ayodhya remembers the incident in which he had shot the attacker in school. He knows he is still reeling under trauma. His inaction may lead to another death. "Ayodhya!!"-Gharial thunders. Ayodhya remains resilient in his position. "He he he... Ha ha ha..."-Sagar scoffs amidst coughs. Blood oozes from the corner of his lips. His teeth are marked with red. Gharial looks into the beautiful cateyes of Sagar. He holds Sagar's head with one hand and plucks out Sagar's right eyeball with the other!!

Sagar screams his heart out and starts beating his limbs. Gharial pulls out the other one too. Sagar's struggle is becoming uncontrollable even to Gharial. Gharial starts knocking Sagar's head continuously as though he is possessed. The skin on Sagar's forehead peels off, revealing some white matter.

Sagar hangs on, holding Gharial's hip for support.

"Do you know when you are hurt the most? When you feel like taking the help of the very person who has hurt you!"-Gharial shares a thought.

Ayodhya is pained! For a moment he feels like attacking Gharial but his senses get him back to reality. Once fallen in to Gharial's eyes, there is no other way than face him. Sagar can't see a thing but he feels his past. He wants to apologize to his mother but he can't speak. His eyesight is lost. He lies draped in a muddy apron soaked in blood. He lies on the ground sobbing and trying to say something. "Bee..whol..zhem... aaa."-his words are unclear.

But it is sure that he is recalling the abuses he had hurled at his mother even though his intentions were not to hurt her. He is remembering the shouts at Ayush even after he had won him the case.

Sagar is recollecting arguing with his father on his career. And more importantly he is realizing that his sacrifices were right...but also that he over-thought about the outcomes. He wants to tell it all right now to his mother and to Ayush, but he knows he can't and that all his dreams for the future are a waste, now that he is leaving the world in some time. He feels some dreams occur solely with the purpose of remaining as dreams. But dreams are where some people live their lives... those who are forsaken by reality. "Don't pledge what you can't afford to lose."-Gharial pulls out Sagar's ears.

Sagar, though, laughs weirdly. His condition does not make it look like a laugh but he does. He strangely feels bold... bold to talk openly with his mother.

When death is near, you humans act way too courageous.

Sagar seems to be talking to Jackpot that he too is joining him, leaving all responsibilities and duties behind.

"The world's greatest feeling is the one of escaping accountability."

Sagar puffs out a long breath. He remains still, with an everlasting contentment on his face. His eyes appear as though they are closed.

Ayodhya stays back, hiding behind the men... One of the men is coming around! He moves his foot a little, felling a wooden bar. Gharial's ears pick up the sound instantly! Ayodhya knows he can't afford to hide now. Gharial moves swiftly, like a spider on seeing its prey entangled in the web. As he nears the cupboard, Ayodhya dashes out, pulling Gharial's feet with him. Gharial falls down but manages to get back to feet in a matter of seconds. He tries to grip Ayodhya but Ayodhya has smeared on himself some oil kept next to the cupboard. Gharial's hand slips!!

Ayodhya brings out a kick, spinning on the other leg. It lands on the back of Gharial's cheek. He is thrown down straightaway! His hat is blown out. He holds his face, painfully squeezing his eyes. Ayodhya attacks again, this time bringing down a gun on his head. He is careful not to get too carried away.

Gharial falls again. But immediately grabs hold of Ayodhya's wrist. Ayodhya struggles like every time he does in his nightmares.

Finally, Ayodhya lets go of the shirt he is wearing. It remains in Gharial's hand while Ayodhya slides away. Gharial pounces. Ayodhya slides again behind a huge table. Gharial takes the opportunity, blocking the exit for Ayodhya by moving the table to a corner. Ayodhya is trapped at the right angles of the walls of the hall to his sides and the table's corner in the front. Gharial goes back by a step and bangs against the table. Ayodhya is squeezed against the corners of the wall. Although he shields his abdomen, he is grievously hurt. His palms and face have taken the blow.

Gharial moves back again. Ayodhya turns to his sides to let his hip face the ramming. Gharial rams in such a way that the walls shake!

Ayodhya would have been cut into two had he not changed his position! Gharial moves the table away. Ayodhya is seen cringed and motionless. Gharial walks with hands spread, to grab him if he tried to escape. He has closed his eyes but is visualizing Gharial's movement. He judges the proximity and swings his feet with the palms planted on the ground. Gharial is forcefully hit on the neck. It was unexpected! Gharial had thought that Ayodhya would try escaping through the table. Ayodhya rolls and dodges to reach the center of the hall. "Who taught you to face me?"-Gharial turns around. "A cockroach!"-Ayodhya strikes with all his energy on Gharial's head! The memories of sleepless nights, the fear of the trio, the pain of solitude, the worry for grandpa, gave Ayodhya enough energy to knock off Gharial.

Gharial is felled! Blood runs down from his head. Ayodhya gets away swiftly. But he cannot manage to stand on his feet. His hip is wounded badly.

Gharial lies down, trying to get out of the pain. Ayodhya squats away from him, judging whether Gharial is really hurt to be struck again. Suddenly, the floor under him rumbles violently! He is shocked! "Is it an earthquake?"

He immediately thrusts his feet against the rumbling to move to hide at a safer location. Gharial crawls under the table! The ceiling of the hall comes down!

The building Soman had planned to bring down was the hospital itself!! He wanted to see each of his accomplices dead before he joined hands with the ministers of Dweepa. And the method he had chosen to demolish it was Resonance!!

Every object possesses a frequency at which, if it vibrates, resonance takes place, leading to uncontrolled vibration and destruction of the object. The frequency is an inherent property of the body. He had witnessed it on TV when he was in college. The singer had broken a glass tumbler with just her voice.

He had had the construction of the Heaven Seven hospital in such a way that the geometry and the weight of the building led to resonance in a stipulated timeframe for a specific forcing function. Today, it is the conclusion of his rigorous planning.

There is dust all around. Gharial coughs and walks with great difficulty, towards Ayodhya. He can see Ayodhya's feet. Ayodhya is immobile, although not totally hurt. Gharial slowly moves the plaster away from Ayodhya's chest. Ayodhya is almost unconscious. Gharial now has all the time in the world to think of killing him in the most horrendous way!

This is the difference between my stories and that of your fellow humans. Mine is not always the happy ending one. I am realistic... I sometimes wreck hearts!

20 AN ACT OF PROVIDENCE... OR IS IT?

Gharial stands in front of Ayodhya. Ayodhya's eyeballs roll in again and again within the shades of the dark sunglasses, in his attempt to fight unconsciousness. The manner in which Gharial stands, the way Ayodhya lies on the ground, and the intensity of the situation... it reminds me of something... Wait... Oh no! How did I? How did I forget that moment? That instant... that even I have pushed beyond the curtains of infinity, is beckoning me.

It is compelling me to pull you five centuries back... to the most capricious period ever... in the history of the world. Wait...wait...

The year is 1556.

The winds howl eerily. The dust on the plains of Panipat settles down just the way the particles far, far away in a neighboring galaxy, disperse after a supernova. The night is cold. The Golden Bird has spread her wings in full bloom- from the oases of Kabul to the sultry waters of Tuticorin, from the moist sands of Gwadar to the jungles beyond Rangoon. She quietly slips in to another of those dreamy nights she has been witnessing since thousands of years.

The scene at a distant camp, miles away from Panipat, opens up. The fire at the center of the encampment dims slowly as though an invisible thief is trying to put off the lights to steal the thunder the night is going to witness.

"Pour some more oil!"-a voice orders a soldier.

A young boy, probably thirteen, in the finest of clothes and jewelry, stands confused at the ways of the world. In front of him lies unconscious the greatest warrior ever to have walked on the silky plumage of the Golden Bird. And to the boy's right stands his caretaker, handpicked after his father's untimely demise, offering a dagger clad with gold and drenched with sin.

"My master, I request you to make haste. The moment is ripe for you to earn the title of a slayer."-the caretaker interrupts the awe and admiration with which the boy looks at the man... his hero... his icon. There is a divine sign of an indomitable spirit even in the closed eyes of the man lying chained, with dusty beard, bloodied moustache, hair spread across the sand and a solidified bleed in the right eye.

"Samrat Hemu!!"-exclaims the boy, brightening his eyes. The wind turns strangely violent for a moment!

The royal guards shiver at the very thought of a conscious, unchained and unhurt Samrat Hemchandra Vikramaditya. They want to pacify their pounding hearts with the sight of lifelessness in the body of the grandest Emperor of the Golden Bird lest another of those invincible battles he waged turn them into dust.

"My master, pardon my words. But it does not suit for a prince to refer to his enemy with a royal title. His heart is filled with hate and tongue is smeared with poison. The right thing to do is to slit his throat and be immortal in the glorious pages of history."

"A prince knows about royalty better than a servant. And Prince Jalal knows it even better!"-the tender heart of the young lad slams the order given in the guise of a suggestion by a battle-hardened, brutal and apathetic Bairam Khan.

"O great Prince, I neither am a man of nobility nor am I capable of appreciating the royal protocols. But as an aged, experienced servant of the crown it is my duty to insist you to earn the coveted title by slaying the maggot that has been made to beg for life by our brave soldiers."

"No uncle Khan, he is unconscious and probably even dead."

"He isn't!"-Bairam Khan's voice shivers.

The mouths of the royal guards run dry!!

The young confused eyes full of questions that the adult eyes hate, hesitate.

Bairam Khan is losing his cool. "Had you not been the son of Humayun..."-he thunders within the safe havens of his molten mind.

"It was a wish of your father to kill the enemies of the great Empire."-he uses the last salvo.

The two innocent eyes gradually mold into a terrifying pair, the fruits of which would be seen in the aftermath of the Siege of Chittorgarh a few decades later. The young boy finally walks the way the grown-up world wants him to.

The dagger effortlessly pierces into the great emperor's neck. The seeds are sown!

Bairam Khan steps in and with all the hatred he has for the enemy, bring down his heavy sword on the throat of the most supreme martyr in the history of the Golden Bird. An era ends before taking shapes after the first ray of hope...

Let me turn back a fortnight before the chilly night.

The fall of the year is quite cold. Samrat Hemu stands on the ramparts of the Red Fort, facing the setting sun. His heavy, silk robe teases the passing wind to shake its state on his broad shoulders. The Samrat too seems to taunt the wind to shake his faith... in liberating the Golden Bird of Mughals whom he knows as hordes of invading Mongols.

He commands me to turn back and take him through the journey of his life as Basant. His poor father is rich in knowledge. He teaches a young Basant about Science, Mathematics, the Scriptures and Philosophy and about how to possess an insatiable thirst for knowledge. "Basant, we are in a very difficult age. By the wrath of the Almighty, we're ruled by merciless foreigners; freedom still seems to be a distant dream. When you grow up, I want you to strive to uproot foreign authority and establish native rule... for the people are dejected beyond relief... When you feel tired of working towards that goal just pick a random man and look into his eyes... And you'll see the pleadings and prayers."

Basant's eyes take a silent oath to break the shackles of slavery. He goes on to grow up as an honest man unwavering in his resolve. Soon, his qualities are recognized by the Suris who have recently defeated the Mughals. He rises from a humble position of a raw material supplier, a market superintendent and finally as the Prime Minister of one of the scions of Sher Shah Suri. But the scion has given in to carnal pleasures and there is rebellion all around. Basant is immediately dispatched to crush them.

Basant's military conquests are at a scale previously unheard of. One by one he wages twenty-two battles against his opponents. His inspirational orations fill his men with insurmountable spirit. His military tactics checkmate his enemies. As I witness the grandest victories of a single man in history, he, with sheer military acumen, strength and courage, leads his men from the front to win... all... of those twenty-two battles. His enemies are shattered. Nobody has the temerity to rebel.

Meanwhile, Humayun dies. A nation craves. Basant attacks. In the Battle of Delhi, he drives away the enemy and graces the throne. His grand coronation as Samrat Hemchandra Vikramaditya has been the much talked about topic world over.

He has brought me back to his present. He now stands at the Red Fort, drawing out plans for the future of his country in his mind. The preparations for a final assault on the Mongols to liberate Kabul are underway.

"Hail the Samrat!"-a man, much younger, stands behind him.

"Hasan Khan?"-the Emperor is pleased to see one of his trusted generals.

"Your Majesty, the cannons are all ready to spit fire. The elephants and horses are all set to race to the battlefield. The morale of the men is high and they are all raring to go."

"That's great. Have the reserve soldiers been briefed about their role in the battle?"

"Yes Sir. They are practicing the commando tactics since a week now. Shamsher Khan is training them."

The Samrat smiles and gently pats Hasan Khan.

"Your Majesty..."-the strong, dauntless Hasan hesitates.

"Yes Hasan?"

"With your great foresight and vision we have been successful in fulfilling our dream of freedom. There is no rebellion erupting in Bengal, no jauhar forced on the Rajputana and Delhi is breathing easy. Your Majesty's leadership has won us twenty-two straight victories. I am lucky to belong to this period in history and blessed to have fought alongside you."

The Samrat keeps his hand on Hasan's shoulder- "We all are lucky to have seen this day, Hasan. Our country will not see barbaric acts again. We will never be razed by invasions. I've charted out steps for the progress of this great motherland. We'll discuss someday after the battle."

"But... Your Majesty..."-for the first time, the Emperor witnesses the bowed head of Hasan Khan.

"Pardon me Your Highness but I could not bear it within myself."

"What is the matter, Hasan?"-the Emperor's assuring broad arms soothingly rest his shoulders. His head rises.

"Shamsher Khan told me in the morning that he had a strange supernatural feeling that we are going to lose this battle... and our lives. I feel that it is a bad omen."

The Emperor's face beams with a soft smile. "Is that all?"

"Your Majesty..."-Hasan wants the Emperor to take his words seriously.

"I think it is the wish of God to fight another day. He has seen defeat and death for us this time."

"There is a saying in the scriptures. 'Do your duty and leave the fruits to me. I will decide the outcome'. If defeat is what He has decided for us, then by His name we should welcome it. But let us do our duty because the struggle for freedom is not by Hemchandra and Hasan against the Mongols. It is about the people of the land against foreign rule. Today the Mongols are menacing our people. Tomorrow, it can be the Europeans."

"Your Majesty, I still believe it is madness to venture into a battle when the outcome is known."-Hasan Khan is still apprehensive.

"In a battle, Hasan, if the cover of purpose is blown away, all that lies beneath is madness!!"-the Emperor walks down the stony pathway with Hasan by his side.

"Someone is mad for the throne. And someone, for freedom."

The Emperor mounts on his elephant. Hasan Khan looks on. The breeze is cruel.

"We have seen decades of Mongol atrocity. We have seen towers of skulls. If we lose this war, their rule can go unchallenged for centuries. There could be more sufferings and servitude... More towers... But the spirit of freedom will never be erased. If we win, Hasan, we give people liberty. If we lose we give them hope. Don't you think they deserve at least an ounce of hope?"

He turns to Hasan at the partition in the parapet- "I am sure we'll go down in the annals of history as the freedom fighters of this noble land. Today it is us. Tomorrow someone in the Rajputana may rise against the Mongols and someone in Bengal against the Europeans. Someone... rises."

Days pass by to make way for the day of the battle. It dawns on the open fields of Panipat. It is all set to receive the ephemeral guests. Survival is the prize in the game of death. You either lose the war and lose life or win the war and lose humanity. It is a loss either way. The only victor is I, myself, for I teach you, learn from you and teach others whatever I learn from you.

Shamsher Khan, a lieutenant in the imperial army awaits the order from Hasan Khan. He is in charge of the strike unit. He has been bestowed with the title- 'Lion of the battlefield' by the Emperor after the Battle of Bengal. He possesses with him the heaviest sword in the army- 'the sword of the lion', the one presented by the Emperor himself from his own repertoire.

I remember the Emperor's words when he gifted it. "Even death cannot separate you from this sword."!

Hasan, on the other hand, has taken up the task of protecting the Emperor's left flank. The Emperor is seated on his war elephant-Puru. His armors are challenging his enemies to breach them. His eyes are the only unprotected parts in his body. He ponders over the bitter enemies who have lined up like a swarm of insects. Hasan is mounted on another war elephant-Sikander. Sikander had suffered injuries in the Battle of Bengal. But it appears that Sikander hates the Mughals more than Hasan and the Emperor themselves do. Despite the grave wounds, he had charged ahead to ram two of the opposing elephants, each almost twice his size, and finally led to the breach of the walls of the fort. Today, he was so adamant to join the war that he created a lot of fuss at the stable for resting him.

The whole arena is quiet except for the occasional war cry emanating from both sides and the impatient trumpeting of Sikander who wants to see action right away.

A flag flutters in solitude atop a pole on the side of the Imperial Army of the Samrat. The wind hurries to get away from the path of the clash. An ominous, momentary vacuum fills the battlefield between the two armies.

The next instant witnesses the unleashing of mounted up animosity, greed and an itch to feel the sword make that zipping sound as it rips off the viscera.

The battle rages. The Emperor's fighting is a sight to bewilder. It is for no ordinary reason that he has won twenty-two consecutive victories. Hasan Khan, fighting with all his strength, sees from the flanks, a personification of death in his Emperor. Shamsher Khan on the other hand, has struck deep into the Mughal formation. The way he rolls a head every three seconds seems to end the battle in quick time. Defeat seems imminent to the Mughals. It seems all over. The Emperor scans the arena to see if any of his men are badly hurt. The battle is almost won. But 'almost' is a deceptive word.

Hasan Khan smiles at the Emperor and raises his axe. The Emperor, though, waits in his Howdah for what he thinks is my ploy, the method I use to meddle with human lives to assert my presence- an act of providence!!

Let me tell you something I've always tried to make your race accept- there is no such act. It is just a label formed by your race to hide behind after I cast indecipherable puzzles at you. There are some games you're made to play without you knowing anything about. Coincidence is my ploy; act of providence is subtler. Butterfly effect is hogwash. It is all about me. You may not like it but I love playing cruel jokes... and remind you that your race is just a big loser!

Finally, it arrives. The split-second that turned the destiny of the Golden Bird and led to it being torn apart across its delicate plumage, the result of which can be seen even to this day!

An arrow from one of the Mughal archers is deflected by one from the Imperial army. And who does it head to? The Emperor himself! Where does it target? To the only unprotected part of him. Blood springs out from his right eye!

"Nirmal!"-the dauntless Emperor pulls out the arrow and hurls it out. His mahout responds immediately amidst anguish, looking at his master's blood, by removing his turban and giving it to the Emperor. The Emperor removes his helmet, ties the turban across his eye. His soldiers can't believe their beloved emperor has been injured. They stand stunned, fixing their sight on him looking at his futile attempt to arrest bleeding.

The Emperor gauges the situation. He senses the worst.

"Don't worry about me. Free yourselves from these ********! Take them down!!"-he yells at the top of his voice.

Probably it was the only occasion his troops disobeyed him. The Emperor, for the first time, repents at the affection for him in their eyes as they still stand numb with cruel shock. He laments their love, for he feels every second spent in shock is drifting victory away from them. Presence of mind is the need of the hour. But he knows. The place he has carved in their minds is dearer to them than their own precious lives.

Being a soldier's king, he regrets the imminent slaughter they are going to suffer, more than his own fall.

He knows he is going to faint sooner or later. He waves at Hasan Khan as the soldiers fall easy prey to the Mughals. Hasan Khan rushes at him, as Sikander stands alongside Puru.

"Master... They won't obey!"

"Hasan, don't worry if I am caught. Make your escape plan. Every drop of my blood that drips on this holy land will reverberate with the ultimate service I have offered as a son. Go, Hasan. Don't be foo..."

Hasan glimpses the fast approaching enemy. He gets down on his horse and makes a quick getaway, turning every now and then to see his pet Sikander being chopped part by part by Mughal soldiers. Sikander gives out the last trumpet by raising his half cut trunk oozing blood and falls on his knees. He has served the motherland well. More Mughal soldiers climb on him and quench their thirst for blood by spearing him wherever his skin is still visible.

A gallant soldier like Hasan Khan who had, in the past, held back forts against raging armies, fails to hold back his tears as he witnesses from a distance, iron chains being wound across the neck of his unconscious master.

Panipat calms down for the second time. There are bloodied bodies of able men everywhere you see. Mughal soldiers compete for gains after an act of wastage. An artillery man spots a silk crown of a nobleman of the Imperial Army. It is studded with diamonds. He immediately picks it up and inspects. But before he could dream about the life it can offer, he feels the smooth slice of a Mughal sword along his abdomen. A Mughal cavalryman has given away to greed. He is overcome by success at snatching the crown. He rides his horse errantly, giving out cries of thrill after wearing it.

His horse falls on his front legs stumbling over a giant body. The cavalryman slowly recovers from the fall and inspects the cause. Shamsher Khan's headless body lies laden with mud on the soil of Panipat. His broad chest braves the cold wind that now has the courage to blow across the battlefield; his right hand still clutches the sword, ready to fight again for his motherland.

The famed 'sword of the lion' attracts the cavalryman. His lust wins over his already weakened senses. He slowly tries to separate Shamsher's hand from it. An 'act of providence' intervenes again. A powerful, unusual lightning at an unusual occasion chars him to death. It is that act your historians failed to notice although they did about the first one... Some events are meant to go unnoticed. They happen; they set off a turnaround into motion without anyone even getting a scent of. They quietly slip away into the slimy sands of memory of those who are a part of it!

Hasan Khan pleads to God in his mind to make him aware of Shamsher's fate. As he passes by a mound of bodies he notices Shamsher's head lie a few yard away, almost buried. Hasan prays for Shamsher- a loyal soldier, a faithful friend, a true Afghan. Shamsher's eyes are visible, staring at the skies and begging for another life to the Almighty -for Delhi, for Kabul...

The field appears red with flying dust. Hasan Khan on his horse merges into another dust that is created by me. The one of past!

There is a secret I've given away to your race... on how to undo my work...

To derail a civilization, deny it its history. And then, savor the civilization unfurl a history of denials. History is not what is kept open in front of you. It is what lies behind you. It's my product. It's unfair...

21 THE LAST WORDS

Gharial seems to be in no hurry to kill Ayodhya. Despite the injuries inflicted by Ayodhya and the oozing blood across his hatless face, he stands sizing his options.

His putrid curiosity to see the face behind the hankie and the eyes behind the sunglasses draws his hands towards Ayodhya's face. He is careful though. He spots a pistol tucked in Ayodhya's belt. He removes it, points it to Ayodhya's head and bends down cautiously. He has never been so anxious, so human... He slowly takes off the hankie and the pair of sunglasses from Ayodhya's face.

The biggest secret of Ayodhya comes crashing down into his deathly eyes! The jolt he experiences is of epic proportions!! His thoughts freeze!!!

He retracts swiftly, pointing the pistol at Ayodhya! His mind blanks at the sight!

In front of him lies Kunj Bihari Yadav!!!

It is the same Kunj Bihari who was left to choose between two deaths by Gharial at the ATM's air-conditioner. The monster can't tolerate the filth that was thrown away to die, lying right there. His eyes turn demonic; probably he himself would fear looking at.

"What if he gets away again?"- his mind thunders.

"What if he gets away again?"-his veins pump up.

"What if he gets away again?"-he gets more violent in his thought.

"WHAT IF HE GETS AWAY AGAIN!!?"-his mind quits!!!

He aims at Ayodhya's face and fires!!!

Well, history is bound to repeat. That is the pattern I have set for you. I am too slow to make any changes by myself. My only role is in setting the mood for gamble and letting the dice of your fortunes roll. To load them in your favor, is your job.

The blood from Ayodhya's forehead creeps down to his fingers like an overflowing stream. The stand he had taken against Gharial has become his last. A mammoth episode of resistance has again come to an end after a gallant struggle.

Ayodhya had judged quite astutely that he had to somehow take Kunj's place in the eyes of others, after the name he had carved out for Kunj. The BlueTube videos of Kunj had further cemented Ayodhya's decision that if there was a leak of identity that it was a YIT Dweepa alumnus involved in the tussle with crime, Kunj would have been the first one to be defused. He wanted people in the world of crime to associate the name Kunj Bihar Yadav with his own face. He also wanted a method to shield himself with an armor of deception.

As a college student, he had intelligently identified a quality of humans that lies buried in the depths of conscience- the frowned habit of stereotyping. He knew stereotyping was superior to facts. Facts are questioned, stereotypes are paid obeisance.

He had successfully harped on the tendency. Jackpot was so blinded in typecasting that he did not even get the slightest idea that the 'Bihari' himself could be Ayodhya and they were not two different persons. Ayodhya had reinforced his belief over and over again. A top selling book and a subsequent movie too had helped Ayodhya immensely in achieving it.

Well, these days Kunj Bihari Yadav stays in mainland India and has established his own venture dealing with auto-machinery. His venture is going stronger day by day, and is all set to grab a considerable share of market from the current players. He is a proud national of a diverse country... A proud Bihari!!

Ayodhya's legacy is going down in my bosom as one of the unheard, unknown sagas.

And the irony of life is all evident on the floor of the restricted hall of the demolished Heaven Seven. The noble, unblemished blood flowing down along Ayodhya's fingers spread further, unifying with that of the most iniquitous, crime-filled and sordid blood from Gharial's eye!

And in Gharial's hand lies Ayodhya's Selfie!!!

Gharial is out on a hit-wicket!!

An hour passes by. Ayodhya shakes his head a bit to the left. He can feel the pain on his shoulder squeezed partially under the reclined cupboard that holds almost all the matter that has come down from the hall except a few pieces of plaster. The hall was specially designed against resonance, isolated from the rest of the building but Sagar's grenade had weakened it.

The dawn comes as a harbinger of hope on Dweepa. Gharial's hands move on the soft granules of the sands of Dweepa's shores. He opens his eye to the deep, blue, spotless sky, one side of which is hidden by his nose and a feathery protrusion of the spirit-smelling dressing.

Gharial can feel the tightness of the iron cuffs on his wrists. He can still stand up, he knows. He gets back to his feet and turns around to find nobody. It is an unused stretch of graveyard, not visited even by the ghouls. He finds the cuffs running into a chain fastened to a ball of stone. A huge ball of stone!

He tries retrieving his hands from the cuffs but to no avail. He tries pulling the stone and is marginally successful in bringing it out of the sand it is sinking in. To his back lies a mound of sand, high enough to check tides of the full moon. He understands he has been left to die by Ayodhya! He can either go down with the sinking ball into the sand with every passing wave of death or keep it on the surface by using all his strength and then die of exhaustion and starvation. Gharial pulls it out again.

Ayodhya stands far away, on one end, witnessing Gharial's struggle for life. He is not killing Gharial. No! He has reasoned himself well. And the reason is the one that makes it a memorable event in me.

"I believe that the best judge is TIME!!!"

"I have been a killer already and it took away my childhood."

He has left Gharial to me!

I'm overwhelmed at this gesture. That is why I had remarked earlier that it is a never before affair. Nobody has ever allowed me to take the reins. Never has anyone thought that I have the capacity to set things right. But Ayodhya is special. He knows I am a part of nature and hence bound by the obligation to establish natural balance with minimum changes and minimal charges.

He leaves from the shore, his figure symbolically wavering in the winds against the rising sun. He has his own share of unanswered questions.

Gharial retrieves the stone ball fifteen times in the hot morning before collapsing on the sand in despair.

More than half of the ball is sunk. He desperately tries pulling it out but in vain. An hour later, his wrists experience a powerful pull into the sand. His fingers are buried. And his forearms are next.

He tries to retrieve his arms in a futile attempt. He looks at the seamless horizon, lying down. It appears to bring back to him his homeland. He can see his island sailing towards him and his people opening their arms to welcome him.

It is his home, the place he spent his childhood away from the rest of the world. The Sentinelese Island!!

It is the only landmass in India untouched by Indians. Gharial was born there as a non-Indian. He spent his younger days happily fishing and hunting. He was known for his physical strength and intelligence. As luck would have it, a team of scientists of a research institute abducted him when he had swum away in search of the slimy mollusk that had given him a slip. Hardly did he know that it had given him the slip of life. The scientists wanted to study the behavior and adaptive abilities of the sub-human. He was kept in solitary confinement and observed. He was given various life-threatening tasks to carry out. And when all the tests were complete, he was cast out into the unknown ocean of ruthlessness which is known in a softer term called 'society'. He neither could understand the language nor could he know the reasons his innocence was shoved under the carpet of norms. As decades rolled by, he finally learnt the trick of the trade, that in the market of life, everyone was to be tricked and everything was to be traded. He finally molded himself into the pugnaciously constrained social order. He sacrificed his natural qualities for an artificial tag. He gave up his identity as a human to take up the title of a citizen!

He strived for years to learn to read and write, something unique that his island had lacked. It was something new. Writing became his lifeline when he learnt he can earn his lobster by creative-writing. But the reality of the literary world opened up quite early as he completed his first work.

He approached several publishers but in vain. His obsession for writing was not allowed to find an end. Each rejection of his work inched him closer to becoming a human-monster. Even after multitudes of refinement, one of them had opined that his work was too crude to be published. Gharial had responded quite creatively. 'A book should be like a tasty wheat roti. Let some originality remain even if it is a bit rough. Too much processing will make it too refined. It looks good but its reality comes to light only the next morning'. He was sidelined.

He had some companions who wrote for money. Gharial's natural instincts prompted him to stand out. He slowly moved to writing for fame. "Who remembers an ordinary person? It is my moral responsibility to be famous."-he judged. He wrote another one. A book that spoke of class, a work of excellence... But alas!!

The critics of the world of literature laughed at him. They laughed at him for the clichéd story that was already aplenty. He understood- "All that I wanted to ask, know and tell have already been asked, known and told, probably including this one. The only one remaining is to never be late into the world."

He had attempted a third one. It was to be an out-of-the-box, the-world and anything potential of enclosing.

He thought and thought and thought. He dwelled in the fictitious world of his own. He fought, killed, died and got resurrected. But that was not enough. He wanted to write something that nobody would have dreamed of- a never before, never after story. Every day as he cooked his food or ate his supper, he lived it. Every night as he slept, he lived it. Every morning as he strode, he lived it. His thoughts became intense. He lived it so much that he ceased to have a life. He slipped into stress. When it was complete, the critics again, stood up to their name and criticized him. "Critics are a non-creative group thriving on a creative group who don't give a damn about them."-he moved on but saw himself cordoned in a non-existent world not allowing him back into the real world.

He was so stressed that he went to the trio for a consultation. And my vices landed him up at their table just when they were in need of a tool!

He was shown the reality of reality. He fell in his solitary ward, longing to get back to the fictitious realms. The trio, against their profession to control every aspect of a human body like pulse and breath, went on a path of unprofessionalism by controlling a life!

Least did they know... An overpowering force was fledging its wings in a faraway place, right under their sensitive noses.

It is evening in Dweepa. Ayodhya lies down on the cool mosaic of his flat. His wounds are healing. He has come to know of Tintu's fate. He feels awkward for repeating the same blunder time and again. He never seeks friendship with anyone until they leave him forever. Be it Tintu or Sagar or Asrar or even Kunj. Ayodhya always stopped at pact. He never went further. He never knew that beyond a deal lies friendship. He thought it was enmity. Well, enmity is just too much friendship. He always miscalculated.

But when he finally thought of proceeding to the next step, Anca happened.

He slowly gets up against reeling head, slowing limbs, paining eyes, boiling forehead and running nose. He knows he has got fever. He walks to the kitchen and picks up a few ripened gooseberries. He starts chopping, hoping for Tintu to show up all of a sudden.

"Tintu died saving a child. Unbelievable... Every ordinary being has a special person hidden within. And time brings it out in the least expected way."- he puts the pieces in the mixer, adds some water and turns on the machine. "Not Ajay, not Vijith... But it is Tintu who is the real hero. Because a real hero is the one who does not get paid for being one. But perhaps, sometimes pays."-he empties the jar in a vessel, adds sugar and starts stirring mildly. "Tintu was a celebrity. No, he did not have fans following him. But I always admired him and his carefree life. It is not fame that makes us celebrities. It is the extent to which someone celebrates our existence, even if there is only one such person. Tintu is certainly a bigger celebrity than the movie stars... and was more handsome than any of them!"

He gulps the juice and goes to bed. When he opens his eyes, it is the next morning already. He can hear the crows and feel the sweet air from the window. He has sweated a lot. Office time has long elapsed. He rushes!

At the office, the situation is grim. A lot of anxious faces greet him silently. He tries assessing the situation. Pillu walks by- "Where the hell were you?"

Ayodhya knows that Pillu is deliberately loud. "I'd gone to order special toilet papers."

"What special? Why? I mean what?"

"Papers with your name imprinted on them."

"What's going on?"-Ayodhya asks another of his colleagues as soon as a dumbfounded Pillu leaves.

"Dweepa is going to sink!"

"It is all across the news. The company is moving to mainland in three months. Everyone is busy with packing up. The Sea Rail is all full. Minicoy is already teeming with crowd. So there are ships sailing from next week to Kochi and Karwar for evacuation."

Ayodhya immediately understands! The political top shots have been driven by desperation. Dweepa is an expensive island. In fact, it is the most expensive island in the world. Soman's mission has been derailed after the red light his life faced. The protests have intensified after the revelation at the Heaven Seven Hospital. Sagar has become an unexpected sensation after his body was found in the debris. The chief minister and his men have hatched a perfect plot to deviate the burning issue. They have lit the first flash of rumor in the dry grass that the minds of the islanders are. Rumors are sometimes what reach you earlier than they should. Nevertheless, they are lit.

Ayodhya is just another drop of water that the society of Dweepa is made up of. And he has made up his mind in uncertain waters. He wants to forget everyone who was a part of his life in his stint at Dweepa. He just does not know why.

He intimates his mantra to his boss and goes to the human resource department, popularly called 'the HR'. The officer is not at her seat as usual. Her subordinate, very much in her mold, asks him to wait at the conference hall, reminding him again and again about the coffee dispensing machine.

When finally, the officer arrives with an overdone face and Anca by her side, Ayodhya gets a chance to talk to the lady- "Madam, I'm quitting."

Anca eyes him, trying to know if he is willing to speak to her. Ayodhya's eyes are fixated on the officer's face. They don't deviate. Anca still maintains her gaze on him.

"You have signed a four-year bond; you remember? Two lacs?"-the officer asks, etching her nails. "Yes Madam. I am willing to break it."

She stares back sharply at him as though asking- "Can you even clear an exit interview?"

She doesn't know that things generally don't matter to him. Breaking a bond is the path to freedom. Breaking bonds is to solitude. And Ayodhya doesn't mind both.

Two days pass by. He has paid the bond amount... In just two days. He has also paid the extra amount for not serving the notice period... all in two days. And the officer remains uncommitted on the issue of a piece of paper called Service Certificate. She cites hectic schedule in moving the office out of Dweepa.

Ayodhya leaves his flat, bundling up his luggage. "Grandpa has not answered my call. He might have thought someone else could be trying to trap him. But Soman's death is all over the news... Then why is he still so unresponsive? Is there a new enemy?"-he starts off to the port.

His Yezdi has already secured a place on a ship. He hurries in the swarming crowd to reach the ship. He manages to read the blurred alphabets painted on the huge ship- Rajarajeshwari. People seem nervous. Everyone is in a dash to get in as soon as possible. They fear Dweepa sinking anytime soon. The Dweepa politicians and their associates cite moral responsibility to stay back until the last of the islanders is moved out. The netizens laud the gesture. Ayodhya, however, has judged rightly that they are going to bring more of the elite Indian class to Dweepa after a few weeks. They are going to share the island between them.

He sees people thronging the entrance to the ship. "Had they been queuing, each of them would have been on the deck by now."

The ship is set to sail. It is the last one for the evening. The panic peaks!

"Hooooh"-they howl together. A violent stampede begins. Ayodhya is close to the water, at the edge. He struggles to hang on with the luggage. He has to somehow get in. His Yezdi awaits him.

Suddenly, the people on the deck throw down ropes to climb with. Some men latch on as though they are storming a fort. Ayodhya manages to get hold of one. As he starts pulling himself up, his arms start shivering at the weight of his luggage trying to pull him down. He hangs on. Inch by inch, he climbs just the way he has handled life so far. "This is the rope of time that we pass through to reach the deck called goal against the pull of luggage called responsibilities."

He doesn't know... There will always be someone to lend a hand! Someone unthinkable!

He almost makes it to the deck. His hands become painful, not able to support him any longer.

Alas!

He lets go of the rope to ease the intense pain!! He is completely in the air, all set to crash into the waters!!

And all of a sudden, a hand from the deck clasps his palm tightly!

Ayodhya has closed his eyes, not able to muster enough energy. The hands of the stranger pull him up into the ship with ease. Ayodhya falls in! He is on his knees, pressing his arms. A few minutes later, his eyes shine!

The grasp!! The grip of the unknown hands has uncanny similarity to that of the dreaded monster he had fought! He feels he can't mistake that. "Gharial!! I even fought him in the nightmares!!"-he immediately looks up!

There are many people around. Many, many people around. He can't find Gharial. He gets up and struggles his way along the fleet of steps to the highest point on the deck, pushing others and thrusting himself. As soon as he reaches the point, he ponders around impatiently...

At the far edge of the ship, looking away into the sea, stands a tall, sturdy man... hatted! Ayodhya's heart pounds!!

He gets down from the point, takes a couple of steps in the direction... but... stops!!!

He stops because he knows he needn't check. He stops because he has faith in me!! To leave the matter to me is one thing. To trust me, to believe my actions is another...

And Ayodhya has proved that he is completely aware of my enigmatic role. He knows I can take care of the situations and he need not display lack of trust. Trust bonds us together... me and Ayodhya.

He finds a corner for himself to settle down. He does not spare a second look at the man.

The journey begins. It is a sore one. People are desperate to reach Karwar.

The next morning, the ship anchors at Karwar Port. Ayodhya undertakes another long, tiring journey to Sarovar Nagar. He is eager to see his grandfather, now that everything is over. His mind jumps with the fact that he can now peacefully stay with his grandfather with whatever small job he can work in.

He reaches Sarovar Nagar. It has changed. His house is now well hidden from the streets. A fly-over passes in front of the next lane. The lush trees that were there just months ago have been supplanted with the pillars of the metro rail. He speeds to his house. It looks cold. It looks barren. He feels a nervous unease in his stomach. "Grandpa? It's Ayodhya! Grandpa?"-he pushes the door only to find it locked.

"He is admitted in the hospital."-the lady next door speaks to him after about more than two decades. "Gandhi Hospital!'

"Thank you! Is anything serious?"-the ends of Ayodhya's ears feel immense pain.

"His..."-she stops seeing her son brush the curtains and come out. "Your uncle and aunts had assaulted him sometime back. He regularly suffered hemorrhage. Two days ago he passed out at home. We took him to hospital."

Ayodhya nods and leaves immediately in an auto rickshaw. He grips the iron bar of the vehicle and turns his wrists over, to overcome anxiety. He waits through the whole journey braving the traffic jams testing his patience and the signals teasing him with the countdowns. It takes about half an hour to wade across the sea of vehicles. He bends down and stresses his eyebrows to look upwards at the building of Gandhi Hospital opening itself up from behind a canopy of treetops.

He pays the driver and rushes in. A few minutes of frantic search in the wards filled with wailing grown-ups and crying children lands him up at the bed his grandfather has closed his eyes on... forever...

"You're his relative?"-a nurse asks.

He nods. "Sign this..."-she holds a document. He obeys. The doctor barges in. He is on his rounds. "We are sorry. He suffered internal bleeding and it was too late..."-he waits for Ayodhya to react. Ayodhya stands silent. "Go to the office. Some formalities are to be finished."

A few weeks of perilous solitude pass by in the memory of his grandfather. There is no day or night that goes without him shedding silent tears remembering his grandpa.

"Your grandson's attendance is low."

"But isn't he on the higher side of the class average scores?"

"I'm sorry, he is mad with cricket."

"He's mad for books too. And it has a better word... passion. Aren't you an English teacher?"

"Your grandson hit Nijju in the class."

"I always taught him to end a fight. I'm sorry I deliberately left out the methods."

The rare complaints and the rarest of interventions are the only few thoughts he can remember as of now. I can help him with some more but my job is the opposite. He knows he has to move on. He knows how much his grandfather hated sulking and dwelling in the past.

You humans... listen to me... You very well know that you glorify the past. But do you know that you also neglect the present and fear the future? No, you don't. Well let me tell you, future is created by connecting dots of present. Listen to me, I am vouching for it...

Six months have gone by. His attention has turned to managing the property his grandfather has left behind for him- the land, the farm houses. The enigmatic Blue Bell Villa is still to be located.

He has started growing pulses and oil seeds in his farm. He has planted fruit trees all along the thirty acres and placed a series of baskets along the fence. The workers he has employed on contract are charmed. He has instructed them to fill water on hot afternoons for birds to drink.

He lives in his home on weekdays, visits the farm on weekends and stays at the farm houses. He has applied for a job in Sarovar Nagar and is awaiting the decision. He knows how difficult it is to get into a company.

He follows news everyday about Dweepa. The island is still standing strong and firm as it always did. The select few from the mainland, involved in businesses and dealings that supersede the law of the land, have bought space on the island and have built numerous mansions, malls and resorts. Dweepa that was out of mainland India is now out of India.

The former islanders are taking to streets to protest the injustice but are largely unsuccessful. It is just a matter of me erasing the incidents from the country's history as I have always done.

Ayodhya finally gets a call for the interview, after about a month. They are a start-up and are looking for software engineers. He accepts the offer. Everything is smooth for now, of course, at my mercy.

His neighbors eye him every day as he passes by. They talk, gaze, stare... For reasons unknown. Some even make it clear, loud and clear- "Look... Look... Look... He is the boy who brought ill-luck to the family. I don't understand why he is still living!"

Ayodhya does not pay attention although somewhere in a corner of his heart he too is human. When people talk about you, you should know that you possess something they want... dearly.

They try to pound you with words, devour you with snarls and consume you with stares. They are fragmented pieces of Gharial. He isn't gone. He resides in each one of them... in parts... The only thing that keeps him beneath is the number. Your life is a game of numbers. Sheer numbers... The moment the number swells up into a mob, his fragments piece up together and he returns!

The night that is cast on Sarovar Nagar is a peaceful one. But in Dweepa, it is not!

Swarga, the chief minister's official residence bears the same ominous look of the times of Gharial. The Chief Minister gets down from his cot in the middle of the night to pacify his arid throat. His feet wander sideways in the dark to feel a pair of night-shoes. But they are wading across the chill water surrounding the cot.

"Moti... Hey Moti!!"-he yells for his servant in his old habit. It takes him a minute to realize that he had Moti ousted from the island in the exodus he had orchestrated. He sighs and walks barefoot for the first time after entering politics. There is water on the floor everywhere... Bed room, kitchen... He decides to check the drawing hall. Lo and behold! The hall too is carpeted with water, the reflection of the furniture dancing over it.

"Help!"-Chimpu is running around, out of his house!

"Dweepa is sinking!!!"

The chief minister is shaken! The rumor has finally been realized!!

He tries calling the guards. But it is a private island now. Literally!

The nearest point for choppers is Karwar but the lines of communication are cut due to stormy rains. He drags his feet to the window. The swimming pool seems to have encroached upon the garden. The roads remind him of Venice... The tour he had been to for a private wedding with the tax payers' money.

He returns home. Earth shakes fiercely. The glassy decorative frames, the heads of bisons and leopards on the wall and the photo of his that others worship crash down on the floor. He drops down on the sofa thinking of the reports of geologists and other scientists who had declared Dweepa a permanent island. A long hour elapses. For the first time, he rises, walks to the table and takes out the photo of God. He sits silently, recalling the series of misdeeds, the most recent being the killing of his predecessor.

There is mayhem everywhere. People are settling their scores by beating up their superficial friends. Everyone is running around. There is competition to reach the highest points in the buildings. Some have brought their cars outside and are banging against those of others in panic. The truth lies drawn and displayed. Dweepa is painted naked.

In about thirty minutes, the most beautiful of islands on earth has vanished without a sign!!

Dweepa has sunk quite contrary to the scientific conclusions. There is no big reason. Simplicity of nature is more complex than the sophistications of mankind.

Nature and I, both of us, conspire to maintain the balance of entities. Probably it is her way to cleanse herself. I've never denied her help and struck at the most opportune moment because, after all, I am a moment, I am an eon. And of course, who can utilize me better than I do?

But I must admit, sometimes I don't understand her intentions and thoughts. I try my best to know but they get so vastly multi-directional that I will have to drive beyond my limits. She is just like any other woman... enigmatic.

Ayodhya has been working diligently. The start-up has just celebrated its first anniversary. Ayodhya is now handling a senior position although he envies the intelligence and the levels of success other colleagues, much younger than him, possess. He sometimes feels inferior to them. But his was a different past he knows. He manages to save his self-esteem.

But a bigger challenge is what he sees every day on his way to work and back. He looks out of the window near the signal at Charlie Bazaar. The grave of his grandpa silently rests next to the road. His heart yanks momentarily... It makes him forget the heat he feels by the touch of the wristwatch and the shirt collar... every day. Today is no different. It pained for a moment.

He has reached home after being thoroughly washed by the jeering of his neighbors- “Look at him, he killed his mother to take birth.”

He feels like shifting his house. He knows... The Blue Bell Villa is there somewhere, waiting to be occupied. He is tired of the people around and the dirt and dilapidation in his house. One of today’s comments passed at him was about being like a Dracula in a ghostly home. He decides to clean his house temporarily before shifting to the Blue Bell Villa. He also hopes that the treasure hidden in it may help him establish a start-up.

He picks up the broom and starts with the ceiling. Twenty-seven years it has been since the house was sparkling the last time! He has finished cleaning the interiors in two days. The next evening, he scrubs the stairs of moss. He has uprooted weeds, and cleaned and trimmed the shrubs in the garden. He has made it a habit to broom his house every day and mop it twice a week.

Today, as he bends down under the table to sweep the floor, he notices a folded piece of paper. He throws away the broom and struggles to get to the paper. His heart jumps as he opens it!!

It is the last letter from his grandfather!!!

The mail exchange between them was not electronic but postal. Ayodhya knew that if phones could be tapped, emails could be hacked into as well. Postal mails, he felt, were secure, confidential and more importantly, they carried a touch!!

They carried a touch of hearts through the hands that moved cursively with the paper to bring out those beautiful emotions. That watery mark between the letter 'd' and 'm' in 'grandma' was a drop of tear that made Ayodhya realize that his grandfather was experiencing one of the cherished moments about his grandmother. And a rupee was all it took for his grandfather to make Ayodhya touch his words to the heart whenever hugged it dearly.

Ayodhya holds in his palm, the last letter from his grandfather that was not posted. He spends a few minutes going through it.

His eyes fill with tears as he closes it and presses it against his chest.

It starts with a general advice to him on why he shouldn't laugh at people when others comment about them in their absence- The very person who jokes about others feels that you will laugh at him in his absence too.

It talks about why Ayodhya has to mix with people-

'Don't live alone. It is impossible to keep running from pillar to post all your life. Time relocates them farther and farther. If you really want to live alone, laugh with others. Talk with them before they do. Be foolish, be expressive. Let them not realize your loneliness and question about it. Don't give them a clue. Make them feel that everything is fine with you. Don't gain their sympathy. That is real loneliness. Can you now live alone? Think about it.'

Ayodhya runs his thumb across his eye, giving out bursts of tears.

'I really can't ask you to continue or stop the daring work you are doing.

But always remember one thing. Courage is a junction where wisdom and foolishness meet.

Appu, if there is one book whose last few pages always remain unread, it is the book called LIFE. Do you think you'll be like this forever? No! Not even for a moment. Time is a ruthless deceiver, Appu. I fell for it. I want you not to. Someday I will vanish from the face of the earth. Ignore my grave. It is just my erstwhile body. It is not me. Someday you'll vanish too. So remember to live. Go. Find the Blue Bell Villa by yourself. Life is a journey meant for the path. The destination is not'

The letter is not complete but the message is!! Ayodhya rests against the wall. He weeps... weeps bitterly for an hour before he slowly gets back to his feet.

He walks out of the pathway to his house and starts cleaning the gate. It is ridden with thick layer of dust. He sighs and brings out a bucket of water and a cloth. He cleans the huge gate for a few minutes. Some of his neighbors come out of their homes to witness the phenomenon. He knows it but doesn't react. They start talking among themselves. More doors open. Many of them he sees for the first time.

For the first time in his life, he wipes the dusty name plate engraved on the pillar of the gate. The engravings are blurred over the years. He decides to install a new one. He pulls out and throws away the old plate in the garden.

The same evening, he brings a new name-plate. The name he has given is THE BLUE BELL VILLA!!!

What he couldn't find, he has made!

He logs in to JunkdIn- an online portal for people in various professional fields, to upload information. Anca's profile is visible with her resume. He chooses to ignore. He is learning the art.

Every day when he goes to work and stops at the signal, he tries to ignore his grandfather's grave that is next to the road, lying just two steps after hopping over the cemetery's compound he leans against. He succeeds eventually...

These days he doesn't even remember. At the signal, he just observes the countdown on the signal's digital display or plans the rest of his day.

He would be traveling to Meghpur next week on official duty for six months. He has packed his stuff. He hears a lot of noise outside. The good neighbor who had admitted his grandfather to the hospital is vacating the house. He releases the curtains back and walks in to the kitchen feeling low.

He sometimes asks himself as to why he was the only survivor in the wrangle with crime. He doesn't quite get an answer. The reason yet, is simple. No, it is not that I had a penchant towards him. Yes of course I intervened to save him but that is not the reason he survived. Others had a life before they died. Ayodhya sure lived but did not have a life. Sagar had his share with Soor. Tintu had a good time scouting for LED TV, watching movies and with Pheno. Jackpot was once in love and was loved back... Ayodhya was breathing away all his past cautiously. He had to live. I can't let him otherwise.

A week has elapsed. It is twilight and he is heading to the railway station to board the train bound to Meghpur. He can see the road-widening in progress near Charlie Bazaar. The heavy movers are uprooting trees and anything in their glorious path to progress.

As the auto rickshaw pulls off a stunning turn to beat the morbid advantage the black jacketed motorcyclist has, Ayodhya's eyes fall on to the right. One of the backhoe loaders is mowing down the compound of the cemetery. He quickly turns away. The rickshaw halts at the signal. The grave of his grandfather lies in the path of the monstrous mover. Ayodhya does not turn although he knows it is inching towards the grave with every portentous rotation of its wheels. He sits still. His vision of the dusty picture of Kanaka Sundari on the windscreen is getting more and more blurred. A greasy curtain forms in front of his eyeballs. He slowly wears his pair of sunglasses. The auto rickshaw driver spares a surprised stare at him.

The noise of the mover is getting heavier and heavier. He blinks to let go a teardrop but doesn't turn. The countdown at the signal speaks of the proximity of the mover to the grave but he doesn't turn. The grave is finally overrun! He closes his eyes tight!

The signal turns green and he moves on in the dusky evening of Sarovar Nagar.

He reaches Meghpur after a tiresome train journey. At the railway station, he is thronged by the auto rickshaw drivers. "Rainbow Mall."-he enquires. An auto driver agrees.

As he rides along the busy streets, the driver remarks- "Sir? First time to Meghpur?"

"Yes."

"I am Ram Gopal. I know this city inside out. If ever you want to go for sightseeing, you may contact me. My number is on the panel."

"Ok."

"Sir, actually many people don't know short-cuts. I am an expert in it. If you take this route, you will reach the Rainbow mall in minutes. See there? That main road? It is the ACP Sagar Road that will lead you to the mall directly."

"What road did you say?"-Ayodhya leans front.

"ACP Sagar Road."

Ayodhya can't believe it! He sticks his neck out and glances around. The addresses on the hoardings of the garage, the restaurant, the retail store...

"ACP Sagar was a Police officer in Dweepa. The island that went down the sea?"-the driver explains amidst showering of select abuses at pedestrians.

"Yeah."

"He killed Gharial and laid down his life to save millions of citizens. Haven't you heard of him?"

"I did hear about him in the news."

"Yeah, same guy."-he drops Ayodhya at the mall. "If you want to know more about him, come to the mall this Sunday. They are going to inaugurate the statues in the center of the mall."

"Statues?"

"Yes. Of ACP Sagar and Head Constable Jackpot who was always with him. He died on a show, fighting Gharial."

Ayodhya nods involuntarily. The next Sunday he waits, one among the many citizens who have swarmed the mall, to celebrate their champions.

"See, he is our star. He studied in Meghpur University where I too studied. You remember? I had taken you to the University last month?"- a mother asks her little son. The boy nods.

The statues are inaugurated amidst pomp and vigor. The media persons throng the first row of the dais.

"I would like to request the mother of ACP Sagar to please share a few words with us. Please welcome Dr. Parvati!!"

She stands on the dais, trying her best to smile. She succeeds eventually, now that Ayush is working. After Sagar was awarded the Ashoka Chakra posthumously, his popularity had spread across the globe. Suddenly, Ayush became a sought after person for potential employers!

The gathering applauds as she bows down with a Namaste. Ayodhya too applauds with the crowd. He catches a distant glimpse of her. He feels an unusual contentment. He doesn't know that she is the same Dr. Parvati who had saved his life as a new born, raised him in his early childhood and left him to paddle through the rough waters of life!!

She is the same professional he hates.

Such is the twist of fate. He just doesn't know. He stands there, admiring her for her son. It is like the Blue Bell Villa. He just doesn't know where it exists but has considered his own home to be it.

He heaves in gladness to see Sagar finally getting the much deserved recognition. He gasps at the sheer strength of mine. He respects my strategies. His thoughts naturally fall on Kunj Bihari Yadav whom he hasn't met since college. He searches about him in JunkdIn. Kunj's entrepreneurship venture is all over Goggle. He obtains the contact number. Someone at the call center answers.

"Can I get to meet Mr. Kunj Bihari Yadav?"

"Sorry Sir, his wedding is going to take place in Bihar."

"Oh? Is it with Pooja?"

"Yes Sir."

"When?"

"Next week."

"Can you give me the address? I am his classmate in YIT Dweepa."

"Sure Sir, just hold on."

The next week he shows up at the wedding venue. There are many people gathered around. Damsels in colorful attire have lit up the atmosphere. Some have locked their arms in those of their princes lest a wily seductress snatch them away. The occasion has marked the onset of the season of bonding beyond friendship, helping them offset the presence of public. They boldly share some moments of unhindered isolation by utilizing their swelling numbers. After all, distributed attention is also a form of privacy.

Ayodhya stands across the road wearing simple clothing and envying the sight. He knows he can never be there.

But he admits in the depths of his mind- "Some girls look stunningly beautiful. Being just friends with them is an insult to them."-he slowly starts walking for a strange shelter under the darkness of a banyan tree.

"And being more than just friends... is again an insult to them."-he looks, as he walks, at his reflection on the windscreen of an expensive car parked nearby.

"Better standard of life is not a measure of better way of life."-the memory of his grandpa's words ring in his ears as it always does whenever he feels that no girl is stupid enough to fall for a horrible-looking guy that he is. Even though he doesn't like it, he can sense the repent in a girl's eyes whenever she catches a glimpse of him by mistake.

His eyes fall on the banner- 'Pooja BE Electronics WEDS Kunj BE Mechanical'.

"A perfect interdisciplinary marriage! Guess their kids will go on to learn Mechatronics"

He walks to the entrance. "Excuse me Sir?"-a guard in plain clothes stands next to him. The guard's clothes look better than Ayodhya's. He turns. "Can I please see your invitation?"

"I don't have one."

"I am sorry Sir. This is a high-profile wedding. The bride's father is a businessman and there are security risks. That is why I asked. Do you know Ms. Pooja personally?"

"No."

"Are you a friend of Mr. Kunj then?"

Ayodhya goes quiet.

"Then I am afraid you may not be able to attend the ceremony."

"It is fine, I understand."

"Thank you Sir."-the guard expresses gratitude. Ayodhya holds an envelope he wants to gift them. He finds an easy way to bypass security at the other end of the building. "Hey, can you give this to the wedding couple?"-he asks a kid playing with a balloon. "I'll buy you chocolate."

"Then buy it first!"

A while later Kunj hurries in his wedding suit, out of the entrance, with the boy. "Where?"

"Here."-the kid shows him the spot Ayodhya had handed it the gift. All Kunj can see is the empty street in the pristine darkness of the night marred by twinkling decorative lights... nothing different from the Ayodhya that he knows. And clutched in his hand is an envelope containing a piece of note wishing him a happy married life, and a portion of hurriedly arranged paper with an advice scribbled hastily-'Spend on your marriage, not wedding'.

But sandwiched between the two papers given by Ayodhya, pressed between Kunj's rubbing fingers, is Ayodhya's college ID card!

Months after months roll by. Ayodhya's job at Meghpur is finished. He returns to Sarovar Nagar. Six months is all Sarovar Nagar has taken to surprise him. All his erstwhile neighbors who tormented him at every opportunity have dissolved in the air!

Sarovar Nagar has changed. New faces, new lifestyles, new looks and new noises have made Ayodhya feel light. He walks down the road. Nobody says a thing. They are all busy with their lives. He walks slowly, unable to believe my work.

He enters his house. Six months of neglect is all evident. He cleans his home again. He wipes the newly mounted name plate on the gate pillar and trashes the old one lying in the garden with one last attempt to read the engravings on it but in vain.

In fact, the old plate also reads THE BLUE BELL VILLA!!

His ancestors had not hidden any secret treasures under the villa. It was the family values and the morals that were passed on from generation to generation, a treasure that they preserved. It was all about gaining the unknown. Because they knew that loss was not just losing. Loss was also about not finding what had to be found... The inner self!

It was about escaping the traps of the materialistic cravings, about compromising with things that were not really needed and yet longed for. It was about searching, about creating what could not be found. It was all about the reaching beyond what was known as the end!

The Blue Bell Villa is everything that you humans possess but are on a lookout. It is that unknown you, you probably will never be able to realize. It is my ace! My joker!

The treasure it possesses has not helped Ayodhya found his start-up but has definitely helped him start up all over again.

He closes the gate and turns to walk back.

"Hi!"-a soothingly beautiful voice sails through his eardrums. The most beautiful picture that anyone lucky enough to have the power of sight can behold, stands in front of Ayodhya... A girl in a Kerala saree!

"Hi"-Ayodhya mumbles under his breath.

"I am your new neighbor."-she smiles confidently. Ayodhya, on one hand, bewilders her boldness, and on the other, he stands bewitched!

"She wouldn't have been so beautiful had she been a shade lighter."-he admires her dusky complexion.

"I just shifted here a few months ago."-she turns to the opposite side, momentarily, and Ayodhya gasps at her long, moist, dense hair running down to her shin. She turns back with a smile. Her hair questions Ayodhya whether there is anything beyond her, worthy to look at. The way he looks at her... Well, I don't think he would notice even the mammoth Gharial standing behind her.

He notices her prominent cheeks that make a hill under her eyes but taper down the jaw-line, still giving a slim look to her face. Her big, bright eyes lined with kohl make him feel lost. But her voice demands his attention. He is in a queer mix of feelings. He hasn't quite savored her eyes yet.

"Can you come to my home for dinner? I love cooking and there isn't anybody I can dine with."

"Ok, ok... ok."-he nods nervously.

"What's your name?"-she smiles, her eyes contracting beautifully as her cheeks presses them in.

"Ayodhya."

"Oh, ok. My name is Tintu."

Ayodhya stands in surprise!

"Tintu?"

"Yeah, strange name you may feel. But you'll get to hear these unusual names in Kerala. Tintu, Jojo, and what not... They are gender-neutral as well."-she brushes her hair involuntarily.

“Are you from Pathanam Thitta?”-he asks with a glow in his eyes.

Her eyes glow brighter, putting his to shame!!

“Yes, very much. How did you guess so accurately?”

“Well, just...”

“Have you been to Kerala before?”

“No... I just... guessed.”

“Wow, that’s unbelievable.”-her eyes look at both of Ayodhya’s eyes alternately, quickly.

“I am going to get some milk and grocery. You want something to be bought for you too?”-he offers, unable to pull out of the magic her eyes cast on him.

“Yeah, some curry leaves.”

“Ok.”-he seems happy, very happy, with her as his new neighbor. This is a new experience for him.

He fetches all the items at a nearby store and starts a slow stroll back to his home. He hears a faint noise the children in the neighborhood are making. “Uncle... uncle...”-they seem to be playing around with grownups just the way he used to before he had moved out to a boarding school. He remembers calling Mr. Hemant out of the house to play with him- “Hemant Uncle!!”-his fond memories return for a moment. He looks at me through the eyes of his mind and smiles. He bows down at my power to stir up events and condense them back. He loves my game. He admires my act of stealing away his childhood well before he even got a scent of it. He thinks of me and arrives at a decision-to take a dive into the watery mirage called life before I snatch it away.

Soft fingers grip his left palm. He turns back. A small boy, three to four years old, stands panting for breath. "How many times should I call you, uncle?"-he manages to blurt. Ayodhya is shocked!

"Can you get me the kite back? It got trapped in the twigs of that tree."-he points at a nearby tree. "Sure."

"Thanks, uncle."

Ayodhya's mind revolves around me again.

He stands under the tree and jumps with his hand stretched out. He misses the kite. He tries again... and misses again. He stands looking at the kite that reminds him of the reaches of life that always evaded him... the slippery, deceptive ones that dodged him... The ones about which he had felt he hadn't tried enough.

He thrusts the milk packet into the kid's hands, rolls his sleeve and this time, leaps high... at life!!

So... That's it, dear reader.

I know it is time to say goodbye. How ironical, I limit myself by an external constraint, which again, is I!

I will not end it with 'and then he lived happily ever after' because unlike you I'm not privileged to stop seeing after a point. Every time I end a story, I see another story unfold. In fact, for me, there is no start or end. It's hard to be immortal.

I understand I was quite cynical in my words to you, dear reader. But I had to. And I am not sorry for that.

It is because I control you. I free you. I do everything that I have to do of you. My ego is just.

I know that you are as unsung as Ayodhya in your own right. But you're quite extraordinary in my eyes. Your achievements need not be measured in how much your own kind recognizes you. It is I who decides your worth. I place situations in front of you. I know your lifespan. It is lying so neatly drawn in front of me. Before you coalesce with nature I will make sure I give you those precious moments of joy that you always longed for. I'll also make you regret every misdeed you've committed.

I've disappointed you on many occasions. I've not given you what you expected after all the efforts you made. I've done that for a reason. I want to give you circumstances you are meant to be in. I want to fulfill everything you're worthy of. I will not leave you unfinished even if you disagree when you leave. I'll settle all your businesses right here, right now. As you move to the final few words, I've unfurled a new chapter in your life. Whether you are a bubbly, energetic young person or someone lying on your bed looking into the eyes of the humongous figure of death almost breathing into you, doesn't matter to me. All I see are the end points. So go out there, live it. Live it as much as you can because now I am with you and someday, I will be all by myself.

Rest assured unless you choose to be Ayodhya!

ABOUT THE AUTHOR

The author was born and brought up in the garden city of Bengaluru. He started writing at the age of seven but never thought of publishing the work until he wrote his first full-length novel. He is a cricket enthusiast and an ardent follower of former Indian Captain Rahul Dravid.
The Blue Bell Villa is his first attempt at writing fiction.
You may reach out with your views and feedback at thebluebellvilla@gmail.com

www.ingramcontent.com/pod-product-compliance
Lightning Source LLC
Chambersburg PA
CBHW021213260626
47172CB00002B/413
* 9 7 8 9 3 8 6 4 8 7 5 4 4 *